The Falmouth Connection

Joana Starnes

ISBN: 1500740411
ISBN-13: 978-1500740412

∘⚬ℰ 9ℰ⚬∘

To Pat and Sophie

Thank you for the tremendous help,
for all the support and encouragement,
for the laughter and the happy times we spent together
either face to face or with a couple of screens between us.
You know this story would not have been the same without you!
Thanks ever so much for everything!

∘⚬ℰ 9ℰ⚬∘

New Characters
(IN ORDER OF APPEARANCE)

In addition to well known and much loved characters, some new ones are added to this story. Those in bold are the most relevant. The others are largely listed as a memory aid.

Mrs. Pencarrow: *Mrs. Bennet's aunt (her mother's elder sister)*

Sarah: *Mrs. Bennet's maid*

Norwood: *Mr. Darcy's valet*

Lord Langthorne: *Col. Fitzwilliam's father*

John: *Mr. Darcy's footman. Acting valet in Norwood's absence*

Joseph: *Mr. Darcy's coachman*

Peter: *Another one of Mr. Darcy's footmen*

Mrs. Polmere: *Mrs. Pencarrow's housekeeper*

Mawgan: *Mrs. Pencarrow's footman*

Gorran: *Another footman of Mrs. Pencarrow's and Morwenna's brother*

Mr. Perren: *Mrs. Pencarrow's butler*

Morwenna: *One of Mrs. Pencarrow's maids*

Gemima Gardiner: *Mrs. Bennet's mother*

Lord Trevellyan: *Mrs. Pencarrow's neighbour and Justice of Peace*

Mr. Penderrick: *Cornish neighbour and former schoolfellow of Mr. Darcy's*

Densil, Merryn: *Locals in Lord Trevellyan's employ*

Tressa: *Another one of Mrs. Pencarrow's maids*

Dr. Polkerris: *The local doctor*

Mr. Tregarrick: *Captain of 'The Rashley'*

Tregony: *Helmsman on 'The Rashley'*

Chapter 1

"Cousin Elizabeth, this is utterly preposterous!" Darcy heard through the open window as he approached the front door of the parsonage and he involuntarily turned towards his cousin, only to notice his brow arching in what he could only assume was a diverting mirror of his own turn of countenance. His jaw tightened. Under different circumstances he might have turned back, but devil take him if he was about to walk away and allow that pompous fool to continue speaking to her in this intolerable fashion!

"Basingstoke indeed, and at such short notice! Why, the very notion!" Mr. Collins was heard complaining further and a soft voice that Darcy readily recognised as Mrs. Collins's tactfully intervened.

"I am quite certain it could not be helped, Mr. Collins," she quietly supplied. "Sometimes matters are out of one's control."

He could not hear *her*, Darcy noted with some concern, which could only mean that she was too vexed to trust herself to speak to her infernal cousin. Pursing his lips, he took the last few steps and forcefully employed the knocker.

It was not long until he and Fitzwilliam were shown into the parlour, only to see that he must have been in the right, judging at least by Elizabeth's countenance and heightened colour.

She barely curtsied and it suddenly occurred to him that, instead of being of assistance, he had in effect hindered her in her endeavours, for of course she would not feel at liberty to discuss family matters in his presence.

A sudden warmth coursed through him at the thought that this was bound to change, and soon. The worst was over – the pain of self-denial, the torment of indecision. All he needed now was the opportunity. The chance to declare himself and secure her hand.

He all but smiled at the thought that, in a day or two, he would have the right to speak for her. Stand between her and her foolish cousin and silence him in a trice.

1

He seemed apt enough to silence him already, thank goodness, Darcy noted, as the man had of course ceased his remonstrations and stood to deliver a deep bow to him and a noticeably less servile one to his cousin. In his turn, Darcy acknowledged him with a nod and turned to greet the ladies. He bowed to Mrs. Collins, but it was Elizabeth he glanced upon as he quietly offered:

"My apologies. I hope we have not called at a bad time."

"Impossible, Sir!" the parson interjected. "You could never call at a bad time. *I* must apologise for the commotion you must have overheard – a trifling family matter, that is all," he added and Darcy could not fail to see Elizabeth's chest rising in indignation at his dismissive tone.

"Can I be of any assistance?" he asked – of her again – and *again* it was the insufferable man who answered.

"You are too kind, Mr. Darcy. Nay, nay, do not distress yourself. I can only assure you we would not dream of inconveniencing your esteemed aunt and her relations."

Elizabeth's dark eyes shot daggers at her cousin and she pursed her lips as she sat down again.

"There is no inconvenience at all," Darcy resigned himself to address his host since all previous attempts to address another had been purposely thwarted. "I should be glad to be of service if I can."

"Sir, your condescension is vastly appreciated. Indeed, just the same as your most amiable aunt – "

A strange noise that sounded suspiciously like a muffled snort came from behind him, giving Darcy to understand that Fitzwilliam was labouring as much as himself under the necessary burden of keeping a straight face at the parson's fawning – and indeed at hearing Lady Catherine being described as *amiable*, of all things!

Fitzwilliam, however, was the least of his concerns and Darcy turned towards Elizabeth again.

"May I be allowed to know what distresses you?" he asked very quietly and could not fail to register and wonder at the look of extreme surprise she flashed at him.

Why she should be surprised, he could not fathom. Surely she did not think that his offer of assistance was meant for *Mr. Collins!* Or had she failed to see that he would like nothing better than to safeguard her interests? Perhaps she did not see it, but then he had been far from obvious lately and *had* struggled to limit his attentions so as to avoid giving rise to expectations while the matter was still undecided.

It was decided now. He *would* stand beside her.

And it was positively liberating to show it at last!

Still, she did not answer. It was Mrs. Collins who quietly supplied:

"An express has just arrived from Longbourn, Mr. Darcy, requesting that my friend curtails her visit – "

"Good heavens! Not bad news, I hope?"

"No, not as such. There is no mention of a mishap or anything of that nature. It appears though that Mrs. Bennet and her daughters – and Elizabeth in particular – are requested to travel urgently to Falmouth to attend their relation."

"I was not aware you had family in Cornwall, Miss Bennet," Darcy observed blandly for want of a more inspired comment as he endeavoured to recover from the shock of the unwelcome news of her imminent departure.

That was not good. Not good at all! She could not leave before he had a chance to privately address her!

"Neither was I," Elizabeth spoke up at last and the very sound of her voice was a welcome balm to his severe disappointment.

Before she could add anything further, the infuriating parson cut her off again:

"How can some people be so overbearing, I shall never know! *Who* is this person who believes herself in the right to issue such summons, and at such short notice? Indeed, Cousin Elizabeth, the very notion that she should be allowed to take precedence over Lady Catherine's interests – "

"Would you kindly allow *me* to be the best judge here as regards Lady Catherine's interest?" Darcy burst out, riled in no small measure by the entire business and no less by the man's presumption and constant interference. "Pray continue, Miss Bennet."

She flashed another glance at him, but looked away as she spoke again.

"It appears that there is a great-aunt I have never heard of, a Mrs. Pencarrow, who resides somewhere near Falmouth. She is advanced in years and her health is failing. She would like to see us all before she grows any weaker. My mother writes that they have made arrangements to set off directly and that I should join them on the way. We are to meet in Basingstoke by Thursday at the latest."

"But surely they can see you must not travel unattended!" Mr. Collins interjected and for once Darcy found himself in agreement with the vexing man.

"Of course," Elizabeth retorted with poorly concealed impatience. "Our maid Sarah is already on her way to join me here. We shall travel post together."

"What, unescorted by a manservant? Cousin Elizabeth, surely you know that Lady Catherine cannot bear the notion of two young women travelling post by themselves. It is highly improper! Young women should always be properly guarded. I am quite certain her ladyship will be most seriously displeased to hear it and will insist I send a servant with you, but I cannot see how I can spare Thomas at such incredibly short notice."

"You need not concern yourself," Fitzwilliam suddenly spoke up from behind him, to Darcy's unconcealed surprise. "I am due to travel to Portsmouth before too long in any case. It will be my pleasure to escort Miss Bennet and her maid on their journey," he concluded, and Darcy all but scowled.

'You will do nothing of the sort!' was his first instinctive thought, before he recollected that Fitzwilliam could not have had any prior knowledge of his own interest in the lady and no inkling that it was *his* place and no one else's to guarantee her safety. He would know soon enough though, Darcy all but smiled, as he quietly determined there was no time like the present.

"That would not be necessary," he said flatly. "Rather, there is no need for you to travel post. I can take you to Portsmouth myself and Miss Bennet is most welcome to travel as far as Basingstoke with us as soon as her maid arrives."

The utter shock in Fitzwilliam's countenance came as no surprise for, after all, Darcy had not once in living memory offered to squire him around the country as he had travelled to his other assignments. Whether the Colonel had understood the implications Darcy could not tell, but he would have to be enlightened later. It was Elizabeth he would rather speak to now, and his eyes flew to meet hers, already fixed upon him with a look of consternation. He paid no heed to Fitzwilliam's shock or the parson's sputter and addressed her instead:

"I hope you would allow me the satisfaction of ensuring that you are safely delivered into your family's protection, Miss Bennet," he earnestly offered, the same warmth spreading through his chest as her eyes widened further at his words.

⋘ ⋙

"Dare I ask what has just happened there?" Fitzwilliam drawled as they made their way together along the gravelled walk that joined the Hunsford church and parsonage to Rosings.

Darcy's lips involuntarily turned up at the corners.

"What should you wish to know?"

The Colonel shrugged.

"Oh, you know me, I daresay that *everything* would just about suffice," his cousin drawled again and this time Darcy laughed in earnest. "But before you start, pray allow me to thank you for your uncommon attention to my comfort. I am deeply touched!" Fitzwilliam grinned widely, in a manner so highly reminiscent of their boyhood that Darcy was hard-pressed for a moment to remember that they had outgrown the years when such a grin would surely warrant a mock punch in his cousin's shoulder.

To his credit, he did not succumb to the temptation but offered a light quip of his own instead:

"I am glad to hear it. That is precisely what I was aiming for."

"Oh, well done, you! So come, let us have the rest of it now, shall we? I cannot remember the last time you have gone so far out of your way for a young lady – literally. I trust you know what you are about, showing such marked attention. I can think of a few ladies of our general acquaintance who would have been inclined to order wedding-clothes for less than that."

"I daresay in this case they would be required," Darcy drawled in his turn and at that, Fitzwilliam released a sudden disbelieving laugh.

"So this is it then, the moment we have all been waiting for? Oh, Lady Catherine will be thrilled to hear it! She has been dropping you more than enough hints that it was high time you considered marriage."

"Oh, hold your tongue!" Darcy retorted with a chuckle, then instantly sobered. "At least this swift departure serves a purpose, inconvenient as it turns out to be. I do not wish for Lady Catherine to be within fifty miles of *her* when everything is brought out into the open."

"I am astonished you have managed to keep it under wraps so far, but I should imagine it was highly recommended. As soon as Collins is informed, then he can surely be trusted to let the cat out of the bag – or I should say, the tiger! Darcy, there is but one favour I would ask of you, in the name of all the scrapes I got you out of – "

"*You* got *me* out? There was I thinking that the boot was on the other foot."

"Regardless. Now, this favour. I will owe you for all eternity if you allow me to be in the room when you share your news with Lady Catherine!"

They could not fail to laugh at this like two errant schoolboys, then Darcy sobered once again.

"Much as I would wish to oblige you, I fear it cannot be done. As I just said, I *will not* speak now – and by the time I do, you will be with your regiment."

"Damn! I quite forgot. How utterly vexing! You know how I detest being thwarted in my amusements – and to miss something as grand as this is a grievous disappointment. Nevertheless, I cannot really fault you for not wishing to provoke her while Miss Bennet is still at the parsonage."

"Indeed. And I daresay that the established form is to speak to the young lady first, before informing all and sundry," Darcy smiled.

"I beg your pardon?"

"Nothing out of the common way, Cousin, surely! You must agree that the proposal should come before the announcement."

"Are you saying you have *not* proposed?"

"Not yet – I should have wished to do so before she leaves Kent, but – "

"Your maddening self-assurance borders on arrogance, you know? Dash it, Darcy! I thought everything was settled."

"It shall be, soon – unless you think she might refuse me?"

The ludicrous notion could not fail to make them smile.

"I would not go that far," the Colonel retorted, "but do you not think you should have secured her hand before starting to crow over me about your triumph?"

"And so I would have – but you *would* persist in poking about in other people's business."

"Never mind that. Well? When will you speak out?"

"That, I know not. Miss Bennet is bound to call on the morrow to take her leave of Lady Catherine. I could offer to escort her back to the parsonage or, failing that, I could address her at some point during our journey – though I would have hoped for a better setting than the private parlour of a country inn."

"Again, Darcy, if I did not know you better I would have thought you savour of too much self-assurance. What does the setting have to do with it?" the Colonel scoffed.

Darcy shrugged.

"I do not expect *you* to understand."

"My coarse regimental manners offend your scruples, do they?" Fitzwilliam drawled, clearly not in earnest, nor in the least put out.

"You can say as much," Darcy retorted, like-for-like, then quietly offered: "Do you not think the setting would matter to *her?*"

"Be that as it may, you have little choice – in Kent at least. What should it be? Lady Catherine's drawing room? Her manicured garden? Or would you settle for the esteemed parson's parlour?"

Darcy cringed.

"Heaven forefend! No, I was holding hopes of a forest walk. Miss Bennet is quite partial to them."

"So what was my role supposed to be in this affair? Escort Miss Lucas? Or hold the fort at the parsonage until your glorious return?"

"I have made no plans – which is just as well, for they would have had to be amended. I can only hope she would be willing to take a turn with me when we stop to bate the horses or something of that nature."

"I shall do my best to orchestrate a moment – "

"Cousin, I earnestly beg that you would not!"

"And why is that, pray? Have you no confidence in my strategic talents?"

"I have no desire to employ underhand manoeuvres, that is all."

"I see. So I should not feign sleep then, as soon as her maid dozes off in earnest, by way of example…"

"You most certainly should not! If you imagine I would conduct my courtship within your earshot, Cousin, you are woefully mistaken!"

"I daresay you may be in the right – otherwise you would never hear the end of the matter," Fitzwilliam ribbed, not unkindly, and the other laughed.

"Well, if I am allowed a suggestion," the Colonel resumed, "you might wish to consider stopping at Seale, seeing as you are so particular about the setting. The views from the Hog's Back are quite astounding, and you might go as far as thinking the village name auspicious, for *sealing* your fate."

"And this is precisely why I have no wish to conduct my courtship in your hearing, Cousin. He who would pun would pick a pocket – not to mention that, even for you, *that* was a dreadful pun."

"Oh, suit yourself," Fitzwilliam shrugged. "Just do not come begging for assistance when the fount of wisdom is closed and out of reach."

"Need I remind you that founts do not close, Fitzwilliam? Nay, they dry up – if there ever was anything in them in the first place."

"As I said, suit yourself. You are an ungrateful wretch but still, blood is thicker than water so I suppose I should wish you well. Have you prepared your speech? Of course – what am I saying! I forgot whom I was talking to. You had it all written down and memorised, I should imagine. For your sake, I hope you did not leave it lying around for Lady Catherine's maids to find it. On the other hand, if you were wise enough to leave out the lady's name, then we shall have a gleeful dinner companion in our aunt for once, which is just as well."

"Fear not, Cousin, I am not quite so staid as to write down my speech and memorise it. I should imagine Mr. Collins was likely to resort to *that*. There are a few salient points which cannot be omitted but otherwise I believe I could be trusted to go *ad libitum* without mishap, once I have assured her that my affections are not the work of a moment."

"No one who knows you can ever assume that any of your decisions are the work of a moment – least of all one as momentous as that."

"To own the truth, Fitzwilliam, I cannot vouch for how well-acquainted Miss Bennet might have grown with my – "

"Pray tell me you have given yourself the trouble to *talk* to the lady, Darcy!" the Colonel interjected with something like affectionate exasperation. "A fair amount more than you did in Kent, I would dearly like to hope."

"If you were expecting yet another tale of love performing miracles, Cousin, and altering everybody's ways – "

Before he could finish, Fitzwilliam groaned.

"So you have stood tongue-tied throughout! I thought as much. Thank goodness you are handsome, Darcy, and a man of means," he remarked, only partly in jest, and at that his cousin violently bristled.

"She would not accept me for either of those reasons!"

"What for, then? Your cheerful and easy conversation? Your smooth ability to please? Your dancing skills and your propensity to use them?"

"Fitzwilliam, are you purposely determined to be vexing or is it merely one of your many inborn talents?"

"Never mind mine – we were discussing *yours*."

"I have no notion why you would seek to undermine my confidence, but you shall not succeed. She will understand. Once I have explained how I have fought to overcome my scruples as regards our union – "

The Colonel's head turned sharply at that.

"Once you have explained *what* exactly, pray?"

"Had you but met them all, you would already know. Miss Bennet's connections are not the sort you might expect, Fitzwilliam. She is of course a gentleman's daughter, but her mother's relations are objectionable in the extreme. A country-town attorney and a London merchant and, as though the lack of fortune and connection was not bad enough, her mother and younger sisters are uniformly bent on deporting themselves with no propriety whatever! As for the parson, you have seen him. She cannot fail to understand that only the utmost force of passion could have overcome such weighty objections to our marriage. You know as well as I do that, in your father's eyes and Lady Catherine's, this union is nothing but a severe degradation, yet it matters not! Now that you are acquainted with her, I trust you will agree that Miss Bennet is worthy of any sacrifice."

"Heaven help us!" the Colonel muttered in lieu of any other answer and suddenly reached to grab his cousin's arm.

"What the deuce are you about, Fitzwilliam?" Darcy blustered, snatching his elbow from his cousin's grasp.

"We are already on Lady Catherine's doorstep," the Colonel pointed out and the other looked up to see that he was in the right.

The garden entrance was a stone's throw before them but Darcy failed to see anything ominous in that.

Nothing more ominous than the usual, that is, he inwardly amended, then lost no time in observing as much.

"It seems we are in dire need of a serious conversation and if you imagine it could be held at Rosings, then you are a greater fool than I think you at present. And believe me, that is no mean feat, at this point in time."

"What the devil are you speaking of?" Darcy impatiently inquired, but had the good sense to follow his cousin's advice and abandon the gravelled walk to Rosings in favour of a narrow path that led towards the woods, along a very tall yew hedge, uniformly straight and very neatly cut.

"Come with me! I have a great need to rave at you at my leisure and I do not wish to have to choose my words or keep my voice down," the Colonel forcefully retorted and was silent, until the path took them beyond the park paling, at which point he spun around. "I can only hope I have misunderstood," he suddenly began. "Pray tell me you were not about to make the litany of Miss Bennet's unsuitable relations the salient point of your marriage proposal!"

He did not wait to have the answer couched in so many words but, having read it in his cousin's countenance, the Colonel threw his arms in the air.

"Of all the asinine – nay, idiotic notions! Darcy, have you utterly lost your mind? What sort of a courtship, what sort of a proposal is this, that begins with insulting your ladylove and all that she holds dear? You think she is beneath you? Then do not propose! Go and marry elsewhere or turn into a hermit, but do not imagine this is the way to win her heart!"

"I have no wish to either marry elsewhere or turn into a hermit, for that matter. Besides, I already have her heart."

"Oh, you do, do you? What makes you so certain?"

"You would not understand. You were not party to our conversations – "

"I was party to a number, over the past fortnight. There is a chance that you might have her interest, though I cannot imagine how the deuce you managed to secure it if all you ever did was in the vein of what I have witnessed. But be that as it may. Let us say you *do* have her interest. God's teeth, let us say you also have her heart! How long do you imagine you can keep them, if your notion of lovemaking is to shower her in your contempt?"

"Contempt? *For her?* Fitzwilliam, you are so far off the mark I could almost laugh. Sadly, I do not find it in the least diverting!"

"Off the mark, am I? Is it not contempt to say that she has no fortune, no connection, her mother and sisters are a mortifying nuisance and her cousin is a fool?"

"It has no bearing on her! I do not choose to marry her *because* of them, but *despite* them."

At that, the Colonel's hands came forcefully together in loud mock applause.

"Oh, Darcy, how magnanimous of you!"

"What on earth is *that* supposed to mean?"

"You are a man of reasonable understanding, Cousin. Can you not exert yourself and imagine Miss Bennet's reaction, when the one who has raised her interest and affection marches in to tell her that although her world is beneath contempt, in his condescension he will have the generosity to overlook it? Do you honesty expect her *gratitude* for that?"

"You twist my words. I am not Lady Catherine!"

"Then why do you choose to sound so much like her?"

Darcy scowled at that, then gave a swift and dismissive wave.

"There is no use in speaking to you when this mood is upon you, *that* I know of old. You will excuse me, Cousin, there is a journey to Portsmouth I should be arranging."

"Have it your way, then! Oh, by all means, *go.* Go and propose to her by listing all her failings and see what good it does you. But do not imagine that I shall spare you the *'I told you so'!*"

Whether the goading was deliberate or not, it served its purpose. Darcy turned back, his fists tightly clenched.

"Firstly," he enunciated, "her circumstances of birth, fortune and connection are not her failings, but her sheer misfortune. Secondly, it is in no way a concern of yours. Thirdly, should it have been, I would have dearly loved to see you practise what you preach. Welcome Mr. Collins with open arms. Be proud to introduce the country-town attorney and his coarse wife as your new relations. Delight in having Mrs. Bennet drink tea with our aunt – or indeed your parents. Come now, Fitzwilliam! Is this truly what you would have done?"

"I would certainly not have shown such blatant lack of consideration towards the woman I professed to love! Nor would I have set about to hurt her feelings in the midst of my proposal," the Colonel shot back.

"I have not set about to hurt her feelings!" Darcy defensively replied, only to be rewarded with a derisive snort.

"In that case, you either are unable to comprehend human interactions, or you are the greatest fool in Christendom!" Fitzwilliam forcefully retorted. "Honestly, Darcy, must it be spelled out? Do you not think she cares for the people you are about to scorn? She may not like them, she may not approve of their conduct, but they are her nearest and dearest, her family, for goodness' sake! What purpose does it serve to denigrate them in the same breath as offering for her?"

"I have already told you: it serves to show that my choice to offer for her is not a whim, but a hard-won decision."

"For which she should be grateful until her dying day? Is that the sort of marriage you aspire to?"

"Of course not!" Darcy bristled.

"Then what do you envisage?"

His brow raised in unconcealed contempt, his cousin scoffed:

"You have met her. Spoken to her – more than I have, you claim. If you have not seen it yet, I shall not waste my breath to make you see it now!"

The Colonel rolled his eyes.

"I am asking what *you* are seeing, you pompous know-it-all."

More than a little stung and at the limits of his patience, Darcy burst out:

"What gives you the impression you have the right to ask, or that I would bare my soul to *you*? Today of all days, when you have been nothing but a nuisance?"

To his surprise, his abrasive retort did not provoke his cousin into another verbal lashing. He did not even seem offended, but merely smiled as though confronted with the antics of a misbehaving child.

"Fair enough," he conceded at length, without rancour. "Still, by my way of thinking, rather than abusing her relations, you might do well to bare your soul to *her*."

Chapter 2

"I thank you, Norwood, you may leave me now," Darcy dismissed his man, then walked over to his writing table.

Three letters lay there, still unsealed, and he cast a cursory glance over each, to ensure that he had forgotten nothing, before he sat down to seal them all. One was for Georgiana, another for his steward and the third for his business agent, to announce his slight change of plans and, in the latter, to also convey instructions which could not wait until such time that he would finally return to town.

The task accomplished, Darcy refilled his glass and ambled to the window. Norwood had drawn the heavy brocade curtains, but Darcy pulled them back again. The windowpanes were cold, which was no surprise for April, especially as the night was crystal-clear.

A bright moon, not yet full but very nearly so, illuminated the surroundings in great but strange detail. It was almost too easy to spot the church in this sort of light, despite the distance. Equally so, the parsonage – the squat, unappealing building, slightly to the left of the church tower.

Candlelight shone at two, nay, three of the upstairs windows, and Darcy wondered which one might be hers. Was she penning a letter? Or writing in her diary – of the prospective journey, and perchance of *him?* Was she ensconced in bed, reading her book, her candle on the nightstand? Or was she caught in last-minute preparations for their departure on the morrow? The last conjecture was not very likely. Doubtlessly she was not the sort to leave matters unattended, past their time. Nay, she must be reading, propped up on her pillows, he thought, and a smile fluttered on his lips.

He took a draught of the ruby liquid. Not long now. Not long till the morrow when, God willing, the deed would be done!

It might have been already – yet it had not, Darcy all but scowled. He should have known that, when she came to pay her respects to his aunt, that pompous fool, the parson, would choose to walk with her to Rosings and then back to Hunsford, thus depriving him of the opportunity of escorting her back himself – and bare his soul, as Fitzwilliam had put it.

The recollection brought a snort, and this time Darcy scowled in earnest at the thought of his cousin and his dashed impertinence. The fact that he was two years Darcy's senior clearly gave him the mistaken notion that he was still allowed far too much licence! All well and good, this high-handed, flippant elder cousin manner when they were in their boyhood, but now, at eight and twenty, he was not of a mind to tolerate it further, Darcy forcefully determined, and drained his glass in a burst of vexation.

He walked back to the port decanter and refilled it, but did not return to the tall windows. Instead, he lowered himself in the winged chair next to the writing table and stretched his long legs, crossing them at the ankles. He reached for his port and took another sip.

To be fair – once he had simmered down sufficiently for fairness – perhaps he *did* owe his cousin a debt of gratitude for opening his eyes to the fact that, rather than being taken in the spirit it was meant, the candid recitation of her relations' failings and of his own misgivings might have served none of its intended purpose.

He had meant to show that he gratefully acknowledged the great difference between her and most of her relations. He had meant to convey the depth of his devotion – for surely nothing less would prompt him into such a *mésalliance!*

She had no notion, really, of his station in life. She had no notion of the circles he belonged to, no notion of what was expected of the master of Pemberley – and indeed its mistress. She had to be enlightened, somehow. She had to understand that her connections could not be permitted to attract the censure of everyone around him and cover the Darcy name in ridicule!

Of course he had not set out to injure her feelings, to offend and insult her with the honest confession of the scruples that had long prevented him from contemplating their association – and Fitzwilliam should certainly have seen it!

Still, there was no denying that the man was in the right, his intolerable manner notwithstanding. He *might* have been the greatest fool in Christendom for choosing the very time of his proposal to impress upon her that they would have to distance themselves from her relations, soon after their marriage.

To some extent, it might have been ungentlemanly, ill-judged and inconsiderate to say as much at that point in time – not to mention unnecessary too, for she must be aware of it already. Surely it was readily apparent to someone as astute as her!

Not that he was inclined to foster closeness with some of his own relations either, Lady Catherine in particular, Darcy thought, sipping his port again, and all but choked on it as a reluctant half-laugh overcame him.

The previous evening her ladyship had been in high dudgeon, ever since Fitzwilliam had casually mentioned over dinner that her nephews were making plans to curtail their visit by two days.

Although disguise of every sort was his abhorrence, Darcy had eventually seen some wisdom in letting his cousin offer his summons to Portsmouth as the only reason for their early departure. Deceitful as it might have been, it was by far the less contentious option. Nevertheless, before Elizabeth called at Rosings to bid her adieus, a reference *had* to be made to their intention to escort her and her maid to Basingstoke and, without hesitation, Darcy had taken it upon himself to do so, directly after the second cover was laid out.

Fitzwilliam's expectant countenance, on the other side of the table, riled him in great measure. Unlike his cousin, Darcy was not looking forward to the confrontation that would undoubtedly arise once he had disclosed his matrimonial intentions. Much as his cousin chose to treat such matters lightly, for his own part Darcy felt there was a vast deal to be said for family unity and concord.

Of course, concord could scarce be hoped for, once his aunt was in the know, and Darcy half-suspected that Lord Langthorne, Lady Catherine's brother, would be far more likely to take *her* side rather than his. In time, his uncle might be brought around, but Darcy was in no humour to hasten that discussion and would have certainly preferred that Fitzwilliam did not look quite so much like the cat that got the cream!

Predictably, Lady Catherine had much to say about their travel arrangements and the impropriety of two gentlemen escorting a young lady who could not claim the ties of a sister, cousin or, heaven forefend, wife.

The maid's presence was summarily dismissed as insufficient and Darcy was challenged to give his opinion on whether he would have thought it proper for *Georgiana* to travel with two gentlemen who were not her relations, her reputation protected by no more than a maid.

"Far be it from me to compare their social standing, Nephew," her ladyship had seen fit to add with a disdainful shrug. "Frankly, Miss Bennet can hazard her reputation if she chooses and it would be the least of my concerns were it not for the fact that she is connected to my parson and any whisper of gossip that surrounds her will therefore touch *me*," she had ill-humouredly remarked, unknowingly raising her nephew's ire at the dismissive reference to Elizabeth's reputation, as well as the suggestion that he would knowingly put her good name at risk.

"I beg you would not distress yourself, Lady Catherine," he had offered, rather crisply. "Times have changed, and so have the morals. No aspersions can be cast on either yourself or Miss Bennet if she chooses to travel escorted by her maid, in the company of longstanding acquaintances of reputable character."

"I trust you are speaking for yourself, Darcy," Fitzwilliam had quipped from the other side of the table, only to have two pairs of eyes instantly turned upon him to glare in disapproval.

"Your levity is misplaced and your choice of topic inappropriate, both for the dinner table and your present company. Kindly remember you are not sitting by the bivouac fire, Fitzwilliam!" Lady Catherine had sternly remonstrated, as though the recipient was a misbehaving youngster, wet about his ears, rather than a Colonel in His Majesty's army, recently turned thirty and having served with honour on many battlefields.

The Colonel had readily apologised, but Darcy could not fail to note that his eyes were dancing. He could easily conjecture his cousin thinking *'More's the pity'*, and he was in the right. However, he remained blissfully unaware of the other reason for his cousin's unholy merriment, namely that his own raised brow and baleful glare had perfectly – and uncannily – mirrored Lady Catherine's.

Glass in hand, Darcy stood and returned to the window.

The same lights burned at the parsonage, in the same places.

She should set her book aside and go to sleep, for a long day awaited on the morrow, he thought, and then chastised himself for his overbearing manner. It would serve him to remember that he could not very well aim to direct her as he did Georgiana – not that she would allow him to get away with it in any case.

Darcy smiled again, warmth spreading through his chest at the recollection of their past exchanges and the delightful manner in which she had seen fit to challenge some of his words and actions.

A worthy companion, a discerning equal, not a fawning miss with no mind of her own.

It was to be surmised that it was her father from whom she had inherited her ready wit – and thankfully none of his eccentricities and occasional want of decorum. Rather grudgingly, Darcy allowed he should feel some gratitude to the older man and perchance some compassion as well, seeing that he would soon be deprived of his worthiest offspring. It was plain to see that, of all his daughters, it was only Elizabeth whom the older gentleman respected, which showed him to be a man of sense and understanding. Of all the avalanche of undesirable relations that should be kept at bay, perhaps an exception should be made for Mr. Bennet. Elizabeth would undoubtedly be very pleased with *that*.

Little as he knew of the master of Longbourn, Darcy vaguely remembered that he was exceedingly fond of reading. The library at Pemberley could not fail to impress him, then – and Elizabeth would surely be proud to reveal such a remarkable collection to her father.

He took another sip of port, his eyes softening as he pictured her in the library – and, before he could control them, his unruly thoughts rose in a whirlwind to instantly place her all over the house, not least in his own chambers. His mouth suddenly dry, he carried the glass to his lips and took a long, steady draught, this time tasting nothing of the sweet, distinctive flavour.

Wholly unrelated to the port, heat rose and spread through him at the tantalising picture that his mind had so readily conjured. Her lovely form, barely covered by a nightdress. In his bed. In his arms. Finally his.

He swallowed hard and leaned his head against the window, relishing the touch of the cold glass panes upon his feverishly hot brow, full of feverish thoughts.

Not long now, the Good Lord be praised!

Not long till the morrow.

"Sleep well," he whispered towards the parsonage, still graced by the three squares of light, one of which concealed the greatest treasure. "God bless you and keep you, and grant you nothing but sweet dreams, my love."

Chapter 3

Having reached the parsonage, the carriage rolled to a stop and Darcy sprang out before the door could be opened for him, and the step lowered. He sensed rather than saw John, one of the footmen, readying the step for the expected addition to their party, but he paid the man no heed, his eyes suddenly drawn to the opening door.

It was still far too early for daylight, and only the setting moon illuminated their surroundings. He had arranged an uncommonly early departure, so that they would arrive in Basingstoke by nightfall, without the need to spend the night along the way. It was a foolish, ridiculously prim precaution, no doubt subconsciously inspired by Lady Catherine's strictures – for of course no aspersions could be cast upon Elizabeth's character if she travelled post and stopped, attended by her maid, at the same inn as other travelling companions. Nevertheless, he would do his utmost to keep her name free of the merest hint of blemish – much as he would have loved to extend the time they spent together on their journey.

He cast his fruitless thoughts aside as the door opened fully into a bright rectangle of light that made him squint. A maid came out carrying a lamp and a very young lad with a torch made his way from around the back, presumably the kitchens or the servants' quarters.

A manservant emerged with a small trunk and then another maid, presumably the one sent down from Longbourn. They were closely followed by the vicar, who hastened to bow to the esteemed caller and thank him repeatedly for his condescension, before rushing to instruct the manservant to place the trunk in such as way as to avoid upsetting the current arrangements. Unwittingly, the commotion behind him drew Darcy's attention and he turned to see the reverend, tugging the trunk himself this way and that, for the manservant's efforts were deemed insufficient. A brief smile fluttered on his lips at the sight of John's obvious exasperation – and no less to see Mr. Collins nearly loosing his footing when the small trunk gave way.

By the time Fitzwilliam had chosen to emerge to pay his own respects – or be entertained by the goings-on behind the carriage – Darcy had lost interest in anything but the rectangle of light that was the open door, for within it now Elizabeth stood framed, a small satchel in hand, escorted by her friend Mrs. Collins.

They did not appear to have seen him, which was no surprise, given his dark cloak and their transition from the indoor brightness into the poor light.

"I beg you would forgive me, Charlotte, for causing this upheaval – and no less for depriving you of two whole hours of sleep," he heard her say, genuine concern beneath the jesting manner, before she turned to clasp her friend in a tight embrace.

"Have a safe trip, Lizzy. I am so relieved to know you shall be well looked after," Mrs. Collins offered and, a moment later, having presumably spotted him and his cousin, she turned to greet them and thank him again for his kindness to her friend.

"Think nothing of it, Ma'am," he replied promptly. "'Tis a pleasure. Good morning, Miss Bennet, Mrs. Collins," he bowed to both, while other greetings were exchanged with his cousin, and above the softly-spoken voices the parson's tones rang out, bidding pompous adieu to his relation, thanking *him* again and – strangely – Lady Catherine, although she had of course not graced them with her presence.

Amid the flurry of inconsequential exchanges, Darcy walked towards her.

"Miss Bennet, would you allow me?" he quietly offered to hand her in the carriage and, with a word of thanks to him and another farewell to Mrs. Collins, she let him do just that.

The maid followed her in – a thin little thing, young and very quiet – and then Fitzwilliam, who had the grace to choose the seat across from the maid. Before long, every requisite civility was duly offered, the trunks secured and instructions given for the speed to be kept down till daylight, so Darcy took his seat and gave the signal for departure. The carriage door was firmly closed behind him and, from up top, Joseph the coachman was heard urging the team on.

⊱❦❦⊰

A new day was dawning, but it was still dark. If anything, it was even darker than when they left Hunsford, for the moon had set and the sun was yet to rise. He could scarce see her, and yet the notion that she was indeed there, bound on a daylong journey in his carriage, with him, was so novel and so utterly delightful that Darcy's lips shaped themselves into a smile.

His smile grew warmer at the thought that this was but a prelude to the journey they would be undertaking soon after their marriage, when he would bring her to his home. A prelude indeed to all their future journeys, he thought with both delight and keen impatience for that blissful time to come at last.

For a moment, he wished she was sitting alongside him. But nay, it was a foolish thought. As yet, he did not have the right to put his arm around her, or entice her to rest her head on his shoulder. They were not alone – and they were not wed.

It was far better, on reflection, to have her on the seat before him. The light was slightly better now and he could just about distinguish the contours of her lovely cheeks and perhaps her eyes – did she just look towards him?

The others were asleep, or seemed to. The maid certainly was, she had not stirred for ages. Neither had Fitzwilliam – but, after the conversation on their return from Hunsford the other day, Darcy could not trust that he was really sleeping. Well, hang him! There was nothing untoward in what he was about to say, in any case.

"Are you comfortable, Miss Bennet?" he asked in the darkness and unexpected joy coursed through him when he heard her soft reply.

"I am. I thank you."

"Should you wish to sleep, there ought to be a cushion placed beside you."

"I thank you. I have found it."

The rumbling of the carriage wheels was all that could be heard for a short while, until she spoke again:

"Mr. Darcy?"

"Miss Bennet?"

"I do not think I had the opportunity to properly thank you for your kindness in offering to convey me to my relations," he heard her say, with clear hesitation.

"My pleasure, Miss Bennet. Anytime."

❦

The carriage lurched over some rut or stone and, at the sudden jolt, Darcy all but jumped. Damnation! He *had* fallen asleep, despite his best endeavours – and had lost goodness knows how long of the treasured joy of travelling with her!

He glanced towards her. He could see her now, quite clearly, and he could not but feast his eyes on the glorious picture. She was still asleep, her head resting on the windowpane rather than the cushion and he could barely restrain himself from reaching to move her to a more comfortable place. Offering his own shoulder for the purpose was sadly not an option, nor could he gather her sleeping form into his arms, so Darcy shifted in his seat with a frustrated sigh.

Her bonnet was a tad askew, he noted, and auburn ringlets had escaped from their confines to spread around her temples. His eyes drifted of their own volition to her lips – full, perfect, rosy and ever so slightly parted. His mouth went dry again – and not for want of water. Temptation lured him, his eyes still fastened on her lips, then darting to take in every touch of the enchanting picture, before returning to her lips again, as a tantalising notion dawned. He might just be allowed to kiss her, later on that day, once he had proposed and had been accepted. He did not smile at the attractive prospect. Instead, he swallowed, willing time to fly.

Another sudden lurch and her eyes flew open, then widened in shock as they encountered his. It was plain to see that, dazed by the abrupt awakening, she had forgotten where she was, along with all the reasons why *his* countenance should be the very first thing that her eyes would alight upon.

He all but smiled, mesmerised by the notion of meeting the same look of stark surprise on the first morning of their marriage – and indeed until she had grown accustomed to awakening in his arms. The prospect was so thoroughly engaging that he forgot to feel embarrassed at having been caught staring. Barely suppressing the urge to grin like a fool at the sheer joy of waking up beside her, he merely sat there, watching every play of confused thought upon her lovely features, until wakefulness finally settled in, and comprehension dawned.

"Good morning, Miss Bennet," he whispered at last, to be greeted by a very quiet, "Good morning to you, Sir."

She did not – *would not?* – look his way for longer than a moment, her cheeks overspreading with a charming blush. So much for Fitzwilliam only grudgingly allowing the other day that he had her heart and interest, Darcy all but scoffed. Nevertheless, he was not about to wish for his cousin to awaken and witness the evidence for himself. The intimacy of the present moment was far more delightful.

He turned towards the window, unwilling to discomfit her any further with conspicuously fixing his eyes upon her. No real loss, for he could still see her out of the corner of his eye. Still rosy-cheeked, she was biting her lip in an adorable picture of self-conscious confusion – and it was the vilest torment that he could not declare himself *now*, this very moment, and set her heart at ease that her interest was returned in full.

Suddenly, he saw her shiver, and unfortunately could not tell whether it was because of the morning chill – or the dreaded prospect of making her life without him. If it was the latter, sadly he could not reassure her yet. However gratifying the alternative, he rather hoped it was the morning chill that made her shiver. At least for that he *had* an instant remedy to hand.

He reached beside him, where a number of travelling rugs were stacked, neatly folded. He should have offered one this morning, when they set off on their way – but he had been too drawn into the delight of her sheer presence and then he had fallen asleep, like the veriest clod! With a grimace at his own unmitigated folly, Darcy lifted one of the rugs from the large pile.

"Would you care for this, Miss Bennet?" he quietly asked.

The look she turned upon him gave him to think that, for some unfathomable reason, she was prepared to say no, before she ascertained what it was that he had offered.

"I thank you," she replied. "It would be most welcome," she added and shivered again.

Darcy lost no time to unfold the rug to its full size – and thought better than discomfiting her further by reaching to fit it neatly around her slender form. He sat back, allowing her to settle it around herself, then earnestly remarked:

"I should have offered one last night – that is to say, earlier this morning, on our departure. Forgive me. I was… distracted."

"Think nothing of it."

"Would you like another?"

"I… I believe I would."

"How thoughtless of me! You must be chilled to the bone."

"'Tis nothing but the early morning air," she shrugged, accepting the second rug – and this time he did reach and carefully settled it around her, to prevent her having to uncover her arms.

Liberating – aye! It *was* liberating to no longer labour under self-imposed restraint. To cast pretence aside and openly court her; and care for her, as he intended to, for the rest of their lives.

"There will be breakfast and a warming drink at *The Fox and Hounds* in Reigate – unless you would rather we stopped sooner?"

"I thank you, no. I am much warmer now."

"I am glad to hear it."

She said nothing further and turned to the window, her eyes flickering over the ever-changing sights. He said nothing either and looked out as well, merely as a guise, for the corner of his eye was still firmly fixed upon her. How childish – and yet how exhilarating! Every moment was exhilarating, when it was shared with *her*. Even the most childish of flirtations and spying on one another out of the corner of one's eye.

He could wager that this was precisely what she herself was doing and Darcy fought very hard to conceal a traitorous smile. Two could play that game if it made her happy, he determined, not at all mortified by the immature antics, but pleasantly diverted and vibrantly alive.

◦৹৹ ৹৹৹

Elizabeth let out a small sigh and bit the corner of her lip.

How utterly provoking that Sarah was still not showing any sign of imminent awakening! She could not blame her, not after the arduous journey she had undertaken in such a dreadfully short time. Nevertheless, she would have greatly preferred Sarah was awake, especially as Colonel Fitzwilliam also perversely persisted in abandoning himself into the arms of Morpheus.

With great caution, Elizabeth stole a glance towards the Colonel and pursed her lips. Now that was a fine to-do! He was utterly lost to his surroundings, his chest rising and falling with the slow breath of peaceful slumber, and was showing no signs of rousing himself either.

'*Aye, rest, why not indeed,*' she inwardly grumbled at the unsettling notion that no one was awake in the speeding carriage, apart from herself – and *Mr. Darcy.*

Elizabeth barely suppressed a huff as she pondered the wisdom to feign having succumbed to tiredness again. But it would not do. The nervous excitement that held her in its grip would certainly ensure that she would fool no one. There was no hope for her to lay convincingly still for any length of time.

She stole another glance, this time to the gentleman seated right before her. She could not see him well, not from the corner of her eye. A short while earlier, she had almost suspected him to be doing precisely the same – surreptitiously watching her – but she was swift to see sense and discard the foolish notion.

From the very beginning of their vexing acquaintance, he had displayed very little interest in her and her pursuits and she could not imagine why this should alter now.

Having said that, it *had* been disconcerting to find herself a few minutes ago at the receiving end of something very much like considerate attention to her comfort. Not to mention the open, almost friendly turn of countenance. Elizabeth could not doubt she must have stared at *that* – so very unexpected, especially of late, when he had uniformly chosen to present nothing but a stern *façade* to the world around him.

She heard, nay, sensed him move, and stole another glance towards him, only to note with some satisfaction that he seemed to have produced a book from a light travelling case. She gave silent thanks for the small mercy, for this removed the unpleasant notion that she should eventually make some vague attempt at conversation.

He did not seem engrossed in his employment though. Had she not known better, she would have been inclined to think that he was watching her over the top of his leather-bound volume.

She briefly thought of looking, if only to reassure herself that she was mistaken, but then rather cowardly settled for the corner of her eye again. And now he *did* look up, she could scarce doubt it – but he appeared more interested in his cousin than herself. She turned her head, by the smallest fraction. Aye. He was insistently regarding his cousin; seemed even to lightly prod his knee with his own, as if to ascertain that he was indeed sleeping – or aiming to wake him, presumably as tired as herself of this extended *tête-à-tête*.

She pursed her lips again, wishing – for the eleventh time at least – that she was not indebted to him of all people for conveying her to Basingstoke to *rendezvous* with her relations. She wondered once more at his willingness to do so, as the countryside scrolled at speed before the carriage window.

Another sigh escaped her, louder this time and, to her vexation, it appeared that Mr. Darcy heard it, for he lost interest in his cousin's slumber and turned to look at her in earnest. A sudden jolt coursed through her at the steady glance of those dark eyes she had grown accustomed to regard as heavily disapproving. There was no disapproval now, she thought in passing, refusing to acknowledge the strange intensity in them – as well as her own extremely foolish jolt.

"Are you well, Miss Bennet?" she heard him ask, very quietly.

Had it come from any other man, Elizabeth would have been grateful. Under the circumstances, she was not.

She pursed her lips again.

"I am. I thank you," she brought herself to say, knowing that she had to.

"Is there anything you need?"

Had she not known better, Elizabeth might have suspected there was solicitude in his address. She did know better, though.

It could not be. Not from *Mr. Darcy!*

"I thank you, no," she instantly replied, wishing he would return to his book.

He did not.

He closed it, his finger still keeping his place between the pages.

"With any luck, we should be in Guildford by noon. We are making good progress," he assured her and Elizabeth could only nod.

She turned to the window again, hoping to convey that she was *not* disposed for conversation. However, for a man who prided himself on his understanding, Mr. Darcy appeared uncommonly obtuse at the moment, for he did not resume his reading, but cleared his voice instead.

"Have your relations indicated how soon they might arrive in Basingstoke?" he asked.

Elizabeth frowned.

"From what I gathered, they should have arrived last night," she answered, pushing back the travelling rugs and reaching for her satchel.

She rummaged for a moment, until she found what she was seeking. If pointedly staring out of the window did not persuade Mr. Darcy to leave her to her own devices, then perhaps feigning interest in her own book would!

She opened it at random and fixed her eyes upon it. And yet, over the top of her volume, she could still see, without purposely looking, that his own remained closed in his lap. She pursed her lips again and her eyes narrowed, willing him into silence. Just as the thought occurred, she all but laughed. That she should be scheming to avoid *Mr. Darcy's* chatter, of all people!

She did not laugh but – to her utter shock – *he* did, or rather chuckled softly, and Elizabeth involuntarily looked up, half suspecting that the rumbling of the carriage wheels must have been playing tricks on her; must have tampered with her hearing.

Surely Mr. Darcy was far above something as plebeian as *chuckling*, she inwardly scoffed – then all but gaped at the contrary evidence before her. There he was now, his gaze fixed upon her, a half-smile playing on his lips, his proud patrician features softened into barely suppressed amusement.

She stared again, quite certain she had never seen him thus. Devoid of stern reserve, he seemed almost human – and in truth, more than a little handsome, a fleeting, errant thought intruded.

In response to both the errant thought and the disconcerting countenance before her, Elizabeth arched a brow.

"May I inquire into the source of your amusement?" she asked despite herself and the infuriating man this time smiled in earnest.

"But of course. I was merely entertained, Miss Bennet, to note that despite firm opinions to the contrary, we *do* seem to be reading the same books after all," he observed, turning his own volume upright so that she could see the title.

She cast her eyes upon it, only to concede that he was in the right. Apparently, they were both reading the second volume of Mr. Southey's *'Letters from England'* which, for some reason of the author's, were presented as though written not by the Englishman he was, but by a Spanish traveller to his confessor.

Elizabeth still failed to see the diverting side of the coincidence however, until all of a sudden she remembered the conversation – or rather verbal fencing – that they had engaged in, during their dance at Netherfield last autumn.

Her companion must have seen her comprehension dawning, for he resumed with the same half-smile:

"All that remains to ascertain is whether we read them with the same sentiments, is it not, Miss Bennet? So may I ask, what is your opinion of this fictitious Don Manuel Alvarez Espriella?"

Her brows arched again – both of them this time. Whatever had possessed him to discard the habitual hauteur in favour of this disconcerting jesting manner? She all but shrugged – unladylike as it might have been. It was his own affair, and she refused to ponder for another moment over Mr. Darcy and his whimsies.

"I cannot deny that he describes well, with keenness of eye and vivacity of spirit," she owned at last. "Yet, while I cannot fault him for his style, I am singularly unimpressed with the way he approached his subject matter."

"Indeed. He *does* write well, but he is horribly anti-English!"

"I daresay he deserves to be – "

"...the very man he is impersonating."

"... precisely whom he claims to be," they both said at once, and for a moment Elizabeth vacillated between laughter and vexation.

For some unknown reason, she succumbed to the first – only to veer towards the second once Mr. Darcy chose to overstate the matter:

"I take it then that our responses are not so different either, in this case at least. Dare I ask about another, Miss Bennet, or would I be stretching my beginner's luck?"

"We are not gambling, Mr. Darcy," she observed, tilting her chin, and the gentleman promptly retorted with another crooked smile.

"I should hope not, Miss Bennet, seeing as gambling is such a hazardous and objectionable pastime."

She stared – again. Had it been any other man, she would have readily concluded he was flirting – either that, or he was in his cups! Since it was *Mr. Darcy* though, in all honesty she would have been more inclined to believe the latter – unlikely as that might have been, particularly at that hour in the morning – rather than imagine he would choose to *flirt* with her.

"So, what shall it be, Miss Bennet?" he prompted. "Dare we compare our views on yet another volume?"

She gave a dainty shrug.

"Oh, why not? There is a long journey all the way to Guildford…"

"In effect, we shall have to stop within the hour. The horses must be bated," he casually observed.

Elizabeth pursed her lips. Of course. She was not travelling post, with a fresh team of hired horses at each stage. She had all but forgotten. Of course the noble beasts would have to be rested, fed and watered, which would imply further delay – and longer time spent with this exceedingly odd version of Mr. Darcy.

"So may I ask, what were you reading before Don Manuel's *Letters*?"

Her chin came up once more, with the same defiance.

"*The Romance of the Forest*," she retorted promptly – and was thoroughly amazed and, in truth, slightly provoked as well, to hear him chuckle yet again.

"Forgive me," he offered, before she could decide between inquiring what it was that amused him or denying him the afore-mentioned satisfaction. "I should not have laughed and I beg you would pardon my ungentlemanly conduct. My sole excuse is that I *have* seen that turn of countenance before – the other time I was asked to despise you if I dared. May I assure you once more that no thought could be further from my mind."

Her lips twitched, as again she swayed between laughter and vexation – and again, to her slight shock, settled on the first. It was an extraordinary notion to have laughed, genuinely laughed with Mr. Darcy twice, in as many minutes! Still, this jesting, boyish stranger was so far removed from the Mr. Darcy she had grown accustomed to that the notion was considerably less surprising.

The same could not be said of *him* though, and Elizabeth wondered what on earth possessed him to deviate so widely from the reserved manner he had uniformly given her reason to expect. Suddenly, Colonel Fitzwilliam's intimation that he was generally different was no longer quite so laughably far-fetched.

"I daresay I have already mentioned this also," her companion resumed, the same half-smile playing on his lips, "but I would never wish to suspend any pleasure of yours, so if you are still of a mind to scandalise me, pray continue – although I would suggest you do not use Mrs. Radcliffe's novels for the purpose. I must confess I have found them rather pleasing."

"How about Madame D'Arblay's?"

"Engaging."

"Mrs. Edgeworth's?"

"Inspiring."

"Mr. Richardson's?"

"A passable read – except perhaps for *'Pamela'*."

She arched a brow.

"How so? Do you dispute the value of the message?"

"I would not dream of it, Miss Bennet! No, I was merely bored."

Despite herself, Elizabeth laughed again – with him rather than at him – for the *third* time in as many minutes. In truth, she *could* think of a volume or two which stood a better chance to scandalise him, but suddenly found she was not so keen to take that path today. Disconcerting as this strange shared good-humour might have been, it was still preferable to spending the entire journey at each other's throats.

"I daresay we could move on to playwrights and poets, but you must allow me a moment to gather my wits. I am still reeling from the shock of hearing that *you* would read novels – and that you were bored by a moral tale," she said with an impish smile, only to see him promptly return it.

"By all means, Miss Bennet, take all the time you need."

She glanced out of the window, playfully pondering what should she mention next – or rather, devising tempting ways to trip him. However, before the matter was decided, a new voice, rather thick with sleep, suddenly broke her train of thought.

"Good morning, Miss – Sir. Pray forgive me, Miss Lizzy, I've been lost to the world. I trust you didn't need me…?"

Having spent a long time wishing that Sarah would awaken, it was rather strange to feel disappointment now, Elizabeth thought in passing, before turning to her mother's maid to reassure her that there was naught amiss and nothing needed doing.

Their conversation must have woken Colonel Fitzwilliam as well, for he stirred, greeted them and then groaned quietly as he readjusted his position.

"I should be glad to stretch my legs at last. I hope we stop soon," he remarked to no one in particular as he cast a glance out of the window. "Ah. Not long now, if I am not mistaken," he cheerfully added, then shifted in his seat and groaned again.

"Are you well, Cousin?" Darcy asked, a slight edge to his voice and at that, the Colonel arched a brow.

"Well enough, I thank you. Stiff as a board, though. No mean feat, staying frozen in one attitude for ages," he casually observed, and the other snorted, for some reason Elizabeth could not fathom.

Nor could she grasp the Colonel's meaning some time later, when she chanced to overhear him muttering to his cousin:

"As I said before, heaven help us. I have given myself a bad back – and what for? Honestly, Darcy! *Books?*"

Chapter 4

For Elizabeth, breakfast at *The Fox and Hounds* in Reigate was an astonishing affair. The repast was welcome, as was the chance to escape the confines of the carriage – but it was the company that made it little short of extraordinary.

She had walked into the inn expecting to breakfast with Colonel Fitzwilliam and Mr. Darcy – or at least her representation of them. She had surmised that, in the face of his cousin's engaging manners and readiness for conversation, Mr. Darcy would revert to his reserved and taciturn self, much as he had on each of his visits to Hunsford.

Nothing could have been further from the truth.

To her great surprise, Elizabeth found herself sitting down for breakfast with a seemingly younger version of Colonel Fitzwilliam and with another gentleman she barely knew. Someone inclined to talk. Someone who would smile. Someone who would light-heartedly advise his cousin that the time might have come for him to sell his commission and retire to the fireside, for surely he must be too old for active service if his back was injured by a mere carriage ride. Someone who, finding himself teased in his turn about his sudden inclination to sample the delights of Portsmouth, would show no dignified displeasure but laughingly observe instead that stranger things have happened.

Elizabeth very nearly dropped the serving spoon to hear Mr. Darcy laugh, quite persuaded that, to the best of her knowledge, she never had, throughout the course of their acquaintance.

He seemed unusually disposed to do so now, more than once, as the gentlemen kept up their conversation throughout the morning repast, their easy banter putting Elizabeth in mind of the affectionate ribbing between brothers.

It required a great deal of effort for her to remember her manners and not stare at such a disproval of the image she had formed of him, especially as it was plain to see from the Colonel's lack of surprise at his cousin's manner that to him *this* Mr. Darcy was the norm, rather than the solemn, reserved version she had come to know.

Having seen this unexpected side of him, Elizabeth thought in passing that his friendship with the ebullient Mr. Bingley was no longer mystifying and it came to her that she was presumably now seeing Mr. Darcy as Mr. Bingley knew him, when his sisters were nowhere in sight.

The notion triggered another recollection. Even Mr. Wickham, despite his understandable resentment, had allowed Mr. Darcy to be sincere, honourable and agreeable, amongst his equals in fortune and consequence.

Yet *she* was not. The thought gave her pause. In those respects at least, she was not his equal – nor was she part of his inner circle. And it was very puzzling to ponder why exactly he was suddenly treating her as such.

The perplexing notion was soon put aside however, for the Colonel chose to start regaling her with tales of their boyhood, far too entertaining to permit distraction.

Again, she would have assumed that the solemn and reserved master of Pemberley would not take kindly to humorous disclosures from the days when he was none of the above.

She was again mistaken, for he merely chuckled as Colonel Fitzwilliam chose to reminisce over a time when they had conspired to hide a very destructive ferret in his chambers and were hauled over the coals in the late Mr. Darcy's study for the damage caused.

"We gave nothing away of course, for our unwilling guest had not been released yet, and we were not about to feed him to the lions," the Colonel chortled, then turned to his cousin. "Poor Uncle George, he was mad as snakes. Still, I daresay we would have got away with it were it not for that weasel, Wickham. He could not wait to go tattling to your father – and *that* just days after you spared him a well-deserved thrashing for spilling a whole bottle of ink over the map that you had drawn."

"Yes, well! Not the first kindness wasted on the scoundrel," was all that Darcy muttered, his countenance suddenly darkening into the same forbidding lines that Elizabeth could not fail to recognise, from the day when the two gentlemen had come across each other on the main street in Meryton.

The Colonel must have seen the change as well, for he swiftly added:

"But never mind that now! Forgive me, Miss Bennet, for bringing up names wholly unconnected with the present party. I daresay you would like to know what happened to the ferret – "

"I most certainly do," she smiled, "but in any case, you need not apologise, Colonel. In fact, I am acquainted with Mr. Wickham," she offered, not quite able to restrain herself.

It was not good manners, *that* she knew full well, to attempt to wheedle further hints as to their history, but the opportunity was too good to miss. By the looks of it, Colonel Fitzwilliam was a far better source of information than Mr. Bingley, since he was such a longstanding fixture in his cousin's life.

Unfortunately though, and with some misgivings, Elizabeth noted that the sole result was to make the gentleman uncomfortable, for all he said was:

"Oh?"

She did not reply at once.

It was Mr. Darcy who supplied in her stead:

"He has taken a commission in the regiment stationed near Miss Bennet's home. I came across him in Meryton last autumn."

The Colonel turned to his cousin at that and, to Elizabeth's surprise, his countenance twisted into something odd. Something that could best be described as... compassion?

"I am sorry to hear it," he said at last, confirming the strange notion, then he forced a smile as he turned to her again. "As I am for *you*, Miss Bennet," he added in a poor attempt at lofty humour, which Elizabeth found suddenly provoking – so much so that she felt compelled to retort:

"I cannot imagine why. Mr. Wickham is well liked in Hertfordshire."

"Is he!" the Colonel said tersely then frowned, his mien and tone sobering and turning very earnest as he added, "I am heartily sorry to have ruined the genial disposition of the morning by mentioning this man, Miss Bennet. I will only add that although he is very skilled at making friends, he is less capable of retaining them. Mr. Wickham is not a man to be trusted!" he concluded with great emphasis and at that, from the other side of the table, Mr. Darcy released a loud huff of vexation.

"Would you be so kind as to change the subject, Fitzwilliam? I daresay we have imposed upon Miss Bennet for too long," he interjected sternly, in a manner that resembled the Mr. Darcy of Netherfield and Hunsford, rather than the cheerful stranger she was travelling with today.

"Of course. Of course. Forgive me. Now, Miss Bennet, as I was saying earlier, the ferret…" he rather awkwardly endeavoured to do as he was bid.

For her part, Elizabeth tried to listen and laugh at the right point in the narrative, but the light-heartedness was gone, and so was her interest in the Colonel's conversation. It was impossible to dismiss what had just happened, to ignore his truncated revelations and not wonder at his forcefulness of manner when he had spoken so decidedly against his erstwhile companion.

Given his lifelong association with Mr. Darcy, one thing was certain: unlike Mr. Bingley, the Colonel must have been fully informed of their transactions. Moreover, he was an honourable man, of sense and feeling – so the fact that he was *still* on his cousin's side and so violently opposed to Mr. Wickham was worthy of careful consideration.

Elizabeth remembered having laughed at Jane when she had endeavoured to clear both parties of blame and explain it all through some misunderstanding. The notion seemed far less ludicrous today. But then there were the references to Mr. Wickham's less than noble deeds, as far back as their childhood. They painted a very different picture, one that could not be dismissed as a misunderstanding.

Was Jane closer to the mark in this as well? Was there truth in her assumption that there might have been more to the story? That no man of common humanity, no man who had any value for his character could treat his father's favourite in such a manner? That a friendship between one who could act with so little feeling and one like Mr. Bingley – or like Colonel Fitzwilliam, for that matter – would be incomprehensible?

Was it possible that, same as in his boyhood, Mr. Wickham might have made use of what he could, for his own ends?

Still, she could not see how Mr. Wickham would profit from blackening Mr. Darcy's name – from vexing a powerful man who had the standing and the means to crush him for a great deal less than slander.

Why would Mr. Wickham lie – what purpose would it serve? Besides, there was truth in his countenance and manner!

Yet there was truth as well, and righteous indignation, in the Colonel's countenance a short while earlier. It was impossible to imagine how such conflicting notions could be reconciled!

Thus distracted, Elizabeth did fail to laugh at the right places in the Colonel's subsequent narrative – and the gentlemen could not fail to notice.

Breakfast finished on a decidedly less carefree note than it had begun, and Mr. Darcy was in a vastly different humour by the time his coachman came in to announce that the horses were well rested and they could resume their journey at his party's pleasure.

His humour was in fact so altered that he positively snapped at his cousin when the Colonel inquired whether he was of a mind to take a turn with Miss Bennet beyond the confines of the coaching inn, rather than repair directly to the carriage. Unjustifiably put out, to Elizabeth's way of thinking, he scathingly retorted:

"It *might* have been an option, were it not for your tales of ferrets that spoiled the day and distracted everybody!" he burst, sounding so much like his forbidding self that Elizabeth's brows arched in ill-disguised amusement.

She failed to see how tales of ferrets would impact on the pleasure of a country walk, but it was diverting to note that apparently Mr. Darcy could not keep the pretence of good-humour for too long, even in his cousin's comfortable presence.

His lips tightened in a line of displeasure, Mr. Darcy pulled his gloves on. Then, with a sigh, he at least had the grace to turn to her and apologise.

"I beg your pardon, I have spoken out of turn. I should have asked. Would you care for a stroll, Miss Bennet, before we resume our journey?"

"I thank you, no. We had much better set off," she answered, quite proud of being able to keep the unholy merriment from her voice and countenance.

It was diverting and very gratifying indeed to see that, baffling moments of light-heartedness aside, Mr. Darcy was not much different from her original view of him – and she was not going to delay their journey for the doubtful pleasure of a walk in his mercurial society!

"But of course," was all he said, a touch of sarcasm in his voice, turning another glare upon his cousin.

At that, Elizabeth arched her brows again as they retraced their steps to the waiting carriage. Sarah had resumed her place by then, as had the footmen, after partaking of their own repast someplace else in the inn, in the quarters reserved for attendants, and Elizabeth made her own way within, before either of the gentlemen could offer their assistance.

The journey began in stony silence, and soon both herself and Mr. Darcy chose to return to their books. In his corner, the Colonel shifted, cleared his voice twice and coughed repeatedly, until his cousin looked up from his employment.

"Shall I procure you a flask, Fitzwilliam? Have a care for your health, I beg you! Your throat seems as afflicted as your back!" he scoffed, and Elizabeth lifted her book for better to conceal her amusement.

She could not screen it from both gentlemen at once though, and could easily surmise that the Colonel must have noticed her smirk, for he shot her a matching one in return.

"Forgive me for disrupting your reading, Miss Bennet," he chose to address her. "May I ask, or would it be impertinent, about the purpose of your journey into Falmouth?"

Elizabeth looked up from her book.

"Not at all, Sir, but I fear I cannot enlighten you. The express I received did not supply details. I was merely told that Mrs. Pencarrow would like to acquaint herself with my mother and her daughters."

"How strange that you have not known of her existence before. This seems to be the case, if I understood you rightly?" the Colonel pressed on and at that, his cousin lowered his volume, seemingly inclined to speak – presumably to censure his relation for his intrusion in the affairs of others.

He held his peace however, and Elizabeth chose to answer:

"It is, and I *am* surprised. I would have thought I knew everything there was to know about my mother's relations."

'*Along with everybody else in Meryton,*' Mr. Darcy's turn of countenance seemed to convey, before he turned towards the window.

Elizabeth pursed her lips, determined to ignore him.

"From what I understand, my grandmother was her sister," she informed the Colonel. "At present, this is the full extent of my knowledge on the matter," she concluded and raised her book again.

Colonel Fitzwilliam, however, seemed inclined for further conversation.

"I trust you shall like Cornwall very well. I have travelled there on occasion, but no further than Padstow, on the northern coast. *You* have visited in the south, have you not, Darcy? My uncle had acquaintance in the area and he was very fond of sailing in...?"

"Talland Bay, near Polperro," his cousin almost reluctantly supplied.

"Aye, Polperro. A delightful coastal village, I remember your father saying. He mentioned your involvement in a sea rescue there once – did he not?"

"Not another tale, Fitzwilliam, I beg you," Mr. Darcy muttered, and again Elizabeth was inclined to smile at his unaccountable ill-humour.

She turned her own eyes upon the gentleman in question.

"A sea rescue, Sir? You are a man of many talents, Mr. Darcy. I never knew you were versed in the art of sailing."

"I am not, Miss Bennet. My father was."

"But... a sea rescue?"

"Merely a group of young people venturing out at sea in a craft that was far too light for the purpose. Besides, I had little involvement in the matter."

"You are too modest, Cousin," Fitzwilliam interjected. "My uncle told a very different story."

"It was a long time ago. Facts tend to get strangely distorted," was all that Mr. Darcy was prepared to offer, before returning to his book again.

Elizabeth sighed. It was going to be a dreadfully long journey!

To make matters worse, at her left Sarah had apparently fallen asleep again! She pursed her lips and, rather than choosing to play umpire to the cousins' rather childish disagreements, she settled into the cushions and closed her eyes. Feigning sleep was equally childish, she determined, and presumably cowardly as well, but at the moment it seemed the most palatable option – as long as she could be trusted to keep herself convincingly still.

She did keep still, although it required the most valiant effort especially when, a few minutes later, she distinctly heard Mr. Darcy whisper:

"Fitzwilliam, I *beg* you would desist from your misguided efforts! Do you imagine it was in the least helpful to bring up tales of me rescuing damsels in distress?"

⁓⁓⁓

"Miss Bennet? Miss Bennet?"

The soft, kindly tones registered vaguely with her, yet not enough to fully bring her from her slumber. A moment later, while still quiet, they took a commanding edge as the gentleman instructed:

"Would you attempt to rouse your mistress, pray?"

A set of hands – Sarah's, rather than Mr. Darcy's – shook her arm lightly, just enough to wake her, and Elizabeth opened her eyes.

Hm. Apparently her feigned sleep had turned real. She blinked, stirred – and suddenly smiled at the recollection of the last words she had heard before falling asleep. Mr. Darcy rescuing damsels in distress! Who would have thought? Now that might have made for a *very* entertaining story. Such a shame she was not likely to cross paths with Colonel Fitzwilliam again, after this. She most certainly would have enjoyed wheedling it out of him. Her smile grew wider and – to her great surprise – it was instantly mirrored on the countenance before her. Ah! So the mercurial temper had veered back towards good-humour yet again.

"Forgive me for disrupting your rest. We have arrived in Guildford," he offered softly and, for some reason, reached to hold her hand.

She looked down in surprise at their joined hands resting in her lap, atop the travelling rug. She could not remember wrapping herself in it. Sarah must have done so – unless, yet again, it had been him?

Elizabeth felt sorely tempted to shake her head, or rub her eyes, or rouse herself fully in some other way, in the vain hope of making sense of Mr. Darcy. It was a fruitless effort though, and she did not attempt it. She withdrew her hand, sat up and pushed the rug aside.

They were now alone in the stationary carriage – the others must have made their way into the inn already – and the door stood open attended by a footman, who maintained his post seemingly oblivious to the pouring rain.

"Oh! I am sorry to have kept you," she said to both – well, in truth, more to the soaking footman, yet it was Mr. Darcy who replied.

"Think nothing of it. Come, let us go in."

He got out and came to stand in the rain across from the footman to hand her down, then ushered her to the entrance of the coaching inn where, under the protection of a wide porch, Colonel Fitzwilliam was waiting.

"I bear ill tidings, Darcy," he announced as soon as they joined him. "There is not a private parlour to be had for love or money. Shall we seek another place to stop?"

Elizabeth's eyes flashed up to him in some surprise. She would not have imagined Colonel Fitzwilliam to be so fastidious! Mr. Darcy, aye, perhaps – but why should the Colonel object to having to sit for a while with other travellers?

True to form, Mr. Darcy did not look best pleased. Nevertheless, he rejected his cousin's suggestion.

"I should imagine not. We cannot trawl through Guildford in search of other places, not in this sort of weather," he added with a slight gesture at their wet apparel. "Besides, this is the best coaching inn in those parts. I cannot vouch for any of the others."

"Are you quite certain?" the other persisted, and Mr. Darcy's features tightened in displeasure as he shrugged.

"It cannot be helped."

A moment later though, an oddly diverted smile fluttered on his lips and he added:

"It seems I shall have to stake my best hopes on Seale after all."

For some reason, the other laughed warmly at that and gave his cousin's shoulder an affectionate pat, giving Elizabeth to understand that, while she slept, they must have resolved their former differences.

"You do that, Cousin," he said kindly, then rubbed his hands together. "Come, let us get away from this blasted chill and see what sort of fare could be got at the best coaching inn in Guildford. I am famished, I can tell you that."

❧ ❦ ☙

The fare was good and the company reasonably cheerful but, to Elizabeth's increasing irritation, Mr. Darcy's mood seemed to sour again on the next leg of their journey and get progressively worse with the passing hours.

Judging by his frequent complaints about the weather, it seemed that the driving rain had a great deal to do with his ill-humour and the Colonel showed himself unstintingly in sympathy with him over that. He knew his cousin well and must have been privy to his strange abhorrence of bad weather but her own patience had begun to run thin with Mr. Darcy and his temper.

That a grown man could be so put out by the vagaries of the English climate was bordering on the ridiculous. One would have thought he had been blessed with perpetual sunshine over the hills of Derbyshire! On the whole, he was behaving increasingly like a petulant, overindulged child.

It required a fair amount of self-restraint to keep herself from telling him just that and, with the greatest effort, Elizabeth endeavoured to ignore him. It was easier said than done. There was little she could do to occupy herself – or rather, to distance herself from her vexing companion and his excessively tolerant cousin. She could not feign sleep – she was too irritated. She could not read – the light was poor, due to the low, dark clouds rather than the time of day. She resigned herself to staring out of the window, more than a little disappointed that the famed views from the Hog's Back were obscured by the dreary, grey folds of rain and mist.

By the time they had left the only inn in Seale – just as beset by travellers, so that a private parlour simply could *not* be had – the driving rain was still showing no sign of abating and Mr. Darcy's countenance had turned so dark that, in the dimming light, it seemed almost purple. His concern unremitting, the Colonel laid a hand on his cousin's shoulder.

"Are you well, Darcy?"

"As well as can be expected," came the tired reply and Elizabeth saw Mr. Darcy bow his head to pinch the bridge of his nose between thumb and forefinger, before spreading his hand to rub at his temples as he released a long sigh.

Colonel Fitzwilliam gave him an affectionate pat and a wistful smile and, having witnessed that, Elizabeth finally found it in her heart to be a little charitable.

In view of his earlier kindness and attention to her comfort and moreover in the face of his cousin's obvious concern, perhaps she ought to give the gentleman the benefit of the doubt and allow that perhaps he *was* in pain. Her countenance softened, as did her eyes when she trained them upon him.

"Headache, Mr. Darcy?" she asked gently and, at her sympathetic tone of voice, he looked up.

"I... Aye, Miss Bennet. A sudden headache..." he allowed.

"Exacerbated by the weather, I assume?"

For some reason, his lips twitched at that.

"It appears so."

"For my part, I have always found that it is more likely to pass in quiet solitude. Now, solitude cannot be had," she added lightly, "but perhaps if you were to sit still and close your eyes...?"

His lips twitched again almost in a real smile at her reference to the lack of solitude, then the smile grew warmer.

"I thank you, Miss Bennet. I shall take your very good advice."

And so he did. He closed his eyes with another sigh and somewhat of a wince and remained still under her gaze, softened into compassion. He did seem exhausted and in pain and, but for the wince – or precisely *because* of it – he did look rather handsome, she thought in passing, before setting the intruding thought aside.

She looked away, straight into the Colonel's steady gaze.

"You know, Darcy, there is always the morrow – or perhaps the carriage," he pensively offered, to Elizabeth's sudden vexation.

Could he not just let the poor man be? It was plain to see that the Colonel's words had brought no succour. Quite the opposite. Mr. Darcy's eyes flashed open and his countenance twisted into insurmountable vexation.

"The morrow, Fitzwilliam? Have you not listened to a word I said? And worse still, *the carriage?*"

The Colonel, however, would not be put off.

"Fastidiousness has its rewards, Cousin, but beware of the price."

Mr. Darcy scowled.

"I – am – not – fastidious!" he enunciated, his voice low and hard.

The reply was an affectionate but disbelieving shake of his cousin's head along with a quiet chuckle and, abandoning the losing battle, Mr. Darcy gave a dismissive wave and an exasperated huff, then turned towards the window.

"Colonel," Elizabeth calmly intervened, "perhaps we ought to let Mr. Darcy try to sleep."

Two pairs of eyes turned upon her at that, with oddly matching warm looks of gratitude and reassurance, but the Colonel was the only one to speak up.

"Of course, Miss Bennet – and I shall do just that."

༺ ༻

The drumming of the rain on the carriage top was still driving him to distraction – futile anger, because it was too late now anyway. It was dusk and too late for a walk even if the rain stopped. Moreover, they must have been less than ten miles from Basingstoke.

Fastidious! The intense vexation he still felt at his cousin's words was well on its way to bringing on a real headache. How was he to propose to her on the morrow, in Mrs. Bennet's hearing? If he heard that harridan again, crowing about his ten thousand a year, there was no way under heaven for him to refrain from stirring the old tirade about unsuitable relations into his proposal! As for the carriage, heaven help us! Aye, he would gladly have Fitzwilliam wait out in the rain – and perforce the poor blameless maid, into the bargain – but how the deuce was he to bare his soul to her, propose to her and, with any luck, kiss her – in his *carriage*, for goodness' sake? Or by the side of the road, like a common ploughboy? Or worse still, in the courtyard of a country inn, milling with all and sundry?

He clenched his fists as he recalled the half-a-dozen times when he had come upon her on the woodland paths around Hunsford and Rosings. Had he not been such an unmitigated fool, had he not wasted all that time wrestling with difficulties of his own making, he would have taken one of those golden opportunities and by now they would have been engaged!

He swallowed again, well-nigh choking on his own vexation and took a long, deep breath, endeavouring to cease agonising over matters that could not be altered. Endeavouring to concentrate instead on the only gleaming light in this frustrating tangle.

She loved him. He had long thought as much, but her earlier kindness could not fail to prove it yet again.

The welcome balm spread into his chest and he opened his eyes to let them feast upon her as best he could, in the fast fading light, while he brought the precious recollections to mind, one by one.

Her gentleness. Her warm compassion. Her sweet concern for his comfort – and, by far the most rewarding, her taking Fitzwilliam to task in his defence!

The adorable notion suddenly made him chuckle and, to his delight, this must have drawn her notice, for she looked up to him and her countenance softened once more into a smile.

"Am I to assume you are feeling better, Mr. Darcy?"

"I am. And I have you to thank for it," he daringly offered.

The unintentional forthrightness gave him no regrets. This precious journey was about to end! He could not declare himself in the hearing of a very vexing cousin and a maid, but at least he would tell her *that*.

"Not at all, Sir. I have done nothing."

"I cannot agree – but let us not argue over it."

A mild laugh was her sole reply and for a while there was silence. The maid was very quiet – but then so she had been throughout the journey, bless her soul. Perhaps she was asleep again. As for Fitzwilliam, he was not stirring either. Whether his cousin was awake or not, Darcy did not care – it was a mercy that he had the kindness or the common sense to keep his mouth shut.

"Miss Bennet?" he began, knowing that he had to.

"Yes, Mr. Darcy?"

"Will your stay in Falmouth be of some duration?"

"At this point, I fear I cannot say. Why should you wish to know?"

"I was merely wondering when would you… er… and your family return to Longbourn."

"I have no notion. But I can only assume it would be sometime next month. We cannot impose for very long on our relation."

"No, I should imagine not," he allowed, knowing full well that the great-aunt would be driven to distraction within a se'nnight by the younger sisters' antics. "Then perhaps I could call upon you at Longbourn in the summer?"

He could not read her turn of countenance – he could barely see her now – but there was no mistaking the extreme surprise in her voice, when she answered:

"Of course, if you wish."

Why should she be surprised rather than glad, he truly could not fathom. Oh, for the freedom to speak now!

43

He could not – but he *would* leave her with at least some indication of his thoughts and intentions.

"I do. You see, Miss Bennet, there is something I most particularly want to speak of."

"And can it not be said now?"

'Now? Was she so certain that the others were asleep?'

"Unfortunately not – much as I would wish to."

"On the morrow, then? To spare yourself a journey into Hertfordshire, if nothing else?" she archly prompted, her merry tones now a disembodied voice in the darkness.

Warmth coursed through him at her adorable impatience and suddenly exploded, flooding his heart. She was as eager as he to settle the matter! He *would* try, by Jove! He would do his best to address her on the morrow and, despite the impending nightmare of her relations' presence, he *would* try to abide by the firm intention to speak to her of love, and not of pride.

"I should like that very much. Aye, Miss Bennet. God willing, on the morrow," he said softly, his countenance warmed by an unseen smile.

Chapter 5

"But, Lizzy, really? *Mr. Darcy?*" Lydia asked for what must have been the seventh time – and this time Elizabeth did not even try to stop her eyes from rolling.

"Yes, Lydia! Mr. Darcy. Now could we move on to another subject?"

"No, Lizzy, we certainly *cannot*," Lydia said with great determination. "I declare he must be enamoured with you, to squire you about the country in this fashion. So much the better! You will be rich – and better still, you will no longer have an eye for Mr. Wickham, so you can leave him to me," she said and twirled about the room, then dropped unceremoniously on one of the sofas.

"Lydia, I wish you would leave Lizzy be," Jane interjected sensibly, but by then Elizabeth was too tired to see sense and subdue her temper.

"If you had anything other than flirtation, love and officers in your head, you would understand when I tell you that Mr. Darcy is no more enamoured of me that I of him!"

"So you will persist in accepting Mr. Wickham's attentions?"

"Probably not," she candidly owned, the Colonel's words still fresh in her memory. "But we can speak of Mr. Wickham later. Now, would you take Mamma her tea and let me talk to Jane?"

"Mamma must be asleep. You know she keeps to her bed in the mornings, especially when she is unwell."

"I did not know she was unwell," Elizabeth replied.

Few and far between were the days when the mistress of Longbourn did not complain of an ailment or another, so the intelligence did not surprise her. Still, she would have hoped that, in the excitement of travelling to meet this mysterious relation, her mother would not need to seek further excitement in complaints.

"Mamma was well enough when we arrived," Jane supplied, as though she had read her thoughts, "but when she learned that, after all this rain, the river burst its banks and the ford might have become impassable, the ill-tidings have brought on a headache."

"I see. So is the ford impassable now?"

"I know not. Papa is to set out with Mr. Darcy to investigate the matter."

Unlike her mother's habitual response to any inconvenience, this *was* highly unexpected, so Elizabeth's eyes widened.

"With Mr. Darcy?" she exclaimed, astonished.

"See, Lizzy? He *is* enamoured with you. Why else would he be courting Papa's favour?"

"Hush, Lydia!" Elizabeth burst out with great vexation.

So the gentleman in question still seemed intent on baffling her then, as if yesterday was not enough. Considerate – silent – jesting – complaining about ferrets – throwing a temper tantrum over the English weather – in pain perhaps, and oddly vulnerable – recovered, chuckling in the darkness and offering to call at Longbourn, of all places. And now investigating the state of the ford with her father!

No plans of that nature had been voiced last night, during the light repast they all sat down to before retiring. Her father had requested it was served – once he had recovered from the shock of seeing her arrive escorted by Mr. Darcy and his cousin – but did not touch it, merely kept the others company as they ate.

As for herself, Elizabeth was too tired to do it justice. She was too tired to speak even, and – true to form – Mr. Darcy did not say much either. It was the Colonel and her father who seemed happy to strike up a conversation, only to find that it effortlessly flowed, much like the wine they had ordered. By the time Elizabeth decided she needed her bed, they were doing battle with the third carafe, while debating over the Peninsular campaign and the shocking way it was reported in the papers.

She had previously assumed that Mr. Darcy must have made his own escape soon after, but since she could not remember any talk of burst riverbanks, impassable fords or the need for investigation, she could only conclude that such matters must have been discussed after she had left them.

Elizabeth all but giggled and shook her head, not quite able to picture Mr. Darcy imbibing with the Colonel and her father – or indeed with anyone – and willingly engaging in lengthy conversations.

For some reason despite having seen him light-heartedly bantering with his cousin on their journey, she rather doubted the same genial manner might have emerged in her father's presence.

The thought gave her pause. Perhaps it had. Perhaps this was precisely why her father was prepared to ride out investigating fords with a man whom, much like herself, he could scarce abide.

Not that *she* found Mr. Darcy as intolerable as ever − not after yesterday. She did not *like* him −… No, that was not strictly true. She did like the facets encountered over breakfast. And speaking of breakfast and the ensuing warnings, she was no longer certain she could or should detest him on account of Mr. Wickham. But that was neither here nor there.

"Oh, Lizzy, only *think!*"

"Believe me, Lydia, I *am* trying to − if you would only let me! Come, take Mamma her tea − wake Kitty − find Mary −… "

"I will not! You are sending me away so that you can confide in Jane, but I want to hear it too. I am not a child anymore, and I would like to hear of your beaus as much as anybody. Come, Lizzy, do tell! You spent a whole day in his carriage, surely you have something to impart! Did he hold your hand? Did he ask for a private interview? Did he flirt? Goodness, no, what am I saying? Of course he did not *flirt* − who can imagine Mr. Darcy flirting! Was he all brooding and romantic, then? Oh, Lizzy, just think − and he said you were not handsome enough to tempt him. Oh, what a laugh! Who would have thought it? Mr. Darcy!"

"Hush, Lydia!" this time Elizabeth *and* Jane urged, both at once, and Jane stared at her sister in concern, as Elizabeth's mouth literally fell open.

Yes, he *did* hold her hand.

Yes, he *did* ask for an interview − or at least asked if he could call at Longbourn.

Yes, he *did* flirt − after a fashion.

Yes, he *had been* brooding − and perhaps romantic!

What sort of a world was this, were *Lydia* made her see things that she had not?

And there was more − things that Lydia would not understand and never thought of mentioning. He had been mindful of her comfort. He had brought her into his inner circle. He had curtailed his visit with his aunt and had gone out of his way to convey her to her relations. He had even silenced Mr. Collins, when he most needed silencing – and had now moved on to staying late into the night with her father and planning rides to ascertain whether the ford could be crossed in safety.

"Good heavens!"

Was Lydia in the right? Was Mr. Darcy in love with her? Was he about to propose – to *her*, of all people? Was *that* why he had been so vexed by the wet weather and the lack of a private parlour?

"What is it, Lizzy?" Lydia piped up.

"Lizzy, are you unwell? You have gone very pale!"

Elizabeth pursed her lips and forgot to reply, as compassion softened her troubled mien. Poor man! He will be disappointed and she was sorry for it. What a blow must this be, for so proud a man, to learn that his affections were not returned!

His affections?

Good Lord, was she blind? How did she not see it? Or had she been misled by her own former dislike of him into thinking that he disliked her also?

The unexpected word almost made her start. *Former* dislike? Where did that come from? She disliked him no longer – after just *one* day? After just one day of revelations? After just one day of casting his reserve aside?

Why now, though? Once Lydia had begun to nudge the pieces into place, others followed, until it was plain to see that he had singled her out as far back as the ball at Netherfield. Throughout his stay in Hertfordshire he had shown more interest in *her* than in any other female. So why had it taken him so long to discard his reserve?

More to the point, why did it matter? She *was* going to refuse him, was she not?

"Good heavens!" she repeated, this time with a loud gasp.

"What is it, Lizzy?" her eldest and her youngest sister chorused and then Jane added, "What is wrong?"

Wrong? *Wrong?* This was a *disaster!* It had just come to her – their final conversation in the darkened carriage. He had asked for permission to call on her at Longbourn, presumably with the intention to propose, and she had urged him to speak up on the morrow! Now – today!

'I should like that very much. Aye, Miss Bennet. God willing, on the morrow.'

Poor man! He must have thought she was encouraging him – while all she aimed for was teasing him out of the notion of calling upon them in Hertfordshire.

"Good heavens!" she said, for the third time.

"Lizzy, *would* you stop saying that!"

"Hush, Lydia!" came the familiar admonishment, just from Jane this time, followed almost instantly by an urgent, "Lizzy, look!"

Had it not been for Jane squeezing her arm, very tightly, Elizabeth would have missed the warning, just as she had missed Lydia's outburst, the ensuing reprimand, the knock on the door and Lydia's voice piping up again to ask the caller to come in. She winced at the tight squeeze – but her head snapped up, only to see the door opening to admit Mr. Darcy.

"Jane, do not leave me!" she whispered in something very much like panic.

Had she been in command of her senses, she would have laughed. With a small difference – *'Jane'*, rather than *'Kitty'* – this was, word for word, exactly what she said when she had been confronted with Mr. Collins's imminent proposal. Was she forever doomed to enlist the help of one of her sisters, in order to escape her suitors?

Poor Mr. Darcy, the thought intruded yet again. How disagreeable must it be for him, if he ever learns that he was in the same boat as *Mr. Collins*.

Her highly-strung mind jumped erratically from one thing to another – from Mr. Collins's imaginary boat to Polperro and then to damsels in distress, before she suddenly clenched her fingers together in her lap and willed herself into some control over her scattered senses. When she thought she had achieved it, she stood up.

"Mr. Darcy. Pray come in, Sir," she offered, then looked back down towards her elder sister, her eyes pleading.

"Of course, Lizzy," Jane reassured her in a whisper, before instructing Lydia, unusually sharply, to sit still and keep quiet – or else leave the room.

Making a show of pressing her lips together, Lydia did not budge.

'Of course not!' Elizabeth all but groaned, knowing full well that wild horses could not drag her away from a scene such as this. More worrying still, whatever Lydia learned would soon be broadcast over seven counties! For a moment, she contemplated the wisdom of walking out with Mr. Darcy, but thought better of it.

If Lydia was the price for Jane's support, then so be it!

With a deep, steadying breath, she walked towards their visitor.

"Good morning, Mr. Darcy. I hope you are well rested."

"I am, I thank you, as I trust are you."

"Would you not sit down – unless you are pressed for time? My sister tells me you have agreed to ride with my father to ascertain whether the ford can be crossed in safety."

"I have. We are to depart shortly. I was… hm!… hoping to see *you*, though, before I left."

It was cowardly in the extreme to feign forgetfulness – and yet that was precisely what she did.

"Oh? Were you?"

"I was. If you remember, there was something I most particularly wished to speak of."

She swallowed.

"Oh, yes, of course. Pray, be seated. Would you care for tea?"

"I thank you, no. I…"

Darting swift glances towards Jane and Lydia, Mr. Darcy walked towards the sofa that was nearest to the door, and waited. She joined him there and sat down, yet apparently that was not what he was waiting for, as he did not take a seat, but came to stand behind a nearby chair, fidgeting with his cuffs. It was so extraordinary to see *Mr. Darcy* fidget, that unreserved compassion flooded her again, chasing away the cowardly notion of suggesting that he should not speak now, but call at Longbourn after all.

No, she could not do that, she determined in the face of his acute discomfort. She had to let him say his piece, now, and be kind in her refusal. He would be hurt, but he would heal. He had his family – … No, the family included Lady Catherine. Well, at least he had his cousin. He *would* heal, and the sooner she allowed him to begin, the better. It was not fair for her to do otherwise. After all, it was not in her nature to torment a respectable man – as she had already said to Mr. Collins.

'But this is not Mr. Collins!', a sharp thought intruded, making her wish she could cover her eyes, run from the room and hide until the spinning haze that clouded her mind receded.

"Miss Bennet, I…" he began, then darted a look at Jane again.

With a deep breath, he finally came to sit beside her.

"Miss Bennet, is there a chance to talk in private?" he asked with some determination. "I am not comfortable speaking of it in your sisters' presence."

As nearly everybody is wont to do, at some time or other in their lives, Elizabeth understood exactly what it pleased her.

She understood him to mean *'sister's'*. That, coupled with his frequent glances towards Jane's side of the room, painted the most rewarding picture. Sudden, blessed relief coursed through her and she all but laughed in sheer delight at her own folly, to have lost her senses over nothing!

"Mr. Darcy," she said with a wide smile, "was it *Mr. Bingley* you wished to speak of?"

"Mr. Bingley!" Darcy exclaimed in his turn. "No, I do not wish to speak of Mr. Bingley!" he forcefully retorted – and at that, predictably, both Jane and Lydia looked up.

Before Elizabeth could feel concern for her elder sister – and indeed before she could fully comprehend precisely *why* the forceful retort seemed to please her rather than bring back the turmoil – equally predictably, Lydia spoke up:

"Mr. Bingley! Is he coming back to Netherfield, Sir?"

Two pairs of eyes turned upon her with silent but stern warnings and the elder sisters prayed that she *would* take heed. As for Darcy, he decided to attend to the interruption – albeit with considerable vexation.

"No, Miss… er… Lydia, I should imagine not."

"He is not? How horrid! He is not giving up the lease though, is he?"

'Hush, Lydia!' would not have been civil enough for company, which is why Jane and Elizabeth simultaneously decided to drop the *'Hush'*.

"I really cannot tell. Why should you wish to know?"

"Because then he will never come back again and Jane will never see him."

"Lydia!" they both urged, even louder, and at that she impatiently shrugged.

"Oh, la, Jane, what does it signify? Why can I not ask? You have been pining for him these five or six months together. Do you not wish to know whether he is coming back or not?"

"Lydia, *enough!*" Elizabeth commanded in the most determined manner.

As for Jane, she seemed to have forgotten how to speak. Extreme concern etched in her countenance, Elizabeth stood from the sofa with a swift, "Would you excuse me, Mr. Darcy?" and walked up to her elder sister.

She would not discomfit her by making a scene and putting her arms around her. She merely took her hands and asked, "Jane, would you not go to our mother?" before pursing her lips and almost hissing over her shoulder, "As for you, Lydia, you most certainly *should!*"

Lydia narrowed her eyes and folded her arms in defiance. Jane merely shook her head.

"I am well. Go to Mr. Darcy," she softly urged and, reluctant as she might have been to leave her, Elizabeth felt compelled to follow her advice.

She found the gentleman standing by the sofa, his eyes fixed on Jane's pained countenance. She did not sit, and neither did he.

"Miss Bennet," he brought himself to ask, very quietly, "Was your sister much attached to Mr. Bingley?"

Mortified in extreme by the entire debacle, Elizabeth could only offer:

"Forgive me, Mr. Darcy, but I cannot discuss my sister's sentiments with you."

"But your sister Lydia – "

"Has spoken out of turn!" she concluded, very firmly, then instantly regretted her sharpness of both tone and manner, for it was Lydia who deserved it and not him. On an impulse, she laid a hand on his sleeve. "I must apologise, Sir," she said with a tentative smile. "Not only for the unmerited sharpness just now, but also for having to ask you to postpone our conversation. It seems…" she trailed off, with a slight gesture meant to indicate that she was needed elsewhere.

"I understand. Forgive me for having intruded for so long," he offered, reaching to gather the small hand still resting on his sleeve.

He held it pressed between his palms for something that, by every standard, was a *long* time. Still – erroneously or not – she did not withdraw it. Suddenly, a smile fluttered on his lips.

"There is still Longbourn, Miss Bennet, is there not?"

The warmth in his eyes was unmistakable, as was the underlying message, and Elizabeth accepted both with unthinking pleasure, inordinately relieved that nothing had to be decided *now*. That she was suddenly freed from the fear of making a terrible mistake – one way or the other. His all-but-declared interest was gratifying, or at least had become so of late, and she could not help feeling thankful for his understanding and his patience. She had not orchestrated a respite – he had offered it freely, and at that very comfortable thought, her lips curled up into a smile.

"Indeed, Mr. Darcy. There is always Longbourn."

She saw him swallow hard, before he carried her hand to his lips. They were warm and – strangely – both firm and soft at the same time, and his tingling breath sent a very foolish flutter right into the pit of her stomach, when he whispered against her skin:

"I thank you, Miss Bennet."

He did not release her hand, but pressed it to his lips once more – a firm kiss that seemed to brand itself into her very flesh – before he gave the deepest bow, relinquished her fingers, farewelled her sisters, and was gone.

⁖ ⁘ ⁖

Elizabeth exhaled, very slowly, as soon as the door closed behind him. Before she could turn though – indeed, before the click of the closing door died out – Lydia spoke up from behind her.

"Goodness, Lizzy! What on earth was *that?*"

Elizabeth sighed. It was a hard task, to educate a sibling who would not be educated – presumably because, much as herself, Lydia was of the opinion that such strictures ought to come from a parent, not an elder sister.

Although concerned on Jane's behalf, Elizabeth could not bring herself to be truly angry with their least guarded sibling. Not just for opening her eyes to Mr. Darcy's feelings – ludicrous as it was to be indebted to *Lydia* for that – but also for unwittingly bringing about the very respite she now rejoiced in.

With a smile at the tangled business, Elizabeth walked back to her sisters. She sat and took Jane's hand and a glance passed between them, but it was Lydia that Elizabeth turned to at last.

"You dear, foolish thing! Did Jane not ask you to be silent?" she remonstrated, with more kindness than she had ever felt for her youngest sister.

"But no one ever speaks of matters of consequence!" Lydia burst in great frustration. "Everybody beats about the bush and nothing ever gets resolved, can you not see it? Should not Mr. Darcy tell his friend that Jane has been pining for him?"

"And what good would it do, sweetling, if Mr. Bingley no longer cares for me?" Jane said, very calmly. "What good would it do, other than expose me to ridicule for my disappointed hopes?"

"Oh, Jane! I have not thought of that! Ridicule? My goodness! Lizzy, do you think Mr. Darcy would spread horrible stories – ?"

"No, Lydia. Of course not."

Lydia released a relieved little huff.

"Jane, I am *that* sorry! I swear never to tell another living soul that you are in love with Mr. Bingley."

"Lydia, do not swear."

"Not a living soul, that is, who does not know already," Lydia smirked and the other two shook their heads in mild reproach.

"But never mind me now," Jane valiantly added, straightening her back. "What of *you*, Lizzy?"

"Aye!" Lydia forcefully interjected. "What just happened? He did not propose – then why did he come, just to hold your hand and be silent? Oh, Lizzy!" she suddenly exclaimed, covering her mouth in horror. "Did I ruin it for you as well?"

"No, sweetling, you have not," Elizabeth smiled, then decided to be truthful. "Much as it pains me that your unguarded comments distressed Jane, I am rather glad that Mr. Darcy did not propose today – and for that I must thank you."

Lydia stared.

"I shall never understand you," she declared. "He had not proposed – and you are *pleased* about it?"

With a light, sudden laugh, Elizabeth came to put her arms around her.

"Yes, Lydia. I am *very* pleased."

"But he will, though. Will he not? He must! Jane, have you not seen how he could not keep his eyes off her? And how he kissed her hand? I thought I should swoon!"

"I am very happy you did not," Elizabeth quipped. "Now, Lydia, this is a dreadful hardship, I am sure, but do you think you could refrain from mentioning this to *everybody?*"

"I do not think I could," Lydia answered candidly and the other two could not fail to laugh. "Can I at least tell Kitty? And Mamma?"

"You can tell Kitty, although there is not much to tell. As for Mamma – "

"*Not much to tell?* Lizzy, are you blind? Have you not seen him?"

"Nevertheless, there is not much to tell as yet. Which is why I wish you did not raise Mamma's expectations – or, for that matter, Papa's dread."

"So, just Kitty?"

"Just Kitty. As long as *she* can keep it under wraps as well."

"You know not what you are asking, Lizzy! Very well. I shall hold my tongue. But you owe me three trimmed bonnets and the use of your green shawl for that!"

༺ ❦ ༻

Warm peals of laughter rang from within when Colonel Fitzwilliam came to knock on the door of the private sitting room that the Bennet family had engaged at *The Falcon* in Basingstoke. The laughter ceased, but it was still glowing in the young ladies' eyes when he was invited to come in.

"Good morning," he bowed to all three, then smiled towards Elizabeth. "Forgive my intrusion, Miss Bennet, but I was hoping you would do me the honour of introducing me to your relations."

"It would be my pleasure. Jane, Lydia, this is Colonel Fitzwilliam, Mr. Darcy's cousin. Colonel, may I introduce my eldest sister… and my youngest," she indicated, then gestured for him to take a seat.

That, he did; and to Lydia's sharp disappointment his admiring glance settled on Jane, as was always the case with every new acquaintance. She sighed – but would not lose hope.

"*Colonel* Fitzwilliam? Would that be infantry, Sir?"

"Cavalry, Miss Lydia. The Third Dragoons."

"Better and better! And you are Mr. Darcy's cousin. Hm… I wonder how it is that Mr. Wickham never mentioned you. He mentioned Mr. Darcy, and not in a good way, but – "

"Lydia!" the sisters chorused again, rolling their eyes in amused exasperation.

"What have I done *now?* Can I not even speak of Mr. Wickham?" Lydia exclaimed in disbelief and, at her childish frustration, the Colonel could not fail to laugh.

"Forgive me, Miss Lydia. I fear I may be to blame for your sister's reticence. Miss Elizabeth," he turned to his former travel companion, "I must beg your pardon – and my cousin's too, but he is not here now – for mentioning that man yesterday. I fear I have ruined the enjoyment of the moment, because my cousin cannot bear to hear him spoken of. I know and I am sorry, but some things *must* be said. At the very least a warning, especially in view of your remark that he is well liked in Hertfordshire. I hope he is not too well liked, or at least not enough for him to be able to impose upon anybody. I cannot reveal details, they cannot be shared. But I have to say that this man has repaid my uncle and my cousin's unremitting kindness in the most infamous manner. A snake warmed to their bosom would have been less vicious! He is a wastrel and a scoundrel and had made it his life's work to poison everybody else's, for his own ends. You say, Miss Lydia," he added to the young girl, who was listening with rapt attention – as she often did to everything bordering on gossip – "that he has spread unpleasant rumours about my cousin. I cannot imagine with what sort of falsehoods he has imposed upon you, but I beg you would not credit a single word he says. I know him and I can vouch for the fact that he cannot be trusted – never, not in any way!"

He stopped, drew breath and smiled at his companions.

"Pray excuse me for ranting in this fashion. He has greatly injured those very dear to me and I should hate to see him injure others – nor can I forgive him. Neither can I forgive Darcy, truth be told," he added with a half-laugh, "for insisting that I do not call the rogue out for the distress he caused us. And now, Miss Lydia," he smiled, "I daresay we have done our duty, mentioned Mr. Wickham so, by your leave, let us speak no more of him – 'tis bad for digestion. How are you enjoying your trip to Falmouth?"

"Very much, Sir," Lydia blinked at the sudden change of topic. "But we have only started on our journey."

"And I hope you can continue it in safety."

"Aye – you must be thinking of that vexing ford."

A soft knock was heard and Sarah entered, bobbing a swift curtsy to everybody present.

"Yes, Sarah?" Jane prompted.

"I am come to fetch Miss Lydia, Ma'am. Miss Kitty needs her."

Lydia rolled her eyes.

"*Now?* But – "

"Go, Lydia," Jane urged softly. "You can return directly."

"But, Jane – !"

"The sooner you go, the sooner you will return," Elizabeth urged, barely restraining herself from shaking her head at her youngest sister's manifest unwillingness to leave the Colonel's company.

She rather hoped he did not notice, gratified as he must be by the young girl's interest. Would it not be wonderful if, for one day at least, she did not have to blush for some of her relations, she thought in some vexation, and endeavoured to distract him.

"It was most kind of your cousin," she interjected, for want of a more inspired comment, "to ride out with my father to ascertain whether it could be crossed."

"I was disappointed to find I could not join them, but it appears that there were only two riding horses to be had at the inn – and I must say, I was not eager to follow them on foot. As for my cousin, you are presumably aware by now, Miss Elizabeth, that he seems bent upon looking after as many people as he can – some more than others," he added with a warm smile and seemed delighted to have made her blush.

No, she was not aware of the best traits in Mr. Darcy's nature and she blushed even more at her earlier blindness, as well as at the implication in the Colonel's words and his obvious intention to show Mr. Darcy to her in the best possible light.

She came to see it now, he had done precisely that, throughout the entire journey. He must be well informed then of his cousin's intentions and seemingly keen to promote them as best he could. The thought pleased her, on more than one count – no less for his obvious acceptance of her.

She smiled at that, then blushed anew at the notion that he assumed – expected – she would welcome Mr. Darcy's suit.

Would she? Would she welcome it – him? Would she say '*yes*' when this man whom she had understood so little and mistakenly thought the very worst of would come to Longbourn to propose to her?

She swallowed, forcing the thought aside.

A respite. Till the summer. She would not ponder now!

"Does he look after you as well, Colonel?" she asked with an arch smile, to break the silence.

"He labours under that misconception," the Colonel laughed, "but I would like to think it is the other way around. In any case, my temper is not ductile enough for his liking and sparks fly oftentimes, as you may have noticed on our journey."

"I cannot imagine what you mean," Elizabeth laughed.

"Can you not? I thank you for your kindness," he retorted. "I fear I frustrate my cousin with my propensity to often disagree with him as to the best possible course of action. To his great satisfaction, his other friends are more accommodating – Mr. Bingley, by way of example. Now that is a friendship made in heaven," the Colonel added with a chuckle, "at least, to my cousin's way of thinking. For my part, *I* think it might do him a world of good to have his views challenged on occasion and if he marries wisely I trust he will enjoy the benefit of that," he casually observed, seeming even more delighted by Elizabeth's renewed blush at the excessively broad hint. "But as for Mr. Bingley, he needs guidance and Darcy loves to give it – so I daresay both parties are pleased with what they have got."

"I have not noticed that Mr. Bingley is in great need of guidance," Jane interjected very quietly and the Colonel turned to her at that.

"I was not aware you were acquainted with Mr. Bingley."

"We have been introduced last year," Elizabeth supplied, with a small grateful thought for Kitty and whatever reason she might have had to request Lydia's company and assistance.

"A pleasant, gentleman-like man, is he not?"

"Indeed," Jane concurred, although the remark was addressed to her sister.

"Still, it seems that despite his amiable nature – or perhaps because of it – he *is* in need of guidance, particularly in those aspects which can severely influence the course of one's life."

"Oh?"

"I have reason to think Bingley very much indebted to my cousin for having lately saved him from the inconveniences of a most imprudent marriage. It must have been a great discomfort for Darcy to interfere in so delicate a matter, but my cousin is nothing if not a slave to his perceived duty," the Colonel smiled warmly.

He received no answer from his fair companions.

The eldest appeared to have lost all interest in his communications and was staring at her hands, while Miss Elizabeth's eyes were fixed on her sister. Suddenly, Miss Bennet looked up.

"And did he give you his reasons for his interference?"

"He told me none of the particulars – merely that there were very strong objections to the lady. My cousin's firm opinion is that his friend was imposed upon, and that he could do a great deal better."

"I see," Miss Bennet said and stood.

Her sister followed suit and the Colonel was prompt to spring to his feet as well.

"Lizzy, you will excuse me," Miss Bennet added, very quietly. "One of us should see to our mother."

"Jane – !"

"Pray, do not fret. I shall see you shortly. Colonel," she farewelled him with a nod and the gentleman bowed to her retreating back and remained standing, waiting for the second Miss Bennet to resume her seat.

She did not.

"I fear I must leave you as well, Sir," she offered instead. "My family is in need of me at the moment."

"But of course. I trust I shall see you at dinner," he civilly added with a deep bow and followed her out of the now empty sitting room, wondering in passing what on earth was ailing Mrs. Bennet that she required quite so much attendance.

The room was not empty for too long. A few minutes later Lydia burst in, followed by her marginally older sister. She cast an eager look around, as though the occupants might have been hiding behind the door or the back of the sofas, but when the inescapable truth could no longer be avoided, she folded her arms over her bosom and gave a huff of unconcealed vexation.

"And now he is gone!" she pouted. "Oh, *hang* your bonnet and your horrid ribbons, Kitty!"

Chapter 6

The ford was passable.

They had at least been able to ascertain *that*, after a length of time spent atop barely manageable mounts that seemed intent on heading the wrong way and splashing about in muddy waters.

Mr. Bennet was in a strangely cheerful frame of mind and seemed indifferent to the antics of the stubborn beasts. If anything, the older gentleman was much more agreeable than his companion expected; more communicative and less eccentric than Darcy had ever seen him, with the obvious exception of the previous night.

Apart from the pair of intractable horses, the only other vexing matter was that, unlike himself, Mr. Bennet seemed bent to delay their return to the inn by every means possible. In truth, Darcy could scarce blame him, seeing as no one in their right mind would choose to relinquish the pleasure of a morning ride – albeit on hired cattle – for the dubious delights of Mrs. Bennet's company.

Not for the first time, Darcy wondered just how a man of such obvious discernment would have chosen to make a woman of inferior intellect his life companion. Yet there was enough beauty left in the lady's middle age for Darcy to suspect that, as many before him, Mr. Bennet might have had his head turned by a pretty face.

He sat up straighter in the saddle with a frown at the sudden thought that many would undoubtedly say the very same of *him*.

He shrugged. Hang them all! He had never made it his life's object to bow to tittle-tattlers and let them influence his choices!

Rather more unsettling was the old adage claiming that if anyone wished to know how a woman would age, they should look to her mother. The notion all but made him shudder. Surely not! Surely nothing short of a miracle – or rather wicked spell – would make Elizabeth turn into her *mother*.

Despite the garish picture, his countenance softened at the thought of her, and of the smile on those tempting lips when she had

60

confirmed that, delays and vexing interruptions notwithstanding, she *would* await at Longbourn for him to declare himself.

The warmth the notion brought was suddenly replaced by sharp impatience. With any luck, she would not have to wait *that* long – and neither would he! Most of the day and an entire evening still lay comfortably ahead. Perhaps a private moment might be found at last, and he could address her!

Impatience spurred him on and, in his turn, he urged his mount forward – only to send the unruly beast into restless, uncoordinated bounds. He tightened the reins and barely suppressed an oath.

"You seem uncommonly mismatched with your horse this morning, Mr. Darcy," Mr. Bennet observed with a quiet chuckle and it was only the unwillingness to offend Elizabeth's father that stopped Darcy from retorting sharply that there was little wonder, for it was not in his habit to ride third-rate cattle!

He held his peace and the other said nothing further, but merely chuckled once more and urged his own horse on, with better results.

Thank goodness, they were nearly there. The rooftops of the inn could just about be spotted over the low coppice that bordered the road, smoke billowing from the many chimneys. There was every reason to believe that, as the road turned, they would see the courtyard.

When the road did turn, Darcy noted with a muffled snort that there was something else to see as well. His cousin was strolling on the grass verge with a Bennet on each arm and was apparently having a grand time with it all! How did he bear their company and their inane chatter, Darcy could not pretend to know. Presumably all those years of active service had inured him to the society of scatterbrained flirts. Or, he thought, a touch more charitably this time – at least towards his cousin – perhaps the dreadful dangers of the battlefield had made him more inclined to find pleasure in the fleeting moment and any amusements that it chose to bring. Still, this was not the time for such deep musings, Darcy determined, and rode on to approach them and offer subdued greetings to Miss Lydia and the other. Catherine? Kitty? Something of that nature, and it mattered not.

"So, gentlemen, what is the verdict?" Fitzwilliam inquired.

Darcy allowed Mr. Bennet to speak up for both.

"I daresay there is hope of going through without being overset," Mr. Bennet shrugged but, for his part, Darcy felt moved to elaborate.

"The water levels seem to have gone down, now that the rain has stopped. If it stays fair, there should be no danger."

"So you will be leaving on the morrow, Mr. Bennet?" Fitzwilliam pressed on.

"I believe so. Eighteen hours should provide ample time for silliness and packing. Speaking of which, young ladies, have you succeeded in emptying *all* your trunks about the place? For, if that be the case, you had much better return to put them back together."

"We have not, Papa," Lydia answered promptly, while the other fidgeted.

"I see. Well, Colonel, I have done my best to rescue you from the society of two very silly girls, but it appears you shall have to bear it for a little longer."

"It shall be my pleasure, Sir," Fitzwilliam smiled and the girls turned to beam at him.

Mr. Bennet shook his head.

"Come, Mr. Darcy, let us return these worthy stallions to their stalls before they lose their patience," Mr. Bennet added and rode on and Darcy was only too pleased to follow.

He did not tarry in his chambers for more than a swift bath and a change of attire, then promptly made his way towards the parlour the Bennets had engaged, impatient to see her. To his disappointment, there were only two people in the room: the middle sister, the bookish one, and – horrifyingly – the mother!

"Oh, Mr. Darcy! A pleasure to see you, Sir," the matron greeted him loudly while her daughter curtsied. "I have been unable to thank you as yet for your great kindness of bringing Lizzy to us. I trust you will forgive me. I have been unwell and kept to my chambers. But Mr. Bennet tells me we can set off soon, early on the morrow, and the good tidings have revived my spirits. And yourself, Sir? I hope you are well."

Civil replies were duly made, while Darcy strived to find a way to extricate himself and, more importantly, discover Elizabeth's whereabouts without raising Mrs. Bennet's undue interest.

It could not be done, he ruefully determined. That woman had the nose of a well-trained bloodhound, once she caught the scent of eligible suitors for her daughters! The services of his own, equally well-trained but far more discreet people would have to be employed.

In some haste, he returned to his quarters to summon Peter, the second footman, and charge him to locate Sarah, the maid who had travelled with them from Hunsford, and enquire where the two eldest Miss Bennets could be found.

The need to involve servants riled him, as it brought the risk of speculation spreading like wildfire through his household. Still, it could not be helped. His people were the best that could be got, and drilled to respect their master's wishes and his private nature, but no man in his right mind would expect even the best of servants not to gossip. Well, be that as it may. They would all know, soon enough.

Peter was gone for a long time – or it merely appeared so, due to his own impatience. He returned at last, to say that the eldest Miss Bennets were in their chamber. He was sent out again to ask, through the same maid, whether Miss Elizabeth Bennet would allow him the pleasure of her company on a country walk.

This time the footman returned promptly – presumably not requiring as long to locate the maid or the Miss Bennets' quarters – to let him know that Miss Elizabeth Bennet sends her regrets, but she is much engaged with preparations for their departure on the morrow and she cannot be spared for a country walk.

The message riled him, especially because it was conveyed through servants, who were now informed of her rather unceremonious refusal.

He struggled to allow that it could not be helped, but the sensible approach could not curb either his disappointment or his impatience to see her. He could not ascertain how long he would have to wait – nor how to fill his time as he did so.

The passing notion of setting off on a walk alone was instantly discarded. He would much rather remain where he was until she would be free to join him, rather than run the risk of wasting more of the precious time left until her imminent departure. Reading was just as summarily dismissed. He lacked the patience now and besides, Don Manuel's *'Letters'* would only remind him of the delectable time spent in the carriage and make him long for her presence even more.

That it should have come to *this!* Waiting, pacing in his chambers like a schoolboy kept on tenterhooks by his first *amour*, when the society of worthier women had instantly been his, for the asking!

Nay, not worthier women, he amended with a smile – not that. Of greater standing perhaps, and greater fortune and connections, but not worthier. None worthier than *her*.

So he still paced, wondering if he should have worded his message better. Of course he should have! What he should have asked was whether Miss Bennet would care to inform him *when* she would be free for a country walk. He had expected an immediate concurrence, naturally; but still, he should have taken the preparations for departure into account.

That she could have walked with him and attend to her preparations later was an equally reasonable expectation, to his way of thinking, but he would not censure her for deciding otherwise. Much like himself, she would attend to duty before pleasure and it boded well, for the mistress of Pemberley would have many duties. It was reassuring to see that his trust in her good sense and diligence had not been misplaced.

Reasonable arguments kept coming in great number – all in order to subdue his disappointment and ensure that he would *not* succumb to the urge to send another message, again through the servants, and be shown as the veriest love-struck mooncalf!

By the time another hour and a half had passed however, reasonable arguments had begun to ring vexingly hollow.

How long would a sensible, efficient woman require to pack? Could the menial task not be left to servants? Perhaps, but she must have grown accustomed to doing a great deal for herself, as the Longbourn household must have been quite small and the services of the few available servants routinely claimed by others, who were neither sensible, nor half as efficient. Perhaps – …

Oh, what a clod! Perhaps she *had* finished her preparations. What did he expect? That she would *send* for him? What sort of fool would expect such unladylike behaviour? She might be in their sitting room, even then, awaiting his arrival!

He turned to the small looking-glass to readjust his neckcloth, in slight disarray after all the shuffling and the pacing. If she was not, then he would have to endure yet another dose of Mrs. Bennet! Oh, be that as it may. Even *that* was better than more pacing.

The blasted folds would not fall into place and he cursed, wishing for Norwood. He should have brought his man along, rather than rely on John's limited skills. The deuce! Now he had made it worse!

Oh, Fitzwilliam would laugh! And, no doubt, liken him to a fluttering miss preparing for the ball.

To his flaring vexation, the door opened and the very man bounded in, as though conjured by his thoughts. Darcy spun around, with about as much good-humour as a goaded bear.

"Have you had your fill of country walks and mindless flirts?" he asked gruffly.

The other laughed.

"You are in fine fettle! What has brought on this charming fit of temper? Oh, leave your neckcloth be, Darcy, it looks well enough. As for those young ladies, I daresay you should be kinder to your future sisters."

Darcy snorted.

"How you can tolerate them, I shall never know."

"They are pleasant, good-humoured girls."

"They are shrill and silly. What on earth can you find to talk to them about?"

"We are not all driven to elevated conversations, Cousin. Sometimes idle chatter works just as well – or better."

"I hope you are not of a mind to offer for one of them! It will not serve you. They have not got a sou."

"So you have told me. Will you not cease tormenting that neckcloth? Oh, let me fix it for you!"

"Never mind that now. Have you seen Miss Bennet?"

"Which one?"

"Fitzwilliam," he warned darkly, "I am in no mood for any of your sallies."

"I did not think you were – but no, I have not seen her."

Before Darcy could vent his frustration on his blameless cousin, the door opened again to admit John.

"Yes? What is it?" Darcy inquired brusquely.

"This young lass is here to see you, Sir."

The young lass was Sarah and Darcy all but breathed a long sigh of relief. So she *would* send word!

The young maid curtsied.

"Mr. Bennet sent me to ask if it would please you both to join the family for dinner."

"Anything else?"

"No, Sir."

Darcy huffed.

"Wait. Has your mistress – … Has Miss Elizabeth Bennet finished her preparations?"

"Sir?"

"The packing. The preparations for the departure on the morrow."

"I believe so, Sir, but I cannot say. I have been helping Mrs. Bennet."

But of course!

"Then, is she… are they assembled for dinner?"

"They are to dine at four, Sir, in their parlour. Not Miss Jane, she is not feeling well. She'll be dining in her chambers, and Miss Lizzy also."

"Oh! I see… I thank you. You may go now."

"Yes, Sir. But beggin' your pardon, Sir, is there a message for Mr. Bennet?"

"A message…?"

"Pray let Mr. Bennet know that I shall be delighted to join him and his family for dinner," Fitzwilliam intervened, skilfully smoothing over Darcy's distraction. "But I fear that my cousin must decline. He is much caught up in some business," he added, to Darcy's enormous gratitude at his cousin's presence of mind and ready understanding.

"Thank you," he chose to put his gratitude to words, as soon as they were left alone. "I did not think I could bear it."

"Without some compensation," Fitzwilliam completed the unfinished thought. "You would do well to practise though, and hopefully get better."

"Better at what?"

"Tolerating dinners with her family. You cannot shut yourself from them forever."

"Perhaps not." But he *would* endeavour to, for as long as he could.

"So, dinner in your chambers, then?"

"So it seems."

"A shame about Miss Bennet being unwell…"

"Aye. In more ways than one!"

"Of course. I hope she has not caught something from her mother. I understand Mrs. Bennet was feeling rather poorly and required her daughters' attention."

"I do not doubt! But fear not, Fitzwilliam, whatever Mrs. Bennet had is not contagious," Darcy scoffed.

Fitzwilliam shook his head at the irreverent remark, but chuckled nevertheless.

"Perhaps Miss Bennet had over-exerted herself caring for her mother."

"Perhaps. But I wish…"

Darcy did not finish – nor did he need to.

His cousin laid a hand on his back.

"I know, old chap. I know."

⊱⊰

They had not done a single stitch of packing. As soon as she had extricated herself from the Colonel's presence, Elizabeth had followed Jane to her chamber, knowing full well that it was there she had rushed to, not their mother's. She could barely contain her indignation at the Colonel's thoughtless words, much as she knew that he was not to blame – that he was not aware to whom exactly he had made the incensing disclosures.

No, he was not to blame. The blame rested very firmly in another place. Her indignation swelled and mounted to murderous anger, this time directed exactly where it ought to be. *Mr. Darcy! He* was to blame for her sister's suffering – today and for six long months!

She snorted loudly. To have thought him different! To have thought, after a mere day of kindness, that the leopard would have changed his spots! He was as despicable as she had always thought him. A proud, horrid man with nothing but disdain for the feelings of others – and nothing, *ever*, could atone for that.

She found Jane sitting on her bed and the frozen mask of pain terrified her. She rushed to hold her very tightly, rocking her gently as one would a beloved child – and then the tears came, for both. Tears of sorrow and humiliation in Jane's case, Elizabeth surmised. In hers, they were tears of impotent fury at the vile man and the pain he had caused; tears of anger at herself and her unsurpassed folly to have believed him different, even for a day. To have been so shamefully taken in!

Not really knowing how it came about, they found themselves lying down on Jane's narrow bed, still holding close, tears mingling –

and for a long time they let their anguish and their anger run its course, until their tears were spent.

Jane sought her handkerchief and Elizabeth did likewise. They wiped their eyes, smiling at each other, then Jane gave a little sound – half muffled sob, half rueful chuckle.

She playfully pressed her sister's nose.

"Your nose is red."

Elizabeth chuckled in her turn.

"And so is yours."

Jane reached to put an arm around her sister, then kissed her still damp cheek.

"Thank you, dearest," she whispered, then sat up. "Well!" she said, with an air of finality. "Enough now. Come, let us do something."

"What would you wish to do? I know what *I* would, but – "

She did not get to finish. Jane's rueful laugh cut her bellicose declaration short.

"It would serve no purpose, dearest, would it?"

"It would give me a great deal of satisfaction, and that is purpose enough!"

"Leave be, Lizzy," Jane said tiredly. "Why should you spoil your chances with – ?"

Elizabeth gave a harsh disbelieving laugh.

"Do you imagine I would accept him *now?* Knowing *this?* Jane, how could I?"

Jane sighed.

"He has been kind to *you.*"

"No, he has not!" Elizabeth forcefully retorted as she sat up in her turn, then stood to walk to the washstand and remove the signs of the long spell of weeping. She cast a glance in the looking glass, then turned back to her sister. "We look a fright," she said, with a half-chuckle.

Before Jane could make a reply, the door opened without warning and Elizabeth sighed to see their mother bursting in.

"Girls, girls, good tidings! Your father has returned and said the ford can be crossed. We set off on the morrow, at first light – is this not grand?"

A false smile pasted on her lips, Elizabeth had to agree for once with her mother's opinion. Good tidings, aye. The morrow could not come soon enough!

"Make haste then, and gather your belongings. You have not unpacked a great deal, Lizzy, have you? Good, good. Now, I shall have some tea and I will get Sarah started on my trunks. Have you seen Lydia? Or Kitty? Well, they *must* be found. But... are you well, Jane? Your colour is so high! You are not coming down with something, are you?"

"A headache, Mamma," Jane dissembled. Coming down with unrequited love and extreme humiliation surely did not count.

"You should conserve your strength. Lizzy can help you pack, can you not, dear? I shall send Sarah as soon as I can spare her."

She bounded out again, her usual self, thankfully unobservant of everything she did not choose to see, and they were left alone again to give each other comfort in a circumstance so distressing that nothing could be done to set it right.

When Sarah came to convey Mr. Darcy's invitation to take a turn with him around the inn, Elizabeth could not believe her ears. It was Jane's common sense that helped explain the matter.

"I assume he has no knowledge of the Colonel's disclosures," she said blandly, but her angelic forbearance only added fodder to Elizabeth's ire.

"Then I suggest he is informed – and promptly."

"Leave be, Lizzy. Nay, forgive me, you must do what you think best. But, for my part, I should not wish to see you face a violent quarrel with Mr. Darcy just to be my champion. It serves no purpose. Just leave be."

It was therefore thanks to Jane that a message was sent to let Mr. Darcy know, most restrainedly, that Miss Elizabeth Bennet sends her regrets but she cannot be spared for a country walk. And later, when the family was at dinner and another message arrived from Mr. Darcy to ask if he was allowed to send for an apothecary to attend Miss Bennet, he was merely told that they are most obliged, but Miss Bennet did not require the services of an apothecary.

For her part, Elizabeth wished she could ask Sarah to say, with the right touch of sarcasm, that Mr. Darcy needed not trouble himself further. Miss Bennet and her sister were persuaded that he has done *quite enough!*

Chapter 7

As he made his way downstairs, Darcy was met with the habitual commotion expected of an inn, even at first light – or particularly at that time of day, when most travellers would choose to embark on their journeys to be assured of covering as much distance as possible until darkness forced them to seek shelter again.

She could not be found – she was not in the hall, nor in the courtyard, although he could spot Mr. Bennet supervising the securing of several trunks at the back of a pair of carriages, which were presumably the family conveyances.

For want of any other option, Darcy stepped out to greet him only to note, once he had done so, that the hallway he had so recently vacated was now bustling with a flurry of activity, led very vocally by Mrs. Bennet.

"Kitty, where is your pelisse, dear? Lydia – your shawl. You left it in the sitting room. To your good fortune, Sarah found it. Mary, confound that book, the light is far too poor at this time of day. You had much better put it in your reticule and free your hands to assist me with these two hat boxes. Oh, Colonel Fitzwilliam! How kind of you, Sir, to awake so early to see us off. Sarah, will you assist Miss Jane? And have you seen Miss Lizzy? Oh, where is that girl? I am all aflutter!"

For once in agreement with Mrs. Bennet – except perhaps the flutter – Darcy made to walk back into the hallway. Where *was* Elizabeth? Before he could step in, Mrs. Bennet burst into the courtyard, leading the procession.

"Oh, Mr. Darcy, you are here as well. How kind! Come girls, make haste! Mary, can you not see the Colonel offering to hand you in the carriage? Thank the gentleman, girl! Lydia, no, dear, do not rush into *that* carriage, you are travelling with me, and so is Kitty. Oh, Colonel, you are too kind, much obliged. Mr. Bennet? Have you seen Lizzy yet? Send Sarah, will you – ...? Ah, Sarah, there you are. Do pop back up to see what is keeping Miss Lizzy. Nay, nay, there is no need, I can see her now, she is coming down the stairs. Lizzy! Come, Lizzy, do make haste, dear. Now, Sarah, I need you to hold on to that. And this. Oh, mind that box, now!"

Darcy heard no more – or chose not to hear it – and his glance darted to the top of the stairs. She was there now and his eyes roamed over the beloved countenance he had not seen for over sixteen hours.

She did not look at him but at her skirts, held out of the way so that she would not trip. He stepped closer, to meet her once she gained the lowest step.

"Good morning, Miss Bennet."

Her eyes flashed up, dark and very tired, faint shades of purple under them. Would that he could kiss them! She should not have tired herself looking after her sister, but it did not surprise him.

He had long known that they were very close.

"Good morning, Sir," she replied – rather tersely, he thought in passing, before reaching for her hand.

"Have a safe journey," he whispered, then smiled as he earnestly added, "I shall look forward to being reunited with you at Longbourn before long."

She withdrew her hand, clasped it on her reticule and her eyes flashed at him again.

"Pray, do not!" she said, very firmly.

"I… beg your pardon?"

Her lips tightened, then opened again, to deliver clearly and crisply:

"I should not want you to be *imposed upon*, Mr. Darcy. I am of the firm opinion that you can do *a great deal better*."

He smiled, warmed by her understanding. How thoughtful – and how noble of her to word it so! He would not have her doubt herself, though. Not now, not ever!

"Perhaps, Miss Bennet," he conceded with a warm smile. "But only in the eyes of others. I can do no better, to my mind."

Her eyes opened wide at this and a strange look, akin to astounded indignation, flashed in the dark depths.

"You, Sir, are beyond belief!" he heard her say, and there was something in her voice and mien that made him fear it was not meant as a compliment.

71

Confused, Darcy frowned, but there was no opportunity to request clarifications. She was already in the courtyard, gained the carriage in an instant and hurried in, briefly relying on her father's hand for assistance. Mr. Bennet followed, the last to take his place, and the carriage door was closed by some obliging servant.

Still dumbfounded, Darcy raised his hand as the two carriages sprang into motion, first one, then the other. She must have missed it, in the dim light before dawn, for his gesture of farewell was in no way acknowledged.

⊱⊰

"So – that is that," Fitzwilliam observed as they made their way back into the inn. "Now you are safe and you need not keep up the pretence any longer," he added lightly. "I can make my own way to Portsmouth by stage coach, you know."

"Nonsense. Of course I shall drive you. Besides, I am in need of an occupation for the upcoming month."

"A month! I should hope not, Darcy. I am to report in Portsmouth in ten days."

"Oh, shush! Would you care for breakfast? It would be rather foolish to return to our beds again."

They *did* settle for breakfast and, over his second cup of coffee, after some pondering and being teased for his distraction, Darcy finally brought himself to ask:

"Fitzwilliam, did you notice anything strange in Miss Bennet's manner this morning? And before you ask which one again, I give you fair warning, I *shall* pelt you with bread-rolls if you do!"

"Oh, I am safe from you. You would never disgrace yourself with such unseemly conduct," the Colonel quipped, but leaned to move the basket of bread-rolls out of his cousin's reach nevertheless. "No, I did not," he finally answered, "but I confess I was not watching. Why would you ask?"

"She seemed rather… edgy, and she said something odd, about her not being good enough for me – and that I was beyond belief."

"Well, as to the final point, I daresay she was right on the mark."

"I fear she did not mean it as a compliment."

"And neither did I," the Colonel retorted, only to find that, in a flash, the other reached into the basket for a bread-roll, which was propelled with uncanny accuracy at his head.

72

Fitzwilliam's hand shot up, palm forward, and easily caught it – he rather prided himself on his impeccable reflexes, which had saved his skin more than once – then reached to drop it back into the basket.

"Forgive me, Darcy, I cannot assist you," he soberly offered. "I have not been party to your conversation. I was otherwise engaged."

"Squiring the younger ones, no doubt."

"No doubt," the Colonel casually conceded.

"You do find astounding ways to waste your time, Fitzwilliam!"

"And you can be a dreadfully boring old stick-in-the-mud!"

⁘

Darcy could not wonder if his cousin *did* find him boring on the way to Portsmouth. He was not inclined for conversation. His eyes were far too often drawn to the empty seat before him, and his thoughts to the strange emptiness in his heart.

He had missed her after leaving Netherfield for town, but this was worse. A great deal worse, for some unknown reason. Perhaps because the promise of happiness was so close. Perhaps because he felt cheated of the moments he could have spent with her, on their last evening in Basingstoke. Perhaps because he was in love and did not much know what could be done with this staggering new feeling. This acute sense of loss, when she was not beside him. The hollow chest. The pining. Oh, he *was* turning into the veriest fool!

Thankfully, Fitzwilliam left him to his thoughts and did not try to cajole him into better humour. Perchance he understood that this time he would not have succeeded. Perhaps he had his own thoughts on his mind.

They reached Portsmouth by noon the following day. There was no rush this time, so they did not push the horses. A very decent dinner could be had at the inn where Fitzwilliam chose to settle until his presence at the regiment was actually required, and the cousins lingered before the fireplace with their glasses of port, their long legs stretched comfortably before them.

"Will you not stay for a few more days?" Fitzwilliam suggested. "I know I teased you about your willingness to sample the delights of Portsmouth, but I daresay there are plenty to go round. We can even sail for a day or two, if you wish."

"Tempting. Yet I should be in town."

73

"Why? You said yourself you are in need of an occupation until Miss Bennet is returned from Falmouth."

"Be that as it may, there is something that must be set to rights."

"And what is that?"

"I fear I did Bingley a disservice when I discouraged him from his plans to marry. I was convinced his feelings were not returned and that his offer would be accepted just as a means to an end. But I have recently learned that I was very wrong."

"What about the strong objections to the lady?"

"Oh, that! Well, if I can overlook them, then surely Bingley can."

Fitzwilliam laughed.

"I wish you could hear yourself sometimes! You sound incredibly high-handed. If you can, then he can also," he mimicked. "It is he who will have to live with those *'objections'* as you put it, and not you."

"They *would* be closer to him, I grant you, unless he drops the lease of Netherfield. But we would still be sharing the same unsavoury relations."

The Colonel looked up sharply from his port.

"I beg your pardon? What did you just say? *Whom* did Mr. Bingley wish to marry?"

"Elizabeth's eldest sister – Jane."

As Darcy soon found out, for an officer and a gentleman, Fitzwilliam was outrageously *au fait* with a sizeable collection of round oaths commonly heard only from the mouths of troopers.

And then he learned why.

Had he not been so shocked, he might have followed suit.

و§و §او

He was stunned. Winded.

A long time ago, as a boy, he had fallen from a chestnut tree, flat on his stomach.

It felt the same today. Too shocked to move or even wrap his thoughts around what had just happened – or what in God's name was he to do next!

Then anger stirred and flared into an almighty blaze. Livid, murderous anger at his wretched cousin, whose blasted tongue ought to be cut to shreds! His countenance turned purple and the predictable stream of abuse poured forth. To his credit, Fitzwilliam merely sat and took it – as well he should, the cursed unmitigated *fool!*

"But how was I to know? I was merely trying to show her your concern for your friend's –... " he tried to interject at last, only to be silenced by another tirade of well-deserved abuse.

And then the ranting stopped – but not the pacing. He paced in the small distance between the door and the fireplace, until there was every reason to believe that the floorboards would wear thin and that he would get dizzy.

"Darcy – " Fitzwilliam offered, only to be stopped by a raised hand and a vicious scowl.

'What now? What was there to be done?' Darcy fumed as terror overcame him.

She would not readily forgive this! Not a hurt wilfully inflicted on one of the people she loved most – and so callously presented.

He snorted, raking his fingers through his hair. So Fitzwilliam had roundly abused him on the walk back from Hunsford for aiming to explain to her the reasons that had delayed him in offering marriage! At least, in doing so, he might have had *his* say. Might have couched them in his own words, shown his own feelings – rather than having it known to her in blunt, stark terms that he had interfered in Bingley's courtship because of *'strong objections to the lady'*.

How could she fail to ascertain that the same objections applied to his own case as well?

She would not.

Great heavens, she *did not!*

All of a sudden, her parting words in Basingstoke took a new, dreadful meaning. She had not – wisely and nobly – expressed her doubts of being worthy of him. He saw it now, the terrifying truth. She had flung his own callous reference to Jane back in his face, with the stark warning that he should not be looking forward to their reunion at Longbourn.

And to that warning – instead of offering a profuse apology for having wounded her beloved sister – all he had done was to carelessly acknowledge that she was not good enough in the eyes of others, but *he* was of a mind to overlook it!

The very sentiments Fitzwilliam had warned him so forcefully against expressing had been revealed to her, at the worst time and in the worst possible way!

She would not readily forgive it!

It mattered not that it was done without malice and with a clear conscience; with the firm opinion that Miss Bennet would have accepted Bingley's hand for her family's sake and not for her own – or his. It mattered not that he had seen the error of his ways in separating them, once he had learned that Miss Bennet had been attached in earnest to his friend. Still was. Had, as Miss Lydia put it, pined for him for six months together. It mattered not that he had decided to right the wrong and make amends.

She did not know this. All she knew was that *he* was to blame for her sister's suffering – and that he regarded the connection as objectionable in the extreme.

No wonder she had taxed his conduct as beyond belief!

No wonder she had no notion of the powerful feelings that urged him towards the very same connection. He had not expressed them! He had not had the chance to voice those feelings that might have mitigated the hurtful revelations. In the worst possible way, she had been made aware of his contempt for some of her relations – but not his passionate admiration and regard for *her*. And in the coming weeks, her resentment would fester into a prejudice he would have the devil of a job to overcome!

This could not be allowed – he *had* to see her!

Explain. Apologise. Atone.

Yet how? When? And, worse still, *where?*

He had no notion where she could be found. He had not prompted Mr. Bennet to reveal their exact destination. He had assumed there was no need to; that he could wait until their return to Longbourn. This was not an option any longer – but where to go next, he simply did not know.

And Bingley! He *had* to involve Bingley, as the only proof that he was indeed keen to make amends.

"Darcy…" Fitzwilliam spoke up again, breaking his concentration and he spun around, but this time he bit back the sharp retort and the useless recriminations.

This called for a campaign of military precision and at least in *that* his nuisance of a cousin might just have some worth!

Chapter 8

The descent to the bottom of the valley looked as if it would never end. The very narrow road sloped, deeper and deeper, between tall banks overgrown with bushes and with gnarled old trees. Ivy grew freely, hanging from the branches in long, wavy streams, seemingly intent to shut out every hint of daylight and, as the road sloped further down, the surroundings grew darker – then eerily darker still.

Elizabeth could not wonder that, after having negotiated three valleys such as this, her mother had declared that her nerves could not withstand another without the reassurance of her husband's presence, which was why, with great reluctance, her father had resigned himself to travel in the other carriage for the remainder of the journey.

Their destination was not far, according to the guide engaged in the first village they had come across after turning off the main road into Falmouth. Judging by their surroundings though, they seemed hundreds of miles away from any human habitation. It seemed that they had foolishly wandered of their own free will into a land of smugglers, footpads – or, at best, of ghosts.

To their great fortune, so far they had encountered neither – and Elizabeth could only hope that their luck would hold. For the tenth time at least, she wondered what they would find at the end of this unexpected journey. For her part, she dearly hoped it was at least a meal and a warm bath.

Four days had gone by since they had quitted Basingstoke.

The roads were good and fast – at least in the beginning – and they made good progress. Surprisingly, her mother was willing to travel for more hours in the day than Elizabeth had expected, presumably in fear of being trapped by bad weather in yet another inn along the way. Fortunately, the weather remained fair which was a mercy, for the roads worsened considerably after Plymouth, and even more so beyond Liskeard. Narrow and rutted, trapped between tall earth-and-stone Cornish walls, they could easily have turned into veritable mud baths and their journey might have taken fourteen days rather than four.

Elizabeth breathed a small sigh of relief as the road finally began to slope upwards and hopefully would soon bring them back towards daylight, out of the gloomy depths closing in upon them.

She wished she could ask their guide how much further they still had to go. She wished she were certain that he was trustworthy – and that he was leading them to the right place and not to their doom in some deserted spot.

With a start, she shook herself from such grim speculations. Whatever had possessed her to think such foolish thoughts? It must have been the dark, forbidding valley, so different from the open prospects she preferred to see. But at least grim speculations about smugglers and footpads had the advantage of taking her mind from her dark thoughts of Mr. Darcy – the vile, prideful man whose arrogance was just beyond belief!

The conveyance swayed abruptly over ruts or rocks and shrill cries burst from the other carriage. Elizabeth's thoughts turned with warm compassion to her father, on account of the long hours he had spent in close proximity to the three most excitable females in their family at a time when nerves and frequent gasps of fear were, if not tolerable, then at least justified.

The road led further up and then still further, until at last they seemed to have gained the higher ground. It stretched before them now in a wide, level curve that hugged the hillside, but the carriages did not continue much longer on that path.

Instead, they turned into a narrow lane that again sloped downwards, though thankfully not into yet another valley, but to what seemed to be a rambling manor-house.

ᴏᴇ Ꮕᴏ

The journey into Falmouth was unremitting hell.

Frustration, fear and impatience were but a few of the identifiable emotions that poisoned every moment, but Darcy was too highly strung to pick out the rest.

Fitzwilliam had of course remained in Portsmouth so there was no one, not even his vexing cousin, to distract him from his thoughts.

Not that he could have been distracted – but at least Fitzwilliam's presence would have provided a convenient outlet for his manifold frustrations. Since his cousin was not there, this only left his servants, but Darcy was too fair a master to resort to *that*.

Despite his better carriage, better horses and a greater incentive to travel overnight, he had not found them yet – had not caught up with the Bennet party. They could be traced along the way, their passing had been noted at a number of tollgates and a coaching inn, as he had imagined it would be. He held great hopes that such a large, memorable party would be easily spotted and identified.

From Exeter though, he had lost their trace. He could not tell whether they had taken the southern route while he took the north, or whether they had stopped at a more modest coaching inn, the likes of which he would not have considered. Both options seemed quite likely and Darcy cursed his folly of not having inquired at *every* inn, regardless of how lowly or how small. Then he might have known which road they had taken – rather than plough mindlessly on, down the wrong one!

It seemed foolish to turn back now, even if he *was* on the wrong road. The northern route was faster and allegedly better – which was why he had selected it in the first place. If he did not find them on the way, then at least he would arrive in Falmouth not far behind the Bennet party and begin his searches as soon as may be.

Apart from profuse apologies, which Darcy eventually saw it in his heart to accept without snorting, Fitzwilliam did have some pertinent advice to offer before they parted. In fact, his cousin's suggestion was so obvious that it was a wonder how Darcy did not think of it himself. The numbing shock must have been to blame – must have addled his brain, scattered his senses, otherwise he would have come to the same conclusion: that a local man should be engaged in Falmouth, to ask around on his behalf.

He had very little to base his search on. Just the great-aunt's name, Mrs. Pencarrow, and a vague location – Falmouth. Worse still, he did not even know if she lived in the town itself or nearby – and if so, how far.

The cousins had eventually settled that, in view of the family connections, all signs pointed to a woman in her seventies or eighties.

Most likely a widow of middling sort and modest independent income, who was known to have settled there rather than being Cornish born and bred.

Sifting the haystack in search of the needle was of course daunting, but in a world where word travelled easily, where people knew their neighbours' business and an outside settler was effortlessly identified, perchance it was not too hard to locate Mrs. Pencarrow. How many ladies of that name could Falmouth hold?

⁂

The house looked very dark – the sombre walls, the shuttered windows. As the carriages came around the bend, Elizabeth took a sharp intake of breath at the sight of the imposing structure, only two storeys high but very large, a sprawling mass of granite. It seemed extremely old, an ancient manor belonging in a different time, with countless ornate chimneys outlined against the cloudy sky.

They drove to the end of the ever-widening cobbled approach and drew up at the entrance. The vast doors opened promptly, as soon as the carriages had drawn to a halt. An old man, liveried as a footman or perhaps as an old-fashioned butler, came out to greet them, followed by a younger one.

They were shown into what seemed to be a great hall of medieval appearance, intricately carved oak beams supporting the tall ceiling. Everything was dark – the floor, the panelling, even the large suits of armour that flanked the enormous fireplace.

Stunned by their surroundings or perhaps awed by the way their voices rang with an eerie echo in the imposing hall, her mother and younger sisters fell strangely quiet, drawing towards each other as though for support.

Less awed, Mr. Bennet looked around him with quiet interest at the unexpected grandeur of the place and Elizabeth could only assume that the same look of wonder that graced his countenance and Jane's was presumably reflected in her own.

There was no time to exchange first impressions, nor was this the place for it anyway. Through an arched door at the far end of the hall another person entered and, to Elizabeth's unexpressed relief, it was not some imposing figure of a tall dark chatelaine, but a cheerful-looking, rubicund little woman of uncertain age, with rosy cheeks crinkled in a smile.

"You are here at last, thank goodness! You must be so tired. Come, let me see you to your chambers for a little rest and a change of clothes."

At the reassuring sight, Mrs. Bennet found her voice.

"Mrs. Pencarrow, I assume?"

"Oh, dearie, heavens, no! I am Mrs. Polmere, the housekeeper. Come now, Mawgan, you need to fetch Gorran and see to the trunks. And send word for water for the baths. The girls must be told they are wanted above-stairs. Mr. Perren, would you be so kind to let Mrs. Pencarrow know they have arrived?"

The liveried older man left and the cheerful housekeeper led them up a wooden staircase, chatting all the way.

"Dinner will be served as soon as you have refreshed yourselves from your travels. Mrs. Pencarrow charged me to give you her regrets but she will not join you. She dines very early and mostly in her chambers. Later on however, she will make her way down and would be delighted if you can join her in the drawing room after dinner. I hope your journey was not very taxing, but I suspect it was. Hundreds of miles at this time of year! The spring can be quite dreadful sometimes, when it rains. There, now, the bedchambers. Pray choose whichever one you will. I fear the young ladies might have to share, in pairs. We lost the habit of entertaining houseguests a long time ago and most of the bedchambers sadly would not suit – too dreary and musty, and the furnishings have grown rather frayed. I hope we can make you comfortable in these four here, though."

Predictably, Lydia chose to share a bedchamber with Kitty and Elizabeth with Jane, leaving Mary to the quiet satisfaction – or the lonely option – of a room all to herself.

Mrs. Bennet seemed slightly put out by the assumption that she and her husband would share quarters. The habit was discarded many years ago. Still, she felt reluctant to complain and risk offending her newfound relation. That she was in awe of the as yet unknown Mrs. Pencarrow, it was plain to see. It was just as clear that she was delighted with their destination – and her delight was put in far too many words a short while later, when she burst into her eldest daughters' room.

"Girls, what say you of this entire business? Oh, your room is charming – so spacious, even if the furnishings are so old and glum. Still, have you noticed? A butler, a housekeeper, two footmen at least

– those two young men with such strange names – and I daresay a handful of maids too. There is a young girl waiting in my chambers. I have no need of her for I have Sarah, so I can send her to attend you. And this house! A dark old pile, I am sure, but not something you can keep up on a farthing. Your great-aunt must be a woman of means. Oh, can we hope that we are her sole relations? Would that not be grand? Oh, girls, we *must* be on our best behaviour! But then you always are, Jane. You need to curb that tongue of yours though, Lizzy, when we meet her. We should not want to offend her with some saucy speech."

"Perhaps you could also warn Lydia and Kitty, Mamma," Jane suggested quietly but firmly, tired of the number of times when their parent would invariably take offence at Lizzy's willingness to speak her mind, but not at their sisters' glaring improprieties.

"And in any case," Elizabeth decided once more to speak up, "we should not start counting Mrs. Pencarrow's silver before we have even met her. Besides, we are certainly not her sole living relations."

"What are you saying? Know you of any others?"

"*Mrs. Phillips*, Mamma, and our *uncle Gardiner*, if nobody else," Elizabeth offered with a little smile and Mrs. Bennet dismissively waved.

"Of course, of course, but they are family already. I was thinking of others we do not even know of. Well, I trust we shall see soon enough. But I am very sanguine about it. It would be very strange indeed if someone who lives in a house such as this summons us from one end of the country to the other just so that she can look us in the eye."

Elizabeth shook her head and forbore to mention that, if her great-aunt could take offence at anything, it would most likely be avaricious thoughts openly expressed.

Mrs. Bennet left them in her usual flurry and, true to her word, she soon sent the superfluous maid, a cheerful young girl by the name of Morwenna, who was quick to see to the young ladies' baths and their change of apparel so that, an hour or so later, Elizabeth and Jane were able to go down for dinner.

The plentiful repast was served in an imposing oak-panelled dining room, but most of the company was not of a mind to pay much heed to their surroundings, or indeed to do much justice to the fare placed before them, too eager to finish their meal and meet their host at last.

Before long, they were shown into a room just off the great hall.

A roaring fire burned in the old-fashioned fireplace and before it, in a large winged chair, far too wide for the withered frame of its occupant, sat a very old and greatly wizened lady dressed in a widow's garb.

"Come and pray sit," she invited in a voice that carried, without being loud. "Forgive me for not standing to welcome you. I fear that my days of flitting about are over. Come, sit before the fire, warm yourselves and let us be acquainted. As you must know by now," she spoke up to Mrs. Bennet, "I am your aunt – your mother's elder sister. This is your husband, I presume. Pray, sit, Mr. Bennet. Now, would you introduce me to your daughters?"

All five were named, in the order of their ages, and dark, inquisitive eyes settled on each in turn.

"I thank you for bearing the inconvenience of such a lengthy journey just for an old woman's whim. I am pleased to have met you at last. I trust you can stay with me for a while, there are matters that ought to be discussed. Now, there is tea and coffee in the parlour, through that door, the first on your right. Mrs. Polmere will serve you. Even now, she is therein awaiting your pleasure. I would be most grateful if you were to go and have a beverage – while I speak privately with your second daughter. With Elizabeth."

꧁ ꧂

Her relations left a little while ago as instructed, to drink their tea in the adjoining parlour.

Predictably, some showed their surprise at Elizabeth being so singled out. Others showed concern – Jane of course, and their father – but as they could see nothing worrisome in the unusual request and as Elizabeth seemed fairly unperturbed by it, they walked out as well, leaving her alone with their relation.

For many minutes nothing more was said and the two ladies sat, quietly assessing one another. She could not tell what the other saw but as for herself, Elizabeth found an older woman whose air seemed to belie her years and her fragile frame.

Suddenly, the lady's thin lips thinned even further into some sort of a smile.

"You ask no questions, yet it would be very strange indeed if you did not wonder why I should wish to speak to you alone."

"I assumed you would tell me, Ma'am, at your leisure," Elizabeth replied and at that, the older woman's smile widened further.

She indicated with a vague wave behind her.

"You shall find a small urn there, and the tea things. Would you be so kind to pour for both of us? Aye, I *will* tell you – but long tales from the past make thirsty work."

With a soft smile of her own, Elizabeth did as bid, then took a cup of tea to her relation.

"I thank you. Pray, bring your own, then sit. There, if you would, so that I can see you," the older lady urged and Elizabeth eventually took the seat her host had indicated.

Yet no more was said, as Mrs. Pencarrow sipped her tea, her thoughts seemingly in a very distant place until, all of a sudden, she looked up to Elizabeth again.

"You look a lot like her," she said quietly. "Like Gemima – my sister and your own grandmother. It changes nothing of course, but I am pleased to see it. In some ways, it makes my task a little more rewarding, if I can fool myself into thinking I am speaking to *her*," the older lady added with a little wistful smile.

She took another sip of tea, then put her cup down on the small oval table at her elbow.

"It does not come easily, unburdening oneself, but I daresay I require the practice. I shall have to do it all over again before too long, once I have gone through the Pearly Gates. But be that as it may. What I wished to say, my dear, is that I have grievously wronged your grandmother, three-score years ago, when we were both young girls in Bristol. She was my younger sister, my parents' second daughter. It may sound a little fanciful to you, I know, but such are old people and their whimsies. I have chosen you because of who you are – second daughter of my sister's second daughter. There is more to it than that of course, but of this, thereafter. Now drink your tea and listen to old stories. When she was but eighteen, my sister fell in love. I did not know how deeply, not at first, but I *did* know it was a sterling catch. The youngest son of the Earl of Wincarton – a handsome young man, a colonel, and positively stunning in his regimentals! Now I could couch this in all sorts of terms, but the plain truth is that I was very jealous. I did not see why

84

she, the younger sister, should get such a prize! He wanted to marry her, you see, he was very attached. The Earl, however, withheld his consent. He threatened to disown his son if he persisted in his attachment to my sister, but the young man would not be dissuaded. Our father was not rich, but he was a reasonably well-off Bristol merchant and, with the Colonel's pay and my sister's dowry, they were certain they would make ends meet, and be glad of it. But the Earl used his connections and, unbeknownst to his son, he had him transferred into one of the regiments bound to set sail on General Wolfe's campaign, in the Colonies. He had to go, but before he set off he asked Gemima to marry him in secret. Clandestine marriages were a great deal easier those days, one did not have to travel over the Scottish border. My sister, to my great surprise, somehow contrived to persuade our father to allow it. But she fell ill of a fever, a few days before they were to wed. She sent me with a note to her Colonel – but, to my discredit, in my horrible jealousy, I passed on a very different message. I told him that she changed her mind and he sailed off, broken-hearted. I was found out, of course. Before he set sail, he wrote to her to give his blessing, tell her to forget him and be happy. And then he fell, along with General Wolfe himself, on the assault on the Heights of Abraham. Needless to say, Gemima never forgave me. She married Mr. Gardiner soon after, to escape her home, me, all the recollections, and settled in that little town of yours in Hertfordshire – Meryton. She never wanted to hear from me again and in truth I can scarce blame her. For my part, I married Mr. Pencarrow and came to live in Cornwall – he had mining interests here. We dealt well together and his fortunes rose and rose. His mines were vastly successful and he acquired others. At one time, it was said that his income was rising by a guinea every minute! He did well; so well that before too long he could buy this place – Landennis Manor, named after its former owner, Lord Landennis who, at that time, had chosen to sell it and sail away to live abroad. Another tale this, of another broken heart, from what I understood, but I shall not digress into another. My poor husband passed away three years back after a long illness, and I was left alone, a wealthy widow, at liberty to dispose of his amassed fortune – our fortune – as only I saw fit. A pity that there were no children, but it serves no purpose to repine. All my life I only wished I could make my peace with my sister but, to her deathbed, Gemima would not allow it. I shall follow her soon, there is little doubt about it and, while I know I cannot buy her forgiveness, I thought she might have been pleased to have her children and grandchildren better situated. Then again, she might have resented anyone of her line benefiting from *my* money. Regardless, I would much rather not leave it to strangers."

"Ma'am, I…" Elizabeth faltered, "I know not what to say to this."

"There is nothing to say. The papers are drawn already. You and your sisters shall each have a portion. With immediate effect of course, as I would much rather my passing was not awaited with anticipation – "

"Mrs. Pencarrow, we would certainly not – …"

"It was a jest, child," the older woman interjected with a swift wave of a thin, wrinkled hand, and silenced Elizabeth's prompt protests. "Perhaps not a good one, but facetiousness and malice are among the joys of old age. God only knows there are few left. Fine! Jests aside, I would find it rewarding to see my money go to a good use in my lifetime, rather than spend my last years sitting like some evil spirit on my pile of gold. The rest is in my will – provisions for your family and smaller legacies for your mother's siblings. *They* do not seem much in need of anything, from what I gathered. Your aunt Philips has a self-sufficient husband and no children, and as for your uncle Gardiner, I understand he is most successful. Still, with so many children, a legacy might come in handy. It pleases me greatly though that I can make a real difference for Frances and her offspring, what with your father's estate being entailed away from the female line and him so woefully unable to make adequate provisions for his daughters!"

"You must not speak so of my father," Elizabeth bristled, stung. "Besides, may I ask, how do you know quite so much of our circumstances?"

The older lady shrugged.

"Anything can be found, if one has the means and the willingness to find it. Forgive me for provoking you with open criticism of your father. It *is* justified and you would have acknowledged it, were you not so loyal and so blindly attached to him," Mrs. Pencarrow smiled, not unkindly.

"Is there anything you do not know of me?" Elizabeth asked, vacillating between laughter and vexation.

"A great deal, no doubt, but it shall be entertaining to find out. For instance, I would like to know if you have left your heart in Hertfordshire, or anywhere else for that matter."

"May I ask why would you inquire into something so private?" Elizabeth bristled again, not so much at the question as the imposition.

"You may. It *is* private, I know, but it affects me also, to some extent at least. You see, I should wish to know if you have any strings likely to draw you away from Cornwall, because I have determined that Landennis Manor itself, together with the necessary means for its upkeep, should go to *you* – the second daughter of the second daughter."

Chapter 9

A few days had gone by since the astounding revelation and Elizabeth still failed to fully wrap her mind around it.

Heiresses, overnight – and herself more so than any of the others!

'Mistress of Landennis Manor, ohhh, how well that sounds!', Mrs. Bennet would have gushed, had she been informed about it.

She was not, at Elizabeth's own insistence.

Once her great-aunt's intentions were revealed to her, all she could say was:

"Ma'am, that is… unspeakably generous and I thank you – yet I cannot aggrandise myself at the expense of any of my kin!"

To her surprise, Mrs. Pencarrow had merely laughed softly.

"So loyal – as Gemima herself was, before I hurt her so dreadfully, bless her departed soul." And then she shrugged. "You will do what you will, once I am dead and buried. You can sell the old place and share the proceeds at your pleasure. It shall be your choice. Nevertheless, it is willed to *you*. You can keep this from your relations for now though, if you so wish."

"Can I share the rest?"

"You will not need to. I intend to summon them back and tell them everything else myself. But I shall not give them a full account of my history with your grandmother. I am an old woman, Elizabeth, and I would much prefer a touch of warmth rather than antagonism from my newfound relations. You are of course free to inform them of the entire story once I am no more. Would this little deception – or rather lying by omission – be acceptable to you?"

"It shall be as you wish, Ma'am," Elizabeth conceded with a smile.

"In every respect?" the older woman shrewdly prompted.

"In most, I daresay," Elizabeth replied and the other nodded, then bid her open the door into the parlour, to summon her relations.

Mrs. Bennet was overjoyed of course, and very vocal in her glee – *"I always knew how it would be! How generous, so kind!"* – but thankfully not so lost to every sense of decency as to inquire what sum exactly had been settled on each one.

The younger sisters were positively thrilled and as loud as their mother in giving thanks for the fact that they were to have *'a portion'*. Just as herself, Jane was surprised and grateful, and at all times well within the limits of propriety. As for their father, he seemed relieved if nothing else. Truth be told, he might have resented the implication that he had not exerted himself to provide for his offspring as best he could, but it would certainly be a comfort to no longer have to hear Mrs. Bennet bewailing their starving in the hedgerows if the worst should come to pass and he would be no more.

So everything was well after a fashion, but for the deluge of new notions and the new surroundings. Elizabeth could not say how long they would have to stay at Landennis – or indeed whether, as its prospective mistress, she was expected to remain with her great-aunt even after her relations had returned to Longbourn.

The notion was unsettling. This place felt too alien, too different from Hertfordshire to ever feel like home.

On the other hand, she thought with grim satisfaction, it would be gratifying to imagine Mr. Darcy descending upon Longbourn in the summer, only to see that she could not be found. It would be even more rewarding to have him know she wanted her exact location withheld from him.

Or perhaps not. Perhaps he should be allowed to come and hear the full extent of her opinion of him, his arrogance and his selfish disdain for the feelings of others. And then be sent away to reflect and inwardly digest her words of righteous anger, all the way into the north – to Derbyshire.

The notion brought a small smile to her lips and Elizabeth skipped gaily on her way. She had set out that morning to explore the new surroundings and the very helpful Mrs. Polmere had informed her that there was a pleasant prospect towards the estuary or down the other side, towards the bay.

One of the footmen, Gorran, was sent to attend her, and Elizabeth would have eagerly resisted the suggestion, had she known how to do so without hurting the kindly lady's feelings.

On the other hand, this was not familiar territory and it would have been foolish indeed to reject their assistance, only to have them out on the hills looking for her, were she to lose her way.

Young Gorran suggested a stroll towards the river, through the ornamental gardens, and Elizabeth was all too happy to agree. In full spring bloom, the terraced flowerbeds were a delightful mix of colour that could not fail to please the eye as she made her way along the gravelled walks and down the narrow granite steps that linked each terrace to another.

From the old dovecote onwards, Gorran would have led her down the cart track that rose from the valley and skirted the property to join the carriage road further up the hill, but Elizabeth was too enchanted by the lush wilderness spreading in succulent splendour at her feet. Large plants of exotic appearance encroached upon the path on either side – strange varieties, the likes of which Elizabeth had never seen before – and their sheer uniqueness persuaded her to disdain the tameness of the track.

Unfortunately, young Gorran was no gardener and could not offer much detail, not even the names of the astounding plants. He could only tell her that they owed their thriving to the much milder climate and some of them to the salty winds coming in from the sea.

"Are you from these parts?" Elizabeth asked her companion as he obligingly pushed an oversized rhubarb-like leaf out of her way.

"I am, Ma'am. From the village."

"The village?"

"Aye. Landennis village, half a mile that way."

"I see. Morwenna said that she was from Landennis too."

"Aye, Ma'am. She's me sister."

"Oh. I did not know that. And have you both been long with Mrs. Pencarrow?"

"Eight years at Michaelmas for me – five for me sister. Mawgan's newer, he was engaged some three years back, but as for Mr. Perren, he was here from the dawn of time, I reckon. He was butler to the old master – to Lord Landennis, before he sold the place."

Elizabeth nodded, then rather lost interest when a sudden turn showed a glistening stretch of water, ivy-laden trees crowding on its bank. The tide was out, and wading birds ambled through the shallows between the mudflats in search of food, but scattered with piercing, startled cries at their approach.

At the bottom of the hill, a tall stone wall bordered the garden. Her companion guided her towards the gate that led out of the grounds onto a narrow and very muddy road – nothing but yet another cart track, which the one sloping down the hill joined a few yards further.

Elizabeth hopped over ruts and puddles to reach the gnarled tree-trunks at the water's edge. At high tide, the river would lap through their exposed roots, but for now the sandy banks beckoned, with the promise of a better view.

"Could I catch a glimpse of the sea from down there?" she inquired.

Gorran shook his head.

"Nay, Ma'am. We should've walked the other way if you were of a mind to see it."

"The other way?"

"Aye. Up the carriage road and then along the coast path that takes you to Landennis Cove. I can show you now – unless you'd care to stroll some more along the river?"

"I thank you, no. I would very much like to see the cove."

Obligingly, the young man led the way and Elizabeth followed, having decided once again that valleys and Cornish forests laden with boughs of ivy were not to her taste and she would much rather regain the higher ground.

They struck into the track that meandered up the hill between steep banks overgrown with flowering rhododendrons. When the rooftops of Landennis Manor could just about be spotted, they turned into the carriage road, only to leave it soon for a very narrow path that ran along an old lichen-encrusted wall, under stunted trees with branches growing inland, shaped at strange angles by the winds. Gorse grew freely on the other side, the sweet scent of its abundant blooms mingling with the much stronger ones of seaweed and saltwater.

The wind tugged at her bonnet with ever-growing vigour. Yet it was not the fierce gusts that took her breath away once they reached the end of the stone wall, but the astounding prospect that had just opened at her feet.

It was not her first glimpse of the sea. Many years ago, on a trip to Eastbourne, she had gazed in wonder over the sparkling, seemingly endless stretch of blue that reached as far as the horizons. But this was as different from the tame Eastbourne shores as peaceful Hertfordshire was from rugged Cornwall.

It was not the vastness of the sea, but the violent restlessness of it that appealed to Elizabeth's every sense and feeling, answering a deep restlessness within herself that she had never known of, until that very day. As wave after wave broke over the sharp rocks with far-reaching bursts of spray, the roar of the surf called out to her, loud and insistent; just as insistent as the cry of gulls wheeling above, gliding on the currents.

"You'd best have a care for your bonnet, Ma'am. 'Tis blustery today," the young man prosaically advised, breaking the spell.

With a little carefree laugh, Elizabeth shrugged, wishing she was left alone so that she could discard the bothersome item altogether.

"Is there a path to the bottom of the cove?" she asked her companion and the young man raised his arm to point it out.

"There is, Ma'am, but you must mind your step. I fear it might be rather too steep for you."

It certainly was not, Elizabeth determined as they began their slow descent, Gorran vexingly insisting that she should take his hand for safety and support. Much as she did not wish to offend either him or dear old Mrs. Polmere, Elizabeth could not help thinking she had grown rather tired of being treated like a fragile little Miss.

"I thank you, Gorran, for your assistance and for guiding me about," she smiled sweetly once they had reached the shingle beach below. "You may return to the house now. I can make my own way back shortly."

"Are you certain, Ma'am?" he asked, clearly reluctant.

"Oh, quite. I will not lose my bearings, so close to the house."

"But the steep climb, Ma'am?"

"Fear not, I shall have no trouble. Still, to set Mrs. Polmere's mind at ease, and yours, by all means come to find me if I have not returned within the hour."

"If this is what you wish, Ma'am…"

"It is, and I thank you for your kind concern," Elizabeth smiled and at length Gorran left her, still visibly unconvinced about the wisdom of the scheme – and presumably in fear of a stern talking-to from the housekeeper.

Once he had gained the top, he looked back once more, just before the turn of the path was about to take him out of sight and Elizabeth waved gaily, to receive a respectful sign of compliance in return. And then he was gone and she had the cove all to herself!

Feeling like an impish child suddenly escaped from supervision, Elizabeth took her bonnet off and set it aside on a large flat rock, weighted down with a sizeable stone. Then, for good measure, she sat and removed her sturdy boots as well, and likewise her stockings.

The shingle was sharp against her bare feet, but she paid no heed to the discomfort as she ran to the water's edge to dip her toes in the shallow frothing waves that came up to meet her. A squeal escaped her lips at the touch of the shockingly cold water and she hoisted her skirts halfway to her knees to avoid getting them soaked.

She walked along, higher up on the shore this time, waves lapping at her feet, rolling small rounded pebbles over her bare toes, and she lifted her face into the sun and the salty wind. She breathed in with great relish, filling her chest with the strongly-scented air, and an exhilarating sense of freedom filled her heart, more vibrant than anything she had ever felt on her ramblings through homely Hertfordshire.

Oh, she could grow to love *this* Cornwall! Not the dark woods perhaps, nor the forbidding valleys, but the Cornwall of deserted coves, high winds and restless seas!

Suddenly, the notion of making a life away from everything familiar did not seem quite so much of a daunting, distressing imposition. She could be happy here, she determined and, on impulse, she released her skirts to stretch her arms out and spin around in a joyful whirl, not caring one jot about damp hems and windblown tresses.

Had she but known that her every move was watched from the outcrop at the far end of the cliff, she might not have cared overmuch about *that* either.

༄ ༄

The best part of an hour must have gone since Gorran left her, Elizabeth determined, so if she did not wish to have him rushing back for her, she must leave the magical place.

With a great deal of reluctance, she returned to the flat rock where her footwear and bonnet were waiting – much closer to the water's edge now that the tide had gradually crept in – and sat down to brush the dried sand off her feet.

She would return here, and soon – and perhaps bring her sisters with her.

They would love this place! Lydia and Kitty would run barefoot along the beach and spray each other with cold salty water like unruly children and as for Jane, she was bound to become as enchanted as herself with the wild, picturesque surroundings.

Her boots back on, Elizabeth retrieved her bonnet and shook it to remove the sand that the breeze had blown into the neatly pleated folds. There! Now she was restored to a semblance of respectability, she told herself with a smile as she made her way towards the path that had brought her thither.

Climbing back up was even easier than she had expected and she reached the top of the cliff in no time at all. She would have to impress upon Gorran and Mrs. Polmere that she was a strong young woman of nearly one and twenty and not a feeble child in leading strings, Elizabeth thought with a smile as she continued on her way.

Once she reached the end of the coastal path, she was pleased to see no sign of Gorran returning to fetch her, so she could indulge in a few minutes more. She did not turn back to the cove, but instead chose to walk along the carriage road that led up from the house, in the hope of gaining the higher ground and a better prospect.

The road kept rising and, quite close to the top, she found a large squat boulder eminently suited for the purpose. She clambered easily upon it, sheltering her eyes against the sunshine and smiled at the delightful scenery that opened at her feet. The lovely cove was part of it of course – and beyond there was another, then another, fading in greyish haze into the distance. She would be sure to explore them all, Elizabeth readily determined and squinted into the bright light for a better look.

A sudden sound of hoof-beats on the road behind her made her turn with a little start. She looked – then gaped. It could not be! That tall, upright carriage – broad shoulders – dark hair – saturnine looks. Not Mr. Darcy surely – and certainly not *here!* She stared in earnest, then drew a relieved breath. It was not him, but a gentleman of very similar appearance, at least from a distance.

Having noticed her too, the newcomer came closer, drew the reins and brought his gloved fingers to his hat.

"Good morning, Miss Bennet," he casually offered. "May I advise you do not wander unescorted in these parts. I fear this is a far cry from the tame lanes of Hertfordshire."

Elizabeth's eyes widened.

"How do you know my name and where I hail from?"

The gentleman laughed as he dismounted.

"I should imagine everyone on a three-mile radius knows your name and where you hail from, Miss Bennet. But I fear I have you at a disadvantage and since there is no one at hand to perform a proper introduction, pray allow me to introduce myself. Lord Trevellyan, at your service, Ma'am," he bowed, taking his hat off with a flourish, then straightened again. "Would you allow me to escort you to Landennis? I was heading there myself. I have some business with Mrs. Pencarrow."

Still dazed by the encounter, Elizabeth looked silently upon him.

"You will forgive me for my hesitation," she offered at last. "It is not every day that I am greeted by name by someone wholly unknown to me, in the depths of Cornwall. Besides," she suddenly felt inclined to smile, "I have it on some authority that these parts are a far cry from the tame lanes of Hertfordshire."

The gentleman laughed again.

"Oh, you can trust me implicitly, Miss Bennet. Amongst other things, I am Justice of Peace for this parish, so I daresay this ought to reassure you that you shall be delivered safely to your great-aunt's house."

She pondered, and he stretched his hand.

"Shall I assist you off that boulder?"

Before he had finished, she had already jumped.

"I shall walk with you, Sir, if you would do me the kindness of explaining how you know so much about me."

"We are friendly people of simple pleasures in these parts, Miss Bennet, and one of those pleasures is knowing our neighbours and most of their concerns. When someone new arrives, it is soon heard of. For my part, I was privileged to hear more, and even sooner. I have Mrs. Pencarrow's confidence and I knew for a while that she was gathering intelligence of her kin in Hertfordshire. I was told of your upcoming visit and I came upon you on her very doorstep. In truth, Miss Bennet, I have convicted on less evidence than that."

She laughed.

"I would venture to hope they were all merited convictions."

"Of course, Miss Bennet. I would not have it any other way."

Lord Trevellyan offered his arm, and Elizabeth took it.

"Will you be staying long in these parts?" he asked as they ambled down the road towards the house, the well-trained horse following close behind.

"I cannot tell. A fortnight at the very least, I should imagine. Maybe more."

'Maybe a great deal more' she thought, but would not say.

"And how do you like Cornwall?"

"I am very partial to Landennis Cove and the open prospect from the top of this hill, but I have to own I am not quite so fond of the dark valleys."

"Of course. Dark valleys are more suited to dark deeds," he said lightly, then suddenly turned solemn as he glanced upon her. "I was in earnest when I advised you against venturing unescorted, Miss Bennet. This truly is not your tame Hertfordshire!"

Despite herself, Elizabeth shivered at the warning.

"I shall take heed," she brought herself to say.

They walked back, talking of less ominous matters, such as the journey thither and local sights to see. When they arrived at the house, Mrs. Pencarrow seemed quite pleased about his lordship's visit and equally so to hear that he had already made Elizabeth's acquaintance.

Before sitting down to whatever business he had come to transact, he was offered tea and was led into the parlour – and Elizabeth had her own share of mild amusement to note that, despite his lordship's boast of well-informed deductions, he was not as much in the know as he claimed to be. It seemed that, either by accident or by design, Mrs. Pencarrow had omitted to inform him that there were no less than *five* Miss Bennets altogether!

Chapter 10

For his part, Mr. Darcy would not have subscribed to Mrs. Pencarrow's opinion that anything could be found if one had the means and the willingness to find it. Apparently, despite all the means and the incisive willingness, some things could *not* be found – and least of all Mrs. Pencarrow herself.

The local man engaged for the purpose, a middle-aged, sturdy Cornishman, had warned him that Pencarrow "be a mighty common name down these parts."

"Not many of them would have seven English guests by the name of Bennet," Darcy had impatiently retorted and, with a crooked smile, the other man had to concede the point.

He was not seen for over a fortnight afterwards and, had he been foolish enough to pay him beforehand, Darcy would have surmised he was ensconced in some tavern, drinking his ill-gotten gains. Still, as he had *not* been paid beforehand, Darcy could only assume him hard at work in and around Falmouth, looking for Mrs. Pencarrow and her seven English guests.

As for himself, he could not do much. Marooned at the ineptly named *Hope and Anchor* in Falmouth, Darcy could only fill his days with inexpertly conducting his own investigations while he eagerly awaited the local scout's arrival – as well as a reply to the express he had sent Bingley.

It had been dispatched from Portsmouth all those days ago, penned in great hurry and too short to do full justice to the number of things that had to be said. The apology came first, for having so woefully misjudged Miss Bennet's feelings, and on its heels came the open avowal of his firm intention to offer his hand to the second Miss Bennet. And if his friend still harboured similar intentions towards the first, he would be advised to follow him to Falmouth and seek him at the first passable coaching inn into that town – for it was somewhere in the vicinity that the ladies would be found.

Knowing Bingley, Darcy fully expected to receive him in person instead of a reply and dearly hoped that he was not mistaken, for his own hopes of felicity seemed to rest heavily on the said friend's shoulders.

There was nothing more to be done, just grit his teeth and bear with the wait, but the highly disappointing days of fruitless searches followed by evenings of enforced inactivity cooped up at *The Hope and Anchor* were the longest he had ever known.

On the eighteenth day, his forbearance was finally rewarded with one arrival out of two – the very one most eagerly expected. Soon after luncheon the local scout returned, and Darcy bade him sit with undisguised impatience.

The man took the seat, as well as the glass of brandy Darcy offered.

"Well? What news? Have you got anything to tell me?"

"I 'ave, Sorr. An' Ah would've returned a vast deal sooner, Mr. Darcy, 'ad you not sent me out on a false trail."

"False trail? Of what are you speaking?"

"You sent me alookin' for a Mrs. Pencarrow o' middlin' sort – "

"And?"

"She ain't no middlin' sort, Sorr, is the Mrs. Pencarrow wi' seven guests from England by the name o' Bennet. She ain't even livin' near Falmouth but across the bay, some five miles beyon' St. Anthony. She's the mistress o' Landennis Manor an' Ol' Pencarrow's widow – *'A-Guinea-A-Minute'* Pencarrow that's ter say, 'im o' the tin an' clay mines – an' one o' the richest women in the whole o' Cornwall."

⚬৹ৎ ৎৡ৹

"I have a mind to give a ball," Mrs. Pencarrow announced to Mrs. Bennet as they were sitting together in the drawing room with their tea and coffee. "By your leave, I wish to introduce the girls to all my neighbours. They shall meet the most notable ones tonight at dinner and many more at Lord Trevellyan's ball tomorrow, but I should dearly wish to have them known to everybody," Mrs. Pencarrow added, only to receive something that could be best described as an adoring smile.

Mrs. Bennet had scarcely known her mother, who had left this world shortly after her brother Edward was born. Her father did not remarry, but engaged a stream of nurses and minders to see to his children's upbringing. They were often changed, these hired hands, and thus a lasting bond could not be formed between them and their charges – and it was only now, after all those years, that Mrs. Bennet felt anything remotely like a mother's helping hand.

This elderly lady, her mother's sister, had suddenly appeared in Mrs. Bennet's life and, with one touch, had cured all the ills that had plagued her ever since it had become quite clear that she and her husband would never have a son.

They were assured of an income now, one that Mr. Collins could never snatch away. Not only that, but the girls had a portion! She knew not how much, but of course anything was better than nothing. And now the dear old lady was going to give a dinner and a ball to introduce the girls to the local worthies and hopefully promote a match or two. Mrs. Bennet did not think that anyone could have possibly done more.

"Shall I pour you a fresh cup of tea, Aunt?" she asked, but the elderly lady swiftly negatived.

"I thank you, not just yet, I have not finished mine. But pour for yourself, my dear, and afterwards perhaps you might be willing to assist me. There is writing paper on that desk and all the implements. The ball could be in three weeks' time. We should send out the invitations. Would you be so kind to write them down? My hand is not so fine these days, since these old fingers have grown so old and knobbly."

"But of course," Mrs. Bennet readily concurred. "And the girls could help, when they return from their picnic. Jane has such an elegant hand, so neat and distinguished – and Lizzy too, although she hardly ever has the patience to apply herself," she added as she busied herself with preparing a fresh cup. "As for Mary, she is – ... Oh, my goodness!" she exclaimed, so loudly and abruptly that her relation nearly spilled her tea.

"Whatever is the matter?" Mrs. Pencarrow asked in some concern, only to see her niece rushing to the window.

"No, surely not! I must have been mistaken," Mrs. Bennet muttered, only to exclaim again a moment later, "La! Fancy that! It *is* him after all. Goodness! How extraordinary. Oh, forgive me, Aunt," she suddenly recollected her duties to her elderly companion. "There is a gentleman coming up the drive and I never thought I should see him here. I wonder what brings him. Hm! The strangest thing."

"I wish you would not talk in riddles, dear," Mrs. Pencarrow impatiently admonished. "Of whom are you speaking?" she asked just as Mrs. Bennet rushed to settle on the sofa at her side, so that it would not be so obvious that she had been spying on their unexpected caller from the window.

She arranged her skirts, then fussed with her bonnet and hurriedly whispered to her aunt as she did so:

"We have met the gentleman in Hertfordshire. A charming young man, by the name of Wickham."

ୄଈୃ ଈୖ୶

Mrs. Bennet fidgeted with the lace at her cuffs, still reeling from the shock of this most astounding morning.

First, there was Mr. Wickham's visit – so wholly unexpected, so out of the blue! Apparently he was once more their neighbour, for he had come to Cornwall and here he was to stay. A Mr. Penderrick who, Mrs. Pencarrow had corroborated, owned a sizeable estate some five miles inland on the way to Truro, happened to be a former school companion of his from Cambridge and, moved by his plight and reduced circumstances, had offered him the stewardship of his estates – or something of that nature.

Mr. Wickham had not given a great deal of detail and, truth be told, Mrs. Bennet had not paid much heed to every part of his communications. Although charming as ever, she had to own deep in her heart that Mr. Wickham held far less appeal now that he had chosen to resign his commission and be an officer no longer. Besides, thanks to Mrs. Pencarrow, her girls could do a vast deal better than a mere steward, however pleasant his society might be.

Mr. Wickham had been visibly disappointed to learn that the girls were away from home and had extended his visit far beyond what was expected of a customary morning call, presumably in the hope to greet them. As ever, he had shown his knack for amiable conversation and spent a vast deal of time encouraging Mrs. Bennet to speak of their journey thither, the length of their visit and any other plans that they might have.

Still, two hours later, the picnicking party had not returned and in the end Mr. Wickham was compelled to take his leave and express his hopes to renew his acquaintance with the rest of the family at some other point in the future.

Mrs. Bennet had made no effort to detain him. There was little to be gained from his society these days. Her darling girls could now have the pick of the local worthies.

Indeed, why settle for Mr. Penderrick's steward when any of them could have Mr. Penderrick himself? Or so Mrs. Bennet thought, until her aunt inadvertently disabused her of the delightful notion when she revealed that Mr. Penderrick already had a wife and child. A pity, that, but Mrs. Bennet saw no reason to repine. There would be others and she could hardly wait for tonight's dinner – as well as the delightful prospect of *two* elegant balls.

Once Mr. Wickham left them, she was all too keen to gather the writing implements and assist her aunt in making notes for the grandest event that Landennis Manor had hosted in the last two decades. Yet she had scarce been employed in this rewarding manner for an hour when, through the mullioned windows, she could espy a most fashionable-looking carriage drawing up at the door – and who should descend from it but *Mr. Darcy!*

To her embarrassment, Mrs. Bennet had to own that, unladylike as it might have been, her mouth had simply fallen open and, worse still, had remained so for several moments. She had barely succeeded to gather her wits by the time the old, creaky-jointed butler had come in to announce the *second* unexpected caller of the day.

But no, this would not do! In forty-four years – well, forty-three, since she had learned to speak – nothing had ever stunned her into silence and *nothing* would today, Mrs. Bennet wilfully determined, and recollected herself enough to introduce the gentleman to her aunt, offer him refreshment, inquire into his comfort and ask to what happy circumstance did they owe the pleasure of his company.

He had some business in the area, Mr. Darcy claimed in his habitual clipped manner, and was reluctant to pass on the opportunity of calling upon them and ensure they had arrived in safety to their destination. A smug smile and a nod greeted his words for, by now, the albeit predictable but well-oiled mechanism that was Mrs. Bennet's mind was fully restored to its proper function.

Business in the area, was it? What sort of business might it be, that brings a young man, not yet in his thirties, to the remotest part of the country – hundreds of miles from his haunts in town and twice as far from his estate in Derbyshire – to call upon a family with five unmarried daughters?

The little cogs quietly whirred and turned.

Lydia? From past experience, youthful good-humour and sheer vitality *had* been known to draw a restrained gentleman. Still, perhaps not. In living memory, Mr. Darcy had not sought her out and the same could be said of Kitty – and besides, bless her soul, Kitty did not have a quarter of Lydia's appeal and charm.

Mary? Her bookish ways might have recommended her to someone who was also bookish but nay, Mary was too staid and far too plain, the poor lamb.

Jane? Dearest Jane could move a saint with her astounding beauty. Who would not want her? Well, that foolish man did not – Mr. Bingley, the undeserving cad! It should serve him right if his best friend were to marry the woman he had courted. For her part, Mrs. Bennet dearly hoped that her darling child had ceased pining over that horrid, horrid man. Whoever needed Mr. Bingley *now*, with his pitiful five thousand a year, when the sweet girl could have a match of ten thousand, or very likely more?

And what of Lizzy? Ha! That would be a fine to-do, after slighting her upon their first encounter. Still – there was merit in the thought. It would not be the first time that strong dislike had melted into strong desire. There was plenty of fire in Lizzy that could draw the quiet, reserved moth. Besides, she had that very spark of impudence and her father's sharp wits which, albeit not to everybody's taste, might appeal to a man who was anything but dim.

Hm... Not the average mix, was Lizzy, with some of Jane's beauty, all of Lydia's vitality and fire *and* a brain to top it. Although Jane was her dearest child and Lydia the nearest, the matron was compelled to own that none of them had an ounce of Lizzy's ready wit.

Had she been prone to reflection, Mrs. Bennet would have wondered by-and-by whether her distance from her second daughter might have sprung from being threatened by the superior Bennet intellect. However, the well-oiled mechanism never chose to apply itself to such ponderous matters but fixed instead on clear, uncomplicated thoughts.

Which one of her daughters had Mr. Darcy singled out?

There was one answer. Lizzy. Always Lizzy. *She* was the only girl from Hertfordshire that he had deigned to dance with. *She* was the one whom he had squired across the country in his carriage. *She* was the one to whom he had paid such marked attention at the inn.

Sarah said he had even asked Lizzy to walk with him – and instead the foolish girl had busied herself with the packing! Nevertheless, Mrs. Bennet had seen for herself, on the morning of their departure, that he had made it his particular business to bid Lizzy adieu and *she* had been the only one whom he had shaken hands with. And now he had given himself the trouble to follow hither, hundreds of miles from home, for *'business in the area'*.

Mrs. Bennet vigorously fanned herself with her kerchief, quite overcome by the charming notion. Oh, if it should come to pass! Lizzy wed to Mr. Darcy – if she had read him rightly and if the girl saw sense and set aside her prejudice against him.

Well, why should she not? A passing slight, what did it matter? Surely she would not be blinded to her own advantage for, even with her share of Mrs. Pencarrow's fortune, she could hardly do better than ten thousand a year.

But then, there was also Lord Trevellyan…

Mrs. Bennet had been most gratified earlier in the morning when his lordship had arrived to escort her daughters on their picnic, as arranged. But then, anyone would be gratified by Lord Trevellyan's interest. Mrs. Pencarrow had explained he was a gentleman of enormous consequence, with extensive property stretching for miles on the west side of the river.

Lady Trevellyan – oh, how well that sounds! And it was by no means unlikely. Ever since they had become acquainted, Lord Trevellyan had called upon them often and, although impressed by Jane's superior beauty, Mrs. Bennet had good reason to believe that it was *Lizzy* whom he was disposed to favour.

Two eligible options for her girl – oh, the delightful notion!

It would be so diverting to see them vie for her attention.

Oh, sweet Lord, to be young again!

And then Mrs. Bennet returned to her senses and to practical matters. Diverting, aye, but of no use to her family, in the long run. Nay, it would be so much better if Lord Trevellyan was encouraged towards Jane, leaving Lizzy to marry Mr. Darcy, and then she would have not one but *two* daughters so wonderfully settled.

Surely Lord Trevellyan could be swayed for, as the eldest, Jane was bound to inherit Landennis Manor, and of course Lord Trevellyan would be only too pleased to extend his holdings on both sides of the water.

She *must* be sharp now and assure herself that she had read them rightly, for what use would there be to coax any of them in the wrong direction? She *must* be certain of Mr. Darcy's thoughts – though goodness knows how one was to ascertain them. Four and twenty years of marriage had not taught her to understand the thoughts of a very private man – but on the other hand, she was not too old to remember how a very private gentleman would look when the object of his affections was courted by another!

Mrs. Bennet's lips curled into a smug little smirk. Oh, aye – therein lay the answer. She must see them together, then she *would* know how to act.

Then her lips pursed. If only they came back from that wretched picnic before Mr. Darcy had to take his leave. Goodness, they had been gone for hours! They *had* to return soon. If nothing else, did they not see they must come home before too long to ensure they showed themselves in the best possible light at dinner?

Mrs. Bennet all but gasped. How had it not come to her much sooner? And then was quick to give silent thanks for the thought occurring to her at all, however late.

"Aunt," she spoke up, interrupting the stilted conversation between Mrs. Pencarrow and their guest, "I trust you shall not mind me saying, but I think it a splendid notion if Mr. Darcy could join us for dinner tonight. What say you, Sir? Would that be convenient?"

Although surprised but by no means put out, her aunt was quick to second her suggestion and, to Mrs. Bennet's visible delight, the gentleman restrainedly accepted the sudden invitation.

"Oh, capital! Now, Sir, can I persuade you to have another cup of coffee? Or one of those delicious saffron buns? A Cornish speciality, my aunt informs me, along with these dainty little cakes. May I help you to one? Oh. Perhaps later. Well, I must say we had a most remarkable journey. Have I told you of it? So speedy and through such varied countryside! I have never been to Cornwall – have you, Sir? I knew nothing of the place, the closest we had ever come to the sea was Eastbourne, in the year ninety-eight, but this is so attractive, do you not find it? So very different from every place I have ever seen..." Mrs. Bennet nervously prattled as she struggled with the daunting task of entertaining the most taciturn gentleman of her acquaintance and holding him in place until she could ascertain whether her suppositions were in any way justified.

'Heavens above, how positively vexing! Just how long can anyone stretch a picnic? Where on earth are you, Lizzy? For goodness' sake, come home now, enough is enough!'

She cast another glance out of the mullioned windows, only to see nothing but a disappointingly deserted drive, and prattled on, more desperate than ever for shreds of inspiration – a topic, *any* topic – as the arms dragged sluggishly over the face of the old-fashioned clock.

Chapter 11

Unknowingly of the same mind as Mrs. Bennet in the quest for a topic, any topic, Darcy shifted in his seat and struggled to endure the most excruciating interview he had experienced in his life.

As though subjecting himself of his own free will to over an hour of Mrs. Bennet's conversation was not bad enough, it had become painfully obvious that all his efforts might have been for naught and he would soon have to excuse himself and leave without even having seen her. There was at least the mercy of the impromptu dinner invitation which assured him of encountering her before the day was out, but after the long stretch of frantic searching and painful expectation, the slightest delay was well-nigh impossible to brook.

"Would you care for more coffee, Sir?" Mrs. Bennet pressed him and Darcy found it in his heart to be thankful to the loud and irritating matron for her assistance in extending the already uncivilly long visit – unless she might have guessed his reasons for tarrying?

At that, he all but shuddered. Good heavens, surely not!

"I thank you, Ma'am," Darcy reluctantly spoke up, "but I fear I have trespassed upon your kindness for too long. I shall leave you now – "

"So soon, Sir?" Mrs. Bennet interrupted. "Will you not stay a little longer? My daughters will be so disappointed to have missed you. They are to return shortly, they should have been here by now."

It was very hard indeed to press a point that went against his wishes, so Darcy's lips twitched uncomfortably as he pondered what response to make.

"Would you perchance care to join my husband in the library?" Mrs. Bennet eagerly offered in the ensuing silence, her speech gathering momentum at the fortunate thought. "How foolish of me not to have asked you sooner! I remember you are very fond of reading, Mr. Darcy, are you not?"

However ludicrous the suggestion of a morning caller repairing willy-nilly to the library to avail himself of its delights, *that* was not the reason for Darcy's hesitation. Somehow, the notion of intruding upon Mr. Bennet's privacy – or, worse still, that of the very astute gentleman gaining purchase into his own innermost thoughts – made *Mrs.* Bennet a far more preferable companion, shockingly unlikely as it might have been.

"I am indeed, Ma'am," Darcy brought himself to say, "but I should not wish to distract Mr. Bennet from his private enjoyment– "

"Oh, he would not mind. He always reads whatever he can lay his hands on. And so does Lizzy, she takes after her father. I imagine Mr. Bennet would appreciate some conversation. He would enjoy sharing his thoughts on some tome or other. Shall I...? Oh, never mind!" she cried ever so brightly and, at the sudden change of topic and of tone, Darcy looked up, only to see Mrs. Bennet gaily rushing to the window. "They have returned at last," she announced with great satisfaction – and it took Darcy all the restraint he still possessed to stop himself from following her forthwith.

He stood – there was no way under heaven that he could have remained peacefully seated *now* – and cast what he could only hope was a disinterested glance out of the window.

Three riders were leading the small party and even from that distance he could easily tell that the one on the right was Elizabeth. His eyes widened in a measure of surprise, for he was almost certain that, long ago, at Netherfield, she had claimed she was no horsewoman. He could also spot Miss Bennet – the other side-saddle rider – and a gentleman between them, on a tall bay horse. A groom followed, and a small carriage close behind – the younger girls were presumably unable or unwilling to ride. Yet Darcy's eyes could not be held by the occupants of the carriage or indeed by anybody else as, through the one slightly opened casement, he could hear the trill of Elizabeth's laugh. His glance shot towards her, only to see her gaily saying something to her tall companion, with a bright smile that made his insides turn.

It took the best part of seven seconds to recognise the violent churn inside him as insane, gripping jealousy. Nevertheless, a short while later he had no difficulty at all in recognising the sentiment for what it was, when the tall gentleman dismounted and walked up to assist her in doing the same, his hands firmly clasping her slim waist.

Was there just cause for *that*, Darcy fumed unreasonably and just as insanely. Could not the groom assist her, as he did Miss Bennet – or the young footman, who had rushed out from the house? And now that she *had* dismounted, just how long was he going to keep his hands on her? A second? Ten? A whole damnable minute?

Darcy's jaw tightened and so did his right hand. His fist uncurled slowly, once the blasted man had released her, but his jaw tightened further at the smile she offered for his frankly untoward assistance and at the sight of her taking his eagerly proffered arm. And then he offered his spare arm to Miss Bennet – a clear afterthought – and they made their way towards the house.

Taking a deep, steadying breath, Darcy steeled himself for the encounter, as the new frightful thought wreaked havoc through him.

A rival! Was he then to be plagued with *this* as well, over and above all the other mishaps, errors and misunderstandings that had bedevilled their acquaintance throughout?

'*Heavens above!*' he all but muttered. Was there not enough that he had yet to gain her pardon for the suffering inadvertently caused to her beloved sister? At a time when she was justifiably disposed against him, must he now face a *rival*, of all cursed things?

He took another breath and swallowed, his eyes closing briefly – then opened them to encounter Mrs. Bennet's steady glance fixed upon him, a smile on her lips.

He would not trouble himself *now* with the blasted woman, Darcy instantly determined – though goodness only knew what mischief she might cause if she had guessed the substance of his thoughts. But no, it could not be. That, of all people, *Mrs. Bennet* should outwit him!

If that day ever dawned, he might as well go hang!

The sound of footsteps ringing loudly on the naked floorboards of the great hall brought him back from his vexing ruminations and then *her* voice was heard, distinctive and light, a trace of laughter in it – the very inflection he unconditionally adored.

"That was the most charming place I have ever seen, with the exception of Landennis Cove, which shall remain my favourite forever. A few more spots like these and I shall become firmly attached to Cornwall."

"I take it that you have not gone sailing yet," a deep voice answered, warm and – *confound it!* – pleasant.

"Indeed, I have not. How did you know?"

"Had you experienced its delights, you would have been firmly attached already."

"How so?"

"No description can ever do it justice. You must see for yourself and if you are so inclined, it would be my pleasure to take you out to sea – and any of your relations who might wish to join us."

"A very tempting offer."

"Good! 'Tis settled then. Weather permitting, shall we endeavour to sail out the day after the ball?"

"From what I hear, Fridays are not made up solely of auspicious hours…"

"You have my promise that I shall avoid the inauspicious ones," the gentleman retorted and Darcy heard Elizabeth laugh lightly, as footsteps rang closer and closer to the open door.

"Are you then one of Fortune's chosen, my lord? For you seem supremely confident in your ability to tell the difference beforehand."

Darcy could not hear the answer, if indeed her companion made any, his mind and senses clouded by the horrific question: was she now *flirting* with this other man?

She was not – would not – would she?

No, of course not! What purpose did it serve, to torment himself with such a dreadful notion? She was *not* flirting! He had heard her speak in the exact same fashion to *Bingley*, for goodness' sake, and she would not flirt with the man her sister favoured. She had spoken thus to others, in his hearing. In Hertfordshire, to Mrs. Collins's brothers – Miss Lucas as was – and to the younger Mr. Goulding of Haye Park. To Fitzwilliam even, on occasion. She had spoken thus to –…

Darcy swallowed.

She had spoken thus to *him!*

The staggering notion well-nigh made him gasp.

How had he not seen it? Had he been so blinded by his feelings? Had he seen only what he wished to see?

He had just persuaded himself, with considerable effort, that what he had just heard was not her flirting with another, but her friendly, sporting manner of address that she employed towards *everybody*.

But that meant… Surely, that could only mean that she had not singled *him* out any more than she had singled any of the others!

His fists clenched once more, of their own volition.

Did he not have *this* either? Not even the slight, tenuous advantage of having held her interest once – an interest that might be rekindled, once proper apologies were made for having hurt her sister? Was he even more arrogant than Fitzwilliam had thought him, in his self-assurance, in his assumption of having gained her heart?

The blow was vicious and on its heels came another, finding him so unprepared that he all but reeled. She walked in – and, as soon as her eyes fell upon him, her countenance altered in a flash. Gone was the smile that had fluttered on her lips following the light discourse with her companion. Gone was the easy, carefree good-humour and in its place came sternness and a cautious, guarded look.

No, he amended with a dreadful sinking feeling. Not merely guarded but visibly hostile. Hostile and reproachful. Casting her eyes down, she gave him nothing but a perfunctory brief curtsy in response to his bow and walked up to stand beside her eldest sister and swiftly took her hand. Then, and only then, she glanced again upon him and there was sheer defiance in her steady glare.

Only a dolt would fail to grasp the silent message and, whatever else he might have been, Darcy was not a dolt. He swallowed, with the distinctive feeling of finding himself on quicksand – or in a mire from which he knew not how he could escape.

Somewhere behind him, Mrs. Bennet was speaking, introducing him to the other man – Lord… Something. Lord Trevellyan? Oh, she must *love* her time in the sun, Darcy thought with petulant impatience at the very notion of Mrs. Bennet enjoying the delights of intimate acquaintance with the grandees of Cornwall.

Yet, to his slight remorse at his ungenerous ill-humour, a moment later he was to find himself indebted to *her* of all people, for the unhoped-for assistance.

"Come, Lizzy," Mrs. Bennet urged. "Come, sit with me and leave Jane to prepare a cup of tea for his lordship. Unless you would choose coffee, my lord? Pray, do sit – and you too, Mr. Darcy. And Mary, dear girl, will you not send for more refreshment?"

Miss Mary promptly left to do as bid. Elizabeth, however, seemed wholly disinclined to comply with her mother's instruction to come and sit across from him, but sat next to the table where her eldest sister obligingly busied herself with pouring tea for Lord Trevellyan.

Pursing her lips in something like displeasure, Mrs. Bennet regained her own seat and Darcy all but cringed when the one rejected by Elizabeth was occupied by Miss *Lydia* Bennet.

"How good of you to call upon us, Mr. Darcy," the latter addressed him, her eyes alight, darting from one side of the room to the other. "We were not expecting to see you so soon, were we, Lizzy? What a great pity you have not arrived this morning and then perhaps you could have joined us on our picnic," she gushed, to Darcy's surprise – indeed, to everybody's.

Miss Bennet straightened up from her employment and, along with Elizabeth, directed a levelling glance towards her younger sister.

"Oh, Mamma, it was absolutely lovely!" Miss Kitty enthused in her turn, but her mother did not pay much attention.

Instead, Mrs. Bennet offered brightly:

"That *would* have been a splendid notion, Lydia, my sweet. Indeed, what a pity it did not come to pass! Still, I am pleased to say that Mr. Darcy has agreed to join us for dinner this evening," she added – and Darcy could not fail to see that her second daughter seemed anything but pleased to hear that.

She looked up and frowned, then shifted a little to one side, to make room for her eldest sister on the sofa.

"But Sir," Mrs. Bennet suddenly addressed him, distracting him from distressing ruminations, "I quite forgot to ask. Whereabouts are you staying?"

"I have not determined, Ma'am," Darcy replied in subdued tones. "I have just arrived. I should imagine an inn could be found in the local village."

Mrs. Pencarrow, who had kept her peace since the return of the picnicking party and had merely contented herself with watching everybody with her sunken yet very penetrating eyes, all of a sudden laughingly interjected:

"Oh, nay, nay, Sir, we cannot have that! *Landennis Arms* is but an alehouse for the people in the village and if there is a room or two, they are hardly for the discerning traveller. I should not wonder if you were to find yourself in damp sheets and beset by bedbugs."

With some effort, Darcy suppressed a shudder, knowing full well that *her* eyes would be upon him. He chanced a glance, only to find that it was indeed so and that her lips were curled into a mischievous little smile, as though the notion was highly entertaining.

Was it so very bad, then? Did she dislike him now to so great an extent that she wished his sleep plagued by bedbugs? The thought pained him nearly as much as it riled him – and yet there was something so utterly adorable in her impish turn of countenance and in that little smile that, without intending to, Darcy found himself returning it in full.

Her eyes widened visibly at the sight and for a moment she was positively staring, as though she had expected him to be offended rather than diverted – and then she looked away.

Darcy endeavoured to suppress a sigh at the magnitude of the task before him, his own eyes forcibly opened over the last half-hour to the obstacles he would have to overcome in order to re-establish himself in her good opinion.

Hell and damnation, no, he could not even hope for *that!*

Not *re-establish*. There was good reason to believe that he had engaged her affections and esteem only in his over-confident imagination – and that the task ahead was far more daunting than he had ever thought.

The sigh escaped. He masked it with a cough, then struggled to attend Mrs. Pencarrow, who had resumed speaking:

"I would very much like to ask you to stay with us here at the Manor, but I fear you shall not thank me for the offer. This old place has known a secluded life for far too many years and most of the bedchambers are hardly fit for purpose after nearly two decades of disuse. Still, I should imagine 'tis a trifle better than *Landennis Arms* and all its bugs," she laughed lightly and, despite himself, Darcy found himself warming to the older woman.

That he would have dearly loved to avail himself of her invitation, there could be no doubt. The unhoped-for chance to be under the same roof as Elizabeth and find a way to soften her towards him was as appealing as could be – and yet he did not need to catch her glance to know that he would read dismay in her too expressive eyes. Only a fool would hurt his chances by riling her further so, with some determination, Darcy brought himself to say:

"I thank you, Ma'am, but I should not wish to impose upon your kindness," he quietly offered, then added with the vaguest hint of a diverted smile: "I think I shall pit myself against the bedbugs after all."

A fleeting glance allowed him to see that Elizabeth arched a brow, although she kept staring at her hands and would say nothing. As for Mrs. Pencarrow, she merely returned his smile and bade him do just as he wished, as long as he remembered that the offer stood, if *Landennis Arms* proved too much for comfort.

In the end, it was only Mrs. Bennet who saw fit to protest:

"But, Mr. Darcy, surely you cannot subject yourself to such an inconvenience! As my aunt suggested, you would be most welcome here, Sir, most welcome indeed!"

It was fruitless to wish for the warm entreaty to be forthcoming from the *daughter* rather than the mother. Today at least, it would not come to pass. With a valiant effort at masking his distress, Darcy turned to Mrs. Bennet to thank her for the offer and let her know that he must abide by the original plan. Just then though, from the other end of the drawing room where he sat, quietly surveying the changing scene before him with all its undercurrents and wordless exchanges, Lord Trevellyan suddenly decided to speak up:

"If I may be allowed a say in the matter, I believe I can claim the doubtful privilege of having seen the inside of *Landennis Arms* more recently than most. As such, I truly would not recommend it, Mr. Darcy, for great many reasons, of which the bedbugs form only a small part. But, as a treasured acquaintance of Mrs. Bennet's, you are welcome to come and stay at my house. 'Tis but a short distance around the estuary – and shorter still across it – and I assure you that you can be accommodated without the slightest inconvenience."

Darcy looked up in unconcealed surprise at the wholly unexpected offer – only to meet the other man's cool stare, fixed upon him from under vaguely arched brows.

It was not the deliberately blank look that riled him beyond sense and reason, but the glance full of astonished gratitude that Darcy saw Elizabeth bestow upon the other man. He pressed his lips together, willing his churning turmoil into some measure of tenuous control.

Not a fool then, my lord Trevellyan, but a crafty devil! In one fell swoop – and a rather elegant one as well, Darcy felt compelled to own – he had gathered most of the trumps and all the laurels.

Not only had he steered him away from Landennis Manor and its environs but – *damn him and his cunning!* – by doing so, he had gained the aura of a Good Samaritan into the bargain.

Gallingly, there was nothing he could say other than, "I thank you, I am most obliged" – and he said so, with as much evenness as he could muster.

"Think nothing of it," the other casually retorted, then put down his empty cup. "Well then, if you have no objection, Mr. Darcy, perhaps we should take our leave, seeing as we ought to make ourselves presentable in time for dinner," he added and, once more feeling vexingly outmanoeuvred, Darcy could do nothing but agree.

Adieus were made, restrained and providing little comfort, and before too long Darcy found himself in his own carriage, with Lord Trevellyan leading the way on his bay horse.

The journey took no more than a half-hour. The man was in the right; his house was not far – a grand and very handsome residence, Jacobean in appearance, atop the hill that overlooked the river mouth.

Casting the reins to one of his men and instructing another to see to his guest's carriage and people, Lord Trevellyan motioned towards the entrance and they both made their way within.

"Can I offer you a drink while your trunk is brought up?" the host offered and, once more, Darcy felt that civility compelled him to agree. He followed Lord Trevellyan to a room that presumably served as his study or something of that nature, dark-panelled and very masculine in its *décor*.

"Brandy?"

"Thank you."

Lord Trevellyan poured for both and they sipped their drinks in silence. For his part, Darcy was rather persuaded that he had been brought there for an oblique quizzing and, in order to forestall it, he began at once – much as disguise of every sort was his abhorrence.

"Your kindness is deeply appreciated, Lord Trevellyan. However, I should not wish to impose upon you. As the local inn does not come with good recommendations, I can easily lodge in Falmouth and engage a craft to bring me across the bay – particularly as I expect a friend of mine to arrive in these parts in a few days' time."

"Mr. Darcy, surely there is no cause to lodge across the bay. You are of course welcome to stay for as long as you wish and so is your friend, when he arrives. You have only to send one of your men to Falmouth to await him and escort him hither. As to the local inn, as I said before, the likelihood of bedbugs is the least of your concerns.

From what I understand, it is the haunt of the sort of people who would not take kindly to a stranger in their midst."

"Oh? What sort of people would that be?"

His host smiled.

"Would you not hazard a guess?"

"Smugglers? Pirates? Wreckers?"

His lordship's smile grew a trifle wider.

"Let us just say, your first guess is not vastly off the mark."

"And is the law powerless against them?"

"I daresay I am – to some extent at least. Oh, did you not know?" he added, noting the other's expression of surprise. "Perhaps Mrs. Bennet did not have the opportunity to mention that I am Justice of Peace for this parish."

"I see."

"In answer to your question, I am not so much powerless as disinclined to wage a losing battle."

"How so?"

"'Tis the nature of things that in every part of the world people would make a living by hook or by crook and, after all, we cannot send everybody to Botany Bay. We catch the big fish – or at least we try to. But never mind that now. I should imagine your room must be readied and presumably a bath as well, so you might wish to retire and refresh yourself, since we are to wander back towards Landennis in a few hours. Ah, that reminds me. You might find that our steep and narrow lanes are better suited to riding than to a London carriage. You are most welcome to choose a mount from the stables."

"You are very gracious – but speaking of Landennis," Darcy resumed, refusing to be sidetracked, "I can only hope that the unsavoury characters you mentioned pose no threat to the people at the Manor."

With a swift, stiff movement from his shoulder, Lord Trevellyan drained his glass.

"I am making it my business to ensure they do not," he said at length and Darcy frowned.

"Would that not be best achieved by tackling a known nest of vipers?" he asked with an arched brow and for a moment he was certain that Lord Trevellyan would bristle at his interference.

Whether or not he was tempted to, Lord Trevellyan did not bristle. He merely offered curtly:

"It would not."

In the end, it was Darcy who bristled.

"Then how do you propose to ensure their safety?"

"I have my ways," was all that the other was prepared to offer and at that, Darcy rather lost his temper.

"For my part, I hope they will soon return where they belong!"

"And where might that be?"

"Hertfordshire, of course."

And in *her* case Derbyshire, God willing, but that was something he could not – would not say.

"What makes you so certain that they belong in Hertfordshire?" Lord Trevellyan drawled, riling him even further.

"I fail to understand your meaning."

"Mrs. Pencarrow has informed me that their Hertfordshire estate is entailed upon a distant cousin. A Kentish rector by the name of Collins, if memory serves."

'A Kentish rector? Collins? Heavens above! Him?' Darcy all but gasped.

He was sufficiently acquainted with Mr. Collins to know that the man had about as much affectionate compassion as the gatepost of Hunsford parsonage. Heaven forefend, should anything befall Mr. Bennet, that man would have his family out of Longbourn before he was cold in his grave! Suddenly, in this light, Mrs. Bennet's scheming to get her daughters married no longer held such repulsively greedy connotations.

"You seem uncommonly well informed about their business," he observed coolly, to mask his discomfort at the revelations.

"It is my business to be well informed."

"Is that so?" Darcy snapped, forgetting his manners. "To the best of my knowledge, Mr. Bennet and his family are not of this parish and thus beyond your remit!"

"Then perhaps it might serve you to become better informed," the other drawled, clearly enjoying his advantage. "As such, you might wish to learn they have good enough reason to be of this parish. Or at least one of them has."

Darcy's jaw stiffened.

"Of whom are you speaking?"

"Miss Elizabeth Bennet."

Lord Trevellyan's prompt and confident retort shook Darcy to the core. *No! It could not be!* He had *not* proposed already, surely – and *she* had not accepted!

"What makes you claim that?" he asked through frozen lips.

"Mrs. Pencarrow has chosen to appraise me of her wishes. It appears that each of the Miss Bennets are to receive a share of the lady's considerable fortune – "

"And what has *this* to do with Miss Elizabeth Bennet being of this parish?"

"Everything, I should imagine. You see, upon her great-aunt's passing, of all her sisters, *she* is to be the mistress of Landennis Manor."

Chapter 12

How could the tables *possibly* have turned so completely and in so short a time? A month ago he held all the cards, or at least he thought he did. A month ago he was convinced she was his for the asking – if only he could bring himself to ask. A month ago it was in his power to offer her everything – if only he could set aside all the reasonable objections to their union. A month ago he was persuaded he had her affections, or at least her clear interest.

He could no longer vouch for that. Not only had she been appraised of his efforts to separate Bingley from her sister – which in itself was reason enough to temper any regard she might have had for him – but it appeared now that her perceived regard might well have been a figment of his imagination and that he had misread the signs so wilfully, so completely!

Worse still, she might have gained the interest of another – a peer of the realm, no less – who stood to offer her as much as *he* could and very likely more. A gentleman who, moreover, had not spent the best part of their acquaintance striving to ignore her, but seemed intent to gain her good opinion. A man highly recommended by her great-aunt and so favoured by the older lady's confidence that he had come to know a vast deal more of Elizabeth's circumstances than *he* ever did.

As to her circumstances, their sudden alteration was another blow and a severe one at that. How horribly ironic that the very fact which made her a far more eligible choice as Pemberley's mistress – despite the fortune having been made in trade – could only serve to make her less needful of accepting his attentions!

The thought was unworthy, on more than one count, and Darcy could only reproach himself for having entertained it. Money made in trade or not – what did it matter? He had decided to offer for her when he knew her portion to have been little more than nothing.

As to the other notion, surely he did not wish her to accept him merely for his name and standing. No, of course not! He had long determined she was far above such mercantile considerations. Yet knowing himself devoid of every familiar advantage was alien and, frankly, a well-nigh terrifying thought.

Darcy pushed his food about the plate, then carried a morsel to his mouth, tasting nothing. From his seat, towards the middle of the long dark table, he could barely see her, placed as she was at Lord Trevellyan's side, his lordship having his own place allotted, as the most honoured guest, at Mrs. Pencarrow's right hand.

This in itself was alien. Darcy could not remember the last time he had been placed so far down the table, so clearly *'below the salt'* – if indeed it had ever happened – but this was nothing compared to the lengthy torture of seeing her chat to her dinner companion, with nary a glance in his own direction.

More vexingly still, he was plagued with other glances. From her own seat at the opposite end, near her husband who filled the role of Mrs. Pencarrow's counterpart, Mrs. Bennet frequently fixed her eyes upon him – though what on earth he had done to attract her unrelenting interest, Darcy could not even begin to guess.

He strained to hear what was said at Elizabeth's end of the table. She was listening with a patient smile to something that the man seated at her other side was saying – a gentleman whose name Darcy had not caught. He had made no effort to commit to memory the names of those introduced to him earlier in the evening, too troubled by the notion that of the sixteen dinner guests only half a dozen seemed married and settled. The others were conspicuously unattached – a horde of young men, single young men, milling around the Bennet sisters!

Mrs. Pencarrow was matchmaking, it was plain to see.

Heavens above! What was the woman thinking? Did it not cross her mind that she was in effect marking them out – marking *her* – as a target for every fortune-hunter in the south of Cornwall? Was she about to let them *all* know, along with Lord Trevellyan, that Elizabeth was the future mistress of Landennis Manor?

"So, Darcy, what brings you to this part of the country?" he suddenly found himself addressed, from across the table, by Mr. Penderrick.

It had come as a surprise to encounter his former schoolfellow here. He had forgotten that Penderrick hailed from these parts – but then again there was not a great deal he remembered of *all* his past acquaintance.

"Some business in the area," he succinctly offered and, from her seat, Mrs. Bennet smirked.

"Will you be staying long?"

"I fear I cannot say. My plans are not yet formed."

"You must call upon me if you have the time and then perchance we could reminisce over the good old days at Cambridge."

"I thank you, I am much obliged," Darcy felt compelled by civility to answer, though he truly could not say what would there be for them to reminisce about.

They had precious little to do with one another, all those years ago. Penderrick was a very private man, which in itself might have recommended him to Darcy. However, it did not – but if Penderrick was of a mind to wax sentimental over their *alma mater*, then Darcy could be persuaded to indulge him. If nothing else, he would greatly prefer Penderrick's hospitality to Trevellyan's, if his former schoolfellow was about to offer it, for at least Penderrick would not make him grit his teeth every blasted second, nor force him to swallow the bile of belated regrets and ever-growing jealousy.

"I did not know you were a Cambridge man as well, Mr. Darcy," Mrs. Penderrick jovially interjected. "In this case, you certainly *must* call upon us. Are you by any chance acquainted with Mr. Wickham too?"

The name fell on him like an ice-cold stone.

"Mr. Wickham, Ma'am?" he pointlessly repeated, struggling to order his thoughts and think of something more cogent to say.

Thus employed, Darcy failed to notice that he had at last gained Elizabeth's attention. Her eyes shot up to him, then drifted to his dinner companions, discretely intent upon hearing what would be said next. Two seats away from him, Miss Lydia was a great deal more conspicuous in her interest. She leaned forward, her glance travelling from Mrs. Penderrick to himself, until Miss Bennet quietly addressed her:

"Lydia, would you like me to help you to some of those delicious sweet-peas? I believe they are the first of the season."

Unbeknownst to Darcy, a silent injunction was passed along with the sweet-peas but his attention remained fixed on Mrs. Penderrick, who casually elaborated:

"Aye, Mr. Wickham, our new steward. My husband had recently encountered him in town and had engaged him in that particular function."

Mrs. Penderrick offered something further, which Darcy did not hear, too engrossed by the shocking tidings. Wickham – here? As Penderrick's steward? Had the man lost his senses, to put his affairs into the scoundrel's hands?

But perhaps Penderrick did not know what Wickham was. Having kept himself to himself at Cambridge, perhaps he had no notion of Wickham's dishonesty and dissolute ways.

Darcy all but cringed. Much as he recoiled from the repulsive prospect, this time he would *have* to become involved. Penderrick must be warned of course – not only to safeguard him from that man's scheming, but safeguard the Miss Bennets as well. The very notion well-nigh made him shudder. Wickham settled a few miles from here, aware of the Miss Bennets' change of fortune and at liberty to make designs, to prey upon them!

For the first time since it had happened, a few weeks ago, Darcy found it in him to be grateful for Fitzwilliam bringing up Wickham's name in Elizabeth's presence, on their way from Hunsford. At least *she* had been warned to some extent, during his cousin's rant, that the vermin was not to be trusted.

There was every reason to believe she would warn her sisters too, but perhaps more ought to be said. Perhaps the full truth should be revealed to her, so that she would be left in no misapprehension of the depths the fiend would be prepared to sink to.

Of its own volition, his glance turned towards her. Their eyes met and held – and this time her countenance was no longer a study in hostile reserve. Unspoken understanding glimmered in her eyes instead, as though she fully comprehended how he felt at the very mention of the blackguard's name.

Was that a little smile of reassurance that she had just cast him, the first smile since their morning at the inn in Basingstoke – or was it just the play of candlelight on her flawless skin? He could not tell, for she looked away towards Mrs. Pencarrow, who was just then rising to her feet to signal the withdrawal of the ladies.

At that, Elizabeth rose too, offered a supporting arm to her relation and together they led the procession to the drawing room.

Custom dictated that he remained in place, Darcy knew full well – as did the precepts of common courtesy owed to Mr. Bennet – so, with the greatest effort, Darcy resumed his seat. To his ill-concealed vexation, the company grew louder once the gentlemen were left to their own devices and, if not yet raucous, laughter was at least unrestrained when the young bucks commenced toasting one another – a custom that had never been close to Darcy's heart.

As for himself, he was determined to remain in the dining room for no more than a half-hour, custom be damned and, while forced to stay on this side of the drawing room door, he might as well acquit himself of the unpalatable duty of dropping a few words in Penderrick's ear.

The opportunity was very long in coming – Trevellyan, perversely, chose to be in the way and engage Penderrick in some conversation. At length, he wandered off and Darcy saw his chance. Finding Penderrick alone with the port decanters, he lost no time in approaching him and, reluctant as he was to plunge into the distasteful business, Darcy brought himself to say, with as much evenness as he could muster, as he refilled his glass:

"I trust you will not take it amiss, Penderrick, but may I offer a word of caution regarding Wickham? From my former dealings with him, I feel incumbent upon me to let you know that he is not a man to be trusted."

"Oh?" the other retorted, then soon added. "Aye, come to think of it, I remember now. There *was* some connection between you – "

"There was no connection," Darcy instinctively rejected the repulsive notion, "other than the fact that his father was my own father's steward."

"I see. And did old Mr. Wickham not discharge his duties to your family's satisfaction?"

"Quite the contrary," Darcy replied promptly. "No one can cast aspersions on the father. The son, however, is another matter."

"How so?"

"Forgive me, Penderrick, but I cannot provide details – and certainly not here. I merely wished to advise you to beware of Wickham. He is not what he seems."

"I thank you for the warning. I shall be sure to keep an eye on him. Now, can I pour you another drink? Port, was it?"

With some surprise, Darcy eyed his empty glass. He must have drained it without notice during the awkward conversation. He set it instantly upon the dresser. This was not the answer – and this was most certainly not the time!

"I thank you, no," he promptly replied, then excused himself with a few words and a swift bow.

He cast a glance around him. The gentlemen had by then clustered in two distinctive groups – the roisterers and the quiet drinkers – and, unsurprisingly, Darcy felt he belonged to neither.

Mr. Bennet must have felt the same for, glass in hand, the older man wandered in his direction.

"Not of a mind to join the fray then, Mr. Darcy?" he observed with a smile and a vague motion towards the assembled company.

Darcy shrugged.

"I have not the talent which some possess of conversing easily with strangers or of appearing interested in their concerns," he retorted and the other laughed.

"I must confess I find no fault in that, though others might. Well. I daresay it is at least diverting to watch others play the fools, if one can neither beat them at their game nor bring oneself to join them."

Darcy's lips twitched.

"There is always the library, Mr. Bennet," he offered and, in his turn, Mr. Bennet gave a quiet chuckle.

"Ah, yes, the ivory tower. Not an option for me at the moment, Mr. Darcy – more's the pity – but as for yourself, by all means feel free, if you are so inclined. The fourth door to the right, once you have gained the hall," he indicated, "but mind you do not miscount and find yourself in the drawing room instead," Mr. Bennet added dryly as he turned to refill his glass.

With a bow, Darcy left him and soon left the dining room as well, although of course he did not head towards the fourth door off the great hall – nor was he thoroughly persuaded that Mr. Bennet had expected him to.

He found his way towards the drawing room – *where else?* – and the first person he saw as he opened the door was Trevellyan, in conversation with Elizabeth, her eldest sister and Mrs. Pencarrow.

How the deuce did *he* come to be there already, Darcy could not tell and his eyes narrowed, privately deciding that he had had his fill of my lord Trevellyan!

"Oh, Mr. Darcy, how good of you to join us, Sir," Mrs. Bennet greeted him with audible satisfaction. "Can I offer you some coffee or a cup of tea?"

He settled on the second, cursing his misjudgement. How *was* he to approach her in such restricted company, with Trevellyan constantly in the way and under Mrs. Bennet's watchful eye – and, for some reason, Miss Lydia's too?

The glance he craved was aimed in his direction only once and then she resumed her conversation with her great-aunt and Trevellyan about some altar stones, an ancient relic found on a hilltop not very far from there. The topic soon led to another, something about St. Veryan and some oddly-shaped houses in the hamlet bearing the saint's name – yet another conversation in which he could have no part – and before long the drawing room door was opened to admit the rest of the party.

They came in, ruddy-cheeked, to increase the noise and double the commotion – which would have been a manifest advantage, were it not for the fact that they substantially diminished every chance he might have had to come near *her* – and Darcy shifted in his seat with a huff of insurmountable vexation.

Precisely *what* he had expected from this dinner other than setting eyes on her, he really could not tell – but it was plain to see that whatever it was, it would not come to pass.

One thing was certain: he had to do *something*.

Clearly, he was running out of time!

A chance came at last, a small chance, and only towards the end of the evening, but at least it was better than nothing. At length, she had excused herself and had walked away from the group clustered around her sofa to pour a cup of tea – for herself, or for somebody else – and Darcy promptly followed, not altogether certain what he was about to say, but nevertheless unwilling to miss the very first opportunity for private conversation.

It came to him, just as he approached her.

"Miss Bennet," he began, only to find her eyes rising to fix themselves upon him, once more cold and decidedly guarded.

"Mr. Darcy," she quietly acknowledged him as she set her cup upon the table. "I trust you are having a pleasant evening, Sir," she added, yet there was something in her countenance that suggested she was merely paying lip service to the requirements of common courtesy.

He should have played the game, but he disdained it.

It was no use and there was little time.

"I thank you," was the only concession to civility he was prepared to make, for devil take him if he was about to lie and claim to have enjoyed the wretched evening! "Pray forgive my bluntness," he pressed on, "but may I be allowed to call upon you on the morrow? There is... a great deal to be said – matters to discuss."

She looked away as she pushed the cup and saucer further towards the middle of the table, then her eyes settled upon him again.

"Yes, Mr. Darcy," she quietly conceded. "I daresay there *are* matters to discuss."

Chapter 13

A long night followed. A long, uneasy night in a stranger's house, a man he detested, in all likelihood a rival.

He would have roamed the halls, at war with his thoughts, had he been at home. He was not – so he paced in his chambers until the early hours, struggling to settle upon what he should say, and how.

It was frightfully alien, this notion that sapped his self-assurance, this sense that he was not playing this game with the best hand. No, not a game! It was not a game, by Jove, but the most important step he had taken in his life, and woe betide him if he faltered!

His agitation mounting, he even resorted to the ludicrously unthinkable: he started making *notes*. Swift lines, boldly penned, then crossed out and reworded. Fitzwilliam would laugh to see him do so – damn the fool and his cursed tongue!

Somewhere in the house, a clock struck two by the time he had folded one final, neatly-written piece of paper and walked over to place it securely in his breast-pocket. The rest – a pile of scribbles – were consigned to the flames and Darcy leaned his hand on the top of the marble mantelpiece as he watched them catch fire, each crumpled sheet in turn, and burn to ash.

He walked to pour himself a drink from the well-stocked decanters – if nothing else, Trevellyan was a flawless host – and drained the fiery brandy in one draught.

No more. Everything was settled. John, the footman who was still substituting for his valet, had been instructed to rouse him at seven and no later, and there was nothing he could do but sleep – or, at the very least, try to keep his wits about him and his nervous excitement in control.

 споте дея

It was, he knew full well, a prodigious task – and more difficult still several hours later, when he finally dismounted before the entrance of Landennis Manor and cast the reins of Trevellyan's horse to one of the stable lads who appeared out of nowhere to attend him. A footman opened the great oak doors for him and he was shown into a small – and empty – downstairs parlour.

"Pray, be seated, Sorr," the young footman bade him, "and I'll be sure to announce you."

"I trust the family is not abed," Darcy offered, rather horrified.

He had made every effort to arrive in the earliest hours, before the time when Mrs. Bennet was likely to be about – which answered both the need for privacy and the proddings of nervous impatience – but there was little doubt, he *did* arrive a great deal too early for a morning call.

Thankfully the footman lost no time to reassure him, and with the best possible words:

"Miss Elizabeth told me you are to call this morning, Sorr. She's expecting you and I'll find her in a trice."

He did. Darcy had barely removed his gloves and was about to drop them on a chair alongside his hat, when the door opened to admit her. He bowed very deeply, yet without losing sight of the enchanting picture she presented – without a doubt, the handsomest woman of his acquaintance! Her cheeks glowed – from the encounter? Or perhaps the exercise, for she was dressed for the outdoors, although without a bonnet, and her auburn hair shone with tints of red, where it caught the early morning sun. She curtsied in greeting, then motioned to a chair.

"Would you care to sit, Sir – or would you rather go for a short walk?"

The latter suggestion certainly explained her attire and Darcy could not fail to appreciate her perception, as well as her sterling common sense. Of course she would see that they needed time to speak without the fear of interruption and without the imposition of prying ears and eyes.

He readily acknowledged he preferred the walk and they made their way out of the parlour. She paused in the small alcove by the door to retrieve and don a bonnet she must have left there for the purpose and Darcy's heart swelled at the endearingly domestic picture. He watched her tie the ribbon with swift, deft motions, devoid of consciousness or artifice, into a neat bow just underneath her ear, then push back some unruly tendrils at her temple, purse her lips briefly when they would not comply and push them back again. Then she looked up – and saw his smile – and caught him staring.

He did not mind, but looked away nevertheless, so as not to disconcert her.

"Shall we?" Elizabeth prompted and, with a nod, Darcy followed her out of the quiet house.

They walked in silence along the drive, then up the road that had brought him thither. Belatedly, Darcy offered his arm and she took it, with just a hint of hesitation. She said nothing, nor did she prompt him to begin, and once more Darcy inwardly thanked her for her understanding and her wisdom.

It *was* time to begin though – and he knew his lines. Still, there was nothing pleasant in the first ones and although he knew that they *had* to be delivered, Darcy could not quite bring himself to do so now and spoil the treasured intimacy of the moment.

The path that she eventually struck upon was very narrow, barely admitting two, perforce bringing them closer together, their shoulders touching now and then as they made their way between the old lichen-encrusted wall on one side and the sharp-spiked gorse shrubs rising on the other.

A brief smile fluttered on his lips as the old adage suddenly sprang to mind, delightfully *à propos:*

'When the gorse is out of bloom, kissing is out of fashion'.

Of course, gorse was almost perpetually in bloom and, for a moment of sweet insanity, Darcy allowed himself to ponder stopping halfway along the path and kissing her. She would be shocked – no, hopefully not shocked, but she *would* be surprised that he would choose to come to the point in so unorthodox a manner. Surprised and not necessarily best-pleased, caution advised, and Darcy determined to obey it. He had, after all, given her more than enough reasons to expect an apology from him and it would be unwise to add another.

He took a deep, steadying breath.

"Miss Bennet," he finally began, "as we both know, an apology is in order…"

Her eyes shot up to him and she arched a brow.

"Indeed!" she remarked and Darcy all but winced to note that her tone was almost scathing. "And do you imagine, Sir, that an apology would set everything to rights?"

He sighed. The task before him was as daunting as he had anticipated! Still, at least she was not feigning ignorance as to his meaning. No, of course she would not. It was not her way to skirt the issue, hide behind artifice, or otherwise dissemble.

Nor was it his.

"I do not," he owned. "I did not come to offer empty words –..."

"Then what *did* you come to offer?"

'Everything I have,' he barely stopped himself, at the last moment, from blurting out without *finesse* and her countenance altered as though somehow she had guessed his thoughts nevertheless.

She released his arm and stepped aside, gaining some distance. The path allowed it now. Without his notice, it had slowly widened and, after a few more steps taken in silence as he pondered on how to best convey his meaning, the prospect opened fully into a view over a deserted cove.

She stopped and turned towards him, waiting – and he had no intention to keep her waiting long.

"Miss Bennet, I came to tell you that I did not *know!* I had no notion that your sister favoured Bingley. From observing her countenance and manner, I gathered that although she received his attentions with pleasure, she did not invite them, nor were his sentiments returned. As you well know, I eventually learned I was in error. You must remember the occasion –..."

She nodded without words and he continued.

"I determined then to speak to Bingley – make a full confession."

"And have you?"

"I have written him. I omitted nothing and urged him to follow me to Falmouth. Even now, one of my men is stationed at the first inn into that town, with instructions to show him the way to... where I am staying," he supplied, choosing to avoid a direct reference to his lordship's name.

"And yet he has not followed," Elizabeth observed and Darcy sighed.

"No. He has not. And I cannot fathom why."

"Perhaps there was not much affection on his side," she retorted, then her brow arched once more as she added coldly, "but this assumption is of course lessening the honour of your triumph."

"I was not seeking to *triumph*, Miss Bennet!" Darcy burst out promptly, riled by her wilful determination to misunderstand him.

"Were you not?" she said dryly, her brow still arched.

"Of course I rejoiced in my success, while I was acting under the assumption that I was saving Bingley from a loveless marriage. He is a good man and we both know he deserves better," he added, already regretting his earlier outburst and not entirely convinced that his subsequent attempt to co-opt her into agreeing with him regarding Bingley was all that well received.

"So you have persuaded yourself that Jane would marry him without affection, if he offered?" she instantly parried and Darcy pursed his lips.

This was yet another stretch of dangerous waters and he did not feel secure of his chances to emerge unscathed from a second one.

"I was convinced that your sister held enough affection for her relations to be prepared to raise her family's fortunes at the expense of her own felicity – and his," he replied with some diplomacy and only as he did so he decided that, although he had couched the matter in those terms so as to avoid riling her with an open criticism of her mother, he did not feel he had spoken an untruth.

She did not argue this time and her countenance softened for a moment, presumably at his estimation of her sister's character, before becoming closed once more, and troubled.

"And is this what Mr. Bingley thinks as well?"

Darcy bit his lip, unwilling to acknowledge, at this crucial time, just how much effort he had put into ensuring that this was precisely what Bingley came to think. In effect, he was almost certain that *this* had been the means to persuade him away from the connection: the notion that Miss Bennet would have seen fit to sacrifice herself.

"I endeavoured to correct the misconception, in my letter," he said instead, then added, "I wish I could do more. I also wish Bingley were here…" – *Where the deuce was he, anyway?* – "… as he would make a far better job of speaking to your sister. It may seem callous – or insensitive, at the very least – for me to come now and ask for her forgiveness, or yours, yet I wish there was something I could do to persuade you that causing pain was never my intention!"

Her eyes did not waver from him, alert and searching. She did not look away, not even when he finished speaking. After a period of silence, which seemed to Darcy unbearably long, she pursed her lips and sighed.

"Much as I resented your interference, I find I cannot fault you for your reasons, Mr. Darcy," she finally offered. "I cannot vouch for my sister's forgiveness but... you *do* have mine. Particularly as I have already heard a similar opinion from another quarter regarding my sister's private nature and her feelings which, although fervent, are not as fervently expressed..."

She said something further which, to his frustration, Darcy could not catch. The wind – a mere breeze up to that moment – suddenly picked up in a fierce gust that all but tore his hat off. He removed it, then pushed his hair from his eyes.

"Miss Bennet," he plunged forth, unable and unwilling to continue hedging, "I thank you for your kindness. I can only hope you shall not withdraw it when you hear I cannot stop at that. You see, it is not merely your forgiveness that I came to ask for. I should have gone about this in a better – in the proper manner. I should have told you many months ago how ardently I admire and love you. Pray allow me to do so now. Pray allow me to assure you that I have come to feel for you the most passionate admiration and regard. My feelings would not be repressed – nor should they be! Miss Bennet, allow me to ask, would you do me the honour of accepting my hand in marriage?"

This time she did not look up. Nor did she speak for yet another horribly long time – and the pause that followed was, to Darcy's feelings, dreadful. When she finally did look up, she cast her glance away from him, towards the water.

"Mr. Darcy, I..." She sighed and turned to him at last. "Last time I said these words, they were spoken in anger. Not so now... and yet they must be said. Perhaps, Sir, and with more just cause than Mr. Bingley, *you* could also do a great deal better than settle for a loveless marriage..."

The words sunk in, quiet and horrifying, and of them all, Darcy readily picked the worst.

"*Loveless?*"

"I fear so..." Her hand came up to rest on his bent arm and pressed it lightly. "I... I do not return your feelings, Mr. Darcy.

Forgive me, my manner must have been at fault, but not
intentionally, I assure you. I never meant to deceive you, but my
spirits might have often led me wrong…"

She trailed off and Darcy winced as he read unmistakable
compassion in her eyes. Heavens above, of all the feelings he had
hoped to inspire in her…! His glance drifted to her small hand, still
resting on his sleeve, and he did not look up as she continued softly:

"I hope you will soon recover from this disappointment. I…
genuinely wish I could return your feelings but… truth be told, even
if I did, I would still have wavered."

"*Why?*"

He wondered if she had detected the accent of disbelief and sheer
desperation. If she had, she gave no sign of it. She let her hand drop
and quietly offered, her voice barely audible over the rising wind:

"I have good cause to know that the most ardent feelings fade
when they are not sustained by mutual respect."

Darcy frowned, then swallowed.

"I am distraught to hear that you cannot respect me –…" he
began with some sternness, his voice gravelly, but instantly stopped
as she interjected:

"I was not speaking of myself."

His eyes widened.

"There is no one of the entire breadth of my acquaintance whom
I have ever come to respect more!" he counteracted promptly and
with feeling, but she merely shook her head with a wistful smile.

"Come now, Mr. Darcy," she chided gently. "You have made no
secret of your disdain for my connections. Whatever might have
altered or *will* alter, this, Sir, never shall: they will always be a part of
me, of who I am, regardless of how far I travel – and I cannot
imagine you would ever be at peace with that."

He swallowed hard.

"'Tis but a small price – and a risk I am prepared to take!" he
spoke with strong determination, his eyes intent on hers, willing her
to believe he was in earnest.

She sighed again.

"Perhaps. But I am not prepared to take any risk of the kind. You
see, I believe that I, too, deserve better than half-hearted
concessions."

"You deserve the best that a man can offer, and I was not making half-hearted concessions! I would –…" He stopped and pressed his lips together. "To my misfortune, it seems that I have failed to persuade you of the strength of my affections…"

Every form of reason, everything he stood for, rebelled against the notion of *begging* to be allowed to alter her opinion. Yet reason had no purchase before the wrenching thought that he could not let the unthinkable come to pass!

Good Lord in heaven, he could not – *would not* – lose her!

Panic rose within him, choking, terrifying. He struggled for words – better words, that would serve the purpose. Yet none would come and before he could even begin to gain control over the frightful turmoil, Elizabeth spoke up slowly, with wistful determination.

"You have not failed, Sir and… I understand. You have offered me everything that is in your power to offer and I thank you for it, but I cannot accept it. I hope that in due course you will see that it is for the best and that no good could have come from doing otherwise. I cannot stake my hopes of felicity on sentiments that are at war with pride – and you should not stake yours on one-sided affections."

And there it was, the one argument he could not refute. She did not love him. Never had – and claimed she never shall. Pain twisted deep inside and, even with his senses numbed with shock, he recognised it for the agonising torture that would grip him later, when he would have regained the full capacity to feel it.

He almost wished that she had raved at him, rejected him in a passion for any other reason, for his misguided actions against her sister, even – but not *this!* This was something he could not set to rights – control – alter. And the calm finality of the unvarnished truth was devastating, for this one sentence would not be revoked.

She did not love him.

High above, seagulls whirled and cried, then delved towards the waters, their greyish feathers glinting with the spray.

An alien, dispassionate thought occurred, from outside of him. How frightfully ironic! There they were, in the most perfect setting – the best he could have chosen for his ill-starred proposal. The sea spread at their feet, vast and glorious, and they were alone amidst all this useless beauty.

A man – a woman – before God.

Nothing more. There was nothing else that mattered. Not society and its shallow trappings. Not glittering crowds of small-minded people choked by illusions of their own importance.

This was paradise – the right man, the right woman. *This* was the only thing that mattered, and he had not seen it. Not until now, when it was too late. *Paradise lost...*

Gusts of wind blowing in from the sea swept his hair back and left traces of salty spray upon his lips. He closed his eyes against the wind and against the pain that stirred deep down – an awakening monster.

His eyes flew open at the soft touch of a hand upon his arm and his insides twisted at the sight of her, so close and yet so irretrievably distant. The deep compassion in her troubled eyes made him wish he could lash out, pound the stone wall beside him or at least run from the very worst curse she could have possibly inflicted.

Pity! Good Lord, *pity* was all she had for him!

He drew a ragged breath.

"Pray allow me to escort you to the house," he said, giving silent thanks for the small mercy that his voice did not betray him.

"Mr. Darcy, I... Forgive me for the pain I caused," she said very softly and his heart broke again, into smaller and smaller pieces, at her sweetness and concern.

"I thank you... You are very kind," he whispered hoarsely.

An insane impulse mounted, to lean and kiss those trembling lips, for the first and last time. To reach and hold her in his arms and fool himself, at least for one fleeting moment, that she had not rejected him. That this was not the last time he would ever see her. That she was his to hold for evermore, and they would not be parted.

Not even knowing *why* he struggled anymore, he fought the pernicious urge and won – an empty victory – and she pressed his arm again, then turned away, and there was nothing he could do but follow along the narrow path sheltered by gorse and blasted trees.

They walked in silence to the house. The walk seemed somehow longer this time, and yet not long enough. Before he knew it, they were before the entrance and she consciously offered:

"Would you like to come in?"

'Heavens above, what purpose would it serve?'

"I thank you, no," he instantly declined and she nodded in silent understanding.

The same footman came out and was sent for his horse. And precious seconds ticked away as he both prayed for his escape and yet could not bring himself to leave her. There was nothing he could say – there was so much – and he said nothing.

He pressed his forgotten hat back on and retrieved his gloves from his coat pocket. From somewhere behind, slow, rhythmic hoof-beats could be heard on the granite paving. The lad was returning with his horse – or rather with Trevellyan's.

Trevellyan! Did she hold *him* in her thoughts, in her heart?

Was he one of the reasons why she had refused him?

The pain twisted in a new, savage knot.

Lady Trevellyan?

Good Lord, he would not do this now – he would not toss down *that* poison!

He pulled his gloves on with forceful tugs, fighting against the gripping, agonising notion – and somehow, the excruciating thought brought forth another, subconsciously connected. Good heavens, he had all but forgotten! It must be said, he could not leave her not knowing, unprotected!

Darcy turned towards the approaching footman – the man had to be dismissed before he could voice his thoughts – only to note that of course it would not be a footman bringing him the horse, but a stable lad. The footman had returned as well and he walked right past them with a bow once he had ascertained that they required nothing further and the stable lad promptly disappeared in his turn, having done his duty and placed the reins into Darcy's hand.

He absent-mindedly patted the animal's large neck, then turned towards her.

"Forgive me, Miss Bennet, I have all but forgotten to mention this," he began, as evenly as he could muster.

"Sir?"

"It pertains to Wickham," he offered through stiff lips and her eyes widened in visible surprise at his choice of topic, at this point in time.

Of course, he should have found a better place for it, and better timing too, rather than taint their last moments together with that scoundrel's name.

But it could not be helped.

"It is a matter of extreme delicacy and, as you would imagine, I would not have shared it with any living soul. In this case though I find it mandatory and I trust in your discretion to make cautious use of these disclosures. As my cousin has previously intimated, Mr. Wickham is not a man to be trusted. May I add, in particular, that he is not to be trusted around young ladies of fortune. And the reason why I know this for a fact is that…" He cleared his voice and forced himself to continue. "I know this because he had formed designs upon my own sister."

She gasped but did not interrupt, and for that he was grateful.

The swiftest said, the better, he determined, and pressed on.

"The story of our association is long and rather sordid but, in a nutshell, after my father's passing, Mr. Wickham informed me that he would rather not make a career in the church, as my father had suggested and, as he could not profit from the terms of my father's will, he was hoping for some other pecuniary advantage. His choice did not surprise me. I knew him far too well to be deceived into believing he could ever be a clergyman. He was offered three thousand pounds instead, and he resigned all claims to assistance in the church. However, years later, when his capital was spent, he saw fit to change his mind and ask me to honour my father's promise. I hope you will not be surprised to hear that I have steadfastly refused to comply."

The horse shook his head and snorted, pounding the ground with his hoof. He must have grown restless – and frankly, so had he, Darcy determined, and reached to pat the horse's neck again, in an attempt to still him.

"To cut the story short," he resumed once more, "Wickham did not take it well and his resentment grew as his circumstances worsened. Last summer, his remedy of choice was to make designs upon my sister's fortune. He tried to persuade her to elope with him. Thank goodness, I chanced to arrive in time to stop him – but I shudder to think of him having better luck elsewhere."

Bile rose to his throat at the hideous notion of Wickham having the power to impose upon *her* and he drew a deep breath to subdue the instinctive urge to seek the vermin, and rip him apart!

"Not with *you*," he swiftly added, speaking as much to her as to his own wrenching thoughts. "You have too much discernment to fall prey to his wiles, but I feel you should be informed, so that you could safeguard your sisters. There, now. There, now, lad," he soothingly murmured, as the horse suddenly bridled, nervously tossed his head and whinnied, stomping upon the ground with both his front hooves this time, presumably responding to his own gripping panic, which he must have sensed somehow, in ways unknown to man.

With enormous effort, Darcy endeavoured to control himself, as well as the poor astute beast that stood beside him. Eventually, the large chestnut horse stilled under his hand, allowing himself to be soothed.

"There, now," Darcy repeated softly and was answered with a long, loud snort.

He took another breath, then turned towards her. She was standing on the very same spot, her eyes fixed upon him with a look that shook him to the core. It was suffused with the deepest sadness and, while he could not vouch for its real cause, the raw feeling found its match within him.

The end. This was the end. Implacable.

And it tore at him like nothing ever had.

Instinctively, he stretched out his hand, half expecting it to remain empty. It did not. She placed her own gloved hand in his and he clasped it for a too short, too searing moment, before he stroke the back of it with his thumb, once – and then he let it go.

"God bless you," he whispered before turning away and gaining the saddle with all the ease brought on by years of practice.

He looked down, to see her lips form the word "Farewell."

He nodded, then gripped the reins as he leaned forward and, digging his heels into the horse's flanks, he rode off, hell for leather.

Chapter 14

'This was too much! Too much for just one day!', Elizabeth thought as she snatched her glove off to wipe her tears with her bare fingers.

She all but ran, not to the house, but back towards the path leading to the cove. Yet suddenly she stopped, as though she had collided with an invisible wall blocking her way. She could *not* go there! She could never go there again without being tormented by dreadful recollections.

Without conscious thought, her steps had taken her to the cove earlier in the morning; to the place she instinctively knew would make her feel strong. Strong enough to withstand the difficult time that she knew was coming. She had anticipated a difficult discussion with Mr. Darcy – but not *this!* Not this wrenching pity – nay, more than pity; this crippling self-loathing at having inflicted such pain upon a worthy man.

She did not regret her refusal, nor could she find fault with her reasons for it. The interest sparked on their journey from Hunsford had been blasted by the Colonel's revelations, and although she could now make allowance for Mr. Darcy's actions, their sobering effect remained. Over the last month since their parting in Basingstoke, her resentment had awakened her to all the other reasons why she must reject his offer. And they were valid still, would always be, even if her resentment was appeased by his explanation.

It seemed she understood his feelings better than *he* did, and what he had mistaken for affection was nothing but the appeal of novelty. If he was accustomed to deference and officious attentions of the sort that Miss Bingley uniformly offered, then her own demeanour – challenging, teasing, pert – must have roused his interest. He must have mistaken this interest for affection. And if there was some affection too, it would be short-lived. Assisted by his pride, time would erode it. His words and manner had shown often enough that he would rather be at Timbuktu than in her relations' presence!

How many years – months – would his supposed affections last, once he was plunged into a sea of Bennetism?

The notion did not pain her in itself, for she did not love him. Yet she felt wretched and guilt-stricken about having caused *him* pain, albeit for a short time – and even more so because his final gesture had been one of kindness. In his parting words, he had disclosed family secrets and endeavoured to protect her and her sisters from that vile scoundrel, Wickham.

A passing thought occurred, to distract her briefly from her despondent ruminations: *how* did Mr. Darcy know of their change of fortune? Yet it mattered not, so she dismissed the pointless question.

No doubt, he *would* recover; she should take heart from that. The very same precepts that must have prompted him to leave Netherfield without declaring his regard would soon help him subdue it. But he suffered *now*, and she was sorry for it.

And every time she went to Landennis Cove she would remember how he stood atop the cliff that morning, hair blown back by the wind, his countenance drawn, twisted, his eyes narrowed.

Just standing there, looking out at sea…

ৡৢ ৢৡ

If he should fall and break his neck, it would be a mercy!

It would at least rid him of the pain.

No more! No more! No more!

Under him, the horse laboured, his muscles bunching and relaxing in rapid succession as he galloped along the country road bordered by tall walls made of turf and stone. He allowed his mount free rein, finding the smallest measure of comfort in the speed and the increasing distance from the spot where the injury was inflicted.

She had refused him.

She did not love him.

She would not have him.

His heels dug deeper into the horse's flanks and stone walls interspersed with hedges flew past him in a blur. If only he could leave the pain behind as easily, as swiftly!

He did not know precisely where he was, nor did he care. He had missed the turning into Trevellyan's grounds long ago, but was not sorry for it – he could not, would not return there!

He rode on relentlessly, covering mile after mile. He would stop when Trevellyan's horse could carry him no longer. He would stop at some inn along the way, send the beast back with a messenger who would urge his own men on to come and get him. Take him away from these alien lands, where nothing lurked but the deepest sorrow. She had refused him!

The chestnut horse sped forth, lathered in foam, his breathing laboured. He must have had enough, the poor beast. They had been going at breakneck speed for goodness knows how long.

Darcy released the grip on the reins, as well as the tight clasp of his heels, allowing the horse to choose a calmer pace at last. The wild gallop slowly settled into a canter, then a trot. He rose in his stirrups and cast a look around. He knew not where they had got to; he did not recognise the place, but before long he could spot something in the distance that looked very much like a country inn.

He nudged the tired beast a trifle faster. Aye. So it was. The sign identified it simply as *The New Inn* at Fair Cross. Fair Cross? If he was not mistaken, this was more than ten miles from Landennis.

The canter slowed into a walk and he made his way into the courtyard. He stopped. Dismounted. And only when he did so he felt that every bone and sinew ached from the punishing ride he had subjected himself to.

He patted the horse's neck, then reached to stroke his forehead.

"Sorry, old chap," he muttered and the animal shook his large head and snorted, his ears pricking as his nose came to nudge Darcy's shoulder.

A young man came to take the reins and, running his hand once more over the animal's strong chest, Darcy relinquished him into the lad's keeping.

"Treat him well," he urged the stable boy. "He has had a rough ride."

And he was not the only one…

"Aye, Sorr, I'll be sure ter," the young man retorted and led the animal away, leaving Darcy to slowly walk towards the entrance.

The inn was very small and poorly lit. As his eyes adjusted, Darcy found himself in the taproom, the ceiling so low that he had to bow his head to avoid knocking his hat against the rafters. He removed it, then gave a curt nod to the few old men clustered around the table nearest to the fire, and they took their clay pipes out of their mouths

– or rather, out of their bushy beards – to mutter some sort of greeting in return. A serving wench, half hidden behind the taps, spoke up to ask if there was aught she could she get him and if the gent desired a private parlour.

The gentleman most certainly did – he could not bear company – and was led through a door into a very small room that boasted nothing more than a table, two high-backed benches and a well-tended fire.

"Would you care for sustenance, Sorr, or just ale?"

No, he did not care for sustenance and, truth be told, he did not much care for ale either. Still, Darcy settled for the latter.

It was not long in coming. The wench poured and left him, and Darcy closed his eyes again, leaning his head against the backrest.

What was he to do now? Drink himself into a stupor in a godforsaken country inn? In that case, a jug of ale would not suffice, he scoffed. If that was his game, he should have called for brandy. Yet no amount of brandy would make *this* go away.

He pressed his eyes shut firmly, as though that might have helped.

It did not. The images were there still, behind closed eyes, forever branded in his memory and in every fibre of his being. Her countenance that morning. The searing look of pity. The –...

Good Lord, it would never stop now, would it? It would never leave him, this agonising emptiness, this crushing grief.

A life, a *whole life* without her! How was he to bear it?

How was he to drag himself through each excruciating day?

Poison. Poison. Every thought was poison.

What else could he have done?

A great deal more, no doubt, or at least differently.

Regrets stabbed – relentless, useless, cruel. Would she still have felt nothing but compassion, had he spent every God-given minute of their acquaintance courting her as she deserved to be courted? Had he told her every day that merely seeing her lips curled into a smile made his life worth living? Would she still have sent him away nevertheless?

He folded his arms over his chest; folded them tightly, as if this would keep him in one piece. He heard the paper rustle in his pocket as he did so – still there, ever since the morning – and reached to forcefully pull it out.

He crumpled the wretched sheet of paper in his fist and spun around to cast it in the flames, where it remained for a few brief moments – a glowing, mocking ball of fire – before turning into ash, as everything else had.

ೋღ ღೋ

Trevellyan's horse was rested. Darcy was not. Regardless, they took to the road again together – the same road, back to where they came from, or rather back to Trevellyan's place.

He might as well return for his people and his carriage, Darcy had tiredly determined when the jug of ale was empty and a modicum of sense had returned to him. He would go mad waiting in that godforsaken place for goodness knows how many hours, while Trevellyan's horse was taken back and his own men came up to find him. He was not altogether certain he would not go mad anyway, alone with his tormenting thoughts that would not be silenced – but there was nothing he could do to alter *that*.

He did not push the horse on the way back – he was in no hurry – but the trustworthy creature seemed content to travel at a reasonable pace, presumably eager to be home.

The road was not a busy one and he encountered very few others – some carts, some villagers on foot, a carriage, but no other riders. Just as he was coming up to a small village though, fast clatter of hooves rang out from behind, warning him of someone's approach. Someone in great hurry.

Briefly wondering what was driving *that* poor devil, Darcy pulled the reins and drew out of the way. The clatter rang louder and horse and rider emerged from the thicket but, instead of thundering past, the man forcefully reined in, all but spilling from his horse in his attempt to draw to a sudden halt beside him.

Darcy cursed as he endeavoured to subdue his mount, unsettled by the other's antics, and was of a mind to ask what the devil was he up to when the rider, bespattered in mud from the tip of his boots to the top of his hat, called out to him:

"Darcy! Thank goodness! Is this Falmouth?"

"Bingley!" he cried out in astonishment.

"Is this Falmouth?" the other repeated and Darcy all but huffed.

"No, of course not."

Did it look like a damned *port*, for goodness' sake?

142

"How far are we?"

"Six miles or so, I wager."

It was a great deal further than that to Falmouth, but Landennis was some six miles distant, which must have been all that his friend wanted to know.

"So they have not misled me – this *was* the shorter way," Bingley declared with some satisfaction and reached to wipe the mud and perspiration from his brow.

"Who has not misled you?" Darcy asked, not really caring.

"At the inn where I hired the last horse they told me to head this way, then go across by ferry, rather than take the main road – but never mind that now! Is she well? Have you seen her?"

"I have. And she seemed well."

"Did she mention me?"

Not once – but then, everything considered, Miss Bennet would not have come to speak to *him* of Bingley, Darcy knew full well, so he merely offered:

"There was no opportunity for her to do so."

"Oh. Come, let us not dally," Bingley urged, startling his tired horse into motion.

The poor beast complied with great reluctance and Darcy felt compelled to caution his friend:

"Best not push him too hard. You will not find a replacement on the way, if your mount can go no further."

"How far did you say we were?" the other asked, distracted.

"Six miles."

"Oh, yes, of course."

They settled into a reasonable pace and Bingley inquired promptly:

"Would you tell me everything you know? There must have been more to it than what you sent by letter."

With a sigh, Darcy gave him what he asked for, tiredly expecting a deluge of recriminations. There was not a vast deal to tell in any case apart from Miss Lydia's frank comments but even as he shared them, the recollection of that day when he had been so sure of Elizabeth's acceptance cut through him, sharp and piercing, and he could speak no more. Over the clatter of hooves, Bingley's feeling voice broke the stillness.

"I thank you, Darcy. You have been a good friend to me."

The sudden declaration was sufficiently astounding to bring him from his stupor.

"*A good friend?*" he bitterly scoffed. "I steered you away from her, for goodness' sake!"

"And I have blamed you for it – for it was easier to blame you than myself. But I have had more than enough time to think, as I rode like a man possessed these three days together," his friend added before Darcy could bring himself to make any reply, "and however great your error, mine was greater. *I* should have been the one to ascertain her feelings – and I should not have allowed myself to be steered away. At least you have attempted to correct your error and steer me back. Would to heaven that she would allow me now to correct *mine!*" Bingley fervently added and despite himself, Darcy winced at the searing notion that, unlike his friend, *he* held no such hopes.

"What kept you so long anyway?" Darcy asked, in an attempt to change the subject and at that, his friend's countenance turned stern and dark.

"Caroline," he retorted bluntly. "She opened your letter. Kept it from me. I only learned of it three days ago, from something Hurst inadvertently let slip. He had got wind of it from Louisa –... But never mind my confounded relations! What of *you?* Are you engaged?"

The sudden question hit Darcy as forcefully as a fist in the stomach.

"How did you –...?" he stammered, and then he remembered.

He had put it in the letter – his intention to offer for her.

Darcy bit his lip and his grip tightened unconsciously on the reins, making his horse snort and bridle.

"I am not," he said blandly, the pain vicious. Crippling.

"Whyever not?" the other exclaimed with great surprise. "Heavens, Darcy! What purpose does it serve to dawdle? You must have had the best part of a month – was that not long enough?"

Darcy did not reply. Bitter agony choked him.

A month? An *hour* had sufficed to lay his hopes to waste!

"I would have spoken out ages ago – if only I had your advantage," Bingley added wistfully and with fervour, unwittingly goading his friend beyond endurance.

His countenance set, Darcy dug his heels in the horse's flanks again, too distraught to remember they were meant to spare his friend's hapless mount.

"Beware what you wish for," he shot darkly as he sped away from his nonplussed companion.

"What was that? I did not catch it. I say, Darcy!" Bingley called out in some exasperation.

He got no answer though and, with an oath, he nudged his tired post-horse to follow down the narrow country road.

⁕

A steady drizzle had begun to fall some three miles back and by the time they made their way into Trevellyan's stables and thence towards the house, the pair were thoroughly drenched and chilled to the bone.

"Mr. Darcy! I trust you have enjoyed your ride," their host called brightly upon their entrance, as he emerged from his study into the great hall. "I must say, most commendable of you. Myself, I would have forsaken the rigours of daily exercise in such dismal weather. Oh. This must be the friend you mentioned," he added and stopped, civilly waiting for the introduction.

"May I introduce Mr. Bingley," Darcy tiredly offered. "Bingley, this is Lord Trevellyan."

"You are most welcome, Sir. I daresay you would both wish to rest and change in time for the ball. I shall see to some refreshment too. I trust you shall not object to having it brought to your chambers, seeing as the dining room is now being readied – "

"The ball?" Darcy exclaimed, taken aback.

"Oh. You must have forgotten. The Spring Masque – a Trevellyan tradition," their host prompted and Darcy all but winced.

Of all the blasted notions! But before his strong disinclination for any social gathering – particularly in his current frame of mind – could find civil expression, a sudden thought shot through him.

He would see her again!

The strangest mingling of acute pain and overwhelming gratitude coursed through him and Darcy remained silent, still reeling from the shock of the intelligence and the mix of emotions.

It was Bingley who decisively spoke up.

"I am exceedingly obliged for your kindness, my lord, but I fear I must beg to be excused. There is an urgent call I have to pay!"

"I can only imagine it is the family at Landennis you wish to call upon," Trevellyan astutely remarked, "seeing as they must be your sole acquaintance in the area, apart from Mr. Darcy."

"Landennis?" Bingley asked blankly – which was no surprise, as the name had not been mentioned to him yet.

Slowly recovering from his own inner turmoil, Darcy saw fit to intervene.

"Landennis Manor – the place where Mr. Bennet and his family are staying," he clarified and Bingley nodded with energy, in sudden comprehension.

"Aye, Landennis! Is it far from here?" he eagerly asked.

"Half-hour's ride," Trevellyan supplied, "but in my opinion, you would do best to wait."

"And why is that, pray?" Bingley bristled, in some danger of forgetting his manners.

"You would only arrive to find them in the midst of preparations," Trevellyan replied, his lips curled in amusement at the other's impatience. "They are due to join us here in less than two hours."

"Oh…" said Bingley, visibly thrown off course by the prospect of encountering Miss Bennet in circumstances so different from what he had expected. "I see… A masque. Well, that is most… intriguing. However," he added in obvious discomfort, with a gesture towards his bespattered apparel, "as you can see, my lord, I find myself woefully ill-prepared for a masque."

"Easily remedied, Sir," Trevellyan countered with a reassuring smile. "My man can show you a selection of costumes, ranging from a cavalier's garb to a reasonably accurate copy of Lord Byron's Albanian attire, if you are inclined to go down that path. For my part," he laughed, "I shall go no further than the mandatory mask, but there are plenty of choices for those braver than I am."

"*Mandatory* mask?" Darcy asked, raising a brow.

"Oh, aye. Another part of the tradition – but fear not, in *that* as well, you shall have a variety of choices. My man will show you. Now, gentlemen, if you would excuse me… You shall be well looked after in your chambers, but I fear I must leave you now," he offered and the others bowed.

With a swift bow of his own, Trevellyan left them and repaired to his own study, while the others made their way towards the stairs.

"Devil take me if I am willing to show up before her looking like a fool!" Bingley muttered, then gasped. "Damme! I have forgotten. Seems I have no other option but take your friend Trevellyan up on his offer of a costume."

"Why is that?"

"I came on *horseback*, Darcy!" his friend exclaimed in some exasperation. "My trunk is on the post-wagon. It will presumably arrive in Falmouth in a few days' time, but until then I can only appear at the ball masquerading as a muddy express-rider or a sad impersonation of Lord Byron," Bingley fumed and, despite his anguish, Darcy's lips curled into a little smile as he patted the other on the back.

"Fear not, my friend, your fate is not so cruel. Surely John can find you a suitable third option in my trunks."

⊷⊶ ✿ ⊷⊶

With a long sigh, Darcy leaned his head against the edge of the bathtub and closed his eyes, allowing the steaming-hot water to soothe his aching muscles. He reached to rub one shoulder, then the other, then he let his arms drop with another sigh.

He winced, then swallowed. In less than two hours... His eyes opened, staring unseeing at Trevellyan's ornate ceiling. In less than two hours, she would be in this house, and he would see her for one more time – the last time. Despite himself, the wrenching pain brought out a quiet groan.

"Sir? Are you well?" John solicitously asked from somewhere behind him and Darcy cleared his voice.

Well? He all but laughed – a bitter, tortured sound. He did not laugh. Instead, he conceded it was time to start dealing in falsehoods.

"Yes. Of course," he muttered.

"Shall I send for more hot water, Mr. Darcy?"

"I thank you, no. I would rather have the dressing gown instead."

The man brought towels, then his robe and, dry and partially refreshed, Darcy walked out of the small, warm dressing room into the damp bedchamber.

"Forgive me, Sir, I have not lit the candles yet. Pray let me do so," John offered, prompt to follow, but Darcy shook his head.

"There is no need for now. You may leave me until I have to dress," he casually instructed and the man left him with a bow to return to his duties in the other room.

Darcy half-heartedly resumed towelling his hair, but gave up soon enough. He could not care less if it was fully dry or not and besides the rough handling did no favours to the headache that had begun to plague him several hours ago and was still showing no signs of abating. He was about to cast the cloth aside when his glance was drawn to the small table beside him. A mask was placed there, by Trevellyan's man perhaps, or John. A firm shape lined with satin, in patterns of grey interspersed with black, destined to cover more than half the face. All but the lips, in fact.

He grimaced. It was neither gaudy nor in poor taste, but it still struck him as absurd. He had never been a willing participant in such foolish antics and tonight was *not* the time to start. And yet…

He sighed. Perhaps, tonight more than ever, he *did* need a mask. If nothing else, to spare himself the trouble of struggling to hide the pain that, he was certain, would be chiselled into his countenance for everyone to notice. It would be a relief to see and not be seen. To watch her from a distance, hidden in plain view. To be assured, moreover, that he would not discomfit her with his presence…

He sighed again and cast the towel on the back of a chair.

Aye. Tonight of all nights, he was grateful of a mask.

He rubbed his brow and temples and slowly walked towards the window. The bedchamber was chilly, yet he was still glad of the open casement. He came closer and drew a deep breath of the evening air, made fresher by the rain. It did not soothe his headache, but at least it smelled pleasant. Not of seaweed and salt, not at this distance from the shores, but earthy and fragrant – turf and moist soil and hay – reminding him of Pemberley. Of home.

He sighed once more, dreading the aching emptiness he knew he would find there, and was about to reach and close the window when stern tones, unmistakably Trevellyan's, suddenly reached him from below.

"He has been to *Landennis?* And you have waited all this time to tell me?" his lordship thundered, his angry voice easily reaching Darcy, presumably through another open window below-stairs, or maybe from somewhere outside, somewhere out of sight, where

Trevellyan had secluded himself with his companion, who was now offering profuse apologies.

"I beg your pardon, your lordship. I did not think it was of any consequence – "

"'Tis not your place to make such decisions, but mine!" Trevellyan forcefully retorted.

"I know that now, my lord. I – "

"*You* will return to your post!" Trevellyan sternly cut him off. "Your men will inform me of anyone who goes there. Anyone who as much as pays a call, drops a parcel, delivers a letter, even comes to bring the meat in from the butcher's. And you will not let that man out of your sight. Now leave me. I have a *masque* to host," his lordship added in a tone so scathing that it was plain to see he set no store by that particular endeavour and the light, casual air with which he had spoken earlier of the ball, when he had greeted himself and Bingley – the lord of the manor, welcoming his guests – had been nothing more than yet another mask.

His features tight, Darcy strained to listen, but there was nothing more to hear. They were gone.

He spun back into the room, his fists clenched at his sides. What hornets' nest was this, or rather nest of vipers? *Why* did Trevellyan want him followed – for he could not doubt that the argument had arisen from his own unreported visit to Landennis. More terrifying still, why would he have the place surrounded? Why would he want to know of *anyone* who went there? This suggested something a great deal more sinister than merely keeping track of a supposed rival or safeguarding the manor against the miscreants at *Landennis Arms*.

Hammers pounded in his temples and Darcy bit his lip, endeavouring to set aside the pain of his own crushed hopes. Nothing mattered now more than her safety! What vile deeds was Trevellyan contemplating? Justice of Peace, was he – or a wolf left to guard the town? What was Trevellyan's game? Why did he pursue her? For her inheritance, rather than the God-given blessing that she was? Or for some other reasons of his own?

A wave of nausea threatened and dread gripped him, icy, terrifying – and worse, a thousand times worse than the searing notion of Elizabeth married to another. Was she about to fall into a trap of Trevellyan's making? Had she, her great-aunt and her entire family put their trust in a dangerous man?

Chapter 15

Glittering crowds milled around him on cheerful strains of music coming from the ballroom. The dances had begun already, and she had not arrived! Not yet, he knew it without being told. Mask or no mask, he would have known her anywhere – of *that*, he held no doubt. Where *was* she? Had there been a change of plans? Some mishap, maybe?

At his elbow, Bingley was equally anxious.

"This was a bad plan. I should have gone to call upon her," he fumed, for the seventh time at least and Darcy huffed, heartily tired of hearing it repeated.

He had the greatest compassion for his best friend's plight and no small amount of understanding, but Bingley's unremitting agitation had begun to rile him more than he could own.

"Does Trevellyan know what might have delayed them? Have they sent word?"

Darcy pursed his lips, forbearing to advise his friend to go and ask his lordship. In truth, attempting to find out was not such a bad notion, but Darcy had his doubts that Trevellyan would share that information – *any* information – even if he had it.

"Where is Trevellyan, by the way? Have you seen him lately? Confound these masks, the devil's own notion! Damned nuisance, I call them! Ah, there he goes. At least I can recognise *him*, since his mask and attire are so much like yours," Bingley muttered and at that, Darcy's head snapped up.

His glance shot to the large looking-glass before them, which Bingley had indicated with a nod, and he all but gasped. How had he not seen it? True, he had not paid heed to anyone's attire but now, with Trevellyan's reflection not far from his own, the similarity was blindingly obvious. Stature. Dark hair. Dark grey coats. Even the masks were strikingly alike – grey patterns interspersed with black – and acute suspicion suddenly crept into Darcy's breast.

Was that done on purpose? Had a *particular* sort of mask been sent to his chambers, with ulterior aim? Did Trevellyan have the shocking nerve to contrive to use *him* as a decoy, later in the evening? Make it seem to the inattentive eye that he was of the company, at a time when he planned not to be? All of a sudden, the Bennets' absence was a source of gripping fear rather than personal anguish. What the devil was being brewed, in this hellish cauldron?

He started out of his consuming thoughts when Bingley's hand came up sharply to clasp his forearm. He barely suppressed the urge to forcefully shake it off.

"What is it?" Darcy hissed in an almighty temper – yet all anger left him as soon as he followed his friend's gaze and heard him say:

"They are here! Look! It *must* be them."

All manner of feelings flooded through him at that moment, of which relief held the upper hand. His friend was not mistaken. Amongst the late arrivals, a group of eight stood out as distinctive as could be – to Bingley and himself at least – and just as easy to identify, despite the blasted masks. A gentleman in front, leading two ladies, one tall and fidgeting, the other thin and visibly frail. Behind them, five more.

His eyes were drawn unerringly to *her* and his heart lurched, then began to hammer. He would have recognised that silhouette, that carriage anywhere, even without the added advantage that, apart from the cream glittering mask, she looked just as she did at the Netherfield ball, down to the last detail. The dress. The ribbons and the tiny flowers in her hair.

His heart lurched again and his chest tightened. The longing to approach her was sudden, overpowering – as was the vicious grip of anger at the sight of Trevellyan sauntering in their direction. He spoke to them. He bowed. He took *her* hand and bowed again over her fingers before securing them upon his arm and leading her away towards the ballroom.

Devoid of the power and indeed the will to do otherwise, Darcy skirted the walls of the great hall and followed. Beyond his notice, Bingley did the same, and it was only later, as he stood watching Elizabeth walking down the set at Trevellyan's side, that Darcy belatedly understood his friend to be going through the same anguish, the same hell for, not far behind her sister, Miss Bennet was also dancing with some Cornish acquaintance.

The dances seemed longer than ever and every second pierced him, every twirl, every motion that brought the woman he adored hand in hand with another man. With that sly fiend, Trevellyan!

Would that she was willing to believe him! Allow him to protect her and take her far away from this. Not to Pemberley, his aching heart acknowledged, if she did not wish to go there, but someplace else – someplace where he could be certain she was safe!

"I cannot do this, Darcy," his friend's tortured groan tore him from his equally tortured ruminations. "How in God's name am I to walk up to her *now*? I cannot do this to her – shock her with my sudden appearance. Damn Trevellyan, I should have never taken his advice! I should have gone to her – gone to Landennis. This is no way to do it. Not here and not now!"

The man was in the right, Darcy belatedly acknowledged, once he had brought himself out of his own anguish for long enough to consider another's. Miss Bennet should be warned, they both should.

His heart twisted once more with the pain and pleasure of recognising that the duty fell on *him*. That he should no longer lurk in corners, but approach Elizabeth. Tell her. Have her warn her sister of Bingley's presence. Speak to her once more. Hear her voice. Have her warmth, her fragrance fill his senses. Touch her hand perhaps. Fill this ghastly void!

His voice gravelly, he shared his intentions with Bingley and the outpouring of gratitude from his distraught friend sat ill on him, but Darcy would not dwell upon it. His troubled eyes followed her until the dances mercifully ended and Trevellyan escorted her to one side of the room, to the sofa where her great-aunt was sitting, alongside another lady, presumably Miss Mary. Still, she did not sit. She merely curtsied to his lordship and, when at length he left them, she turned to speak to Mrs. Pencarrow, leaning her head towards her, so that she could hear her better.

With a swift word to Bingley, Darcy made his way around the crowded ballroom, his throat dry, his heart pounding. So did his head in fact – the blasted headache had only got worse – yet that was of no import. Nothing mattered but the forthcoming moments and he walked faster, until he reached her side of the room at last.

She did not notice his approach until Mrs. Pencarrow prompted her with a nod to look in his direction and finally she did so and smiled – only to rob him thoroughly of the remainder of his senses.

Her lips looked fuller and rosier still, under the cream satin of the mask. Behind it, her eyes glittered, their shape concealed, but the sparkling light as wondrous as ever.

Words failed him and Darcy could only bow, to receive a curtsy.

"I was not expecting you to return so soon, my lord," he heard her say. "Were you not about to seek Mr. Penderrick?"

Acute pain slashed through him at her words. Of course. The similar attire and the blasted mask. It was not for *him*, that smile, the warmth in her eyes, the light repartee. She thought... His insides twisted and, through his agony, he forced the mandatory apology out.

"Forgive me, Miss Bennet, for the disappointment I have unwittingly caused, but I am not his lordship," he quietly offered, his words barely above a ragged whisper.

Her head snapped up at that and he could hear her gasp:

"Mr. Darcy!"

The fleeting pleasure at her having recognised his voice was instantly blasted by the way in which her own had faltered and the obvious discomfort she betrayed as she bit the corner of her lip.

"My apologies, Sir," she resumed with feeling. "I have not imagined... I thought you had left the country..."

"I was about to, Madam," he retorted, his own aching discomfort making him sound stern, which was never his intention. He worked to soften his tones as he swiftly added: "I was prevented by a circumstance beyond my control. Miss Bennet... May I have a private word?" he tentatively requested and, with a conscious nod, she indicated her willingness to comply.

They took a few steps further away from her relations and, as soon as he felt he could do so with impunity, Darcy began without preamble:

"You see... a few hours earlier, Bingley has arrived. He feels – we both do – that his presence ought not be sprung upon your sister without warning. Would you be so kind to find the best way to inform her?"

"Oh!" she gasped again and her glance shot to him.

Devil take the wretched mask! Would that he could see her eyes without its damned encumbrance, see her face, and gauge what she was thinking!

"Is Mr. Bingley here now?" Elizabeth asked at last.

"He is. Across the room, next to the second pillar," he instructed and, guided by his words, her eyes drifted towards the solitary figure looking forlorn in its isolation – a gentleman in an ill-fitting coat, too broad-shouldered for him and a tad too long.

"I see…" she whispered, then looked up to him again. "I thank you, Sir, for your thoughtfulness… I shall… I must leave you now… find my sister…"

"Of course…" Darcy replied with a bow.

She did not leave at once, but seemed inclined to say something further. She did not. At length she curtsied and turned away, and there was nothing left for him to do but bow to her relations from a distance, then walk off to find Bingley at his outpost.

"Well?" his friend anxiously questioned.

Darcy sighed.

"She is gone to find Miss Bennet," he tiredly imparted and followed his friend's glance, knowing full well that it would guide him to the very ones that both of them were seeking.

He was not mistaken. He could see them now in a distant corner, in eager conversation. The hated masks ensured that naught else could be seen, yet he could not tear his eyes away and, he assumed, neither could Bingley.

After a horribly long time, the ladies stood at last and made their way towards what seemed to be an open door leading to a terrace.

"Come, Darcy!" Bingley urged and at the same time Darcy moved to follow, not needing his friend's prompting. He had already caught her glance and the nod that seemed to convey an invitation.

They crossed the ballroom with unseemly haste and by the time they reached the doorway the sisters were already outside, standing together next to the stone parapet. As they walked through the door, Darcy could see them clasp each other's hands in a heart-wrenching gesture of tender reassurance and he drew a ragged breath that ended in a sigh. How could they have made such a dreadful mess of the entire business, himself and Bingley? They desperately wanted to keep them safe and happy – yet all they had achieved, with error after error, was to distress them so, and make them wary!

At his side, Bingley must have thought the same – or he must have been steeling himself for the encounter, for he too drew a steadying breath and, removing the darned ornate contraption that concealed his features, he walked steadily on to meet his fate.

Elizabeth withdrew towards the door at his approach to let the other couple talk in private and at that Darcy removed his own mask as well. He could not tell if Miss Bennet had seen fit to do the same in response to Bingley's gesture but unreasonably his own anguish softened somewhat as he perceived Elizabeth attempting to rid herself of hers. She seemed to have come to some difficulty however, for her gloved fingers laboured ineffectively with something at her temple. She sighed in obvious exasperation and removed her gloves but before she could resume her efforts Darcy spoke up.

"Would you allow me?" he quietly offered and, at her silent nod, he cast his own gloves on the wide top of the parapet and reached to find the catch, in the same spot where he had seen her seek it.

He swallowed hard as he felt the softness of her curls under his fingertips – the softness of her skin, just underneath her temple. His fingers slipped gingerly beneath the ribbon around the edge of the smooth mask and breath caught in his throat as they brushed against her cheek. The urge to linger, to prolong the closeness and savour the bitter-sweetness of the moment was stronger than him – a great deal stronger – and he allowed himself a few more fleeting seconds of stolen pleasure before he reluctantly sought the catch again.

He found it easily and also found the tangle – the end of the ribbon had twisted around a hairpin or perhaps the stem of one of the small flowers braided in her hair. With great care, he tugged it loose until the fastening was fully disentangled.

Held in place no longer, the mask fell off her cheek, revealing a sliver of her beloved features. Her eyes shot open – *why had they been closed?* – and she instinctively reached to catch the mask before it dropped off to the ground.

Just as reflexively, Darcy did the same, but she was quicker. Her hand closed on the mask. His fingers closed on hers. Unconsciously, his hold tightened. Soft, warm hands, and very small. Her fingers, curled around the satin-covered shape, were all but hidden underneath his own.

At her faint gasp of surprise or perhaps displeasure, enough sense returned for him to let his hand drop.

"I thank you," Elizabeth whispered softly, though whether for his assistance with untangling the knot or for having released her fingers, Darcy could not tell.

She pulled the contraption fully off her face and cast a troubled glance towards her sister. Yet there was nothing she could see. The other pair had retreated to the far end of the terrace and their backs were turned as they stood close together in earnest conversation, or perhaps one-sided discourse, for it was only Bingley's voice that could be heard in eager, steady murmur. As for the *words*, none could be distinguished – not that either of them would contemplate eavesdropping.

Despite her concern for her dearest sister, Elizabeth glanced away, clearly disinclined to pry. She looked down at her hands, twisting the satin mask this way and that, and it was awfully plain to see that she was most uncomfortable in his presence. Darcy sighed. What else did he expect? Of course she would be ill-at-ease now. Silent. Troubled. She had refused his hand in marriage earlier that morning!

He winced. It seemed hard to believe that it was just a few hours ago. He seemed to have lived through a lifetime of misery since then.

Suddenly, she dropped the mask on the parapet alongside her gloves and his, then glanced up to him and began speaking in a low, strained whisper.

"I must thank you, Sir, for your concern for my sister's feelings… I know it must have been very difficult for you to – "

"Pray, do not regard it," he interjected earnestly. "I would do anything…"

Darcy stopped as her troubled countenance softened once more in compassion and he fought the urge to beg her not to look at him this way.

He drew a deep breath, acknowledging that it was a churlish thought and worse still, untrue. That he would rather have her look upon him with compassion if that was all she had to offer, rather than the anger she had shown in Basingstoke.

"Miss Bennet," he brought himself to say, "you must have long been desiring my absence – … No, I am not necessarily speaking of this very moment," he added, as her turn of countenance suggested she was about to utter some form of civil protest, "but of my departure from these parts. Forgive me, but I cannot leave as yet. There is – …" he stopped, then forced himself to press on with the terribly awkward topic. "I fear there is devilry afoot, and Lord Trevellyan is no stranger to it."

156

There! He finally said it. And yet no sooner did he begin to feel some satisfaction at having brought it out into the open that the mild reproach implied by her next retort made his insides turn again, for the age-old reason.

"Mr. Darcy!" she gently chided. "Your prejudice against his lordship – …"

"This is not a matter of *prejudice!*" Darcy burst out, without allowing her to finish. "You must believe that I am not trying to poison you against a… *a rival*. As of this morning," he added with difficulty, "that would be… quite unnecessary, and I have no rights. But –… Pray allow me to continue, Miss Bennet," he urged, at her evident desire to stop him. "Just before the ball, I heard him speak to one of his men about keeping watch on all who set foot at Landennis and of the fact that he has had the place surrounded. I know not what he is about, but I urge you – … Nay, I *beg* you would allow me to protect you!"

As he finished speaking, he found that her hand was in his, although he had no recollection of just *how* that might have come to happen. Yet she did not withdraw it, nor did she step back, but remained there, silent and very still, for a length of time that none thought to measure. When at last she spoke, her voice caught and faltered and was so quiet that he could barely hear it.

"I thank you. You are… very kind – too kind. Yet I do not wish you to be burdened with such concerns, which are… *must be* for naught. There must be a reasonable explanation for your overhearings. Presumably measures similarly intended for protection – *Mrs. Pencarrow's* protection, that is to say," she swiftly added, in a touching attempt to spare his feelings. "I understand there is a longstanding friendship between my great-aunt and Lord Trevellyan. I cannot imagine her trust to be misplaced. So I thank you again for your solicitude, but you need not fret, Sir. Twice in one day you have done us great kindness and you have received little for your efforts. Pray, Mr. Darcy, do not trouble yourself further on our account – on *mine*. You have done more than enough already!"

Her voice gathered strength as she proceeded and, by the time she had finished, it was warm and firm.

Yet it was not her heartfelt entreaty or her compassionate concern that robbed him of his breath, but the barely perceptible touch, the fluttering caress on the back of his fingers.

157

Darcy swallowed and looked down to their clasped hands – and alongside, her free one, moving as though without deliberate intent, fingertips lightly stroking his suddenly tingling skin, and he bit his lip, wondering how in God's name he was to overcome the desperate need to kiss her!

"Elizabeth…" he whispered hoarsely, not even realising his *faux pas*, and at the sound of his tortured voice she started, withdrew both her hands and brought them to her temples.

"Forgive me!" she burst out. "I am not… What am I *doing?*" she exclaimed in accents of the deepest contrition. "I beg you would excuse me, I must return to the house."

Instinctively, Darcy clasped her wrist.

"Pray, do not go," he pleaded, but Elizabeth shook her head with something very much like anger.

"I must! I had no business to mislead you," she declared with feeling, demonstrating that her anger was directed at herself. "Nothing has changed since this morning, Mr. Darcy, and I should not wish you to think otherwise."

"I beg you would not reproach yourself," he urged and, at her obvious distress, he felt compelled to release his hold, only to see her pick up the discarded mask and hide behind it yet again as she tied the ribbon with swift, nervous motions.

"Elizabeth! Miss Bennet," he amended this time, "is there anything I can say to ease your discomfort?"

"I thank you, but too much was said already. I *must* leave you now. Pray, Mr. Darcy, return home. Return to Pemberley and… find your peace there!" she earnestly entreated and, retrieving her gloves, she tugged them back on with some difficulty, for her hands were shaking.

Darcy's lips tightened at the affecting sight and he forbore to tell her that there was to be no peace for him, at Pemberley or elsewhere. Before he could find something else to say, something that would not seem exactly calculated to distress her further, the sound of footsteps drew his notice to Miss Bennet hurrying towards them – or rather, to the doorway that led back to the house. Her countenance held none of the placid good-humour he had grown to associate with her and the raw edge of pain that had replaced it filled him with shock and horror at the enormity of his past misjudgement.

Darcy instinctively lowered his eyes, lest she see him stare and be mortified by her own display of feeling, but it was not him that Miss Bennet glanced at, a plea in her anguished features. It was her sister, and Elizabeth was prompt to respond.

She left him in an instant and rushed to Miss Bennet's side to clasp her hand in tender reassurance. She offered hurried words of comfort as she helped her sister don her mask again and in her turn hide her acute distress behind the fragile screen covered with gauze and satin. And then she turned to him and curtsied – and a few moments later she was gone, they both were, leaving him crushed by the hopelessness of the encounter and the heart-rending note that it had ended on.

A groan behind him suggested that Bingley was not faring any better – which came as no surprise, given Miss Bennet's obvious distress and swift departure.

With a muted oath, Darcy walked over to his friend. He did not ask him anything, it served no purpose. In the end, Bingley was the one to break the silence.

"She would not even hear me!" he burst out in accents of deep anguish, which Darcy could not fail to recognise. "She said this was hardly the time or the place – and how can I fault her? Worse still, she said –…" Bingley broke off and passed his hands over his face. "She said my comings and goings are so uniformly unexpected that she can only assume I shall be on the move again, and soon, with as little warning. She would hear nothing to the contrary, nothing of my deep regard for her – but said that actions spoke louder than avowals and empty protestations. And then she left and asked me not to follow!" he burst again in something so akin to desperation that Darcy was compelled to lay a hand on his shoulder in understanding and compassion.

"She might hear you on the morrow," he quietly offered, but the other merely shook his head.

"I doubt it. She bade me return to town and seek my amusements elsewhere," he dejectedly imparted, then heaved a long sigh.

Whether he expected sympathy or not, none was forthcoming. Darcy's retort was prompt and sharp:

"If you leave now, then you do not deserve her!" he forcefully exclaimed and at that, Bingley lost his temper.

"Of course I shall not leave! Do you imagine that I would give up? What sort of weak fool do you take me for? Is that what you would do if you were in my place? Give up so easily, if Miss Elizabeth bade you return to Pemberley?"

Darcy's hand dropped from his friend's shoulder.

And then the truth came out at last.

"I *am* in your place," he tiredly acknowledged in a ragged whisper.

"*What?*" Bingley burst, too highly strung for civil repartee.

"She *did* bid me return to Pemberley… and point-blank refused my hand in marriage…"

He was not to receive sympathy either, or at least not expressed in the customary fashion. Bingley merely gave a bitter laugh.

"You poor devil! So this is why you have been such a bear lately. Forgive me, Darcy," he added softly, even before the other could rouse up the energy to reply in anger. "I had not imagined we were both in the same sinking boat. What a fine mess we are in, eh?"

Bingley shook his head and it was his turn to pat his friend's shoulder.

"Shall I tell *you* now that if you give up so easily then you do not deserve her?" he asked with the mildest reproach, or perhaps sarcasm.

Nevertheless, he got no answer. With a great deal of effort, Darcy forbore to mention that the similarity of their circumstances ended at the most salient – and most excruciating point: Miss Bennet's current withdrawal from his friend sprang from hurt feelings but, at some point at least, she *did* love him, and there was some reason to hope that she might love him still. *He* could claim nothing of the sort as regards her sister. Elizabeth had been dreadfully clear on the subject – so how could he blithely dismiss her wishes and be so self-willed as to ask again?

Thankfully, Bingley did not choose to goad him any further. His lingering resentment for Darcy's past misjudgements or for more recent outbursts appeared to have left him. When he spoke again, there was nothing but raw earnestness in his voice as he declared with feeling:

"For my part, I know not how to go about it yet, but I *must* regain her trust. I have to. I cannot lose her, Darcy! Come hell or high water, I am *not* giving up!"

Chapter 16

Reluctant as they both were to further distress the women they loved with their unwanted presence, Darcy and Bingley eventually determined that they could not skulk on the terrace for the remainder of the evening so, having donned their masks again, they made their way back into the ballroom.

Unlike all other similar assemblies that they had attended in the past, this time they remained at each other's side for, unsurprisingly, Bingley was no longer drawn to cavort amongst the dancing couples. To anyone inclined to observe them, they made a strange pair, standing together without speaking, either to each other or to those around them, but it appeared that few, if any, were glancing their way. It was *they* who were keenly searching the glittering crowds for a glimpse of the two eldest Bennet sisters. Not for the purpose of approaching them again – *that* would have been a severe misjudgement – but for the simple reason that neither could do otherwise. Yet they could not be found. Not in the line of dancers. Not with the wallflowers. Not in any of the public rooms on the ground floor, where others were gathered in small groups to sit, chat, flirt or gossip.

The two remorse-filled gentlemen could only assume that the sisters had found a more secluded spot to speak in private and draw strength from each other's sympathy and presence – or simply to avoid another encounter. The notion that they would dread their society to such an extent as to hide from sight weighed like molten lead on Darcy's spirits – and burned likewise – and presumably Bingley was of the same mind, judging by his oppressive silence, so wholly out of character for him.

By the time the supper dance was announced, Darcy felt he could not bear another second of her absence. He would have to endure the torment of seeing Trevellyan escorting her to supper, *that* he knew full well – and even if his lordship would choose or would be compelled by the rules of precedence to favour another, she would not allow *him* to escort her in any case. But at least she would have to emerge from wherever she had secluded herself with her eldest sister. Again, his thoughts must have been in tune with Bingley's, for his friend greeted the announcement with a sigh of relief and a heartfelt "At last!"

Darcy wondered if it had crossed Bingley's mind that, come supper, when masks would be discarded, they would have to seek the other members of the Bennet party and pay their respects, a prospect which ought to terrify Bingley a great deal more than it used to unsettle *him*.

For his part, the notion of an encounter with Mrs. Bennet was no longer greeted with mortification. Indeed, what did it matter what the mother chose to say or do? His deep concern extended only to the reception he expected – dreaded – from the daughter.

Finally, the last strains of music rang in the vast room and the dancing couples bowed and curtsied to their partners. Darcy's eyes sought and found Trevellyan not only because, in view of his choice of mask and attire, he would be easiest to find, but also in the painful expectation that Trevellyan would lead him to *her*. He scanned the group his host advanced towards, and still he could not spot her. Without consciously choosing to, Darcy edged closer, just as his lordship began speaking, loud enough for everyone to hear:

"Honoured ladies and gentlemen, the time has come for masks to be discarded and for you to see if you have been dancing with whom you thought you had – or whether a surprise is in store as regards to whom you shall escort to supper."

Peals of laughter greeted his light-hearted words and, as one satin-covered shape after another started to fall off the countenance of the assembled ladies, Darcy's eyes darted around with unconcealed impatience, still checking now and again whether Trevellyan had spotted her already.

Strangely however, Lord Trevellyan did not seem to be seeking anyone – or at least not Elizabeth. His eyes and full attention were fixed on none other than Mrs. Penderrick. Surprised and intrigued, Darcy stepped even closer and heard him utter with what seemed to be either shock or suppressed anger.

"Madam, I must confess myself mystified. I had imagined you were dancing with your husband!"

The very notion that Trevellyan would keep track of Mrs. Penderrick's dancing partners was extraordinary in itself, as was his choice to question her in public on the subject, but Mrs. Penderrick did not seem to mind. Instead, she offered lightly:

"My husband sends his deepest regrets, my lord, but a sudden indisposition has prevented him from attending. He had no wish to disrupt your arrangements or ruin my enjoyment of the evening, so he suggested that my cousin escorted me instead. We were both certain you would not be put out – in effect, Mr. Penderrick was persuaded you would find it a very good joke."

Trevellyan restrainedly bowed at that.

"Your husband was not mistaken, Ma'am," he said flatly. "I find it a very good joke indeed. Pray excuse me," he offered with another bow and withdrew while Darcy, his eyes still fixed upon him, determined the time might have come to follow him in earnest, lest he lose sight of his lordship in the crowd.

He turned to share his intention with his friend, who had followed him towards the centre of the room bearing a vague resemblance to a forlorn puppy, when a voice behind them made them start.

"Mamma, look! There, look! I do believe 'tis Mr. Bingley!" they heard, quite loudly, in Miss Lydia's unmistakable tones.

What came as a greater surprise was Mrs. Bennet's cool "I know."

The lack of interest must have surprised Miss Lydia as well, for she exclaimed:

"*You know?* Have you seen him already? When?"

"When you were out there, dancing. Speaking of which, your second partner but one, who was that? Mr. Wickham?"

Darcy's back stiffened. He had completely forgotten about the rogue. Was *he* there too?

"No, it was not. I have not come across him tonight. I suspect he was not invited."

"No wonder. He is a mere steward now."

"But, Mamma, *Mr. Bingley!* Does Jane know he is here?"

Surprisingly for someone as chatty as Mrs. Bennet, the answer was a mere "She does."

Nothing more appeared to be forthcoming and, while Miss Lydia proceeded to pepper her mother with more questions, the gentlemen exchanged a wary glance, fully aware of their duty.

They turned and walked towards the matron and her daughter and offered a deep bow. In different circumstances, Darcy might have been vaguely diverted by his friend's fidgeting discomfort at Mrs. Bennet's glare and frosty reception – something he had rarely experienced before, and never from that quarter. Oddly enough, it was *himself* who was favoured with an enthusiastic greeting.

"It is a great pleasure to see you again, Ma'am," Bingley stammered as soon as he found an opening, only to receive a muted "Hm!"

"I trust you are in good health... and all your... er... family."

"We are well enough, Mr. Bingley, I thank you for your concern."

"Mamma, should I not go?" her youngest interrupted, then added in a lower voice, but still loud enough to hear, "You know? To find Jane?"

"You will not find her, dear," Mrs. Bennet impatiently retorted. "She left two hours ago."

"She left?" Bingley interjected and at that, Mrs. Bennet's eyes were again fixed upon him.

"She became unwell," she said with clear emphasis. "Something must have disagreed with her. Lord Trevellyan was very concerned of course, not to mention disappointed, but he was most gentlemanly about it, very understanding. I daresay he would have liked to escort her home himself, such a charming young man and so attentive, but with a ball to host..."

The lady shrugged daintily, and Darcy arched a brow.

He wondered if Bingley had caught the implication, but to him Mrs. Bennet's game had become quite clear. Her coldness to Bingley might have been prompted by maternal affection, after all the suffering he had inflicted upon her eldest daughter, but there seemed to be more to it than that. Bingley was no longer the best possible suitor, and the matron's eye was fixed on a far more advantageous connection for Miss Bennet – Trevellyan, no less!

Having Mrs. Bennet for an ally was as novel a concept as could be and might even have been an entertaining one, had he not known full well that her schemes and wishes were not likely to affect his lordship's choice – or Elizabeth's.

Darcy bit his lip and, before he could bring himself to openly ask a question he already suspected the answer to, his newfound ally voluntarily supplied:

"I am sorry to say that Lizzy had insisted on accompanying her and would not be dissuaded despite my best efforts. She was adamant that she ought to be with Jane and that Mrs. Pencarrow might need her also – my aunt left as well, you see, she was feeling rather tired. Too much exertion at her advanced age, you know. And Lizzy would not leave them – the dear girl, so dutiful and affectionate. Well! I trust you know that you are always welcome at Landennis, Mr. Darcy," she offered warmly, "and at Longbourn of course, when we return to Hertfordshire, though I have no notion how soon that would be."

She fanned herself, then pursed her lips and added, pointedly looking straight over Bingley's shoulder:

"And I suppose you can bring your friends, if you so wish…"

Mr. Darcy might have been moved to assist his beleaguered friend or at least extricate him from the inauspicious spot, but suddenly he had no thought to spare for the other man's predicament for, somewhere across the ballroom, he espied Mr. Bennet slowly ambling in their general direction, presumably to escort his wife to supper. Alarmed in no small measure, he turned towards the matron.

"I trust the young ladies did not travel unescorted! I had assumed that Mr. Bennet left with them, but I see now that I was mistaken," he anxiously remarked and, with a wide smile, Mrs. Bennet was eager to reassure him.

"Of course not. Your thoughtfulness does you credit, Sir. Nay, nay, they were well looked after. My aunt's footman was sent to attend them and Lord Trevellyan most particularly insisted on sending some of his men too."

He did?

"Pray excuse me, Ma'am," he abruptly offered with a perfunctory bow. "I fear I must leave you." He feared a vast deal more than that just now, but it was nothing he could share with Mrs. Bennet. "Bingley, may I have a word?" he added and his friend was swift to follow, grateful for the excuse.

"I thank you for extricating me just now – " he began, but Darcy would not let him finish.

"Never mind that! Have you seen Trevellyan?"

"I saw him leave the ballroom a short while ago, when Mrs. Bennet was enthusiastically inviting you to Longbourn," Bingley supplied with patent bitterness. "Why should you wish to know?"

"I need your assistance to locate him, if he is still around. But I fear he is not – and we need to go!" he forcefully added, to the other's surprise.

"Where to?"

"Landennis."

"*Landennis? Tonight?*"

"Aye! As soon as possible!"

And pray that all was well there – or at least that they would not arrive too late!

⁂

All was not well at Landennis, but for none of the reasons Mr. Darcy feared. Mrs. Pencarrow was unwell. Soon after their arrival home, everyone could see that her extreme fatigue was real, and not a mere subterfuge to lend weight to Jane and Elizabeth's wish to leave the ball. Her countenance was pale, ashen even, and she could barely stand. With no difficulty, Elizabeth persuaded her great-aunt to retire.

Once left to their own devices, Elizabeth and Jane determined they were not of a mind to sleep – nor could they, given the night's events. Instead, after exchanging their attire for warmer and more comfortable dresses, they sought the privacy of the small downstairs parlour with soothing cups of tea before them, for a long sisterly conversation that hopefully would soothe them far more than tea could. Everything was too new and unsettling, but sharing thoughts and confidences made them both feel marginally better.

The same could not be said of Mrs. Pencarrow for, an hour or so later, just as the sisters were considering retiring to their chamber, Mrs. Polmere came to tell them that her mistress had taken a turn for the worse. Her breathing was laboured and she was complaining of pains in her chest and flutterings to her heart. Instantly forgetting their own comparatively lesser troubles, Elizabeth and Jane rushed to their great-aunt.

She greeted them with a small self-deprecating smile.

"It seems I am even more feeble than I have imagined if a short outing such as this is apt to put me in a state," she whispered, struggling for breath, then winced and put a gnarled fist to her chest.

"Do not strain yourself to talk," Jane urged and Elizabeth was swift to second her, then turned to the housekeeper.

"Has this happened before?"

"A few attacks now and again, but none so bad. I think we ought to send for the physician."

"I wish you would not speak of me as if I was not here," the lady protested. "As for the physician, he must be at the ball."

"The apothecary then, Ma'am, from the village," Mrs. Polmere offered, only to have her suggestion dismissed with a wave and a derisive snort.

"What good would that do? His draughts are useless, and who should know it better than myself? He has tried to foist them upon me for long enough."

She coughed again and Elizabeth determined she would brook no opposition.

"Would you send Gorran to seek the physician and Mawgan to fetch the apothecary, pray?"

"So my word counts for nothing, does it?" the older woman grumbled, but Elizabeth smiled.

"Quite the contrary, Ma'am, we are all working to ensure it would remain the law at Landennis for many years to come. Now, can I get you something? Orange water, or a cup of tea?"

"I thank you, no. I have had more than enough tea for one evening."

"Would you allow me to sit with you, then? Read for you perhaps? Might that help you sleep?"

The older woman's lips formed a tired smile.

"If you wish… Aye. Thank you. I would like that…"

They both remained with her, while Mrs. Polmere left to instruct the footmen. She was not gone for long, and she seemed very vexed when she returned to tell them that Gorran left on horseback to seek the physician at his house and then wherever else his people might suggest he could be found, but the other footman, Mawgan, was nowhere in sight.

"Most irregular, this!" the housekeeper fumed. "I can get no inkling of his whereabouts. Mr. Perren is of a mind to have a stern word with him when he deigns to return."

"Let us not trouble Mrs. Pencarrow with this now," Elizabeth advised and the housekeeper was swift to see the wisdom of it and grow silent.

Before too long, Mrs. Polmere left them and sent the young maid, Morwenna, to attend her mistress and be there to carry any instructions the young ladies might have. Yet for now there were no instructions as Mrs. Pencarrow drifted, Jane kept watch and Elizabeth read aloud. There were no other sounds in the darkened chamber – just the old woman's laboured breathing and the gentle cadence of old poems read in youthful and very soothing tones.

و

Trevellyan was nowhere to be found. Not in the supper room, where the guests mingled or sat at several well-laden tables. Not in the card room, the great hall, the ballroom, the terrace, the library or the study. Nor anywhere else they could think to seek him, for that matter. The servants, when applied to, offered nothing but port wine, burgundy and the suggestion that they sit down for supper – and Darcy suddenly determined they had lost too much time already. With a swift instruction to Bingley to await him on the gravel walk outside the house, he repaired to his chambers to find John.

Damnation! He had forgotten about Peter, his other footman, who was still in Falmouth pointlessly keeping watch for Bingley's arrival. A message should be sent to him on the morrow, to leave his post and rejoin his companions and his master – but this was of no use to Darcy *now*. It would have been a great deal better if Peter was at hand as well – he needed as many trustworthy men as he could find – but it seemed that John must needs suffice. If only he could be easily located! As for the coachman, he might as well be left behind. Poor Joseph, at his age of five and fifty, he could be relied upon to drive the carriage, but he would be of little use tonight.

Thankfully, John was quick to answer the summons of the bell and, by the time Darcy had replaced his dancing shoes with sturdy boots, his man was in his chambers, awaiting instructions. He was merely told to grab a coat and follow but, quite understandably, Bingley was less likely to obey without question, so Darcy was not surprised when he encountered his friend in the designated spot, only to find himself pressed to provide an explanation.

There was not a great deal he could tell him – there was not a great deal that he knew himself, other than the unsettling overhearings earlier that evening and the number of occasions when Trevellyan had acted in a suspicious manner, so he shared them with his friend in hurried whispers as they swiftly made their way along the narrow footpath.

"But this is not the way to the stables," Bingley belatedly remarked, only to receive a terse "I know."

"Are we to go *on foot* and tarry, when so much is at stake?"

"'Tis faster this way. Come!"

He had no doubt about it. By the time the horses were saddled and they rode around the estuary, the best part of an hour would have gone – a long time, which they could ill afford. Besides, he wished to give as little away as possible as regards his actions and intentions.

By the time they reached the riverbank, Bingley was beginning to catch on:

"You aim to row across!"

"Aye. There are boats moored at the pier. I saw them yesterday."

"And do you know the way?" Bingley persisted – vexingly more prone than ever to question him at every turn, which was presumably why Darcy was nettled into scathingly retorting:

"No, Bingley, I *do not*. I just thought it was the best night for an exploration!"

Yet he was already regretting his untoward outburst as soon as the harsh sarcasm left his lips so, with a quick apology, he motioned across the water where, on the hilltop opposite, in a wide gap between the trees, a dark shape punctuated by a few dots of light and crowned by several chimneys was outlined against the late night sky.

"That is Landennis Manor, over there," he informed his friend and with a nod Bingley followed, thankfully desisting from any further questions.

Luck was on their side. They easily found the pier – a dark shape on the moonlit waters – and there seemed to be at least two boats to choose from, with their oars still in. Darcy frowned. He vaguely remembered having seen more than two the other day and wondered if the notion to row across might have occurred to others.

He shrugged. Be that as it may. Still, they would be wise to watch out for company when they reached the other side. As for the crossing, they should do their best to keep to the tree-shadows hugging the riverbanks until they found a narrower stretch of open waters – either that, or wait for a cloud to conceal them from whomever might be watching. Otherwise, in this blasted moonlight, they would be sitting ducks!

"Shall I do the rowing, Sir?" John obligingly offered, but Darcy was prompt to reject the suggestion.

He could not sit still – he had to do *something*. Anything that might keep his thoughts at bay. He took to the oars with skill and caution and the dark boat glided noiselessly through the shadows, with nothing but the occasional muted splash. And nothing broke the stillness of the night but the cry of peacocks, forlorn and eerie, calling out behind them on Trevellyan's grounds.

ஒஜ ஓஓ

"What news, Mrs. Polmere?" Jane asked when the housekeeper finally rejoined them in Mrs. Pencarrow's chamber. "Was the physician found?"

"Nay, Ma'am. Gorran has not returned and neither has that rascal, Mawgan!"

"We cannot wait much longer!" Elizabeth determined, closing her book and casting another glance at her great-aunt. She was still very pale, and seemed to have fallen into a fitful slumber from which she would occasionally emerge to cough or release a faint groan.

"Shall I go for the apothecary, Ma'am?" Morwenna spoke up from her corner in a low, rather fearful whisper and Elizabeth looked up.

"I daresay 'tis time," she decided. "But you cannot go alone."

"I shall go fetch one of the other girls," Mrs. Polmere offered turning to leave, but before she could do so Elizabeth stood.

"No need. I shall go with her."

"*You*, Ma'am?" Mrs. Polmere and Morwenna spoke in one voice, visibly shocked.

From the other side of the large bed, Jane gasped:

"Lizzy, you cannot!"

"Of course I can! Morwenna will lead the way. I will keep her company. We shall be in the village in no time."

"Any of the other girls can keep her company, Ma'am! Or Mr. Perren," Mrs. Polmere protested. "Besides, if I may say so, any of them are bound to know the way better than yourself."

"Poor Mr. Perren can barely walk and would be wheezing by the time he gets no further than the dovecote. As for the other girls, they are scarce more than children. Younger than my sister Lydia. They would be terrified out of their wits, and that is bound to slow them down."

"What of you, Lizzy? Will *you* not be terrified?"

Her sister gave a little breathless laugh.

"Come now, Jane! You know me better than that."

"I shall come with you!" Jane declared firmly, only to see her sister shake her head in protest.

"Surely you can see it makes no sense at all. I can walk faster than you – run faster. No, stay with our great-aunt, and do not fret. All will be well."

Despite repeated reassurances, Jane and Mrs. Polmere remained clearly unhappy with the scheme and Morwenna did not seem too eager for it either, but in the face of Elizabeth's wilful determination, misgivings and insistent protestations eventually gave way. Bonnets and wraps were found and donned, but the offer of a lantern was rejected as superfluous and somewhat of an encumbrance and, with a swift embrace and a light kiss on her troubled sister's cheek, Elizabeth and the young maid took to the narrow road that ran alongside the gardens and sank into the valley to join the cart track by the river.

⚬⚬⚬

The tide was in, which made mooring a great deal easier, for they could tie the boat to the tree-roots and scramble onto the riverbank without having to wade over the mudflats.

They saw no boats nearby, but whether or not some might be moored further away, Darcy could not tell. They moved swiftly away from the water's edge, only to find themselves on something that seemed to be a cart track. Upon reflection, Darcy saw fit to shun it and led the way through the trees instead, to make good use of the thickest shadows. It was not long until he found what he expected – the dark contours of a wall that must be bordering the grounds of Landennis Manor.

Further ahead, the cart road seemed to branch out into another, leading up the hill but, yet again, he chose to remain under the protection of the shadows and kept to the wall, looking for the gate. None was found as yet and Darcy shrugged, conceding that scaling the wall might be their only option, when a faint sound caught his ear. Voices. Light and quiet. Women? Most unlikely, at this time of night. Young lads perhaps, returning to the village?

A possible encounter with a handful of young Cornishmen did not trouble him unduly. Still, it was best avoided, so Darcy gestured his companions to be still and silent. John saw the warning and obeyed at once. Not so Bingley, who walked on – and stepped on some half-rotten piece of wood or something of that nature. Whatever it was, it broke under his foot with a loud *crack*.

⁀⊕ ⊕⁀

"What was that?" Morwenna whispered and her hand closed tightly on Elizabeth's elbow.

"Sh! I know not," Elizabeth whispered back.

It was presumably nothing of consequence – a dead branch falling from a tree perhaps, or snapped under a deer's tread. In any case, they would do well to hurry on their way, so she lost little time in quietly advising her companion that they should do just that.

⁀⊕ ⊕⁀

Bingley's blunder seemed to have had no effect, and they went undetected. More stealthily this time, they resumed their cautious walk along the wall until they found the gate. It was not locked and it did not creak, and the three filed in, then hastened up the hill through what appeared to be an overgrown, ill-tended garden, towards the bulky contours of the house.

Halfway up, the gardens were significantly tamer and they found themselves on gravelled walks rather than a muddy path. Before too long, the house was right before them, emerging from the foliage, and through a pair of mullioned windows left unshuttered, they could see an candlelit room – a deserted parlour.

Just as Darcy was contemplating the best course of action, someone walked in – an elderly lady. Mrs. Pencarrow? No, the housekeeper, more likely. A young maid followed her and began tidying away the cups and other tea-things left on the small round table by the sofa. She gathered everything carefully on a tray, then walked out, taking the tray with her. In her turn, the housekeeper cast a glance around, as if to assure herself that the room was left in order, then blew out all the candles but the one in her hand and, with her own slow exit, the room was left in darkness.

All appeared peaceful in the quiet house. Mrs. Pencarrow must have retired to her chambers and her great-nieces also, leaving the housekeeper to do the last rounds, in readiness for the night.

"What now?" Bingley whispered very quietly – he had presumably learned his lesson, or at least Darcy hoped he had.

"Now we keep watch," came the brief reply.

John was sent to find and guard the servants' entrance; Bingley – to keep the front door in sight. As for himself, he sank into the shadows, a stone's throw from the arched door leading in from the gardens. He leaned against the wall and settled in for a long wait, pulling his cloak around him. It was a cold night and, under the crystal-clear skies, it was getting colder by the minute.

Yet the midnight chill could not defeat the warmth within, at the thought of her somewhere in the rambling house behind him. Readying for the night perhaps, or ensconced under the counterpane already, her eyes closed, her breathing slow and even.

Daylight would revive the pain, no doubt – but that was for the morrow. For now, after his unnamed fears for her safety, it was oddly comforting to at least guard her sleep.

Chapter 17

The track grew muddier once they reached the bottom of the hill, yet they pressed on, slipping and sliding, the silence broken only by their squelching footsteps and the lapping of the water against the riverbank. The silvery estuary on their left was a comfortable companion – open; safe – yet the dark woods to their right brought anything but comfort!

They were no longer speaking – *what was there to say?* – but hurried along the moonlight-dappled track, their eyes instinctively darting this way and that, drawn to any movement in the dark mass of foliage.

The ghostly sway of ivy was the worst – long tentacles trailing from the trees, moving with the breeze that rolled in from the water. Yet, from the corner of the eye, they did not look like the harmless garlands that they were. They were shapes, shadows closing in on them, stealthily sneaking alongside… a mark of peril, of unknown, unnamed dangers.

An owl's sudden hoot made them jump and Morwenna gasped in clear panic, then released her breath in a long sigh.

"Not far now, Ma'am," she whispered, as though to reassure herself as much as her companion, and they pressed on further, only to be petrified again by the piercing cry of some other night-bird whose slumber they must have disrupted.

Birds and ivy! Merely birds and ivy and deceptive shadows in the moonlight, Elizabeth told herself, in a firm endeavour to keep a clear head and not allow the alien surroundings to unnerve her.

Morwenna said herself, it was not far to go, and before too long they would be in the village. See reassuring lights gleam in cottage windows. Hear other sounds – familiar, comforting. Human voices, or the lowing of cattle, or a cock crow, or –…

"Halt! Who goes there? Stop and show yourself!"

The hard, vicious voice rang from somewhere very close and, at the sound of it, terror overcame her, sharp and chilling.

Elizabeth froze, rooted to the spot as the previously quiet surroundings suddenly exploded in bursts of frightening commotion. A shape, dark and massive, sprang into their path a few steps away. Birds scattered overhead with squawks and dreadfully noisy flutter. Somewhere behind, forceful footsteps crushed down wood and bracken, in their haste towards them. And above it all rang Morwenna's scream – a shrill cry of terror piercing the night and giving everything away, their vulnerable presence, their location!

It also reawakened Elizabeth's benumbed senses in a flash, as if she had been doused in icy water.

The foolish, *foolish* girl! They might have stood a feeble chance of escaping undetected, had they withdrawn into the shadows, still and silent. It was too late for such hopes now, and there was naught to do but turn and run! Not back up the path, no, they would be easily spotted, but into the woods, as fast as they could, and hope for a good hiding place, or the chance to outrun their less agile pursuers.

There was no time to deliver instructions other than a firm whisper of "Sh! Stop screaming! Come!" and Elizabeth gripped Morwenna's arm and tugged for her to follow.

She did not. Too frightened to see sense, the girl snatched her arm away and ran back up the path; back where they came from. There was no way Elizabeth could bring herself to abandon the young maid to her fate, much as every instinct told her to dart another way and hide in the shadows. She could only chase after the younger girl, a sickening sound of heavy footsteps squelching in the mud somewhere behind them.

Would that they did not trip, or slip, or fall! Snatching up her skirts, Elizabeth ran faster. Their pursuer was not gaining ground – if anything, his footsteps rang further away but, just before her, something must have happened to make Morwenna dart sideways with a muffled cry of panic. Elizabeth looked up and peered into the darkness, to the left, as louder sounds of several people crashing through the bracken reminded her of the horrible fact that the pursuer they had so far succeeded to outrun was not the only one.

She thought she saw a shadow – two – no, three or more! The fastest shot like lightning through the trees and burst into the path, cutting their retreat, followed in an instant by another, then another. Morwenna whimpered and drew to a sudden halt, then instinctively fell back a step or two, to pull away from the new aggressors.

It served no purpose, for they drew nearer still, fanning out across the track to cut off their retreat. By the sound of it, behind them the fourth seemed to have regained all the distance he had lost, but Elizabeth did not turn to verify the suspicion, her eyes darting to the three dark shapes ahead. Without conscious thought, her hand flew to her throat and she swallowed, her mouth dry. The scream was bubbling inside, she could almost feel it, churning and roiling, pushed this way and that by the icy claw of fear that gripped her stomach, and would not let go. She swallowed yet again, in a desperate endeavour to force the scream down, before it escaped and somehow triggered their aggressors into action.

What did they want?

Thoughts flashed, unacknowledged. She did not dare think them, even – and yet the terror would not shake its hold. Vulnerable. Lost. No protection. Would it help if they begged to be left in peace to continue on their way? Not beg, no, begging was pitiful and feeble!

A show of strength might offer better chances… might offer *some*. Was there a chance that they might cower before the future mistress of Landennis – or would revealing her identity and implicit value as a hostage make matters infinitely worse?

She raised her head and tightened her arms across her chest, as though to brace herself, to keep herself together. She took one further step, which brought her alongside Morwenna and, stiffening her back in a show of confidence she was very far from feeling, Elizabeth was about to demand unhindered passage – and pray that her voice would not falter – when one of the newcomers strode towards them, an air of command clearly evident in his demeanour, even before they got to hear it in his voice.

"What the blazes is this? Who are you?" he asked harshly.

Elizabeth all but gasped and her eyes widened. There was no doubt about it – the voice was Lord Trevellyan's!

Her first reaction was blessed relief. *Thank goodness!* They had not run into some vicious ruffians after all – and there was no threat to their lives, their freedom or their virtue! She was about to rush to him, inwardly laughing at her folly and her fears, when chilling thoughts stopped her in her tracks.

All of a sudden, Mr. Darcy's warning earlier that evening returned to stab her with the sharp, hideous suspicion that perhaps her trust in Lord Trevellyan *had* been misplaced after all.

Why was he here, and not at the ball? Why was he leading a number of faceless ruffians – or men who could easily be considered such – instead of leading the quadrille, or his guests to supper?

She wondered if she should find the courage to ask those precise questions, just as his lordship lost his patience and thundered again, towards herself as much as Morwenna.

"Speak, will you! Who are you? And who sent you here?"

Another whimper came from the frightened girl, and it was this more than anything that prompted Elizabeth to speak up, with as much firmness as she could possibly muster.

"I would thank you, my lord, to leave Morwenna be! She has done nothing wrong – "

She did not get the chance to say anything further. At the first sound of her voice, Lord Trevellyan looked away from the servant girl and spun to her instead, his greatcoat billowing behind him. He drew up sharply, a foot away from her, clearly endeavouring to scan her features in the poor light.

She had no greater success in reading his. The brim of his hat concealed them, as did the fact that he was towering above her and thus the dappled moonlight fell on *her* face, not his. Yet the tone of his voice left Elizabeth in no misapprehension of his feelings, for Lord Trevellyan – their charming and obliging neighbour – shockingly burst out with vicious anger, the likes of which she had never seen him show before.

"*Miss Elizabeth?* What on earth are you doing here, in the middle of the night? Heaven help us! Did you not hear me tell you that it is not safe?"

"I am beginning to see that for myself," Elizabeth icily retorted, her indignation at his intolerable manner having in some measure helped subdue her fear. "Still, it had to be done. Mrs. Pencarrow has been taken ill. She is in need of the apothecary, or the doctor. But Gorran could not find him – that is to say, the doctor. He went out a long time ago and has not returned – ..."

Her words did not seem to put his lordship in a better frame of mind – not that *this* had been her purpose. Neither did he seem at all inclined to apologise for his untoward outburst. Quite the opposite in fact, for he cut in roughly:

"I have business with Gorran. And with the doctor also."

"Gorran is with *you?*" Elizabeth interjected in her turn, horrified to hear of the young man's desertion. "And the doctor? Business? *What* sort of business, may I ask?"

"I fear you may not!" his lordship replied brusquely – then, at long last, seemed to recollect what it was that he was saying. "Forgive me, but there is no time for this," he perfunctorily offered through tight lips. "The doctor will be sent to attend Mrs. Pencarrow as soon as I have finished with him," he added tersely. "In the interim, I sent you the apothecary. Why is he not with you?"

"I know not," Elizabeth retorted, incensed in no small measure. "Morwenna and I set out to summon him – "

"You should have had more sense than setting out into the night with naught but a young servant-girl for protection!"

"My sense or lack thereof is not under discussion at the moment!" she interjected hotly. "Mrs. Pencarrow requires immediate attention!"

At last, her words seemed to sink in enough to make him desist from further remonstrations.

"What ails her?" Lord Trevellyan asked instead.

"I cannot say. She is in pain and her breathing is laboured."

"What sort of pain?"

"Pains to her chest, she told us."

"Damnation!" Trevellyan burst out, then spun on his heels towards one of his companions. "Densil, go and see how soon the doctor can be spared. Take this girl with you, she might be of some use."

"Morwenna is going nowhere!" Elizabeth firmly interjected, even before the maid's hand could clasp itself in fright around her elbow.

"I need her assistance," his lordship retorted without ceremony. "Fear not, girl, your brother will see you safely back to Landennis," he added and, despite his unprecedented brusqueness, his words served to allay some of Elizabeth's concerns.

Regardless of his reasons for changing allegiance and disobeying Mrs. Polmere's orders, surely Gorran would not let his own sister come to any harm!

"Where is Gorran?" she felt compelled to ask.

"In the village. Now, Densil – "

"*Why?*" Elizabeth spun around, endeavouring in vain to catch his eye and make some sense of the entire business. "My lord, I *must* learn the meaning of all this!"

"What you *must* do, Miss Elizabeth, is return to the house! Merryn, see that she gets there safely, then come back at once. Rejoin the others, you will find us there. Come, let us see if they had better luck," he urged the third man, and then turned towards her. "Miss Bennet, I hope you will forgive my abrupt departure, as well as – "

"My lord, I must insist on an explanation!"

"Not tonight, Ma'am! Return to Landennis and, by Jove, pray remain there! Have your people secure the house and admit no one but the doctor. He will be with you shortly, or the apothecary shall, if anyone can find the blasted fool. Pray go now, my man will attend you. Gorran and Morwenna will be sent back when they are no longer needed."

"Needed for *what?*" she asked again, her temper short and frayed.

"All in good time, Miss Bennet. Pray go now! You too, Densil. And mind that girl, would you? See that she does not raise the alarm again. You must keep quiet, do you hear me?" he gruffly addressed Morwenna. "Follow my man, he will take you to your brother."

"Do I have your word on that, my lord?" Elizabeth interjected sternly, only to receive an impatient "Pardon?"

"Do I have your word that she will be delivered safely to her brother?"

"Of course – though I hope she can be trusted not to sprain an ankle on the way. The doctor has his hands full already. Go now, Miss Bennet, before the mischief starts afresh and, by your leave, I shall see you on the morrow."

And with that, he vanished through the trees, along with one of his companions. Densil lost no time in doing as bid and hurried down towards the village with Morwenna on his heels, somewhat revived by the expectation of being reunited with her brother.

"Come, Miss," the man left to attend her urged in a rushed whisper and, with a frown, Elizabeth had to follow.

The pace he set was fast, almost too fast for her, but Elizabeth pressed on, determined to keep up. This man – Merryn, Lord Trevellyan had called him – was one of those sent to escort her and Jane from the ball, back to Landennis. She was sure of it, once she caught a glimpse of his countenance, and also heard him speak.

She wondered if the other two were still lurking in the woods as well. Were they *'the others'* that Lord Trevellyan had instructed Merryn to return to, once he had seen her back to the house?

Or were the others a great deal more than two? Perhaps so – for Mr. Darcy warned that Landennis was said to be surrounded by Lord Trevellyan's people.

Earlier that evening, she had dismissed Mr. Darcy's warning as nothing more than prejudice against his lordship, but it was clear now that Lord Trevellyan's men *were* roaming all around.

She had told Mr. Darcy there must be a reasonable explanation – to protect Landennis.

Protect it against *what*, though? And if Landennis was the place they were protecting, should they not be on its very doorstep, rather than searching through the woods? Searching for what? Or whom? Why was the doctor needed? Why did the apothecary not arrive? Why, moreover, had Lord Trevellyan rushed away from his own ball to roam with his men through the woods around Landennis village? Why would he not explain his actions – what secret was he hiding? Why tonight, of all nights? Or was this conspiracy meant to stretch far further than one night?

He was not there to answer any of those questions and, judging by her earlier frustrated efforts, Elizabeth very much doubted that he was prepared to tell her anything at all. Still, his man was there – and Elizabeth could only hope that his tongue was looser than his master's.

"Did your companions take to the woods as well, after escorting us home from the ball?" she asked between sharp breaths, coming faster with the exertion.

"Nay, Miss," the man answered gruffly.

It was plain to see that no more would be forthcoming. Nevertheless, Elizabeth pressed on.

"But *you* did. Why?"

"His lordship's orders," another cryptic answer came and Elizabeth huffed, about to dryly observe she was not aware until tonight that the men in Lord Trevellyan's employ were also expected to roam over his neighbours' woodland. She found herself too out of breath for sarcasm though, so instead she asked a shorter and more pressing question:

"Why is his lordship sending his men to the woods of Landennis?"

"A spot o' trouble, Miss."

"What sort of trouble?"

"'Tis not my place ter say."

"Whose place is it, then?" Elizabeth asked, quite out of patience.

"His lordship's, mayhap, if he's of a mind ter share it. Now could we hurry, Miss? For he expects me shortly an' I'd much rather not provoke his ire tonight!"

Her own ire repeatedly provoked, Elizabeth made no answer but forced herself to increase the pace, not so much to comply with the suggestion as to vent her frustration at his lordship and his tight-lipped henchman.

Equally frustrating was her bonnet, which seemed to have acquired a life of its own and began to twist this way and that, wildly protesting at the unladylike swift progress. With another huff of vexed impatience, she pushed it back till it slid right off and trailed behind, hanging by the ribbons. The cool night air ruffled her damp tresses and Elizabeth shook her head into the wind, relishing the breeze and the calming sensation. She took a deep breath and, in marginally better humour, she sped forth.

⚬᯽ ᯼᯽⚬

"Did you hear that, Darcy?" What the deuce was it? It came from down there, did it not? From the valley. Do you not think it sounded like a scream?"

Hushed and disembodied, his friend's voice rang beside him and Darcy's eyes narrowed in vexation, wishing Bingley would for once hold his tongue!

'*Aye, damn you! It did sound like a scream. Now be quiet!*' he wanted to burst out as he strained to listen.

He did not burst out, and Bingley held his peace of his own accord. Yet nothing further could be heard over the rustling of leaves until, quite suddenly, a window was opened high above them, around the corner, on the other side of the house. Voices were heard as well, though not the words, but one of them was sufficiently distinctive for Darcy to recognise it as Miss Bennet's, so he did not wonder at his friend's instant inclination to return to his earlier outpost. Still, he restrained him, if only for a moment, to whisper a few stern words of warning:

"We have not come hither for you to play Romeo to Miss Bennet's Juliet! Be sure to stay out of sight and remember to keep silent."

But Bingley snatched his arm away and rushed around the corner, leaving Darcy to peer uselessly into the darkened valley for the cause of the earlier disturbance. Yet there was naught to see, just swaying foliage and ever-shifting shadows.

Darcy breathed out a muted oath. Having plagued them on the journey hither, the useless moon was now behind the clouds! What on earth was happening down there? Would Miss Bennet have an inkling? Would it serve to make their presence known and perhaps ask her? But then he instantly dismissed the notion. Of course she would not know – how could she?

He wondered briefly whether his friend had chosen to appraise her of his presence – but then, judging by the continued silence, undisrupted by cries of surprise, dismay or recognition, he readily concluded he did not.

The casement was eventually closed – Darcy could hear it well enough from where he was – but Bingley did not return, presumably awaiting on the same spot, in the hope that it might be reopened.

Darcy pursed his lips and sighed, wrapping himself in his cloak again, and once more leaning against the cold wall behind him.

Would that it had been *her*, an unchecked thought intruded, before he *did* check it and endeavoured to persuade himself that he did not begrudge his friend a glimpse of his beloved.

If only...

Beyond control, thoughts flooded. And dreams, and aching wishes, and Darcy groaned, allowing them free rein. Ever since Elizabeth's rushed withdrawal from the terrace, he had fought to keep it all at bay – the pain; the crushing emptiness awaiting – and think instead of what had to be done. And now the fragile barricade was crumbling. The floodgates had opened, at the same time as that window above-stairs.

It was not concern for Miss Bennet's feelings or any other equally noble sentiment but envy, pure, shameful envy that had made him stop his friend from – *how did he dare put it?* – play Romeo to her Juliet.

Would *he* have remained silent if it had been Elizabeth up there and not her elder sister? Would *he* have stayed out of sight and held his peace? He knew not – but he suddenly lost interest in the pointless speculation. His senses sharpened and his head came up.

Her voice! He was quite certain he had just heard her voice, coming from somewhere, some distant place before him. Or had he? Darcy shook his head. Was he losing his senses? Imagining her voice to be ringing in the darkness! He *must* have imagined it, for he could now hear nothing more.

He strained to listen yet again, unconsciously moving away from the wall and into the shadows that bordered the footpath as he struggled to pick out sounds and whispers – something other than the whisper of the wind amongst the leaves.

But surely… footsteps! Beyond doubt. Footsteps hurrying up the gravel walk through the gardens. And then, mere yards away and clear as a bell:

"We are here. I can see the house."

This was neither error, nor wild imagination. It *was* her voice! Elizabeth! What in God's name was she doing out there? Good Lord, then… The scream! Had that been *her*? Was she in danger? But no, she did not sound afraid just now – it was a placid statement.

Heavens above, where *was* she? Why out there? And with whom?

No matter – as long as she was safe!

Good Lord, let her be safe – and keep her so!

๛๏๏

"There now, Miss. Make yer way in an' keep 'em doors bolted," Merryn urged as they gained the top of the slope.

From the dovecote onwards, he had left the cart track and had led her through the side gate into the gardens and then up the gravelled walks with practised ease, as though he knew them like the back of his hand, in daylight or in darkness.

Despite herself, Elizabeth shivered at the thought of his lordship's men roaming secretly through her great-aunt's gardens and knowing every corner, every turn, as if they were entitled to be there – or at least as if they *had* been there anyway, oftentimes before.

She shivered again. Did Mrs. Pencarrow know of this? Or was Lord Trevellyan taking advantage of her too trusting nature?

Without another word, his man turned on his heels and broke into a run, to rejoin his companions. For her part, breathless with the swift trek uphill and with the terrors of the night, Elizabeth hurried to the house.

The garden door would not be open, surely. Would they hear her if she knocked? Perhaps not. Perhaps she should walk around to the main entrance.

She rushed forth noiselessly over the damp grass – and stumbled into something or *someone* in the darkness, only to find herself caught and held tightly in strong arms that would not let her fall, yet at the same time prevented all escape!

Chapter 18

Before the cry of utter horror could leave her lips, a deep voice, warm and earnest, stilled her struggles and set her thoroughly at ease – for she would have recognised *that* voice anywhere.

"Sshh. You are safe. You are safe. You need not fear *me*. Forgive me for startling you thus! You have nothing to fear. Thank goodness, you are safe!"

The words did not sink in. Not yet. Not quite. But their fervent cadence reached her, along with the overwhelming certainty that *this* was not some unknown aggressor. It was Mr. Darcy – and she clung to the folds of his cloak with all her might, shaking like a leaf.

Not for fear, though. The fear vanished as if it never was, to be replaced by the strangest weakness. Had he not held her, she might have collapsed, for her knees felt useless, about to give way, and her head was swimming.

'It must be the shock,' some wispy threads of reason sensibly claimed, but at this point she could barely heed them.

Still shaking, and still gripping the folds of his cloak with trembling fingers, she could not think straight. She could only feel. And the only feeling she could readily identify, from the tumult and confusion that seemed to reign inside her, was unspeakable relief that at long last this was someone she could fully trust. Someone who came from her own safe, sane world, and not from this terrifying *other*, where one could not tell one's friends from one's foes!

She was not cold – at least she did not think she was – and yet she felt herself shaking from head to foot with a violent shiver. Or was it a sob? Or both? Most certainly a sob this time, and then another, deep and wracking.

She could not control them, which was terrifying in itself. She struggled for breath – and yet did not withdraw from the tight clasp of those arms, but unconsciously drew nearer.

Support and succour and safe haven. How strange that she had never felt as safe before! It was the oddest certainty that nothing could harm her now, and the relief made her positively dizzy, after the events of this long night, without a doubt the most frightful she had experienced in her entire tame existence!

The sobs subsided, tempered by the novel thought and no less by the equally novel, barely perceptible sensations. A light touch of warm lips on her brow, sliding to her temple. Cold fingertips brushing against her cheek – and yet the trail of their caress was not cold at all. It was hot. And tingling. Another touch of a cold fingertip on her lower lip, in a light stroke, so light that she could barely feel it.

Her senses, previously dulled by the dizzying weakness, came suddenly alive, like hissing candles lit in very quick succession. She felt his breath upon her cheek, warm, rapid and uneven, and her own breath turned fast and shallow, as though to match the pace of his – then grew faster still when the narrow gap was closed and his lips touched her cheekbone. They lingered there, dropping light, feathery kisses, and the cold fingertips were on her chin now, tilting her face upwards – or perhaps she had already done so of her own accord; she truly could not tell.

"Elizabeth..." she heard him whisper, his lips still trailing a soft line on her cheek, and then the whisper gave way to a harsh intake of breath – and his lips were on hers. No longer soft and tentative, but searching. Deepening the kiss over a length of time that seemed to be measured in thundering heartbeats.

Her eyes flew open, yet she could barely see his face. The moon had long since hidden behind clouds and they were in the deepest shadows. She reached up, her hands seeking blindly until her fingertips encountered the hard jaw, the cheeks, ever so slightly rough, not perfectly clean-shaven any longer, and she explored their shape, strangely glad of the darkness as she stroked their contours, never before touched, yet ever so familiar just the same.

Under her touch, the jaw tensed, and she could hear his breath becoming ragged as the kiss deepened even further into something her thoughts could not encompass. In truth, there was no room for thoughts, not anymore – otherwise she might as well begin to wonder what on earth was she doing in the gardens of Landennis in the middle of the night, kissed breathless by none other than Mr. Darcy, whose offer of marriage she had *refused* a few hours ago!

There was no sense, no reason, just the exquisite kiss and the night that suddenly felt warm and gloriously perfect, after the reign of fear and of doubt. Come to think of doubt though, she might as well begin to doubt her sanity for allowing *this* to happen – but as his hands roamed across her back, clasping her so fiercely that she could barely breathe, she closed her eyes again, relishing the madness and the bewildering sensation of homecoming, into strong arms that would keep her safe.

Her fingers travelled to the back of his head to stroke his hair, tangle themselves in it, as he brought her even closer – something she would not have thought remotely possible before – and his lips left hers to drop feverish kisses over her cheeks, her eyelids, only to return, just as insistent, just as searching, hungry. And she could not, would not deny him, any more than she could deny herself. Instead, her own lips parted, to better taste his delectable flavour, and a low sound rose in his throat at that, sending a shiver through her, from her scalp to her very toes.

She must have taken leave of her senses lately – or perhaps it was this most unnerving night, or the soothing darkness, that made her lose touch with the world as it was, or at least as it should be.

What madness had possessed her, to compel her to behave so wantonly, so wholly without boundaries or reason? And indeed heartlessly as well – for would he not be justified in thinking that she had reconsidered her rejection?

Had she? Had she reconsidered? She had not... More to the point, she had *considered* nothing. She had not been guided in the least by reason over the last few moments – minutes – deliciously undetermined time that they had spent together in exquisite abandon, flaunting every rule, every consideration, every precept!

In the end, she could not truly tell who broke the kiss. It might have been herself, in some belated acknowledgement of right and wrong. It might have been him – or perhaps both, in joint recognition of their untenable position, or simply in sudden need of air. Her breath *did* come very fast indeed, in forceful gasps, as if she had just run all the way up the hill, from the village – and his did also. Elizabeth could feel it on her tingling skin and raised her face to it – only to find his lips again with a staggering, explosive burst of joy.

It must have been the need of air then, earlier, and not some other argument that common sense dictated.

Yet common sense *had* to prevail before too long or, if not sense, then decency and also common kindness, for surely she must not continue to mislead him in this fashion!

With a faint sigh, she brought herself to turn her head away. Yet she did not withdraw from him completely, vainly searching for something to say that would convey the substance of her thoughts. Words would not come though, and that was little wonder, for there was no hope to do the faintest justice to the complex turmoil toying with her senses.

Before she even tried, she was thoroughly distracted by strong hands cradling her to his chest, keeping her there, cherished and protected. And warm lips brushed against her cheek, next to her ear, as the deep voice spoke words of deep contrition.

"Forgive me. Pray forgive me! That was... beyond the pale. I should not have taken advantage of –... Forgive me!"

She could not let him continue to apologise for a fault that was as much her own as his – or even more so hers – and so, unthinkingly, Elizabeth raised her hand to his mouth. Another shiver coursed along her spine at the feel of his lips against her fingers. Worse still, she audibly gasped when his hand came up to cover hers and raise it by a fraction, until his lips were pressed against her palm, sending unnerving, nay, highly disturbing tremors through her. Not tremors, but veritable earthquakes!

She swallowed and withdrew her hand, lest the staggering new sensations remove every remaining trace of sanity and compel her to tangle her fingers in his hair again and bring him back to her, his lips crushing hers as they did before, for those glorious moments!

This time she did endeavour to withdraw from his embrace – it was by far the most sensible option – and although her intent was not immediately perceived, or perhaps it was perceived with great reluctance, his hold eventually slackened, and she was released. Yet his hands lingered on her arms, then lightly traced along them until her own hands were in his – which was just as well for, unreasonable as it might have been, Elizabeth felt she could have scarcely borne a full and immediate separation.

"Are you –...?"

"Why are you here?" they began at once, both in hushed whispers.

For her part, Elizabeth could only regret the ill-judged and far too abrupt question, particularly as it seemed to convey the false impression that it was meant as censure.

"I had no intention to cause you any discomfort, I assure you," the retort came, wistful and earnest, making her even more acutely aware of her error.

She hastened to correct it.

"Oh, I *know* that! Pray forgive me, I did not wish to imply that I was anything but glad."

Upon reflection, *that* was the wrong thing to say as well, although for different reasons, and before they were drawn into stormy waters, Elizabeth was swift to amend:

"I am very grateful for your unstinting kindness, Mr. Darcy, and I am distraught to think of the trouble and discomfort you must have endured, but tonight I am very glad to have come across someone I can trust –..."

She got to say no more. Her hands were carried to his lips again, if only for a lingering kiss on the back of her fingers rather than the deeply unsettling feel of his mouth pressed against her palm, and Elizabeth found herself rather relieved by that – and also strangely and perversely disappointed.

"I should have paid more heed to your warning," she brought herself to add before her own unruly thoughts could gain further purchase. "You were right about Lord Trevellyan. He is not what he seems."

"What makes you say that?" he instantly asked, his tone alert and anxious.

For the first time since the beginning of their unparalleled encounter a few minutes ago, Elizabeth was rather sorry for the lack of light. Reading his countenance was something she had never mastered, so ascertaining his reactions from the mere sound of his voice seemed a hopeless task. Nevertheless, she felt compelled to answer.

"He was in the woods... He came upon me as I was walking to the village with Morwenna – "

Her sentence was cut short by his sharp intake of breath and her hands were clasped so tightly it was almost painful.

"Can you tell me where he is now?" he asked after a long moment, in a voice so rasping and so dreadfully uneven that he did not sound like himself at all.

"I... No, I cannot. I heard him say to his men that they should rejoin the others, but he did not say where..."

Her words were met by yet another gasp – nay, by forced deep breaths rather, as though he was struggling to quell the most violent distemper.

"His men! Did they – ... How many?"

"Three. But of those, only one went with him. The other two were sent to attend Morwenna and myself."

"I... beg your pardon? To attend you?"

"Aye. And Morwenna also. Escort her to the village, to her brother."

His voice seemed to falter.

"Forgive me, I... do not seem to understand. I do not wish to... grieve you in any way, but may I be allowed to know... what happened, when you encountered Lord Trevellyan?"

"Not a vast deal," she replied in some confusion and she was further mystified to hear him exhale forcefully – or sigh with incommensurate relief.

"Not a vast deal," he repeated, slowly and distinctly, and clasped her hands again, pressing them to his lips.

Bemused and strangely breathless, Elizabeth resumed.

"We argued. Heatedly. And he seemed very altered. Abrupt, ill-tempered, secretive. Yet he made no secret of the fact that he was most put out to find us in his way –..."

"*'Us'*? Oh, aye, you mentioned someone else. Morwenna, was it?"

"Aye. Morwenna. A maid from Landennis."

"I see... So, you argued. And was that... the extent of it? No one was harmed?"

"No. No one."

"So... the scream I heard, a while ago...?" he inquired with the greatest hesitation.

She understood his line of questioning at last and blushed the deepest scarlet, thankful for the shadows that hid her face from him.

"That was Morwenna," she replied when she found her voice. "Poor girl, she was terrified to see them spring out of the darkness."

"And you?" he asked very softly and at that she chuckled consciously.

"To own the truth, my show of confidence was merely that – a show. I – …"

She broke off once his arms encircled her again and she found herself gathered to his chest, his lips pressed on her brow, as he fervently whispered:

"Thank goodness you are safe! My dearest brave, wonderful, foolish girl, what were you thinking, roaming through the woods at night? If anything had befallen you, Elizabeth – … Good Lord, my love! It does not bear thinking!"

Was it the comfortable darkness that made him so unguarded, Elizabeth wondered in a daze, that made him speak in earnest, soul to soul, rather than act the part convenience dictated? It should have made her ill-at-ease perhaps, yet for some reason it did not. It was a novel and exhilarating notion to learn just how much she was loved – and to what extent she had misread his feelings.

The *appeal of novelty* she called it, earlier that morning – and passing interest mistaken for affection.

No man would spend the night guarding a woman's doorstep for the appeal of novelty or for a passing interest! It must have been the utmost force of passion that had spurred him on, and his every word and deed seemed to confirm it. As for his kiss…

Once more, Elizabeth felt grateful for the darkness that concealed her blushes. This time she made no motion to withdraw. In fact, she was rather tempted to bury her face into his cloak, drawn by the warmth and the appealing scent – reassuringly familiar and ever so delectable – yet, to her almost palpable disappointment, his arms dropped from around her, without warning.

"I beg your pardon. I forgot myself," she heard him whisper and the hands that had lingered on her elbows, to steady her perhaps, dropped away also. "You must be very cold and very tired – I should not have detained you," he added, his voice a study in subdued civility that seemed to belong to stilted exchanges in an overcrowded parlour, but terribly ill-suited to the moment.

"Do not regard it," she earnestly whispered back, unwilling to allow the untimely reversal. "Besides, I am not cold – but *you* must be. Your cheeks are cold, and your hands are icy –…" she spoke with feeling, only to fall silent at the involuntary reference to the earlier moments of exquisite intimacy. She heard him clear his voice, yet he said nothing. In the end, it was Elizabeth who spoke up again, still in a conscious whisper:

"You must come in – warm yourself. A cup of tea, perhaps…"

"Pray, do not trouble yourself. I am quite well and besides, your great-aunt would rightly take objection to – "

"Great heavens!" she exclaimed, his words a sudden reminder of the night's troubles and above all, her duties.

Mrs. Pencarrow! How could she have forgotten that she was meant to hurry in, discover if the apothecary had arrived, see how her great-aunt was faring, relieve Jane…

"E –… Miss Bennet? What is amiss?" she heard him ask, alarmed by her altered tone and manner.

"Forgive me, I must hurry, but pray do come in," she urged and turned away to walk towards the entrance as fast as she could.

To her undisclosed relief, she heard him follow, with a concerned "Elizabeth? What is it?"

She made to answer, but before she could do so the sound of footsteps approaching in a rush from around the corner gave her pause – and no less the unexpected voice which, although hushed, sounded suspiciously like Mr. Bingley.

"Darcy? Is anything the matter? Who are you talking to? Oh, hang it, Darcy, where the devil are you?" the voice burst out in angry whispers, the tones forcefully bringing the said gentleman to mind, even if the petulance and the show of temper most certainly did not.

"Over here!" Mr. Darcy called, not loudly but loud enough to carry and guide the other in the right direction.

Their paths crossed on the carriage approach to the house. Had she not been so preoccupied with other matters, Elizabeth might have found some sympathy for the younger gentleman's discomfort, when he became aware of her presence. As it was, she barely acknowledged his apology for the earlier display of temper as, over and above her manifold concerns, it had just crossed her mind that her companions might have already noticed whether or not the apothecary had found his way to Landennis in her absence. She lost no time to ask – only to receive nothing of use from Mr. Bingley, other than an exclamation of surprised concern.

"The apothecary? Goodness! Is anyone unwell?"

Now that they had emerged from the shadows, Elizabeth could distinguish enough of Mr. Darcy's countenance to see him roll his eyes at the pointless question.

She answered it nevertheless.

"My great-aunt was taken ill. A footman was sent to fetch the doctor, but then I learned that they were both sidetracked by Lord Trevellyan – "

"Trevellyan!" Mr. Bingley exclaimed. "So he *is* involved!"

"Pray, continue, Miss Bennet," Mr. Darcy intervened. "Sidetracked, you said. How?"

"He claimed that they were needed in the village – the doctor and my great-aunt's footman – although he would not tell me why. The maid, Morwenna, was asked to come and lend a hand, and Lord Trevellyan promised that the doctor would be sent to Landennis as soon as he can be spared," she quickly shared everything she knew, then added, "He also mentioned that he sent us the apothecary instead, to do what he can while we are waiting for the doctor. Did he arrive while you were here?"

Mr. Darcy gravely informed her he did not.

"But I can walk into the village to hurry the doctor along," he offered.

"And perhaps discover what Trevellyan is about," Mr. Bingley interjected, to receive a curt "Indeed."

It was not the word itself, but the way it was uttered, darkly and with purpose, that sent a shiver through her. Suddenly, and with great clarity, Elizabeth saw she did not wish to cause to a meeting between Lord Trevellyan and Mr. Darcy – not tonight! On the morrow, in the light of day, things might be different, tempers might have settled. But she could not draw an easy breath if Mr. Darcy was to set out *now* to encounter Lord Trevellyan.

"Perhaps later," she quietly offered. "Let us go in – see how my great-aunt is faring. Her condition might have improved a little. And you both must have a warming drink."

Mr. Bingley showed absolutely no desire to protest but as for Mr. Darcy, he seemed oddly keen to know which way was the servants' entrance.

"Around the corner, to the left," Elizabeth informed him, rather mystified. "Why should you wish to know?"

"I sent my man to find it and guard it. I should speak to him. And, Miss Bennet, since you kindly suggested we should make our way within, perhaps John might also be allowed to guard the servants' entrance from the inside?"

"But of course," Elizabeth readily assented and, with quiet thanks, Mr. Darcy disappeared into the darkness.

Thus, a few moments later, when the great doors were promptly opened in response to a forceful knock, only two people were standing on the threshold. To Miss Bennet's relief, she could readily see that one of them was her dearest sister. However, when the second stepped into the light, it became blindingly obvious that he was *not* the apothecary they were so eagerly expecting, but a very different person altogether!

ᵉᵒⁱᵉ ᵍᵉ

At the sight of the blood draining from her sister's countenance, Elizabeth was distraught at her own folly. She had expected Jane to be in their great-aunt's chamber, and that she would have plenty of time to warn her of Mr. Bingley's presence. How did she fail to see that her elder sister would be so concerned about her that she would want to gain the earliest intelligence of her return to safety?

In lieu of any belated apology, Elizabeth walked into Jane's embrace. The tight clasp of their arms around each other conveyed everything and when they drew apart Elizabeth was vaguely reassured to see that Jane seemed to have regained some of her composure – outwardly at least – and was able to greet Mr. Bingley with a curtsy and a few quiet words:

"Sir. Pray come in and allow me to thank you for escorting my sister."

"You are very kind, but I fear I have done nothing to deserve your thanks. I have only encountered Miss Elizabeth a few moments earlier, on your doorstep," Bingley replied wistfully with a bow and at that, Jane's eyes turned searchingly from her beleaguered suitor to her sister, the wish to ask precisely *what* was he doing on their doorstep at this time of night clearly etched upon her countenance.

Elizabeth felt it was her place to supply the relevant details, but there was a more urgent question that required an answer:

"How is our great-aunt, Jane?"

"I think she is a little better. Mrs. Polmere found a phial that still held some of the draughts the apothecary had prepared for her a while ago and, despite her protestations, Mrs. Pencarrow's was prevailed upon to take a double dose. Her pains seem to have subsided. She is resting now."

"Thank goodness!" Elizabeth fervently replied. "So the apothecary might be of as much assistance as the doctor, or even more so, if he would just turn up!"

"Did you find him, Lizzy? And where is Morwenna?"

Elizabeth promptly shared her modest knowledge as to the whereabouts of Mrs. Pencarrow's maid, her footman and her doctor – which brought them to Lord Trevellyan and thence to the explanation still owed Jane regarding Mr. Bingley's presence on their doorstep.

"Before the ball, Mr. Darcy overhead that Lord Trevellyan had Landennis surrounded. We know not why. So both he and Mr. Bingley wished to offer their assistance and protection."

"Oh! That is… very thoughtful," Jane remarked sedately. "I take it then that Mr. Darcy is here also?"

As though on cue, the gentleman himself appeared in the doorway, followed by another man, who must have been the footman he had mentioned.

"Would you come in, Sir?" Jane spoke up with another curtsy, calmly stepping into the role of mistress of the house and Elizabeth found herself inwardly glad of it and more than a little grateful for, at this point in time, she doubted she could say a word if her life hung in balance.

Her glance had instinctively darted to the door at the first sound of footsteps and her eyes met his with a jolt before she cast them down, her cheeks blazing at the overwhelming thought that this was the first time they were in company together after the unprecedented moments in the garden. That they were in the midst of people, in a lit room – and not in dark surroundings where blushes and the play of emotions on one's features could be easily concealed. That *he* would know, as soon as their eyes met, that all she could think of at the moment was the feel of his arms around her, and his lips on hers. And, judging by the dark intensity she had just encountered for the fleeting moment when their eyes did meet, he must have known it very well indeed!

The door was closed, and the candles ceased to flicker.

Still unable to look up, Elizabeth stood listening to his deep voice as he spoke to Jane and Mrs. Polmere, providing carefully selected snippets of information to justify his presence at Landennis, then requesting permission to station his man at the servants' entrance. And then he left, accompanied by his footman and Mrs. Polmere – and the large room seemed dreadfully empty for his absence. Empty and cold, and very dreary…

Pursing her lips, Elizabeth released an impatient huff. She could not afford to turn into a self-indulgent Miss! Mrs. Pencarrow needed her. Or, if her great-aunt did not need her now, Jane certainly did.

"Come and warm yourself by the fire in the parlour, Mr. Bingley," she quietly invited the gentleman whom her sister did not feel comfortable to address. "You must be chilled to the bone. I shall speak to Mrs. Polmere about some tea. Unless you prefer coffee?"

"I thank you. You are very gracious. But I think I should learn what my friend is proposing to do next. We have not come to trouble you for refreshment," he added with a feeble smile and a half-hearted attempt at an equally feeble jest.

"Of course. But you can at least wait for Mr. Darcy in the parlour," Elizabeth offered kindly.

Much as she had resented Mr. Bingley for what she had perceived as heartless abandonment of her dear sister – and then, after Colonel Fitzwilliam's disclosures, for his gullible nature and his lack of backbone – Elizabeth could not fail to experience at least *some* compassion at the sight of him visibly treading on eggshells around Jane, once they all made their way into the parlour.

There was little doubt he wished to approach her, and the total lack of encouragement from that quarter must have been a severe reminder of his failings. In a very quiet voice, he brought himself to inquire whether she was warm enough, then ask permission to rekindle the fire. Once it was granted, he set to it with purpose – until the flames sprang up again and there was nothing left for him to do but sit across from Jane and diffidently glance upon her, then finally raise the courage to address her, only to receive monosyllabic answers and no smiles.

From her own seat on the sofa, Elizabeth forbore to intervene but simply sat, only half-listening to their stilted conversation as she wondered how the four of them had arrived to such a muddle.

If anyone had asked her a few days ago, she would have said it was all Mr. Darcy's fault. And of course Mr. Bingley's too, for being weak and spineless, but it was Mr. Darcy who was the villain of the piece!

And now she knew him to have acted out of friendship rather than prideful ill-will – and knew just as well that blame should be apportioned equally and fairly. Mr. Bingley ought to have his share for being, if not spineless, then prone to rely on others for decisions that were his alone to make. Jane, for being far too keen to conceal her feelings. Herself, for her wilful determination to misunderstand – how shrewdly this great fault of hers was spotted, and how aptly put!

Which left Mr. Darcy with no greater sin than pride. And if a prideful man was prepared to do his utmost to ensure the safety of the woman who had just rejected him, then his pride must be under very good regulation – and his feelings far too strong to be repressed!

With a slight shiver – not of cold – Elizabeth could not fail to acknowledge that the all-too-short time spent together in the garden had only served to prove this exact point.

Her fingers knotted in her lap, she had long ceased paying heed to her companions. They could have left the room and still she would have failed to notice as she sat staring into the fire, at the red-hot flames that danced around each other, untamed and all-consuming, like a lover's kiss.

◦ৡ৩ ৩ৡ◦

Not far from there, in the servants' wing, Mr. Darcy was just as lost in thought and there was nothing remotely pleasant in his ruminations. Elizabeth's unwillingness to cast him more than a passing glance when they were reunited in the entrance hall had chilled him to the bone with the fear that he had truly gone beyond the pale with the liberties taken earlier that night – and had shocked her dreadfully with his appalling conduct.

That he himself had also been shaken to his core by hideous fears regarding her encounter with Trevellyan and his men was supremely irrelevant – although, even then, Darcy shuddered at the recollection. A dark curtain of boiling blood seemed to have settled on his brain during those awful moments, when all he wanted was to tear at Trevellyan and his band of beasts with his bare hands!

And then the relief, the blessed certainty that the scream in the woods had no sinister meaning; that he had jumped to horrible conclusions, and she was unharmed!

The transition from one state to the other was enough to unhinge any man – but this was no excuse for behaving and speaking to her as if she had accepted his offer of marriage! No wonder she was too uncomfortable to even look at him.

And yet…

"This way, Sir," the housekeeper indicated and Darcy followed with John on his heels, endeavouring to make some sense of very different, breathtaking recollections.

Elizabeth in his arms, stroking his hair, his face, responding to his kisses. As though she *had* changed her mind about him! Or as though she had just been transported by the nerve-wracking succession of events that had assailed her in a single day, only to regret it when the whirlwind settled…?

With a sinking feeling, Darcy felt compelled to own that her withdrawal from him since their return to the house seemed to indicate the latter.

Unless it was just a sign of self-conscious discomfort…?

Damnation! How was one to guess the substance of another's thoughts and feelings?

He drew a deep breath and straightened his back. He would certainly not find the answers skulking in the servants' quarters, so the sooner he concluded his business here, the sooner he might know.

"Mrs. Polmere, what is the meaning of this, pray? Who are these men?" a voice rang before him and the housekeeper stopped to explain the reasons for their presence to the irate old fellow who turned out to be Mrs. Pencarrow's butler.

With a half-hearted apology directed at Darcy, the older man eventually let them continue on their way to the servants' entrance, where John was to be left with a lamp, a chair and a very stout cudgel. Before returning to the others, Darcy felt that a few words of appreciation were decidedly in order, so he turned to his man with a steady glance.

"I am obliged to you, John, for willingly undertaking all manner of duties that go far and beyond those you were engaged for. I shall not forget it," he said simply and the other offered a deep bow.

"'Tis a privilege to serve you, Sir. I thank you," the younger man warmly retorted, palpably grateful for the recognition. "I shall endeavour not to fail you this time," he earnestly added, to Darcy's surprise.

"What are you speaking of? You have not failed me – have you?"

The young man wistfully shook his head.

"You have done me great honour in allowing me to serve you as your valet for such a length of time in Mr. Norwood's absence, but *he* would not have made such a ghastly mistake!"

"What mistake?" Darcy prompted, mystified.

"Turning you out for the ball as a copy of his lordship, Sir! I should have sensed that something was amiss when Lord Trevellyan's valet was reluctant to allow me the choice of mask for you, but – "

"So the mask and the attire was *your* choice, not Lord Trevellyan's?" Darcy interjected without thinking.

"Of course, Sir," his man replied, clearly nonplussed at the intimation that his lordship would go as far as choosing his guests' attire for the ball.

"I see. Well, no harm done. Do not trouble yourself about it," Darcy replied with feigned unconcern, slightly put out by his own slip of the tongue.

More unsettling still, he could not fail to note that he had been wrong twice in one day about Trevellyan. He was humbly grateful for it of course, at least in *one* instance in particular – but it did make him wonder what else he might have been in the wrong about.

With a nod to his man, Darcy made his way towards the parlour, hoping against hope that, as far as Elizabeth was concerned, he would have the wits or the good fortune to do *something* right!

Chapter 19

It was not going well – nothing was – though why the blazes he had ever hoped it would, Darcy could not tell. There could never be a more damnably uncomfortable situation. All four, sitting together in the too quiet parlour – and not an ounce of comfort to be had!

She would not even meet his eyes, but kept hers trained on the confounded square of linen she was embroidering – and so did her sister, who attended to some crochet-work with uncommon zeal.

They were to be envied, Darcy thought with a frustrated sigh, wishing there was something *he* could do to hide the acute discomfort or temper the vexation at not being able to speak to her alone.

He all but snorted. Taking up needlework was sadly not an option, so he stood to pester the fire in the grate again.

"Leave it be, Darcy, I beg you! It was doing well enough," Bingley grumbled from his own seat, clearly labouring under the same frustrations.

His gruff admonition made the sisters look up and, for the most fleeting, most unrewarding moment, Darcy caught her eye. And then she looked away in the same instant, a fierce blush making her cheeks glow.

Darcy's hand tightened on the fire-poker. She would not look at him for longer than a second! She had not glanced in his direction for over a half-hour, ever since he had rejoined them in the parlour.

'You had to kiss her, you unmitigated fool!' Darcy belatedly chastised himself – yet breath still caught in his chest at the exquisite recollection, no matter how ill-judged it might have been.

If they could only *talk!* If only he could get her alone for a few moments. And say what? Apologise, of course – and then? Tell her that he would always love her? Beg her to reconsider – or at least let him court her? *Beg?* Aye, beg, by Jove! On bended knee, if that would help!

He put the fire-poker back where it belonged, absent-mindedly rubbing the dent it had left into his palm, all too aware that although *she* started at the sudden clatter, this time she did not as much as look up. It was Miss Bennet who did, ever so briefly, then she set her crochet-work aside.

"We should see if our aunt is still resting. Hopefully the pains have not returned to trouble her," she said quietly, only to be met with Elizabeth's ready acquiescence.

Darcy's heart sank at her eagerness to leave – although in truth he could scarce blame her. A glance at Bingley only served to show that he was equally distressed by the thought that the woman he loved desired nothing more than to leave his presence. His friend stood and bowed and he did likewise as the ladies glided to the door. Elizabeth walked out first and, with a deep sigh of frustration, Darcy turned to pester the fire yet again.

From his own spot, Bingley began to mutter some complaint. He might have saved his breath. A moment later, Darcy lost all interest in the fire. His glance flew to the doorway, as soon as he heard Elizabeth's exclamation of surprise:

"Good heavens! Mr. Wickham! Whatever brings *you* here in the middle of the night?"

Fire-iron still in hand, Darcy darted to the door.

ೕಲ ಲ಄

With a muted curse, Wickham spun around. Despite the horrific urgency of the situation, he involuntarily spared a thankful thought to roaring fires and sheer petticoats and muslin dresses, as the well-tended fire behind her outlined Miss Elizabeth's shapely legs in the most pleasing manner.

He cursed again, inwardly this time, the rounded oath encompassing the night's events, his useless companions and the harebrained scheme that had kept him otherwise engaged ever since his arrival in this part of the country – when he would have been better advised to show himself at Landennis at least a fortnight sooner and then call every day and do his utmost to secure her hand in marriage.

She looked incredibly enticing, just as she had a few weeks ago, when he had spied upon her from the cliffs overlooking the secluded beach in Landennis Cove.

If anything, her allure was greater than ever, now that he knew the tasty morsel came with a plump dowry – all wrapped up in a neat, delicious package.

Yet it was not his fault that he had not pursued her, any more than all his past misfortunes had ever been his fault.

As always, it was *Darcy's*. Had it not been for his Nemesis suddenly appearing on his very doorstep, he would have found the time to court her, regardless of his other duties. Besides, Penderrick had been overjoyed to hear that his newly-appointed steward could claim an acquaintance with the people at Landennis and could use that connection to their overall advantage to learn as much as possible of Trevellyan's suspicions and intentions.

But then Darcy, damn him, had turned up again like the proverbial bad penny and, true to form, had hastened to poke his nose in other people's business and advise Penderrick that he, Wickham, was not to be trusted. They got a good laugh out of *that* at least, Penderrick and himself.

Still, this was poor consolation in the face of his current troubles. Tonight's harebrained scheme was shot out of the water – literally – and he was saddled with a dim-witted servant and an injured patron, his own share of the loot depending on the latter's safety, and the dangers of detection had just increased tenfold, now that the delectable Miss Elizabeth had happened upon them.

His mind working faster, Mr. Wickham sifted through his options – until a particular dark figure burst out of the parlour and increased his difficulties a hundredfold.

⁂

With a groan, Mr. Penderrick removed his hale arm from around his steward's shoulders and Wickham eased him onto the steps behind them before drawing out his cutlass with a swift, fluid motion.

That useless rogue, Mawgan, had darted out of the door instead of turning back to assist his master, presumably in the hope of absconding before Miss Elizabeth recognised him and exposed him for the turncoat that he was. It would not serve him well. Penderrick would not forgive his cowardly desertion and besides, the fellow who had just darted after him – *Damme! Was that Bingley?* – seemed to be moving rather too fast for comfort.

But Mawgan's fate mattered not one jot and – although he took in everything that happened on the sidelines, as was befitting of a man of his experience and skill – Wickham's eyes remained trained on his chief opponent, who stood before him poised to lunge and just as carefully assessing his own chances. Wickham grinned and could not deny himself the vast pleasure to taunt him.

"Lo and behold," he sneered. "What have we here? I do believe 'tis the knight in shining armour armed with a fire-iron! Always in the wrong place at the wrong time, Darcy, and ill-prepared as well. How do you think your pitiful poker would fare against my blade?" Wickham sneered again and apparently succeeded in giving the other pause, for he saw Darcy swiftly casting around for a better weapon.

Taking advantage of his foe's momentary distraction, Wickham lunged and struck but Darcy, devil take him, had impeccable reflexes! The fire-iron parried the vicious blow – and might have also dented his blade in the process, Wickham noted with an oath. Well, be that as it may! Darcy could duel with a poker if it pleased him, but he would have the devil of a job skewering anyone with the blunt, crude weapon, Wickham smirked. Yet his smug self-satisfaction faded once his opponent turned and twisted, skilfully avoided yet another blow and lunged to grab a blade from the positively medieval display that Mrs. Pencarrow had chosen to adorn her great hall with – to Wickham's detriment and disappointment.

The damned thing was not even secured on the wall and readily came off the panoply into Darcy's hand as the maligned poker clattered to the floor.

It seemed it was now Darcy's turn to goad him.

"You were saying, Wickham?" he shot back with a curl of his lip that his childhood playmate would have dearly loved to reshape with a cutlass.

With a loud grunt, Wickham lunged again, giving his best strike, but blade met blade in yet another parry, and he could only hope that his enemy's weapon was a mere ornament devoid of substance or blunted by disuse and age.

To his ill-fortune, it was nothing of the sort.

'This must be the stuff of nightmares,' Elizabeth thought, overcome with terror, as the scene before her erupted into violent commotion, the sickening clash of metal against metal echoing in the vast empty hall. Hands pressed against her mouth in agonising fear, she watched them lunge, thrust, feint and lunge again, the poor light from the few guttering candles making the scene more terrifying still. Not for herself, not for her own safety but *his*, Good Lord, for *his!*

How could she have been so blind, so dreadfully blind and dense? Why did she need to see him facing mortal peril to understand at last how much he meant to her?

Was she so devoid of reason and imagination that she had to witness this primeval scene before she understood that her whole world would plunge into grief-filled darkness if anything befell him?

She gasped and barely suppressed a whimper when Wickham's blade slashed violently through the air, right through the spot where Mr. Darcy had stood a fraction of a second earlier, and caught the doorframe instead, biting savagely into the aged wood.

For a brief moment it seemed that the cutlass would remain embedded, but the splintered wood promptly gave way at Wickham's forceful tug. His blade freed, he thrust again at his opponent, who skilfully parried, only to be shoved into a large suit of armour that collapsed with an almighty clatter to the floor, and Darcy with it.

Gripped with horror, Elizabeth saw him roll away from the scattered heap of metal, narrowly avoiding yet another blow. Sparks flew off the flagstones laid before the fireplace as the cutlass clashed viciously against them, yet seemed to remain unaffected by the impact. Wickham raised it yet again, and the following blow was frightfully more accurate. It was just the breastplate of the suit of armour, swiftly picked up and used as a makeshift shield, that saved Mr. Darcy's skin – his life, even.

The blow parried, he forcefully threw the heavy breastplate at his foe. Despite Wickham's lightning-fast reflexes, it still grazed his head, sending him staggering back a step, and then another. The brief respite was all that Darcy needed to spring back to his feet, sabre in hand – and deadly. He lunged at Wickham, only to see him bending down as though to avoid the thrust – or retrieve something.

For a moment, it appeared that he was aiming to pick up the fire-iron that Darcy had so incautiously let drop.

And yet it was not so. Worse still, Wickham reached to produce a dagger from his boot instead, and thus the blow Darcy forcefully aimed at him was stopped by crossed cutlass and dagger – an impenetrable defence turned instantly into a dangerous double weapon. Parrying one and dodging the other, Darcy twisted and turned, visibly aiming to come within reach of the ornamented shield mounted on the wall, as part of Mrs. Pencarrow's display of knightly splendour – and it was just as clear that Wickham aimed to stop him.

All those fencing lessons had clearly paid off, the latter inwardly scoffed, for Darcy fought like the very devil, his blade seemingly slashing everywhere at once and so far deflecting all the blows and thrusts. They were now aimed in quick succession, with vicious accuracy and renewed vigour – for Wickham could think of no better impetus than seeing his reviled Nemesis at a disadvantage, his luck fast running out. Nay, fully out of luck already, he amended, and released a sharp bark of laughter when Darcy suddenly lunged towards the shield displayed behind him only to find that, unlike the sabre, it was firmly fixed, and would *not* come off.

As was frequently the case with Mr. Wickham, the one who laughs first rarely laughs best – for the dagger fiendishly thrust at his opponent found the stone wall instead and, to Wickham's dismay and the others' fierce gratification, unlike the cutlass this one did snap on impact, evening the odds once more and bringing an end to Mr. Darcy's disadvantage.

'*Keep him safe! Dear Lord, keep him safe!*' Elizabeth cried in silent prayer as blade met blade again and blow followed blow – yet a moment later it was her own safety that was brought into question as Wickham suddenly lunged in her direction, with the obvious cowardly intention of replacing a lost advantage with another and using her as a human shield.

She darted out of reach with plenty of time to spare, savagely pleased to catch Mr. Wickham's look of shocked frustration at having underestimated her agility and reflexes, and her heart lurched and twisted at the pleading panic in Mr. Darcy's voice, as he cried out to her, his eyes still trained on his opponent:

"Leave! Elizabeth, *leave*, I beg you!"

"'*Elizabeth*', is it?" Mr. Wickham taunted with a sneer, as he thrust again. "Good to know, Darcy. This is –… very good to know!" he grunted, his blows coming faster as he endeavoured to manoeuvre himself yet again in her direction.

"Leave, Elizabeth!" Mr. Darcy called out once more, yet although some form of reason told her she was placing him in greater danger with her presence, Elizabeth could not make herself obey.

Leave – and do what? Hide away in the parlour and not see, not know whether he was safe or not? Save herself and leave *him* to his fate?

'No, foolish girl!' whatever was left of her terrified senses screamed at her. *'Leave Mr. Wickham without the hope of a cowardly advantage and get help. Someone. Mr. Bingley – where was he? And Mr. Darcy's footman.'*

As soon as a modicum of sense gained the upper hand, Elizabeth lost no time to listen. Without a second thought, she darted to the corridor towards the servants' quarters.

She did not get far. Drawn by the commotion, the young man – *John?* – was approaching at a run and instantly dashed past her with Mrs. Pencarrow's ageing butler trailing far behind him, along with Mrs. Polmere and one of the girls.

Her spirits buoyed, Elizabeth gathered her skirts and ran back to the great hall ahead of the slower party – and arrived just in time to see Mr. Wickham felled by the impact with Mr. Darcy's sword-hilt, once it met his jaw with a rewarding sound. The footman's cudgel, unerringly finding Wickham's skull a second later, was mere icing on the cake but no less gratifying, as was the sight of the rogue's limp form crumbling to the floor.

A loud sob broke free of her chest and Elizabeth reached behind her for support as tears of thankful, fervent joy welled in her eyes to behold *him* standing – safe, alive and well! She did not stop to think. She ran to him, as the first woman must have run to the man who fought for her and won. She would have clasped his hand in hers, but for the fact that he seemed unable to spare either. One was still gripping the hilt of his weapon and the other was clasped hard upon his shoulder – so Elizabeth dropped her own hands to her side and breathlessly asked:

"Are you safe? He has not injured you, has he?"

"I am well. I thank you – all is well. But what of *you?*' he inquired swiftly, his glance sweeping anxiously over her as though to reassure himself that she was unharmed.

"Do not concern yourself, nothing befell me. I am – " she hastened to reply, then gasped as her eyes fell away from the dark, mesmerising intensity she had found in his, only to catch sight of his red-stained fingers, still clamped on his upper arm. The sombre hue of his coat had previously concealed it, but against the whiteness of his skin the dark red stood out – as did the staggering truth.

"You *are* injured!" she gasped again, this time in horror. "Your arm! How badly – ?"

"'Tis nothing," he hastily cut in. "A flesh wound, nothing more."

"But you must – "

"Darcy!" Mr. Bingley vexingly cried out, drawing them from the far more pressing matter.

She had not even kept track of Mr. Bingley's whereabouts, had not even noticed him darting out of the front door when the commotion had erupted, but she could see him now, dragging the limp form of the third miscreant, whom he must have managed to subdue outside. Although far more basic, his methods must have been just as effective – the burden he dropped unceremoniously to the floor stood testament to that – and it appeared that Mr. Bingley had received his own fair share, judging by the bloodied and bruised marks that graced his handsome features.

From her own place by the front door, Jane gasped in her turn as soon as she caught sight of him in the candlelight. Her countenance showed clearly how grateful she was that Mr. Bingley's superior pugilistic skills had allowed him to gain the upper hand over his opponent. She must have followed Mr. Bingley when he had dashed outside, drawn just like Elizabeth by the instinctive need to reassure herself of her beloved's safety – however backward both of them had been to recognise the true depth of their feelings until tested by severe danger. The sisters exchanged warm, unsteady glances, still overcome by the lingering effects of the night's terrors, as much as by their own epiphanies.

Around them, the men were aiming to bring at least *some* events to their conclusion.

"We must secure the scoundrels," Mr. Bingley spoke up and it appeared that the tasselled cords destined to hold curtains in place were equally effective in trussing up Mr. Wickham, Mr. Bingley's charge – who, shockingly, was revealed to be Mawgan – and for good measure, the pale, weak form of Mr. Penderrick.

In comparison, the latter had caused but little trouble. He had merely tried to make it to the door, but had soon staggered and was now fallen over, unable to get by without assistance. A brief inspection showed an injury to his chest, which he must have acquired earlier in the evening, presumably related to the comings and goings in the woods that night.

"Splash some water over them, John, would you?" Mr. Darcy instructed. "And then we might find out what this is all about."

A voice – her own – rang loudly, taking Elizabeth completely by surprise.

"All this can wait! They can be questioned later. We should look to your injury, Mr. Darcy."

She could not meet his eyes for above a moment, but briskly proceeded to spur the party into the desired course of action.

"We should return to the parlour, the light is better there. And we must have some water. Nay, Mrs. Polmere, you need not go yourself, Tressa can fetch some for me. Would you go instead and see how my great-aunt is faring? Sarah must be with her still, and I suppose she would have told us if there were any changes, but I would rest easier to know that you have checked. Mr. Perren, if you would kindly remain here and assist Mr. Darcy's man in keeping an eye on these people," she added, largely to make their butler feel of use – for there was little doubt that John, at less than half his age, would have no trouble in maintaining single-handed control over the situation.

Just as she had intended, the older man looked grimly pleased.

"I shall go fetch my blunderbuss, Ma'am," he announced and moved away, swiftly for his years. He shot Mr. Penderrick a dark glare as he hurried past him. "I never would have thought it of you, Sorr! Never – if I live ter be a hundred!"

Still smiling at the thought of the belligerent Mr. Perren rushing to fetch his blunderbuss, Elizabeth finally turned to Mr. Darcy. Her brisk confidence wavered as their eyes met again. Unnerved, she looked away from his distracting countenance to his injured shoulder and quietly prompted:

"Would you come into the parlour, Sir? We really must see to that!"

Just as she half-expected, he resisted.

"You are very kind, but it can wait. I am well – "

"And you shall be even better for having that wound bandaged," Mr. Bingley interjected.

"It can wait," Mr. Darcy stubbornly repeated. "We must secure the house, there might be others above-stairs, and I would dearly like to know what those three were doing here," he muttered darkly.

Quite reassured to have seen them descend from the disused wing and not the one that housed her great-aunt's apartments, Elizabeth hastened to object, but Mr. Bingley was there before her.

"I daresay you can hold your curiosity in check until we have ensured that you keep your blood inside you," he said abruptly and then lost his patience. "Come now, Darcy! Can you not do as you are told for once, and leave off being so bull-headed?"

Curling his lip in distaste at his friend's comment, Mr. Darcy was at last persuaded to make his way into the parlour, along with Mr. Bingley, Elizabeth and her sister.

"Sit there, pray," Elizabeth indicated towards the sofa nearest to the table, then brought more candles and begun to light them.

Towering over his friend for once, Mr. Bingley took charge of the situation.

"Here. Let me remove your coat."

Unable to stop herself, Elizabeth raised her eyes from her employment to watch the obviously painful process and bit her lip to see his handsome features twist and tighten as the well-fitting coat was finally pulled off, along with the waistcoat.

It suddenly crossed her mind that she had never seen Mr. Darcy quite so informally attired. Not even at Netherfield, when she had wandered into the wrong part of the house and found him playing billiards in his shirtsleeves – there was still a waistcoat *then*. The intruding thought lingered, along with the recollection of that distant evening, but both were instantly dismissed a moment later, once she caught sight of the large bloodstain spread widely around a slit in the fine lawn.

"Hm," Bingley muttered. "I should have thought of that. The shirt must come off too. Ladies, would you...?" he tentatively asked turning towards them and, despite her overriding concern for Mr. Darcy's injury, Elizabeth could not fail to blush.

She looked away from the arm that had commanded her attention.

"Of course," she whispered, but Darcy's stern tones stopped her in her tracks.

"Enough, Bingley! Pray leave my shirt be!"

His friend began to protest:

"Then how can I get to – ?"

"There!" Darcy cut him off, reaching to find the bloodied edges of the slit.

With a wince, he forcefully tore the lawn away, then tore again.

It was Elizabeth's turn to wince, once the gash was fully exposed.

"Where is that girl... Tressa?" she stammered. "She was supposed to bring some water. Jane, could you see what is keeping her?"

Her sister did not seem to wonder at the request, nor question why Elizabeth was not going herself, presumably quick to understand that nothing but extreme necessity could have made her leave the parlour. Jane nodded and was about to do as bid when the door opened and young Tressa came in, with nary a glance to the bowl she was carrying, for her eyes were darting excitably around the room to fully take in the novel scene before her. Elizabeth rushed to take the bowl from her – only to splash as much as Tressa over Mrs. Pencarrow's floorboards, not that anybody present cared one whit about them anyway.

"Did you not bring a cloth?" Elizabeth promptly questioned.

"Nay, Miss," the girl answered, hard to tear her glance from the unprecedented sight of an injured gentleman sitting on old Mrs. Pencarrow's sofa. Half-hoping, for his sake, that he was not about to bleed to death, much as *that* would have compounded the excitement, Tressa returned to the matter at hand and swiftly added, "I didn't know ye'd be needin' one, Miss, but I can go fetch somethin'– "

"No, never mind," Elizabeth impatiently waved the suggestion aside. The handkerchief she had half-heartedly embroidered would serve just as well, she inwardly determined, and swiftly picked it from the table to soak it in the bowl of water.

"Thank you," she cast over her shoulder towards the fidgeting girl, then added, much to the latter's disappointment, "You may go now. See if Mrs. Polmere is in need of your assistance," she instructed, then lost all interest in the reluctantly retreating maid and came to sit beside Mr. Darcy on the sofa. "Pray, allow me, Sir," she breathlessly urged, but he shook his head.

"No need to ruin it..."

"It does not signify!" she declared firmly and with the greatest gentleness she reached to dab the wound.

The handkerchief turned red in an instant and so did her fingers and Elizabeth bit her lip again, striving to conquer the sudden ache deep into the pit of her stomach at the sight and scent of blood – *his* blood. She glanced up only once to meet his eyes and found something there, not pain, but something infinitely more unsettling. She looked away. With suddenly trembling fingers, she rinsed the cloth and dabbed the deep cut, then dabbed again, her hand conspicuously unsteady.

She all but started when Mr. Bingley spoke very close beside her:

"'Tis not bleeding quite so much now. You were in luck, Darcy. It seems 'tis but a flesh wound."

"Aye. That was what I thought," the answer came, in an uneven voice.

"I should imagine stitches are in order. Your embroidering skills might come in handy, Miss Elizabeth," Bingley observed lightly, making her gasp.

"Surely, Sir, you are not in earnest! Are you?" she asked in near-panic, dropping the cloth in the now blood-red liquid in the bowl.

"He is not!" Darcy all but growled at his friend. "The doctor can see to it when he arrives."

"The doctor! Oh, where, *where* is he?" Elizabeth exclaimed, unable to take her eyes off the hideous gash.

"Pray rest easy," Darcy urged. "A bandage would serve well enough for now."

"Aye! A bandage!" Elizabeth spoke up, gratefully gripping hold of the returning shreds of common sense. "What – ?"

"This should do," he suggested, reaching for his neckcloth.

Unfastening it single-handedly was clearly a challenge, so Elizabeth said softly:

"Here. Let me do that," she offered in a conscious whisper, her fingers coming up to replace his.

Yet she found herself equally unable to prevail over that most intricate knot. Vexingly, her hands would not stop trembling and worse still, despite all efforts, her eyes would not stay trained on the work of her unsteady fingers. Instead, ever so often, with a mind of their own, they would flash up to his face – so near. Nevertheless, she stubbornly persisted, her brow creased in concentration – until her glance darted up again, and encountered his.

Her hands stilled and breath caught in her chest as yet another strange ache stirred within her, along with the sharp yearning to stroke his face and somehow remove the look of sadness from his eyes. She saw his lips move, saw them form her name, yet no sound came, and the constriction in her throat grew tighter. She felt her cheeks blaze, hotter and then hotter still, and did not even try to fight the recollection of the same lips tasting, crushing hers.

Good Lord, what sort of madness was taking hold of her – was ruling her already? Had she no shame, no decency, no sense of decorum? How could she have become so lost to her surroundings and to every given precept, to the point of wanting *nothing* quite as much just now than leaning closer still, to press her lips on his?

She tore her eyes away and looked back to her useless hands, applying herself to the vexing knot with renewed vigour. It gave way at last and the crisp white cloth finally came undone. With swift determination, she proceeded to unwrap it from around his neck – only to unsettle herself even further as her fingers reached to loosen the starched cloth and brushed against his skin and the thick set of curls she had caressed without any restraint earlier that evening.

She withdrew her hands with a start and a faint gasp and, blushing fiercely, she straightened up and leaned away, her fingers tingling with the delicious sensation and with the shocking urge to tangle themselves in his hair again.

His hand came up and finished the unnerving task for her – and it was no less unnerving to see his throat fully exposed now, the prominent Adam's apple rising as he swallowed hard. He raised his eyes to hers but seemed as self-conscious about offering the neckcloth to be used as bandage as she was to take it.

In the end Elizabeth reached out, still blushing but determined that necessity should override any foolish feeling arising from the unsettling intimacy of tending to his bare injured arm. The eyes met again, and she leaned closer.

"Would you raise your arm a little?" she asked in a whisper.

With a promptly suppressed wince he did as bid, and Elizabeth saw him swallow hard again when her fingers brushed over his hale skin as she endeavoured to apply the bandage.

She did not get far. With a disgruntled huff, Mr. Bingley intervened.

"Here, Miss Elizabeth. Let me do that for you," he said gruffly and met Darcy's glare with a matching frown.

"No, I – " Elizabeth protested, wondering in passing if Mr. Bingley's offer was aimed to preserve his friend from her clumsy efforts – or whether it just stemmed from nothing more than envy.

"I insist!" Bingley retorted, his tone and mien giving weight to the latter suspicion and, although vexed as much as diverted, Elizabeth thought it best to let him have his way.

She rose from the sofa, her place taken by Mr. Bingley, who proceeded to wrap the neckcloth around the injured arm rather less gently than the circumstance required. Mr. Darcy's glare turned into a wince and a fierce scowl when the knot was tied with undue force.

"There! That should serve for now," Bingley said matter-of-factly, only to receive another glare.

"Much obliged, Bingley! How very thoughtful of you," Mr. Darcy muttered, his voice dripping with sarcasm, to receive a matching retort of "Any time!"

"What of your own injuries, Sir?" Jane quietly asked. "There must be some lukewarm water in the tea-urn and another cloth somewhere…"

Mr. Bingley reached up to tentatively touch his cheekbone, his countenance clearly indicating that he would like nothing better than being attended in the same fashion as his friend had been.

Yet the said friend was very prompt to offer:

"Indeed. I should return the favour and see to that bruised cheek of yours," he said tersely, giving Mr. Bingley the distinct impression that in fact he would willingly supply another bruise instead.

"I would much rather not, if it is all the same to you," the younger man retorted as he stood.

Despite herself, Elizabeth's lips twitched at their boyish antics. Her warm glance met Darcy's and his deep scowl vanished. For a glorious moment, all the awkwardness between them melted into the delicious comfort of a shared diverted smile – and then she blushed again and looked away.

Darcy cleared his voice.

"We should see to the miscreants out there," he observed, only to glance instinctively to the door as loud commotion suddenly erupted yet again in the great hall. "What the devil – …?"

But before he could stand or at least apologise for the uncontrolled expletive, the door was thrown open and Lord Trevellyan burst in. His first glance was for Elizabeth, and it was her he rushed to and swiftly clasped her hand.

"You are unharmed! Thank goodness! Good Lord, I should have *known!*"

From his sofa, Mr Darcy raised a brow, but did not comment.

It was Lord Trevellyan who acknowledged him first.

"Mr. Darcy! Thank heavens you were here! I should have –… No matter. So it was you who subdued those rogues."

"With Bingley's aid," was all that Darcy offered, not backward to give credit where it was due.

"What on earth happened here?" another voice rang out and a sturdy gentleman in his middle age joined them from the great hall. "I thought I was summoned to attend Mrs. Pencarrow, but I find another battlefield instead."

Something in his manner told Elizabeth this was the doctor rather than the apothecary, and Lord Trevellyan's words soon came to prove her right.

"Aye. A busy night, Dr. Polkerris. How is your great-aunt faring, Miss Elizabeth?"

"She was resting peacefully an hour ago, my lord," Jane replied instead and, from behind them, Mrs. Polmere spoke up to give more information.

"I just came down from her chamber and she is still asleep."

"Asleep or unconscious?" the doctor brusquely differentiated, but Mrs. Polmere had too much sense to take offence.

"Asleep, Sir, I am sure of it. She has had no more pains since Miss Bennet and I have persuaded her to take some of the draughts you ordered last time."

"Well! Good to know, at least. Then I shall check on her shortly–"

"What of the rogues outside?" Lord Trevellyan asked.

"Penderrick seems stable enough. He is weak from the blood loss, but his injury was adequately seen to. Who attended him?"

"I have no notion. What of the others?"

"What ails them?"

"Nothing that a pitcher of cold water cannot cure," Mr. Bingley muttered. "A few blows apiece. They should come round soon, if they have not already."

"They have," Mrs. Polmere interjected, "but they seem under good regulation. That young man, John, is still seeing to that. And Mr. Perren, with his blunderbuss," she added and Elizabeth's lips twitched again to hear it.

"Well then, I – " the doctor began, but Elizabeth intervened.

"Would you kindly see to Mr. Darcy's injury first, Dr. Polkerris? The wound is quite extensive and it requires your attention."

"No need, not now," Mr. Darcy protested, only to find himself under the scrutiny of several pairs of eyes.

"I daresay you should let *me* be the judge of it, Sir," the doctor remarked with some distemper, then dropped his bag on a nearby chair and came to undo the makeshift bandage.

"There is no rush!"

"Would you be still, Sir!" the doctor admonished gruffly, the long night's toil having presumably brought him to the limits of his patience.

"Miss Elizabeth? May I have a private word?" she heard Lord Trevellyan speak quietly, close to her ear, and could not fail to notice Mr. Darcy looking up sharply, his brow quizzically raised again.

Her eyes moved from his face to his exposed shoulder and remained steadfastly fixed there. She did not look away – not even when Lord Trevellyan felt obliged to repeat his question.

"Of course, my lord. In a short while," was all that she could offer, her attention barely spared from the doctor's ministrations. "I trust it can wait."

Lord Trevellyan sighed.

"Aye, Miss Elizabeth. I daresay it can…"

Chapter 20

The doctor's hands moved swiftly and with purpose. All was in readiness now – needle, thread and scissors, and clean cloths in abundance, and many candles to give better light. Dr. Polkerris looked up from his preparations.

"Is there any brandy to be had, Ma'am?" he inquired of Elizabeth – the only one who had chosen to remain behind.

Her brows shot up and the doctor grumbled.

"Not for myself, needless to say. The gentleman should down some. It will dull his senses."

But the gentleman did not want his senses dulled – not if, heaven forefend, tonight was to be the last he was allowed to spend in her presence.

"I do not need it," Darcy said firmly and at that, the doctor scowled.

"I think you should go, Ma'am," he declared and, despite his own wishes on the matter, Darcy inwardly concurred, unwilling to have her witness anything that might give her unease.

Elizabeth's reply came without hesitation.

"I am not leaving!"

Darcy opened his lips to play devil's advocate, but did not get the chance. The doctor spoke up first.

"I wish you would," he observed sternly. "Your presence causes the gentleman to be heroic – and after a night such as I had, I have no time for heroes or for swooning misses."

His own discomfort notwithstanding – bodily and otherwise – Darcy's lips twitched at the flash of outraged defiance in her eyes.

"Fear not, Sir, I am *not* about to swoon!" she all but hissed and walked with purpose to the drinks tray to fill a glass almost to the brim with brandy.

She brought it back, her stare fixed on the amber liquid, until she came to stand before him, and her eyes sought his. She offered the full glass, her glance warm and pleading.

"I beg you would not try to be heroic," she said softly and smiled when, after the slightest hesitation, Darcy took it from her and drained it in a few long draughts.

"Good. Another," was the doctor's only comment and another dose was duly brought and taken.

Darcy leaned his head against the backrest and closed his eyes.

"Do you need assistance?" he heard her ask a little later, as though from a great distance.

She was not speaking to him but to Dr. Polkerris who muttered something about requiring a fresh bowl of water. He heard her swiftly walk away, her footsteps a soft patter on the wooden floor, and back again. His head already swimming with the blasted brandy, he forced his eyes to open to a blurry vision of her, the doctor, and far too many candles.

"We should begin now, Sir. Are you ready?"

Darcy nodded – only to grit his teeth a moment later, when the sharp pain in his right shoulder came to show that the brandy made little or no difference. He took a hissing breath and swallowed.

"Are you well, Sir?" the doctor needlessly inquired and Darcy could not quite bite back a dry retort.

"Never better!"

The other man chuckled, riling him in no small measure, until the feel of a small hand clasping his removed the doctor from his mind – and went a long way in soothing the hellish pain as well. Darcy's eyes flashed open to find her very close, sitting at his side on a corner of the sofa.

"Hold my hand," she whispered, but he shook his head.

"I do not wish to hurt you," he said with great difficulty and cursed the brandy yet again, as he heard himself slur the words.

"No matter," Elizabeth eagerly replied, only to send the doctor into another fit of passion:

"What is it about tonight that keeps prompting heroics?" he exclaimed. "Bring a chair, would you, Ma'am? Or something else that he could grip. It would do just as well – or even better."

She did bring something.

It felt like some wooden object in his hand and Darcy gripped it for the duration of the lengthy torture, until Dr. Polkerris saw fit to cease using him as a pincushion and put the finishing touches on his injured shoulder, including a firm bandage.

Darcy muttered something he hoped would convey his thanks, his senses dulled even further now that his skin was no longer pierced in quick succession. He heard some sort of clatter, then their voices, low and distant, but he could not make out the words and he eventually stopped trying.

If this was the lull before more pain, then so be it, he tiredly acknowledged with a sigh, grateful for its temporary absence from both his shoulder and his heart.

His eyes still closed, he drifted. There were no dreams of her, yet her sweet fragrance stayed with him, deliciously persistent, as though she were no further than a step away.

৩৫ ৩৫

She was.

She did not dare stir, just sat beside him, her eyes trained on the beloved features, softened in repose after the gruelling trial. She winced at the recollection – the hideous half-hour when she sat and watched Dr. Polkerris perform his task and tend to the injury that Mr. Darcy had incurred in his endeavours to protect her.

She shivered as she thought of it – that frightful time of peril, when she had helplessly witnessed his violent confrontation with that repulsive Mr. Wickham. She felt the sting of tears and fought to banish the excruciating guilt brought on by the very different wound she herself had inflicted, earlier that morning.

Would he forgive her for it?

Was there still some hope for them after all? She prayed it was, otherwise she knew not how she could ever learn to bear it.

Blind! Prejudiced and blind, and woefully unaware of her feelings! Woefully unwilling to admit the salient truths, not even to herself: that she had taken such offence at his initial rejection because she had been drawn to him, from the first moments of their unorthodox acquaintance; that she had purposely steeled her heart against him, had persuaded herself to mistrust his avowals, for fear of allowing his power over her to grow and make her wretched if, in time, his interest in her waned.

She reached out with very careful motions to rearrange his coat, which she had draped over his reclining form as soon as the doctor left them... and lingered there, drawn by the bittersweet desire to run her fingers through his hair.

She reached a little further, her hand poised just above his brow, then paused... nervously curled her trembling fingers... – and promptly withdrew them with a start when the sound of the opening door rang unexpectedly behind her.

She turned – only to encounter Lord Trevellyan's steady gaze. He was standing in the doorway, frozen in his tracks, his grip still on the handle, his handsome features clouded with dismay.

"Forgive me, I –... " he quietly offered but, before he could withdraw and close the door, Elizabeth stood.

"The fault is mine, my lord. I have forgotten that you wished to have a word," she whispered, then indicated the connecting door at the far end of the parlour. "Shall we go into the library and leave Mr. Darcy to his rest?"

"Aye – by all means!" Lord Trevellyan retorted grimly and, taking a set of candles with her, Elizabeth led the way.

ഏറ ഇൈ

Although the candlestick was now resting safely on a nearby table, the flames still swayed and flickered, twisted this way and that by the swift air currents caused by the closing door.

They cast tremulous shadows over the shelves filled with dusty old tomes, hardly ever opened and slowly decaying in the all-pervading salty dampness that clung to the ancient house. The air was stale and musty, but it was the tension in it that made Elizabeth feel she could barely breathe.

One of the three flickering flames crackled with countless little sparks and swayed wildly, then went out with a hiss – and so did another, leaving the room darker still, and dreadfully oppressive.

She could hardly see Lord Trevellyan's face, for he stood away from her, in the shadows of the deep door-recess – until he suddenly walked up and took her hand.

Was it the flicker of the solitary candle that played tricks on tired eyes? Elizabeth rather doubted it, and her chest tightened at the raw feeling she detected in his exposed countenance.

"Can you ever forgive me for being a self-centred *fool?*" Lord Trevellyan began without warning, his voice deep and urgent. "I should not have left you! And yet I did, to chase after my own selfish interests. But you must believe me, I thought you were protected! I thought my men would ensure your safety. Fool that I was, I did not foresee there would be a turncoat at Landennis and he would overcome them. I should have seen it though – and I should have put your safety above all else, just as *he* did," his lordship concluded with sudden bitterness and at that, Elizabeth's cheeks flamed in a sudden, forceful blush.

Naturally, she knew without a doubt of whom he was speaking and the implications could not fail to distress her, as did his self-recriminations. She did not wish to cause anyone pain – yet she seemed doomed to do precisely that, at every turn. She despised herself for her cowardice but, rather than allowing him to continue in that vein, Elizabeth withdrew her hand as she asked quietly:

"Of what selfish interests are you speaking? I fear I do not understand you…"

His mien clouding further at her withdrawal – or her question – or both – his lordship sighed.

"Do you not?"

And then he squared his shoulders.

"Of course, there *would* be a great deal you do not understand and, to my misfortune, I failed to see that I should have been more forthright. This is not the time, particularly as I fear it shall not help my case – but be that as it may," he added with renewed bitterness. "You must hear the truth. I owe you as much."

"The truth, my lord?"

"Aye," he said, exhaling deeply. "And I might as well start at the beginning."

Yet he did not start, but raised his hand to rub his brow. Overcome with compassion at his obvious discomfort, Elizabeth quietly whispered.

"Would you care to sit?"

"I thank you, no. I – "

His lips tightened, then Lord Trevellyan drew a long, deep breath.

"So. The full truth, at last," he said, once more straightening his shoulders. "For a long time now, I suspected – nay, I *knew* that Penderrick was the mastermind behind the local smugglers. The ringleader if you will, offering them the protection of his estate, his connections and his strategic skills," he began and, now that the words had begun flowing, others followed without hesitation. "But recently I came to suspect that there was more – that it was worse than that. That he aimed a great deal higher than smuggling a few casks of tobacco and French brandy. In short, he was in league with the enemy and, under the guise of smuggling, documents were exchanged as well."

"A traitor!" Elizabeth whispered, horrified.

"Aye. A vile traitor, selling his country for thirty pieces of silver!" Lord Trevellyan burst out. "And tonight was my chance to prove it. You see, I knew that something was afoot. My men have kept an ear to the ground and learned that a ship was expected to come to the cove –… "

"Landennis Cove?"

"No. Too great risk of exposure. I imagined it would be Rosteague, halfway to the village. And so it was."

"You knew it was to be tonight?"

"No. I just knew it would be soon. But when the masks fell at the ball and I saw that Penderrick's wife had colluded with him and had passed a cousin of hers as her husband –… "

"Heavens! Was she part of Mr. Penderrick's schemes?"

"I know not, but I doubt it. He is not the man to trust too many with his secrets."

"And yet he trusted Mr. Wickham."

"Another one of my woeful errors! I had not seen in time where he came into it. My men were told to keep him in their sights of course, for no one in Penderrick's pay could be above suspicion. But I have only learned before the ball that he had called *here*. That he had come to renew an acquaintance with your family. Needless to say, I was very troubled. His connection to Penderrick could hardly recommend him! Yet I should have done more, learned more – and sooner! Until tonight, I had no notion of the true reason for their association!"

"And now you know it?"

"I do. Wickham was ostensibly employed as steward, but in fact he was to act as Penderrick's courier for the exchange of documents with his London connection."

"He told you that?"

"Oh, aye. Mr. Wickham was all too keen to incriminate his patron in the hope of a better fate. I spoke to him tonight, and to the others, while I was waiting for you to –... While I was waiting," he quietly amended.

Elizabeth bit her lip and once more cowardly sidetracked the conversation.

"What else have you learned?"

"Not everything, but enough to seal Penderrick's fate. With any luck, Monsieur De La Tour –... "

"I beg your pardon, who?"

"The French spy caught in the cove tonight. My men apprehended him and he was badly injured in the skirmish. This is why I needed Dr. Polkerris. De La Tour *had* to survive, to be coerced into bearing witness against Penderrick. It blinded me, this notion that I was so very close. It blinded me, Elizabeth, and even if you are willing to forgive me, I never shall forgive myself!"

Her breath caught at the sudden intensity in his voice and at the free use of her Christian name.

"You must not – ..." she faltered.

"Blame myself?" he finished for her, although that was not what she was about to say. "But I do. How could I not, Elizabeth? Yet you must believe I thought you were protected! The men who escorted you, your sister and Mrs. Pencarrow to Landennis had strict orders to remain in place and keep watch. Not Merryn, he was told to join those posted around the shoreline, but the other two. I never suspected they would be set upon by Mawgan."

"Set upon?"

"Aye. Mawgan confessed everything. Same as Wickham, he hopes for leniency if he owns the truth. It appears that he tried to sneak from the house after your arrival home with Mrs. Pencarrow and Miss Bennet, to join Penderrick and Wickham in the cove. He saw the men I posted at Landennis and approached them, one by one. They had no reason to mistrust him and apparently he had no trouble in subduing them with an unexpected blow, then tie them up and leave them out of sight in the outbuildings – "

"Have they been found? Are they well?"

"Well enough, but for large lumps to the head, bitter anger at their foe and a severe headache. The apothecary was found as well, by the bye."

"Where?"

"In the disused wing at Landennis, gagged and bound."

"The –... How?"

"It seems Penderrick was also injured in the fray. Mawgan and Wickham spirited him away, but did not dare take him to his house assuming, and rightly so, that it would be watched."

"So they brought him *here*? And the apothecary too?"

"Aye. Mawgan fetched him with the excuse that your old butler was unwell. He did not know of Mrs. Pencarrow's illness, he had sneaked out of the house too early for that. It was this lie that drew my notice, for why would a Landennis footman tell the apothecary's servant he was wanted for the butler, not his mistress? That was when I suspected the apothecary was summoned for a different reason than the one avowed. Besides, it struck me that, given the time when his man said he was called out, he should have long reached you and you would not have gone into the night to seek him. Elizabeth, I –..."

"But how did they get in?" she interjected. "The house was guarded again by that time..."

She mentioned no names, but Trevellyan's countenance darkened.

"Thank goodness that it was," he brought himself to say. "Yet they were unable to guard every entrance."

"But John was posted right outside the servants' door!"

"John? Oh, yes," he seemed to remember. "Mr. –... The other footman."

"Mr. Darcy's footman," Elizabeth thought it was time to say.

"Indeed... Anyway, Mawgan and his companions gained entry through the passage that leads from the outbuildings into the servants' quarters. John and... the two gentlemen were unaware of that."

"And so Mr. Penderrick was seen to at Landennis."

"Aye – the impudence! And the apothecary's folly to go along with sneaking into the house that way. But I daresay he was unaware of the commotion in the cove and, as he was told he had been summoned for the butler, he did not see much amiss in the manner of ingress. He says that it was only when they got to the disused wing that Wickham emerged from the shadows with Penderrick, and that he tended to the latter in fear of his life, for they threatened to run him through with their cutlasses if he raised the alarm. He was most grateful to be merely gagged and bound when the deed was done, and they left him above-stairs before attempting to sneak out of the house again. This time Mawgan went ahead, for his presence in the house would not raise suspicions. But he found that they could not follow the same route, as they would have had to walk past the servants' entrance, which was guarded from within by then."

"So he tried to smuggle them out the front. The sheer audacity! Where did they hope to go?"

"Penderrick had a scheme in place, and stashed funds as well, to get himself out of the country – if only he could make good his escape."

It was thanks to Mr. Darcy that he did not. A great deal more than that was owed to Mr. Darcy, Elizabeth knew full well and, judging by his mien, Lord Trevellyan knew also. His eyes clouded with the deepest sadness.

"I came too late, did I not, Miss Bennet?" he whispered and the formal address rang incongruously with the intimacy of the double-meaning question.

Her countenance turned wistful, her compassion overwhelming.

"I fear so, my lord," was all that she could whisper in her turn and winced to see his features darken with untold pain.

"I thought as much… But I needed to ask."

He looked up and his eyes bore into hers.

"Would it have made a difference if *I* was the one lying injured in that parlour?" he asked with great urgency, as though he could not stop himself.

"If – …"

She shivered. She wanted to say no – for this was the absolute truth at this precise moment, and shivered yet again at the suspicion that perhaps it *would* have made a difference, had Mr. Darcy not given proof of his devotion. Had he taken her at her word this morning, accepted her refusal and ridden away from Cornwall. Had he not shown her that he valued her wellbeing far above his pride and his own safety. Had he not returned to watch over her, kiss her, put himself in danger to protect her.

It did not bear thinking but, had circumstances been different, she might by now be giving her allegiance to Lord Trevellyan rather than Mr. Darcy, for she would not have had the chance to understand him and understand the deeper workings of her heart.

She did not say as much – what purpose would it serve? Yet he seemed to have read the answer in her eyes, for his filled with agonising sorrow.

"He is blessed with fortune, Miss Bennet," Lord Trevellyan said at length, with great difficulty. "I can only hope he knows it." His jaw tightened. "Forgive me, I must –... I shall leave you now."

And, with the deepest bow, he left her to the painful notion that she had deeply injured yet another worthy man that day.

ᴏᴏᴏ

Mr. Darcy did not feel in the least blessed with fortune. He awoke with a pounding, excruciating headache, not knowing where he was, nor why his head felt like all devils were beating drums inside it and were piercing his shoulder with their sharp claws for good measure. Yet the latter affliction soon helped clear his head to some extent and reminded him of the night's endeavours.

He sat up in panic and winced as vicious pain shot through him at the sudden move. Where was she? Was she safe? What happened while he lay there in brandy-induced stupor? Damn the doctor, he never should have listened to his gruff requests that he filled himself with the deuced stuff!

He straightened up, more carefully this time, and brought his hand up to gingerly explore his shoulder. It hurt like the very devil, but at least it was not throbbing – which must be a good sign.

He bent to retrieve his coat that had fallen to the floor when he sat up. Somebody must have draped it over him while he slumbered. The slashed sleeve was caked in blood, but it would have to do.

He spotted his waistcoat, neatly folded on the backrest, and he carefully eased his injured arm in it first, then the other, and buttoned it with some difficulty with only one hand. The coat would be more of a challenge, with an incapacitated arm and without John's assistance, but he eased his bad arm into the torn sleeve nevertheless and groaned as his clumsy attempts to force his good one into the other made the too tight coat press sharply on his wound.

"Blast!" he muttered and pondered giving up – when the door opened without warning, to reveal him to the woman of his dreams half-tangled in his own apparel like the veriest fool.

Darcy made to stand, but she was beside him before he could free himself from the wretched thing.

"Oh, let me help you!" she exclaimed, then added softly but with feeling. "You ought not try to tug the coat back on. 'Tis bound to hurt, the sleeve is much too tight. I daresay a sling might be in order…"

She paused and bent to help him extract his partially trapped hand from the tangled confines of the coat sleeve then, very gingerly, the coat was pulled off his injured arm. She straightened up and looked around for something that could be made into a sling, only to see that nothing would serve except the shawl she was wearing, lightly draped around her shoulders. She removed it promptly, even before Darcy could gather his wits about him and begin to form a civil protest.

The cream cashmere square adorned with a small paisley pattern was already folded into a triangle and she deftly tied the ends into a knot, then wordlessly indicated that it should go around his neck. The smooth fabric stroked his face in passing and he inhaled the floral scent still trapped in its soft folds. She held his coat to help him ease his hale arm in, and then carefully proceeded to guide his other one into the makeshift sling that seemed to have retained not only her deliciously distinctive scent, but her body-warmth as well.

Darcy did not speak – in any case, he doubted that he could – as the folds were rearranged around his elbow and then the coat was with great care brought up to rest over his injured shoulder.

She smoothed it, once it was gingerly draped thus, and Darcy's breath caught as her hand lingered on his lapel, then dropped away with something that his starved senses might have misconstrued as a light caress. She straightened up again and took a half-step back, and Darcy stood.

"I thank you," he consciously whispered.

"Do not regard it. How is your arm?"

"Well enough, considering. What of yourself?" he asked quickly. "And… all the others?"

"Fine. Everyone is fine – except perhaps Mr. Penderrick, Mawgan and Mr. Wickham," she added with a little chuckle, as though endeavouring to relieve the tension. "They are being carted off even as we speak."

"I see. Did you learn what brought them here?" he asked, not really caring, just casting for something that would keep her at his side.

"To some extent," she offered, then proceeded to give him a brief account of everything she knew. "And now they are secured – thanks to *you*, Sir. I... cannot begin to thank you, Mr. Darcy, for your generous assistance."

He frowned, as much at the unwelcome notion of her feeling beholden to him, as at the recollection of everything *else* that he had done – for which she would have precious little cause to thank him. He suddenly realised this was the first time they were alone together since their too short moments in the garden and Darcy's lips tightened at the uncomfortable thought that this might be his only chance to apologise.

"Think nothing of it," he offered quietly, then forced himself to continue. "While on the subject, I... I beg you would excuse my presumption and forgive me for... everything I did wrong tonight," he finished awkwardly, his eyes searching her beloved countenance for any sign that she might be willing to hear him out – though heaven knows what he was to say to plead his case without playing on her sense of obligation, of all cursed things!

Yet she would not look up, but stared down at her hands, a fierce blush creeping into her cheeks. She had caught his meaning, of that he was quite certain, and his heart sank at her withdrawal from him.

At last she spoke, but her glance was still elsewhere.

"There is nothing to forgive," she murmured, her voice the faintest whisper. "You did everything right tonight..."

Everything right! Good Lord, was she implying –...? If only he could meet her eyes! If only his head would cease this infernal pounding. Did she mean what he did not dare hope she meant?

"You are very kind," he tentatively offered, struggling to clear his head and avoid saying all the wrong things yet again.

What... *how* could he phrase it? Was there ever a safe way to ask the woman he could not live without, the woman who had refused his hand in marriage, whether she meant he had been in the right to take such liberties, to kiss her – without completely blasting whatever wisp of hope he might have had?

"I would give anything to turn back time and start afresh, without the dead-weight of my errors," he said instead, then burst out with undissimulated fervour: "I wish to God that we had met *tonight!*"

Her eyes shot up at that, and they were full of tears.

"Excuse me," she said breathlessly – then turned away and fled.

Darcy froze in shock, and shock gave way to anguish. The wrong words – again. Always the wrong words! *What* had he just said to make her run away in tears? What might he have said to make her stay… give him another chance?

The searing pain was overwhelming and Darcy turned to the door with a vicious scowl at the unwelcome sound of Bingley's voice.

"Darcy! Miss Elizabeth tells me you are back amongst the living," he quipped, inordinately cheerful, even for him.

There was no way for Darcy to know that his friend had reasons aplenty to be cheerful. A short while earlier, when the commotion had died out, he had the glorious chance of a private word with his beloved and he could scarce believe his luck, but the frozen agony between them was gone as though it never was. The beautiful angel had forgiven him. She was *his* beautiful angel once again, and had agreed to marry him!

Yet Darcy had no notion why Bingley was in such high spirits and could not care less – for Elizabeth had just followed his friend into the parlour, her eyes warm and smiling through her tears.

"How is your shoulder?" Bingley inquired but Darcy would not heed him, his anxiously searching gaze trained on *her* and her alone.

And then she spoke, her lips still curled up at the corners.

"Mr. Bingley, would you be so kind to introduce me to your friend?"

Their eyes locked and the smile they shared grew wider and then wider still, until it seemed to brighten their ill-lit surroundings.

None spared a glance for the flummoxed Mr. Bingley.

"I beg your pardon?"

"Humour the lady, Bingley," Darcy said, his eyes never quitting hers, heartfelt delight altering his features into something his companions had never seen before.

His brow raised, Bingley did as bid.

"Very well. Miss Elizabeth, may I introduce my strange and headstrong friend to your acquaintance. Darcy, this is Miss Elizabeth Bennet."

She curtsied to his very deep bow, the impish curl of her lips and the glow in her countenance robbing him of whatever was left of his senses. He barely heard the front door open, and it was only Mrs. Bennet's exceedingly loud voice that could reach him in the hazy splendour of the seventh heaven.

With a roll of her eyes, Elizabeth pursed her lips, but the playful smile returned as she curtsied once more.

"Delighted to make your acquaintance, Mr. Darcy," were her parting words, before she reluctantly went to attend her relations.

"Would you mind telling me what on earth was *that?*" Bingley asked as soon as they were left to their own devices, only to gape as the other turned to him grinning from ear to ear:

"That, my friend, is *hope!*"

٭٭٭

"Heavens above! Lord bless me! Just as his lordship said, and worse! But the girls – Mrs. Polmere, where are the girls? Lord Trevellyan assured me that they were unharmed, but –... Ah, Lizzy, there you are, thank goodness. And Jane, where is she? Is my dearest girl safe too? Lydia, Kitty, hush! Hush, I tell you!" she unfairly admonished, her voice easily carrying over all the others.

"But, Mamma –... " Kitty argued, her protestations drowned out by Lydia's impatient demands for detail and explanations, and even more so by their mother's tones, raising in pitch with every passing second.

"Good gracious!" she exclaimed. "Who would have thought? His lordship told us all about it when we crossed paths on our way home and I could scarce believe he was in earnest. Hush, Kitty! Oh, the rogues, the wretched devils, I hope they rot, or hang, or both! Lydia, hush, I can barely hear myself think. Look at that suit of armour scattered everywhere! Where is Jane, Lizzy? Is she well? Are *you?* Good gracious, I thought I should faint dead away when Lord Trevellyan told us what had happened. My poor, poor Jane! And you too, Lizzy. Oh! Oh! The spasms are back – the flutterings. Give me your arm, Mr. Bennet, the faintness is creeping up on me again. I need to sit. Where are –...? Oh, my smelling salts, where are they? Oh, Lizzy!"

The pandemonium her mother caused was worse than the noise and bustle of the duel, Elizabeth uncharitably thought – only to smile uncomfortably a moment later, rather ashamed of her own musings, as soon as Mrs. Bennet seemed to have forgotten all about the faintness and the smelling salts and flung her arms around her, clutching her to the maternal bosom.

229

The look in Mr. Bennet's eyes was a vast deal more affecting and a lump rose to Elizabeth's throat as her father rushed to clasp her hand even before she was released from Mrs. Bennet's bear-like embrace. In a blink of an eye she was in his arms instead and felt his whole frame shaking, as did his voice, low and rasping in her ear:

"My child… My child… Oh, the good Lord be praised! My Lizzy, you are safe!"

Tears welled in her eyes at the open display of feeling, quite unprecedented despite their long-acknowledged closeness.

"Dearest Papa! Rest easy – I am well."

"Truly?"

"Truly. I am well," Elizabeth repeated, only to let her arms drop from around her father's waist and pull away from his embrace as soon as her mother's next tirade reached her ears.

She was no longer in the hall, but had burst into the parlour, her loud exclamations testament to her elevated feelings:

"Mr. Darcy! Bless you, oh, Lord bless you, Sir, for preserving my beloved daughters," Elizabeth heard her mother cry and turned around just in time to see her flinging herself at Mr. Darcy and clasping *him* to her bosom too, with no restraint but with substantial vigour.

The look of stark surprise in Mr. Darcy's countenance was fleeting. No so the violent grimace of pain, and Elizabeth saw him bite his lip and heard the groan he could not quite suppress. Without a second thought, she rushed into the parlour.

"Mamma, have a care! He is injured. Oh, be careful!"

Amid Mrs. Bennet's flustered and profuse apologies intermingled with disjointed inquiries into his comfort, Mr. Darcy straightened and brought his hand up to his shoulder with another grimace before he forced himself to reassure the matron that he was well enough and he had taken no offence. Elizabeth's warm intervention and her readiness to come to his aid almost made him grateful for her mother's onslaught, as did their brief exchange of half-conscious, half-diverted glances and the lingering touch of her small hand soothingly laid on his uninjured arm.

As for Mrs. Bennet, she moved from one gentleman to the other.

"And poor Mr. Bingley too – just look at him! Dear, oh, dear," she exclaimed, clasping her hands together, having belatedly spotted him and his battle scars.

Mr. Bingley was not treated to a similar embrace, which left him to wonder whether this was because the lady had just learned her lesson – or because he was still not quite as high as his friend in her good graces. Yet the lady's fervent gratitude, warmly expressed a moment later, promptly reassured him that the first supposition was correct and not the latter. Mrs. Bennet then proceeded to expound on the healing virtues of various common remedies and some not quite so common, ranging from poultices of bread and milk to boiled elderflowers, or rubbing the bruised parts with brandy or some such ardent spirit.

Quite heartlessly – or so it seemed to Mr. Bingley – his friend was showing no intention of bestirring himself to come to his aid and deflect the flow of unsolicited advice. Neither were the others, but on their assistance Bingley could stake no claim.

It was dreadfully unfair that Darcy's Miss Bennet was at hand to intercede for him and they were now exchanging smiles and whispers – while his own Miss Bennet was elsewhere in the house. But then the thought, instead of feeding the deep feeling of injustice, brought such a wide smile to his lips so as to make Mrs. Bennet wonder why would he be so thrilled at the prospect of having his bruises liberally rubbed with vinegar and brandy. The smile made his face ache, but he smiled wider – for Jane was indeed his own Miss Bennet now, or very soon would be.

Another voice, much more subdued, brought Darcy down to earth from his reverie. As though drawn to his favourite daughter's side by every belated terror, Mr. Bennet came up to protectively wrap an arm around her, his other hand outstretched.

The firm handshake might have said it all.

Still, Mr. Bennet added warmly:

"I thank you, Sir," he said, the words distinct and earnest. "I owe you a debt I could never repay."

Darcy returned the handshake, then bowed without a word and his eyes drifted from the father to the daughter. And yet it was another daughter – the youngest of them all – who visibly swooned at the exchange.

'Oh, my! That glance could melt a rock!'

From where she stood, mere steps away and unusually quiet, for there was a great deal to hear and a vast deal more to see, Lydia missed nothing.

She swooned, but she also pouted, for no gentleman of ten thousand a year had ever looked at *her* that way – and she the handsomest and tallest of the lot!

Well, be that as it may. The man *she* favoured was nowhere near Mr. Darcy in wealth and consequence, but he was a vast deal more appealing to her in everything that mattered. And the joy of it was that, thanks to the dear old lady, her great-aunt Pencarrow, she could follow her heart wherever it might lead her – not that anything had ever stopped her anyway.

Cheered by her musings, Lydia found that the diverting sight of a thoroughly besotted Mr. Darcy was something she would dearly like to share with Kitty. But the silly fool, instead of turning to look in the direction she was indicating, jumped with an *'Ouch!'* and a fierce scowl and then proceeded to take her to task for having pinched her.

"Oh, never mind that now!" Lydia exclaimed and waved her hand with undisguised impatience.

It was too late in any case, for Kitty's loudmouthed admonitions made Mr. Darcy glance to them instead, the heart-melting look replaced by something *very* different. As unaffected by his grimace of displeasure as she had been by Kitty's scowl, Lydia stifled a giggle in her glove.

'If nothing else, it shall be entertaining to have him as a brother,' she incorrigibly determined, then giggled yet again as she wondered when their father would come to see there was *one* sure way to pay off the debt he had just mentioned.

The giggle turned into a playful snort at the most diverting speculation of the evening: just how long would the deep gratitude last, once Mr. Darcy voiced his claim to Lizzy's hand?

Chapter 21

Engulfing shadows… streaks of blinding light… and deep, swirling darkness punctuated with sharp stabs of pain. Wickham's grin, so close – nay, now distorted, distant… and flashing light… Not light, but the glint of Wickham's cutlass as he lunges forward… And his own arm, not moving – why does it not move? Ah, he can move it now, a little. A very little. It *did* move, slowly. Far too slowly. No time left, there is no more time! The strike – the thrust – must parry! Ha, no wonder that his arm could barely move. Wickham's cutlass is already embedded in his shoulder – or is it a dagger? No, a cutlass. Then what the blazes is Wickham charging with? Whatever it might be, 'tis sharp, and stabbing deeper. Time and again, in the same wound. And there is nothing *he* can do to stop it, for he is watching Wickham repeatedly stab at his own mangled corpse.

How strange, watching oneself lying there, dead. Dead – or dying? Galling, either way, and a damned wretched business. And yet Elizabeth is smiling… Stroking his hair and smiling through her tears. Her sweet scent fills his senses, vivid and distinctive, reaching him through the swirling, roiling haze. There is nothing else he can perceive as clearly – except perhaps the sharp pain in his shoulder – but, with determined effort, he might come to ignore the pain and just sense *her*. Seek her – find her. Somewhere.

'Mr. Bingley, would you introduce me to your friend?'

'I wish to God that we had met tonight!'

'Gracious me! Bless you, Sir. The smelling salts. Oh, bless you, Mr. Darcy!'

"Mr. Darcy? Mr. Darcy – Sir?"

Where…? What…?

His eyelids felt as though weighted with lead and his head swam. Mrs. Bennet…? What the devil was *she* doing in his chambers?

"Mr. Darcy? Forgive me, Sir, but I was asked to wake you. Mr Darcy?"

Wakefulness settled slowly and with it came a low chuckle that threatened to bubble into laughter. Poor John, to have been mistaken for Mrs. Bennet, of all people! Not even fitful slumber and the distorting effects of laudanum could fully justify that – or indeed excuse it.

Darcy stirred and reached to explore his shoulder, only to find that he still held Elizabeth's shawl, no longer needed as a sling, but kept at hand nevertheless – a treasured memento. That *would* explain her scent finding its way into his dreams, with all the vividness of a real presence.

If John was surprised to find his master sleeping with a fragrant heap of cashmere by his pillow, he was careful not to let it show, with all the discretion of a well-trained valet. All in all, he had done well, very well indeed, ever since he had been thrust into Norwood's place. He had proven himself more than suited to that particular position. Perhaps it was time to consider Norwood's retirement to one of the best cottages on the estate. He had served his father faithfully for more than two decades, and then himself after his father's passing. He might be ready to pass that duty on. But that would have to be considered later. Darcy pushed the counterpane aside and sat up.

"What time is it?"

"Half past ten, Sir. Forgive me for disturbing you –..."

"You did well. It was time I rose, in any case."

High time, by Jove! Half past ten already. He should be at Landennis, not slumbering here. Was *she* expecting him? She *would* understand that nothing could keep him from Landennis now!

"I wish to be gone within the hour."

No valet worth his salt would even think of asking where, and John did not. Besides, he must have known already.

"Of course, Sir. Although you might have to brook a slight delay. Dr. Polkerris is anxious to see you. He instructed me to wake you, as he would like to examine your wound and change the dressing before he has to leave and attend another patient."

"Oh?"

So the gruff gentleman was paying house-calls this morning. Was it too much to hope that he would be in a better frame of mind today? He did not say as much of course, but merely asked:

"When did he arrive? I trust I have not kept him waiting long."

"He spent the night, Sir. Might as well, seeing as his charges were all here."

"The Frenchman too?"

"Aye, Sir. He was brought in last night, soon after you retired. He is still in a bad way, but the doctor reckons he can patch him up enough to make him fit for prison. And the same goes for Mr. Penderrick."

"What of the other two, Wickham and the Landennis turncoat?"

"They are fit enough, it seems. Lord Trevellyan took them both to Falmouth earlier this morning."

"Ah. Has he set off already, then?"

"Aye, Sir. The best part of an hour gone."

Darcy nodded his sudden satisfaction. He would much rather not encounter Trevellyan this morning now that, the good Lord be praised, his suit was no longer hopeless and his lordship had a very likely rival in him. He wondered if Trevellyan knew it too. If so, there would be sufficient cause for bad blood between them.

He would have to take himself elsewhere, and soon – regardless of whether Trevellyan knew or not. Availing himself of his lordship's bed and board did not sit well with him under the circumstances.

Involuntarily, Darcy's lips twitched. He might have to pit himself against the bedbugs at *Landennis Arms* after all. But then he pushed the diverting thought aside and turned to his man, who was saying something.

"I beg your pardon. Would you repeat that, pray? I was not attending."

"'Tis nothing, Sir. I was merely saying that Peter has arrived. I thought you would wish to know."

Of course – his other footman, left in Falmouth with orders to expect Bingley and show him the way hither.

"I see. You did well to send him word that there was no further need to wait."

"I did not, Mr. Darcy. He arrived this morning, of his own accord – or rather, he came to escort Miss Bingley," said John and, sensibly, went about his business to assist his master in preparing for the day, as though he had not heard the muted oath.

♦♦♦

"There now, Sir, that should do the trick. 'Tis healing nicely, but it must be kept clean and the dressing changed often. Young man, you saw me do it. Do you think you can be trusted to perform the same?"

"I do not doubt he can," Darcy spoke up over John's quiet assurances and both men nodded in response – the doctor in some satisfaction and the footman in thanks for his master's vote of confidence.

"I shall leave you with a fresh supply of lint. And laudanum for the pain, should you require it. I trust his lordship's people can provide the bandages. Any clean piece of linen may be used, or indeed muslin. I shall return on the morrow to see how you are faring, but I see no reason why it should not heal without mishap."

The doctor stood, gathered his belongings and, after the customary exchange of civilities, left Darcy to John's ministrations.

The routine ran like clockwork, timely and precise – only to come undone in its final stages, for the coat selected for the purpose was rather too tight over the thick bandage. As Darcy would not brook calling at Landennis as an invalid with his arm in a sling, a coat with wider sleeves had to be found – and when one *was*, after a vexingly long process of trial and error, the hue turned out to be ill-matched with the rest of his apparel. So a full change was perforce in order and the dressing routine had to recommence *da cappo*, as though he was some sort of foppish coxcomb enslaved by fashion choices, rather than a man of reason, with sensible tastes!

"That would do," Darcy impatiently muttered when John finally got to aligning the points of his collar and smoothing the lapels.

The man stepped back promptly and Darcy's tone softened.

"I thank you for your efforts. Do you know, has Mr. Bingley come down for breakfast yet?"

"I believe so, Sir."

Well! That, at least, was *something* for, all things considered, he had no stomach for a *tête-à-tête* with his friend's sister.

Despite his earlier impatience, Darcy took his time in making his way downstairs. From his post in the great hall, a footman offered him a bow, then restrainedly advised:

"I believe your party is in the morning room, Sir."

The intelligence came with a discreet motion indicating the direction but, truth be told, it was hardly necessary. Miss Bingley's voice – all too familiar – would have served to guide him just as well.

"No, Charles, I will *not* apologise for opening that letter! It had to be done and, but for Hurst and his vexingly loose tongue, it would have solved everybody's problems," Darcy heard her say, from one of the rooms ahead.

Bingley's reply followed, substantially more subdued.

Nevertheless, it carried.

"Lower your voice, Caroline. May I remind you that we are guests in this house," his friend admonished and Darcy's brow involuntarily shot up at the unprecedented sternness.

Welcome and long overdue as it might have been, Darcy had no wish to witness it at close quarters, nor was he of a mind to walk into a family scene. He made an about-turn, only to discover that the well-trained footman had also determined he ought to be elsewhere. As for himself, the library would serve – it was far enough. Before he could put sufficient distance between himself and the Bingley siblings though, he was to hear more.

"As for solving everybody's problems," his friend resumed quite firmly, "you thought of nothing but your own. And I for one think 'tis high time for some unpalatable truths. No machinations would have made him offer for you – *ever*."

"Of *what* are you speaking?"

"Pray spare me the show of outraged innocence! Do you imagine me ignorant of your pitiful little schemes? As soon as you read Darcy's letter, you must have seen that his suit hinged on reuniting me with Jane."

Ungentlemanly as it might have been to eavesdrop, once he heard as much Darcy found it impossible to leave. His brow arched further at Bingley's forthright statement. He did not remember having spelled it out so clearly in his brief message to his friend. In fact, he could scarce remember what exactly he had written, at that time of panic and of haste. Presumably he had wronged Bingley in more ways than one and had severely underrated his perception and his ability to read between the lines.

The younger man, however, was very far from finished. To Darcy's disbelief – for he never would have thought that Bingley had it in him – his friend's tone grew from stern to icy:

"Since you could not physically chase after Darcy and stop him from proposing, your best hope of damaging his chances was to prevent him from bringing me back to Jane."

"Do not speak such ridiculous nonsense! How could I – ...?"

"Indeed. How *could* you, Caroline? I am your brother! Do you care so little for my happiness, my wishes?"

"Your happiness! Your wishes!" Miss Bingley angrily retorted. "Why should I care for yours, when you dismiss *mine* out of hand?"

"Because yours are as selfish as your schemes were pointless. You might have ruined his life – ..."

"Ruined his life!" she scoffed.

"Aye – and mine as well, not that it seems to count. But do not imagine it would have brought you any closer to wheedling a proposal out of Darcy."

"At least it would have spared me the odium of seeing that upstart call herself Mistress of Pemberley!" Miss Bingley venomously burst – at which point Darcy decided that enough was enough.

He strode towards the open door of the morning room, not quite knowing what he was about to say, but grimly determined that no such comments would be tolerated, in his presence or otherwise – and Miss Bingley ought to know that he had overheard her, very clearly. For once, he did not stop to think of the implications and of the fact that joining them just then might embarrass Bingley too, perhaps even more than his harridan of a sister. He did not get far before his friend's next words stopped him in his tracks.

"Did it ever cross your mind that *we* are the upstarts, Caroline?"

"What on earth are you saying? Have you completely lost your mind?"

"You boast of your proficiency in French – and yet the phrase *nouveau riche* does not strike you as fitting. Mr. Bennet's father was a gentleman. As you well know but choose to forget, our grandfather was not."

"You seem determined to vex me at every turn today, but I shall not allow it," Miss Bingley retorted very coldly. "There is no further purpose in this conversation."

"At last we are in agreement! Nor is there any purpose in you being here. So unless you are willing to accompany me when I call upon Miss Bennet and pay off your arrears of civility towards my future wife, you might as well make your way back to town."

"Your future wife? You have proposed already?"

"I have. And she has accepted."

"Hm. I never doubted that she would."

"I did – and sadly with good reason. Yesterday she bid me return whence I came. Praised be, since then I had the good fortune to persuade her otherwise."

"Good fortune!" Miss Bingley scoffed again but did not get the chance to say anything further, for her brother interjected.

"Yes. Precisely. And there is no more to be said but this: if you join me on my call this morning, I expect you to show Miss Bennet all the courtesy due her – or at least all that you could muster – ..."

"Oh, fear not, I have not the slightest wish to join you on your call."

"Very well," Bingley replied coldly. "Then I bid you good day and a safe journey into town."

"I have no intention to leave either."

"You might as well. You are not welcome here."

"Is that so! There are inns in Falmouth," Miss Bingley emphatically declared.

Judging by the approaching sound of footsteps, she was storming away from her brother and aiming for a dramatic exit, Darcy determined. It did not take him long to ascertain that, although he had already distanced himself discretely from the doorway, there was no time to vanish altogether – and he was not of a mind to be caught scuttling away. He turned, took a deep breath and squared his shoulders – then suppressed a wince when sharp pain stabbed through the injured one.

In the morning room, Miss Bingley added firmly:

"I am not leaving Cornwall until I have seen – ..."

Her angry stride brought her to the door, and at the unexpected sight of him she faltered.

"Mr. Darcy!" she exclaimed, her countenance a picture of mortified confusion, before she promptly schooled it into an ingratiating smile. Her eyes shifted to his, assessing, calculating, clearly keen to ascertain how much it was that he had heard.

His mien frozen, Darcy bowed.

"Good morning to you, Ma'am. Bingley," he acknowledged his friend, who had by then followed his sister to the door.

"How good to see you, Sir," Miss Bingley offered and Darcy bowed again, conspicuously laggard in reciprocating.

"You are very kind," he said, his lips barely moving, and his eyes drifted to the lady's brother. "I trust I have not kept you waiting long. Have you sat down for breakfast yet?"

"I have not. Shall we?"

"By all means. I should not wish to delay our visit to Landennis," Darcy replied promptly, his voice firm and measured.

Miss Bingley's glance grew questioning.

"Landennis?" she queried.

"Aye. The country house where the Miss Bennets and their family are staying," Darcy answered flatly, unwilling to beat about the bush. "Will you be joining us, Miss Bingley – that is to say, for breakfast?"

This was a clear indication that he *had* heard a vast deal more than she could have wished, and the lady must have caught it, for her mien darkened.

"How gracious of you, Sir. I thank you," she replied, regardless. "So, what brings you to this part of the country, Mr. Darcy? I had no notion you had acquaintances so far off the beaten track. Will you be staying long?" Miss Bingley asked, availing herself of an arm he did not offer.

Darcy's brow arched at her insufferable presumption.

"As long as it takes," he replied curtly and withdrew his arm.

"Dare one ask as long as *what* takes, precisely?"

Apparently one did dare ask, Darcy thought, his vexation mounting. He had no wish to offend his friend with an open set-down aimed at the said friend's sister, but the well-deserved rebuke would not suffer to be bitten back much longer if she continued probing into his intentions.

A similar notion must have occurred to Bingley, for he interjected:

"Let us to breakfast. Feel free to join us, Caroline, before you return to Falmouth."

"As I said, Charles, my plans are not fixed. Besides, you were interrupting. Mr. Darcy was about to tell me about his incursion into this backwater. I trust you will soon return to more familiar and more civilised society, Sir."

And there it was, the sharp retort! Darcy felt it coming and made no effort to suppress it.

"You must forgive your brother for rushing you, Miss Bingley," he cut in firmly, his diction precise. "He is understandably impatient to resume his courtship – and frankly so am I."

Had he been watching *her* – rather than someone infinitely more appealing – on the evening of their conversation about the very great pleasure which a pair of fine eyes in the face of a pretty woman could bestow, Darcy would have recognised the sequence of emotions as they flitted yet again over Miss Bingley's countenance. Flirtatiousness was replaced by disbelief, then shock, then anger and finally by a painstaking effort at feigning nonchalance. Unconsciously reinforcing the association, Miss Bingley made a very similar response:

"I am all astonishment. *Courtship*, Sir? Good gracious! Should I assume that a local beauty has captured your heart?"

"Pray assume as much as you choose, and unless you believe me actually married, you cannot greatly err," Darcy retorted beyond the limits of his patience, thus affording Miss Bingley the doubtful satisfaction of having goaded him into a conversation that could vex no one as much as herself.

⸎⸎⸎

Not surprisingly, Miss Bingley did not join them for the morning repast. Instead, with a great show of dignity, she offered them tight-lipped wishes of a pleasant stay in this part of the country, then declared her intention to return at once to Falmouth, and thence to town, the following day. Thus, Bingley and Darcy's time in the breakfast parlour was a great deal quieter and more enjoyable than it might have been. One thing was certain – it was very short. Less than an hour after Miss Bingley's own hasty departure, the two gentlemen could be seen riding away in the direction of Landennis Manor.

They did not speak much. One was too happy for conversation and the other much too caught in his anxious musings. Anxious to see *her* – that, he undoubtedly was – yet also dreadfully anxious about the outcome.

It was a source of wonder and, at times, of something very much like panic to note the changes she had surreptitiously wrought in him. Never one for distressing himself with dark imaginings but choosing to tackle misfortune as and when it came, Darcy now found himself doing the very opposite and dwelling on all manner of painful speculations. What if the hopeful signs he had received last night were nothing but a product of overtaxed emotions? What if rest and sleep and the cold light of day had settled her perception back into the old patterns? What if she had simply changed her mind again?

"Look, Darcy! Now there is a fine stroke of luck!"

His friend's cheerful tones, as well as the jolt of his own heart, tore Darcy from his disquieting ruminations when a sudden turn of the road brought them in sight of the very ladies they had ridden out to seek. In unspoken agreement, both gentlemen urged their horses into a faster canter, eyes trained on the slender silhouettes that were by now responding to Bingley's eager wave.

"Good morning to you," the younger man called out when they were close enough for conversation and was answered in kind as he hastily dismounted – a feat which, at the moment, Darcy could not match.

Yet consciousness regarding horsemanship and posture could not be further from his mind. A different sort of consciousness held him in check as he bowed deeply and added his own greetings.

The anxious search for an indication of her thoughts was fruitless. The sun was in his eyes and he could not read *hers*. Yet Elizabeth did not glance away, but smiled; a welcoming, unpractised smile that kindled hope and made up for a great deal worse than the discomforts of riding with an injured shoulder.

"Good morning, Mr. Darcy. I am happy to see that you are well."

'Never better,' Darcy thought – and this time he meant it – but somehow forgot to say as much, mesmerised anew by the sparkle in her eyes. Bingley said something and Miss Bennet made a lengthy answer, but nothing registered with Darcy until his friend felt obliged to prompt him for the second time, with a diverted roll of his eyes that the other did not catch.

"So, what say you? *Darcy!*"

With an effort, he willed himself back from the clouds to listen.

"I beg your pardon. I was not attending."

"Were you not?" his friend teasingly remarked and they all smiled, but it was the warm glow in *her* eyes that mattered.

"I was suggesting we leave the horses here to graze and escort the ladies on their walk. Miss Bennet told me they were on their way to a nearby cove."

"Oh."

"Just around the corner there is a path leading down to it, I hear," Bingley added, unknowingly confirming Darcy's suspicion that it must be the very place that Elizabeth had taken him to, the previous morning.

The brightness of the moment dimmed, overshadowed by the recollections of that place, that time, and all the heartache it had brought him. He fought them off and forced a pallid smile on darkened features.

"Of course. Why not?"

To his great joy and gratitude, Elizabeth's hand was laid comfortingly on his arm for a few fleeting seconds, before she turned to Bingley.

"It was but a passing thought, Sir," she swiftly offered. "We can walk elsewhere. There are countless lovely prospects."

'None lovelier than the one before me', shot through Darcy's mind – and this time it was not just an inward reflection. Unwittingly, he spoke the words aloud and actually failed to notice, until alerted to the fact by Bingley's chuckle and Elizabeth's conscious blush.

There was no hope whatever to creditably cover the slip of the tongue he was not entirely regretting, but he assayed nevertheless.

"Landennis Cove is one of the loveliest I have ever seen," he said and cleared his voice.

"No doubt," Bingley shot back, grinning widely. "Come, shall we? Let us secure the horses. Those stunted trees would serve, do you not think?"

"Pardon? Oh, yes, of course," Darcy concurred at length and moved to do as bid – rather late as it happened for, shaking his head with mild amusement, Bingley was already securing Darcy's mount, just as he did his own.

"Never mind. 'Tis done," his friend observed. "In any case, you can use some assistance," he added with a nod towards Darcy's shoulder, then gave his other arm a hearty pat as he walked past him to the ladies.

With a steadying breath, Darcy followed suit.

Chapter 22

Warm with the midday sun, the scent of gorse blooms filled the air around them as they walked in silence behind the other couple. The crushing sense of *déjà-vu* was overpowering, much as Darcy fought against it and endeavoured to take comfort from her earlier kindness, her closeness – and her touch. Both her gloved hands were on his arm this time, clasped around it and one atop the other, and the subtle difference from the day before, when she had barely rested her fingers on his sleeve, brought the thinnest wisp of hope.

He clung to it with something very much like desperation, in order to ward off distressing similarities that twisted his insides into painful knots. Such as the fact that she was still concealing her face from him, safe under the brim of the bonnet. And, worse still, same as yesterday, she kept her peace and would not say a word.

All-too-vivid recollections of everything that had passed between them the previous morning sapped his confidence – nay, wiped it out completely. Was he a fool to grip onto tenuous hopes?

It certainly seemed foolhardy to tempt fate in this manner and even contemplate pressing his suit so soon, and on the very spot of his earlier rejection. What sort of madness had possessed him to even entertain the notion of asking again *today* – and *here*, of all places?

Ahead of them, Bingley was gaily chatting, asking Miss Bennet if she had ever walked this way before, only to be told that she had not and had been enticed thither by her sister's promise of astounding views. For the first time in living memory, Darcy wished he could trade his temperament for Bingley's – wished *he* could find something to blithely chat about or at least think of some innocuous remark that would break the unnerving silence. Yet every topic he could think of – other than pitiful observations on the weather – seemed charged with uncomfortable associations and thus under an unbreakable embargo.

Suddenly, Elizabeth glanced up.

"Are you very uncomfortable?" she asked, only to throw him into startled confusion with *her* unexpected choice of topic.

His countenance must have betrayed it, surely, for she blushed profusely and then stammered:

"I… beg your pardon… I was speaking of your shoulder…"

"Oh. Of course. Well … 'tis not so very bad…"

"Will you see Dr. Polkerris again?"

"He was kind enough to call this morning."

"And did he offer an opinion?"

"He seemed fairly satisfied…"

"I am so glad!" she replied warmly and, as soon as Darcy thanked her, silence fell again, leaving him to the unprofitable exercise of wishing he could string more than ten words together.

He took a deep breath, urging his senses into focus, and for once the effort brought some scant result, for the passing reference to the grumpy doctor supplied at least *one* topic for safe conversation.

"And your great-aunt? I hope she is recovered."

"I thank you, yes she is, thank goodness."

"Did the doctor ascertain what happened?"

"From what I understand, Mrs. Pencarrow has been suffering with this complaint for a long time – heart trouble. I know not how severe her overall condition is, but for now Dr. Polkerris seems persuaded she is in no danger."

"Good tidings."

"Aye. The best."

"And… hm!… the rest of your family?"

"They are very well, Sir, I thank you, though perhaps less tranquil than expected," she added with a hint of laughter in her voice.

A hint of laughter that spoke to him of other times when archness had not yet given way to strife or to acute discomfort, and something in him stirred back into life at its unexpected call. Sparks of hope. Deep snow melting in the sunshine.

"How so?" he asked, as soon as he could speak.

"As usual, it seems that news travels fast. Our neighbours must have heard that there was some excitement last night at Landennis and so they came to call in unusual numbers, presumably in the hope of learning more."

"How fortunate that you were still able to walk out."

"I am ashamed to say nothing was left to fortune," she declared with another smile, warming his heart further. "When we saw that the first round of callers was followed by another then another, Jane and I decided to abscond as soon as the third wave left. I daresay we should have stayed to brave a fourth one, but – ..."

"I am very happy you did not," Darcy replied promptly, her altered manner enticing him into throwing caution to the wind.

A warm, steady glance was his reward. She was about to speak, but Jane was there before her.

"Beautiful," she breathed. "Thank you, Lizzy. You were right, the views are astounding."

With something of a start, Darcy looked away from his companion – only to discover that the path had opened and he was on the very spot where his sentence had been passed the day before. Salty sea air was blowing in their faces and Darcy's eyes narrowed, hard as he endeavoured to suppress the wince. High above, three seagulls cried and circled, then plunged towards the sea, diving for the odd elusive fish. One of them seemed to have been successful and flew away with its prey, silver scales glinting briefly in the sunshine, while the others remained floating upon the restless sea churned by the breeze into white-fringed surf.

Her countenance distressingly reverted back to sombre consciousness, Elizabeth released Mr. Darcy's arm. His jaw tightened and he sighed.

"Let us sit," Miss Bennet suggested. "The grass must be dry enough."

"No!" Elizabeth retorted swiftly with strong determination and then her tones softened as she turned towards her sister. "Would you not like to walk down to the beach?"

Warm gratitude coursed through Darcy at her wish to spare his feelings, along with another wisp of hope engendered by the notion that perhaps *she* was not happy to remain here either.

"Are you quite certain that the path is safe, Lizzy?" Miss Bennet tentatively queried. "It seems dreadfully steep. Besides, the view must be far better from up here," she added; noticeably less keen than her sister to engage in strenuous pursuits.

"The path is safe. I have walked down many times before," Elizabeth reassured her. "But if you are not comfortable, dearest, we can turn back..." she offered.

"Or we can wait for you up here?" Bingley suggested hopefully, not at all averse to a few moments of relative privacy in the company of his betrothed.

"Oh, no, I should not wish to spoil your fun," Jane protested, slow to realise that she was going the wrong way about it. "I am happy to walk down, if I can take my time."

"Of course. Then let us not linger here," Elizabeth remarked to no one in particular, but it was Darcy who hastened to reply.

"Gladly! Pray allow me," he said, offering his gloved hand, palm up. Elizabeth met his eyes for mere moments, but she put her hand in his without hesitation and they walked down the path together, his spirits soaring with every step that took them away from the cursed spot. Unreasonable as it might have been, Darcy felt as though an enormous weight was being lifted off his chest, and he took a deep breath of the bracing air.

A step ahead of his treasured companion and thus slightly lower down the incline, he turned to face her, their eyes level.

"Thank you," he whispered without thinking.

She did not ask what for, but the hold of her hand tightened. And, for the briefest moment, he imagined that he felt a light stroke of her thumb through the frustrating double barrier of gloves.

If this was a day for reckless impulse then so be it, Darcy suddenly determined and withdrew his hand, whipped his glove off and offered it again, bare – and as exposed as his naked heart.

Bent on removing the offending glove, he had narrowly missed the wistful look of shock mingled with sadness that had crossed her features at his misconstrued withdrawal. But his searching glance, settled on her when he offered his bare hand, could not miss the brightness of her smile as she matched his gesture, stripped her own glove off and placed her hand in his.

Not a light touch, but a firm clasp, fingers interlacing – and at that anything inside him that might have still recommended caution flew on the breeze that blew strongly from the sea. Darcy brought their joined hands up to press the back of hers against his lips and they lingered thus, their gazes locked for the longest moment, his dark eyes burning into hers. Her eyes glowed and shimmered, bright with unshed tears, but her lips curled into a wider smile – and somehow captured Darcy's whole attention. Rosy. Full. Slightly parted. Inches from his own – so close – tantalising!

His senses swam with the heady temptation and blood sang in his veins at their vividly remembered taste. Sweet. Fragrant. Warm and pliant, as they had eagerly responded to his kisses last night, in the garden. And the urge to claim them yet again – claim *her* as his other half, now and forever – rose to a pitch that nearly bordered pain.

"Elizabeth…" he whispered and felt her shiver as his breath brushed against her skin.

The exhilarating proof that she was not indifferent sent white-hot stabs of fierce desire through him, the sort that brought grown men onto the brink of heaven – or of hell.

"How foolish of me! There is really nothing to it," Miss Bennet cheerfully observed behind them, then Bingley replied something, urged her to step this way or that – and Darcy valiantly swallowed an oath at the stark reminder of the world around them and of the very vexing fact that they were not alone.

He let their joined hands drop and turned to resume their own descent, step by cautious step, willing his head to cool and his senses to cease roiling – with about as much success as the legendary King Canute against the tide.

ᴖᴗ ᕫᔭᴖ

Soon, far too soon by Darcy's way of thinking, they reached their destination, but he did not release her hand – nor did she seem in any haste to withdraw it.

Pebbles scrunching under their slow footsteps, they walked towards the water's edge. The beach was a great deal wider now, the rolling surf many yards away from the tideline of dried, tangled seaweed that filled the air with its distinctive scent.

"I have never seen the tide quite so far out," Elizabeth observed, presumably to fill the silence.

"Have you not?"

"No. These rocks – whenever I came here they have been submerged and those enormous boulders have always had the waves crashing against them."

"Oh."

They were fully exposed now, the boulders that she had just spoken of – a massive outcrop closing the cove on their right, or rather separating it from a smaller one, just around the corner.

The work of relentless, all-powerful water could be seen upon them, where it had fashioned channels to rush through from one side to the other, or it had smoothed the hard rock into strange, protruding shapes, or crumbled it at will into little more than pebbles.

"I hope Jane was not too uncomfortable with the steep descent," Elizabeth remarked with a glance over her shoulder towards the other couple.

They had negotiated their way down to the beach at last, Darcy noted, but had apparently chosen to walk towards the other end – which was just as well. He turned his back on them – turned towards *her* – his hand still wrapped around her fingers, and ran his thumb over her knuckles, stroking them lightly, one by one. Yet this time she did not glance up, and a blush crept into her cheeks.

"It is... very peaceful here," she breathed, looking out at sea.

"Yes," he whispered back, although peaceful was not exactly how *he* would have described it.

"Would you care to walk further?"

'Anywhere – with you,' he thought. Or did he say it? No, not this time, although perhaps he should have. No, of course not, what the deuce was he thinking? Too soon. Too soon by far. She had rejected him no further than yesterday, for goodness' sake!

Ahead, waves crashed over submerged rocks, then rolled tamely over sand and pebbles, advanced, withdrew and crashed back in again – an unsettling mirror of his own tormenting indecisions.

He had to choose his moment, choose it with great care, for if he was to blunder into another ill-worded and ill-timed proposal...

Darcy all but shuddered and his countenance turned grim as they walked around the exposed outcrop to their right, their boots sinking deeper in the waterlogged sand as they made their way onto the beach in the other cove which, judging by the dark tidemark on the bare-rock walls, was probably submerged most of the time. He cast an assessing glance towards the sea. The tide seemed safely out, far enough to reassure him that they were in no danger.

So they walked along the water's edge in further silence – for the sound of the rolling surf did not quite count, much as it filled the narrow cove and bounced back from the steep cliffs around them.

Why on earth was it so difficult to speak? Downright maddening as it might have been, the reason for his current crippling shyness was extremely simple: this was not a moment for small talk.

And nothing was worth saying except what was foremost on his mind: would she ever be prevailed upon to reconsider and, more to the point, would she be willing to believe he would do *anything* to bring it about?

A sigh escaped him – yet a moment later all tormenting thoughts were gone, flying in the breeze much like her bonnet, which had just been snatched by a sudden gust and was now rolling away from them, fast gathering speed. They set off in hot pursuit together, Darcy a few steps behind, for he saw wisdom in firstly removing his own hat. He caught up in no time, despite the momentarily impulse of allowing her the advantage. For the sake of her bonnet he thought better of it though, once he saw that, caught by another gust, one coming from the shore this time, it was progressing with alarming speed towards the water. They both changed course, darting the other way, and luckily Darcy managed to retrieve it just in time from the path of a far-reaching wave that threatened to carry it off and make small work of the milliner's skilled efforts.

Wet sand was clinging to the brim and the honey-coloured trimming and he made a half-hearted attempt to shake it off while not destroying the bonnet altogether. He handed it back with a wide smile as soon as she drew to a halt beside him and, at the sight of the poor crumpled thing, Elizabeth burst out laughing.

"I thank you. My fault, I should have known better. A bonnet without ribbons can cause nothing but mischief at the seaside," she said, still trying to shake it clear of sand, before abandoning the fruitless task along with the notion of wearing it again, at least for the moment. She pushed back wavy tendrils, teased loose by the wind and the run, her cheeks glowing with laughter and the bright flush of exertion – and Darcy stood rooted to the spot, entranced by the delightful vision. She had never looked as beautiful before. Never as warm, as full of life, as perfect!

Thank goodness, self-consciousness seemed to have gone from her and wrenching thoughts were vanquished by shared laughter, leaving no discomfort in their wake, no challenge – just the prodigious effort to stop himself from gathering her close.

So perhaps thanks were owed to gusts of wind and flight-prone bonnets – if weather fancies and inanimate objects could ever receive thanks – for the marked constraint between them seemed somewhat lifted as they bent their steps towards the far end of the second cove.

There was one single loss that he could think of: they were no longer holding hands. For some unknown reason, hers were now busily engaged in toying with her crumpled bonnet and with the glove that she had taken off, and Darcy did not feel confident enough to reclaim the sweet indulgence.

They finally reached the end of the pebbly strip, where a rambling mound of rocks was blocking their path. They could have easily negotiated those if fancy took them, but they both readily agreed it might be unwise to venture into yet another cove and risk being trapped by the tide which, any time soon, might be returning.

"We should walk back," Darcy offered, raising his voice over the sound of the crashing waves.

"We should," Elizabeth concurred, but did not move.

They could not see Landennis Cove from where they stood. It was concealed beyond the outcrop they had walked around. But they could see another one now, right across the bay, next to the furthest headland.

"That must be Rosteague," Elizabeth observed.

"I beg your pardon?"

"Rosteague Cove, where the landing was, last night," she clarified as they finally fell into step again to make their slow way back.

"Oh. Was it? How do you know?"

"Lord Trevellyan said so," she offered in passing, before suddenly asking: "Will you be staying long with his lordship?"

"No. I will not."

Elizabeth arched a brow.

"He did not ask you to leave, surely! I can see why, but..."

Her casual remark surprised him. What exactly *did* she see?

"But?" he prompted her to continue, just as a sickening suspicion dawned. Had Trevellyan declared himself already?

"I thought it beneath him, that is all," Elizabeth said softly and the clear trace of disappointment stung, for it implied that Trevellyan had an established claim on her good opinion.

But no, he must be running mad to even think it. She had not accepted Trevellyan's suit, surely! She would have acted very differently last night – this morning – if she was already promised to another. It certainly was madness to torment himself with such speculations, he determined.

251

Besides, he owed her an answer and, tempting as it might have been to blacken a dreaded rival, Darcy could not bring himself to be anything but truthful.

"He did not ask me to leave, much as he might have wished to. I just thought I ought not overstay my welcome."

"So... are you leaving Cornwall?" she asked, so quietly that he could barely hear her.

"*Leave?* Good Lord, no! Elizabeth, I do not *dare* leave!" he exclaimed with feeling.

Her glance shot up at that, and she stopped walking. As though independent of her wishes, her lips formed just one word:

"Why?"

"I was hoping that you need not ask," he offered very gently and reached for her hand. He found it still clasping the brim of the wretched bonnet but wrapped his fingers around hers nevertheless. "I was so sure of my chances when we parted in Basingstoke – only to find that it was nothing but arrogant presumption and in fact I had nothing of what I thought I had. I do not dare leave, for I would fear each moment that every ounce of hope is snatched away."

Her eyes grew very soft and very bright. Her lips trembled and parted to release a sigh, or maybe the beginnings of an answer.

Perhaps he should have waited for it.

He did not. The words burst out of their own volition:

"Elizabeth – is it too soon to ask again?"

The world, his world, stood still as he waited. All was in the open now, too late for caution or concealment, and Darcy swallowed hard, his eyes trained on hers.

Every passing second – or fraction of a second – felt longer than a lifetime, and everything around them seemed suddenly bound by a new set of rules. Unnatural new rules, incomprehensible and strange – for it made no sense why everything should now be forced to happen in slow motion.

Dark-fringed eyelids dropped and screened her eyes from him and the breeze swirled, blowing their hair in their faces. Yet none stirred to push it aside. It was another gust that did so, not that Darcy seemed to notice. The long lashes fluttered, trapping unshed tears – but before he could begin to torment himself with their unspoken meaning, her lips moved.

"I think…" she whispered, then her voice gathered strength and her eyes flew open. "No. 'Tis not too soon," she smiled through her tears and for a moment he was thoroughly robbed of breath – until he put his whole heart into the only words that mattered:

"Then marry me – I beg you!"

And the world was at long last put right, when she simply answered *"Yes"*.

ᴏᏇᏇ ᏇᏇᴏ

Her cheek was warm and very soft against his palm, and he stroked it with his thumb as he laced his fingers through the tendrils round her temple. They were soft as well and damp with the sea air, and her bright eyes seemed to fill the world.

His thumb dropped to her lower lip and traced along it, gingerly exploring its enticing fullness with a light, lingering caress while, left to their own newly discovered purpose, the tips of his fingers stroked their way down to the small hollow underneath her ear, then reached up to find the contours of her cheek again.

His pulse was thundering wildly in his ears, loud and forceful, drowning out the surf and the distant cry of seagulls – and grew louder still, instantly responding to the gaze she settled on him from under part-closed, heavy eyelids. And then, ever so slowly, her lips curled under his thumb into heart-shaped perfection, to drop a light kiss on it and send his skin tingling and white-hot fire racing through his veins.

His hand slid around her neck, revelling in the silky softness, and his lips sought hers – eager, insistent, hungry – only to find that her warm response was fuelling the raging fire into something that surpassed everything he had ever felt before. Nothing compared to this. Not wild imaginings from lonely hours of yearning. Not even the treasured moments in the Landennis gardens, when every stolen joy had been tainted with the chilling fear that it would be his last.

There was no fear now. Nothing but bliss and heady promise – and full lips responding to deep, searching kisses, stoking a blaze that was already beyond reason and control. Her hands came up to hold him very tight; stroke his hair, bring him closer still – and all else ceased to matter, in this world or the other!

With every passing second, the hunger only grew.

ᴏᏇᏇ ᏇᏇᴏ

The sudden rush of water along with Elizabeth's small cry of surprise brought him to his senses and Darcy opened his eyes to find that the returning tide was lapping at their boots.

"Blast," he muttered, his eyes anxiously scanning the way out of the secluded cove. It was already closed and waves were crashing against the massive outcrop, repeatedly sending up powerful streams of spray.

"Come!" he urged, reaching for her hand, and they broke into a run together. It was not far, but the tide was coming fast – or so it seemed to his apprehensive eyes.

"Forgive me. I was dreadfully careless."

"No more than I," she blithely replied between intakes of breath, then added something Darcy could not catch.

"I beg your pardon?"

"I said I do not regret it. Besides, there is no danger – just a little salty water."

"A *lot* of salty water," he amended and, in spite of everything, his eyes warmed at her cheerful acceptance of their foolish predicament.

She truly had no equal in this world – and she was *his*.

"I love you," he called out, the words flying in the wind, along with the sand thrown up by their boots, and with the seagulls.

"This is the first time you said so, if I am not mistaken. You must tell me again, when we are not running from the tide."

"I should have told you every day. I *will* tell you every day."

"I shall hold you to it," she teasingly replied and he smiled back.

And thus, rather than clouded with concern, their eyes were warm with laughter when they reached the end of the cove. Darcy took mere moments to assess the situation, then turned towards her.

"Would you put your arms around my neck?"

"Most certainly not!" she replied hotly. "I will not have you carry me, with your injured shoulder. I can walk."

"No," he retorted flatly.

"Mr. Darcy, this is not the time for a battle of wills!"

"Fitzwilliam," he amended.

"Pardon?"

"My Christian name."

"I see," was her sole response, before walking past him to the water.

He stopped her with a firm hand on her elbow but his voice, when next he spoke, held nothing but persuasive softness.

"Elizabeth? Pray humour me. I would very much like to carry you."

Nothing but *that* could have made her waver – and the warm glow in his eyes sent her pulse racing.

"You are not playing fair," she quietly admonished.

"I never claimed I would."

"What about your shoulder?"

"I could not care less about my shoulder," he declared and put an arm around her. His tone lightened: "Elizabeth, if you do not relent, you *shall* have my shoulder on your conscience, because I shall be forced to drape you over it and carry you like a sack of turnips."

"You would not dare!"

"Try me!"

She pressed her lips together.

"I suppose you would do well to let me hold your hat…"

Darcy handed it promptly and dropped the glove that he had taken off inside it.

"Thank you," he said softly, then clarified in response to her inquiring glance: "For letting me have my way."

Elizabeth made no reply and he bent down to lift her off the ground with his hale arm, firmly suppressing the merest suspicion of a wince when his injured one protested. He draped it around her back and hastened to wade in, mindful of keeping his distance from the outcrop, where the water might have formed deep hollows. He trod carefully and prayed he would not slip or stumble over things he could not see, and send them both crashing down into the water.

It was not so very deep. When the waves receded, it barely came up a palm or so above his ankles, but at their return the level rose as high as his knees, sending seawater seeping into his tall riding boots.

He felt his way to the large flat rocks that now barely protruded from the water and eased himself up on them, while still wondering about the wisdom of the move, for he was far more likely to lose his footing over a smooth surface. Thankfully, the rocks were anything but smooth and the clusters of barnacles and limpets seemed to provide a reasonable grip. If anything, the greatest risk of getting soaking-wet was not so much from falling flat into the sea as from being drenched by the waves breaking into spray around them.

Sure enough, a few high ones came in quick succession, rolling one after the other and sending a fair amount of ice-cold water as high up as their faces. He heard Elizabeth gasp in surprise, but she said nothing. It was Darcy who spoke.

"How are you?"

"Just fine – do not regard it."

He did not press the point, but continued on their way. They were already rounding the small headland into Landennis Cove and he could espy Bingley and Miss Bennet at the furthest end, seemingly oblivious to their surroundings and to the other couple's predicament and antics. It was just as well that they were in no need of assistance, Darcy thought grimly, otherwise they might have had to cling like limpets to the cliff-face in the other cove before their companions noticed there was anything amiss!

The level of the rocky floor seemed to be dropping and Darcy edged himself forward with great care until at last the hard surface underfoot gave way to sand and pebbles and he was safely wading through the shallows towards the water's edge, on the other side.

He took his time, at liberty at last to focus not on the rising tide or the need to find safe footholds but on the sheer joy of holding her. Sharp stabs of pain reminded him of his injured shoulder but he steadfastly ignored them, in favour of her delicious warmth, her treasured closeness and the feel of her breath upon his face.

"Are you contemplating walking out of the water any time soon, Sir?" she suddenly asked.

"No, not as such."

"In that case, I think this is as good a time as any to conclude our conversation."

"Oh? I forgot what we were speaking of."

"You were thanking me for letting you have your way..."

"I see. And?"

"And I was reluctant to distract you while you had other matters to contend with, but I suppose now it would be safe to ask whether I should expect you to be quite so forceful once we are married."

Her tone was arch, but the inquiry seemed to have been in earnest, so Darcy abandoned his own jesting manner.

"I beg your pardon if I was too forceful. Did you mind it very much?"

"Only if it proves to be the norm," she answered truthfully.

"It might," he cautiously owned. "But only when I am not allowed to care for you."

"And what if I choose to value your comfort above my own?"

"Then I hope we shall be able to find a happy medium," he smiled, warmed by her words. "It just so happened that there was no time for a lengthy debate while we were still on the wrong side of the advancing tide."

"And now we are not."

"So I have noticed. And?"

"And it would do your shoulder a world of good if you put me down."

"Did I happen to mention I could not care less about my shoulder?"

"Did I mention that my sister and Mr. Bingley are watching?"

"Oh, are they now! I thought they had not even noticed we were trapped on the other side."

"Pray put me down, Mr. Darcy."

"Fitzwilliam."

"Fitzwilliam, pray be so kind to step out of the water and set me down, or I shall have to jump."

"Of course. Just one more thing, though."

"And that is?"

"As you have rightfully pointed out, we are no longer running from the tide…"

"Indeed."

"So, as requested…" he smiled, only to suddenly relinquish every hint of teasing from his voice, leaving nothing but genuine feeling: "I love you, Elizabeth. And I am happier than I have ever been in my entire life!"

He was not necessarily expecting a reply.

Nevertheless, he got one – and it was highly unexpected.

"Would you kindly turn your back to my sister and your friend?"

He arched his brows, but did as bid.

"May I ask why?"

"If you must…" she whispered, before reaching up to press her lips on his.

Chapter 23

Mr. Bennet was not having a good day.

To begin with, there was the deeply disturbing notion that his dearest daughter, that *both* his eldest daughters had, unbeknownst to him, been exposed to dreadful peril, and he shuddered to think what might have come to pass if those two' young men had not been at hand at Landennis to watch over them – which was precisely what *he* should have done! Not that he could fool himself into believing he might have been of greater use, or indeed any use at all, in armed combat against that vile beast, Wickham. But that was not the point. A father's duty was to protect his daughters, and Mr. Bennet feared he might have failed in more ways than one.

Once he had seen fit to open that particular unappealing box, much like the proverbial Pandora, he found it very hard to force it shut and from within sprang bold reminders of his failings, to prod and niggle and destroy his peace.

The failure to adequately provide for his daughters so that they would be protected if anything befell him was arguably his greatest – and the fact that Mrs. Pencarrow seemed to have willingly stepped into the breach did not lessen his parental guilt one iota!

And then there was the extreme reluctance to involve himself in the education of his daughters. True enough, few men of his generation did and they happily left that task to their spouses – but perhaps they had chosen to marry women of higher intellect than Mrs. Bennet.

And here was another failing for, having made his bed, he should have uncomplainingly lain in it, rather than spend the best part of two decades deriding or deploring his wife's shortcomings as a life-companion. But that was murky water under far too many bridges. The salient point was that he of all people should have taken pains to ensure that the girls would not grow up to repeat their parents' errors.

Jane and darling Lizzy were going the right way about it, the Lord be praised – but the Lord must have known as well as *he* did that their father could scarcely claim the credit.

Mary, bless her, was harmless enough. Still, if she did not get her nose out of her books there was little chance to ever see her married.

It was the last two he should not have neglected. Lydia in particular – for Kitty, the silly chit, followed wherever Lydia chose to lead her. Look at them now: harebrained, loud, unguarded and a nuisance to boot – this morning more than ever!

'*The morning shows the day*' claimed the old adage and he should have taken heed, for the morning had not begun well.

He had roused himself hoping for a lengthy chat with Lizzy and a firsthand account of everything that had happened. Last night, after the carriage had been ordered to convey Mr. Darcy and Mr. Bingley to their lodgings, Lizzy had offered a few snippets, but it was very late, she seemed exhausted and her doting father had sent her off to bed. But in the morning, instead of a leisurely chat to Lizzy over cups of chocolate, he was faced with a crowd of gaggling ladies, young and old, who had come in droves to call at Landennis hopeful, no doubt, of some juicy gossip.

Mr. Bennet had retreated to the library of course – *what was a man to do when faced with such an onslaught?* – and had left Mrs. Bennet, Lydia and Kitty to gleefully dispense the gossip, with reluctant assistance from Lizzy and Jane. But then, when he had re-emerged, he had only learned to his vexation that he had missed his chance to talk to Lizzy yet again for, at a lull in morning callers, she and Jane had absconded somewhere by themselves. Which was another source of worry. The foolish girls, did they not know better? Granted, the miscreants were at large no longer, but after such a night they should have shown more sense than wandering off unattended!

Another brace of callers had made their appearance shortly and, from the darkened corridor that led towards the library, Mr. Bennet had espied some goings-on that had soured his day. On the heels of several prying local ladies, a number of officers had suddenly turned up – six or so, if he had not miscounted – and amongst them Mr. Bennet could easily recognise Mr. Darcy's cousin.

There was no telling what *he* was doing there but, true to form, the arrival of a batch of redcoats had thrown his foolish youngest into a frenzy of excitement.

Predictably, she had rushed out of the drawing room to greet them but what surprised – nay, what vexed Mr. Bennet greatly – was that the brazen girl had bodily thrown herself at Colonel Fitzwilliam!

And, as though that was not bad enough, then and there, in the great hall and right in front of the open door into the parlour – ergo, in full view of the gaggle of neighbouring ladies – she had thrown her arms about his neck and, heaven help us, she had planted a loud kiss on his lips!

Albeit grudgingly, Mr. Bennet felt compelled to own that the man had the decency to not take advantage. Pleased as he clearly was by the enthusiastic welcome, he had endeavoured to salvage what he could from the frankly unsalvageable situation and had followed the harebrained chit into the drawing room, to face what must have been a gaping crowd. It was fair to say that he deserved some credit. After all, it was not his fault that Lydia had flung herself at him and besides, not many would have walked, head high, straight into the lions' den – but then he *was* an officer in His Majesty's army and must have braved peril oftentimes before.

Much as he was forced to see that paternal intervention was in order, Mr. Bennet determined that, since it had waited fifteen years or so, it could wait a few hours more, until the family was left alone.

A stern conversation with Lydia would have to follow later on that evening and her father shuddered at the thought. Equally so at the mortifying prospect of having to speak to the Colonel as well and question him regarding his intentions. Galling, that – particularly as he could not rightly blame the man for the debacle, but what was he to do? The gossips were about to have a field day and they certainly got more than they had bargained for when they had chosen to come to call that morning.

'*A moment's peace! Is that too much to ask for?*' Mr. Bennet wondered in acute vexation as he discretely made his escape from the house – for apparently the library could not offer adequate sanctuary.

A word with Lizzy, that was what he needed, to steel himself for the nasty business.

Caught in his troublesome thoughts, Mr. Bennet did not notice the pair of fine-looking specimens left to graze higher up the road, their reins fastened upon the lowest branches of a windswept tree. He made his way along the path that led to the cove Lizzy favoured – only to stumble upon something that blew his day to smithereens.

Far down the beach, on the left, there were Jane and Mr. Bingley. Far on the right, for some strange reason Mr. Darcy was standing in the water – which was his God-given right to do if it so pleased him but, as far as Mr. Bennet was concerned, he had no business whatsoever to be carrying Lizzy in his arms!

The two men had their backs turned to each other, screening their companions, but the childish scheme was fooling no one. Least of all was it fooling Mr. Bennet who, from his vantage point, had the doubtful privilege to see quite clearly that just then his eldest daughters, his *sensible, decorous* eldest daughters, were shamelessly kissed breathless by their respective suitors. The world must have run stark raving mad – and there was every chance that so would he!

For a moment, he contemplated walking down and asking the two young men to have the kindness to inform him what the blazes did they think that they were doing! Yet the habits of a lifetime were too strong for one of his age and disposition. Mr. Bennet suddenly felt very old and very, very tired. The time for confrontation would come soon enough... Now all he craved was solitude and silence – so, shoulders slumped, he turned and walked away.

⊰⊱

Unlike Mr. Bennet's day, Mr. Darcy's might have begun ill, but it had taken an about-turn for the better. Having returned to Landennis Cove at great personal discomfort, to his unbelievable good fortune he was now leaving it an engaged man. As he walked along the path that curved up from the beach with *his betrothed*, his friend and his future sister, Darcy was not only sensible of his good fortune but also humbly grateful for the bliss that was now his.

Such was the alteration in his spirits that he was barely troubled by the size of the crowd encountered at Landennis when the four finally made their way into the parlour. He had expected a large number of callers – though not at all to come across his cousin, whom he found surrounded by some of his men and a number of young ladies, the most notable of which was Miss Lydia Bennet, hanging possessively on his arm.

"Darcy! At last!" Fitzwilliam came to greet him, emerging with some effort from the crowd.

Much as he would have liked to ask at once what brought his cousin there, civilities had to be observed, and Darcy acquitted

261

himself creditably of the duty to greet Mr. and Mrs. Bennet and be introduced to a number of those he did not know.

To his manifest discomfort, he got a hero's welcome from the lady and most of the guests, but the host looked as though he was pestered by the toothache and the grimace he offered could hardly be regarded as a smile. It was probably the crowd, Darcy assumed, for Mr. Bennet was never one for company and, casting the older gentleman a sympathetic glance, Darcy left Elizabeth to assist her mother in serving a new round of refreshments and walked to his cousin, questions on his lips.

He did not get to ask them, as Fitzwilliam was swift to offer:

"You must be wondering what brings me here. Long story short, we were assigned to the garrison in Falmouth. A shame it had not happened sooner so that you could have travelled with me, but I am pleased to see that you have found your way."

At Darcy's brief nod, the Colonel continued in a lowered voice:

"Dare I hope you have secured everything you came for?"

A wide smile was his answer and Fitzwilliam all but gaped; it was the warmest he had ever seen – on his cousin's countenance, that is.

"I have," Darcy acknowledged. "This morning, to be precise, so I would rather you refrain to comment. It has not been mentioned yet to anyone but Bingley and Miss Bennet."

A hearty pat landed on his shoulder – thankfully not the injured one – and Fitzwilliam grinned widely.

"I am *that* happy for you, Darcy," he said, as quietly as he was able. "I daresay I can wait for the details – such as why on earth would you require the best part of a month to settle the affair."

Darcy rolled his eyes.

"Should you not tell me what brings *you* to Landennis?"

Fitzwilliam shrugged.

"I would have come to call in any case, as soon as I discovered the location. But I got my answer sooner than I thought, and plenty of good cheer into the bargain, when one of your local worthies arrived at the garrison this morning with two neat packages and a very entertaining tale. So – you have finally paid all your dues to Wickham. I was at pains to keep a straight face when I heard. I would have given half – … well, let us say a hefty portion of my soldier's pay to see that duel, Darcy! I daresay it wiped the slate clean in a most satisfying way."

Despite himself, Darcy returned the smile.

"That it did."

Then his smile faded as he encountered Mr. Bennet's glance again. No so much a glance as a scowl, and it seemed aimed in his direction. Aye, so it was, without a doubt. He could not imagine what had soured Mr. Bennet towards him, so soon after last night's outpourings of gratitude. Well, truth be told, he knew what *could* have done the trick but it did not seem likely, for how would the older gentleman already know about it? Mr. Bennet's unaccountable ill-humour was niggling and uncomfortable – much like the feel of salty water in his boots – particularly as he would have wished the older man in a more amenable frame of mind when the time came to ask a particular question.

Fitzwilliam's voice drew him from his musings.

"Darcy? I was asking of your injury."

"I beg your pardon – idle thoughts. As to that, 'tis nothing. A flesh wound. It has been taken care of."

"Well! I can foresee a long night over a bottle of the finest brandy. You should call on me in Falmouth. Are you still staying with Trevellyan?"

"For now. But I shall have to seek new lodgings soon."

"I am surprised to hear you can tear yourself away," Fitzwilliam remarked with a significant glance over his cousin's shoulder.

At that, Darcy turned around, only to espy Elizabeth walking up to join them, and his countenance brightened in a way that made the other chuckle.

"Not without difficulty," Darcy retorted. "Nevertheless, it must be done."

"And why is that?"

"I have my reasons," Darcy said curtly, unwilling to launch just then into explanations as to why it would not do to continue treating Trevellyan's house as his own – or as an inn.

"Can I offer you some refreshment, gentlemen?" Elizabeth asked as soon as she arrived beside them, then added brightly: "Forgive me, Colonel, I have not even had a chance to greet you. Welcome to Landennis, Sir."

To Darcy's satisfaction, his cousin had the good sense to refrain from either oblique comments or congratulation. He merely bowed and declared that the pleasure was all his.

Better still, a few moments later he declared he must speak to one of his men and left them, presumably quick to grasp that there were times when privacy held vast appeal, even in a very crowded parlour – and the day when a man's proposal was accepted was definitely one of them.

"Oh. I did not mean to interrupt your conversation," Elizabeth offered on Fitzwilliam's departure, but Darcy waved in unconcern.

"We were not speaking of anything of consequence," he assured her. "I was merely telling my cousin that I should relinquish Lord Trevellyan's hospitality," he added, only to receive a smile that warmed his heart.

"I daresay my great-aunt's offer stands," she observed sweetly.

The mere thought of being under the same roof as her was exceedingly appealing – perhaps insanely so, given the circumstances. Darcy returned the smile, then sobered. From his place by the mantelpiece, Mr. Bennet was still watching. A long stare, more unsettling than ever.

"A most tempting offer," he replied at last, "but perhaps I should not impose upon this household…"

'*And on your father's dwindling goodwill*', Darcy thought but chose not to say.

"*The Hope and Anchor* in Falmouth would suffice," he said instead. "No doubt some boat or other could be bespoken to bring me across to Landennis Cove to call," he added very quietly and at that Elizabeth's eyes warmed with affectionate mischief and her tones took a matching timbre:

"Are you suggesting secret assignations?"

"I would not dare! Although just now there is little that could possibly appeal more."

Elizabeth smiled back, but did not get to answer.

A few steps behind her stood her father, a stern set to his jaw.

"Mr. Darcy? A word, Sir. In the library, if you please!" he asked – nay, demanded – with far less civility than was his wont. "And I would trouble you to bring the others. That is to say, your cousin and your friend."

Compared to the noisy bustle in the parlour, the library was deadly quiet when the summoned three made their way within, to find a grim-looking Mr. Bennet walking slowly before the fireplace, hands behind his back. He stopped at their arrival and gestured them in, but offered neither seats nor refreshments. Instead, he asked the last one in – Bingley – to be so kind as to close the door.

"Well now," he observed dryly. "Have any of you gentlemen got anything to tell me? I daresay there must be *some* things that I ought to know!"

Darcy's eyes widened. Although at a loss as to exactly how the older gentleman managed to keep himself so well informed, he could see what might have prompted his own summons and for that matter, Bingley's – yet could not fathom why Fitzwilliam of all people was also hauled before the bench. And then his cousin spoke – and Darcy all but gaped.

"Mr. Bennet, I would like to ask your permission to court your youngest daughter."

Unlike Darcy, Mr. Bennet did not seem at all surprised.

"I see. That is most honourable of you," he said but it was anybody's guess whether or not he was in earnest. "May I ask though, is that in consequence of… shall we say, her most unconventional salute?"

The terse words wrought no change in Fitzwilliam's countenance; it remained blank, as if he was reporting to one of his superiors.

"No, Sir. Not at all."

His brows raised, Darcy eyed his cousin. What the deuce was this all about? It had begun to sound as though the young chit had done something improper and Fitzwilliam was stepping into the fray to preserve her reputation. Commendable in theory, but his sensible, astute, well-informed cousin tied for life to Miss *Lydia* Bennet?

Some effort was required to suppress the shudder.

No effort could suppress the gasp when Fitzwilliam spoke again.

"I must own I have formed an attachment to Miss Lydia."

"In just one day?" Mr. Bennet shot back, uncannily voicing Darcy's thoughts.

"Yes, Sir. It happens."

"Hm. Now, I shall not ask Mr. Bingley here, whose attempts at courtship have kept us on our toes for months but what of *you*, Mr. Darcy? Is your own attachment one day old as well?"

Involuntarily, Darcy bristled at both the tone and the implication particularly as, unlike his cousin, he had no recent experience of submitting to authority. Still, he had no wish to antagonise Elizabeth's father, little as he appreciated the manner in which the older man chose to assert his parental rights.

"No, Sir. Several months, rather."

Mr. Bennet arched a brow.

"I see. You will forgive me for observing that I was not aware of your interest, nor of Lizzy reciprocating it, for that matter – until today," he added darkly. "And I am troubled by the notion that hasty decisions seem to follow on the heel of yesterday's events. No doubt, as I said already, we are greatly in your debt but – …'"

Darcy's jaw tightened.

"I am in no position to reassure you that *this* has no bearing," he said firmly. "Only E – … Miss Elizabeth can do so. But I hope she can persuade you that her consent was not based on a misplaced sense of gratitude!"

"Forgive me, I had no intention to offend," the older man said calmly, almost wistfully. "But you must see that exceptional circumstances have their way of influencing matters…"

Darcy's first reaction was to protest – yet suddenly cold doubt seeped in to chill him.

Was there a basis for Mr. Bennet's reservations?

The chill went deeper, as many pieces fitted. She had refused him only yesterday, and even at the ball, during their heart-rending time on the terrace, she had shown him kindness and compassion, but she had still urged him to leave Cornwall and find his peace elsewhere. And had only changed her stance after last night's events – the liberties he had taken, and the duel!

Was there truth then in the sickening suspicion? Did she accept him today out of mere gratitude, perhaps not even sensing its insidious sway, and had given in to gratify *his* feelings?

All the joy of this most glorious day drained out of him, leaving him barren, empty. His voice was lifeless when at last he spoke.

"I shall not make any demands of your daughter, Mr. Bennet. I… would not – could not. If she – … If your concern is proven justified and Miss Elizabeth finds that she regrets having given her consent, then of course I shall not hold her to it."

A look of pained consternation crossed Fitzwilliam's countenance, mirrored almost identically in Bingley's, but Darcy did not look at them to notice. His glance drifted out of the narrow mullioned windows. No one said a word. In the ensuing silence, the bustle from the adjoining parlour reached them like some sort of a discordant, mocking tune, broken at last by Mr. Bennet, who said in a low but very earnest voice:

"I thank you, Sir. Your honourable conduct is appreciated."

"Mr. Bennet, I – ..." Bingley spoke up, presumably struck by the injustice of the fact that, of all three, it was only Darcy's suit that was thus challenged.

He could not know that there was ample reason for it, at least to his host's way of thinking. Mr. Bennet had no doubt of Jane's sentiments for her indecisive suitor. They had been plain enough for months, at least within the family. As for Lydia, she had made her feelings clear earlier that morning – far, far too clear for decency and comfort! But Lizzy, darling Lizzy! Did *she* know what she was about?

Mr. Bennet did not get to hear the case that Bingley was prepared to make. With a swiftly raised hand, Darcy forestalled his friend.

"I hope you would allow me to court your daughter though," he said, slowly and distinctly. "Without ties or expectations and, needless to say, without public announcements. Thus, clear-headed decisions might be taken in good time and when they are... if they go against me, then Miss Elizabeth might proceed without the inconvenience of a broken engagement."

Mr. Bennet settled a long glance upon him.

"That is most considerate. I could not have asked for more," he said at last. "You would excuse me, gentlemen. I must see my daughter."

As soon as the door closed quietly behind him, Fitzwilliam exhaled violently and raked his fingers through his hair.

"Darcy, this is – " he burst out hotly, but his cousin cut him short.

"No more! Not now! Forgive me, I cannot do this now. Pray, be so kind to leave me. Cousin – Bingley – I... would appreciate some time..."

The others stammered something, their features twisted in affectionate concern, but thankfully found it in them to promptly do as bid, in unspoken understanding that at this point in time no words could offer palliation.

Neither could silence.

The now empty room was stifling, oppressive. Releasing a deep breath, Darcy ran his hands over his face, then walked to the window to rest his brow on the small dusty panes.

He could scarce think. He did not *wish* to think. Not anymore.

The enormity of it all could not be encompassed. In mere days – nay, hours, less than forty-eight – he had been taken from abyss to summit and cast back into the same, time and again, and he could not bear it any longer. Not now, when every cherished hope was snatched from his grasp just as he thought that he had reached the end of all his sorrows!

The treasured recollection of those glorious moments in the cove – *their* cove – pierced through him. There was light in her eyes then. There was love, acceptance. Her kiss. Her arms around him. Her half-closed eyes clouded with awakening passion.

His insides turned and twisted, gripped by sudden painful longing.

A mistake… Could it have been? Tangled emotions confused by gratitude? Not that – never that! Though to be fully honest, he would take it gladly. Have her in his life on any terms. With unequal feelings, even with little more than friendship, if it must be so.

Yet, much as something akin to hatred rose in him towards Elizabeth's father for tarnishing this perfect day and crumbling his joy to dust, he knew that the man was in the right: this was no life for his beloved daughter – for this wonderful woman that both of them loved above all else.

He opened his eyes, raised his head and turned to lean against the windowsill, arms crossed over his chest as if to grip hold of himself, keep himself from crumbling to pieces.

He would not hold her to it – of course not! Not against her better judgement, if her better judgement was to steer her away, but the foreseen emptiness was crushing. Life held no flavour and no meaning without her…

What seemed like an age later he was still there, staring at the well-worn floorboards, seeing nothing. Suddenly, the door burst open and was just as forcefully slammed shut – and Darcy's glance shot up to see Elizabeth striding in towards him.

He straightened and let his arms drop. It was plain to see she had been crying. She was not crying now. She came up to him, very close, and reached to hold his face between her palms.

"He is *wrong*," she said quietly, but with great emphasis. "Fitzwilliam, my father is wrong! I have not the slightest doubt and I do not wish to wait. I want our engagement to be announced today. Would that the banns could be called tomorrow! I want to marry you as soon as may be. I love you. I love *you*," she forcefully repeated and her eyes filled anew with tears.

With a ragged breath, Darcy took her in his arms. Almost painfully tight, and very close.

"Elizabeth – ..." he whispered and, before he could even begin to know what he was about to say, her lips came up to silence him with a long, breathtaking kiss.

Had he been able to formulate a coherent thought, Darcy might have begun to contemplate hiring a vessel in Falmouth that very day or on the morrow at the latest, though not to ferry him to pursue his courtship at Landennis but to sail out with Elizabeth into the open waters and ask the captain to perform the rites of a marriage at sea!

✥

"So. You are not to settle at Landennis," Mrs. Pencarrow observed matter-of-factly.

They were alone together in the older lady's chambers as, according to the doctor's orders, to which she was submitting with no pleasure, she was still bedridden, for one more day at least.

Once all the guests – welcome and unwelcome – had finally left, Elizabeth saw fit to come and sit with her great-aunt, not just to keep her company but also to inform her of what had come to pass.

The intelligence was received with no manifest displeasure – but also with a startling lack of surprise. What was it, Elizabeth wondered, about shrewd old women, that made them see further than most? Perhaps they lived vicariously through others and amused themselves with watching younger people go through their lives and follow age-old patterns while foolishly believing they were blazing virgin trails.

"No, I shall not settle here, I am sorry to say," she replied at last.

"Are you? I should hope not. Why would you marry the man, if you are sorry?" Mrs. Pencarrow chortled.

"I was speaking of disappointing *you*," Elizabeth replied, reaching for her great-aunt's thin, cold fingers. "But... I have other sisters, who would be worthier recipients for your kindness."

The older woman pressed her hand, then patted it gently.

"I am old, Elizabeth, and tired. Too tired to begin afresh with a task I thought long completed. My will stands, child. Landennis is yours to do with as you please. I would have liked it to remain in the family, but sell it if you must and dispose of the proceedings as you wish. Or ask another of your sisters to settle here in your stead. After all, you know them better than I ever shall. Maybe one of them would like to make her life here."

In response to the older woman's wistfulness, Elizabeth eagerly retorted:

"*I* would have, Aunt. Gratefully and gladly. But – ..."

"I know. Love got in the way," Mrs. Pencarrow interjected. "You could have had both though, you know. I had great hopes that you would have both. *And* a title to go with them."

"I could have. But it would have been an error."

"Would it?"

"I am quite certain."

"Well!" Mrs Pencarrow stirred and shuffled up against her pillows, then patted the coverlet with impatience. "I shall leave my bed tomorrow, and blast the foolish doctor and his mollycoddling! You must bring him to me, this paragon you speak of, Mr. Darcy, who is worth forsaking Lord Trevellyan's vast wealth and title."

"Mr. Darcy is a gentleman of great consequence himself, Aunt," Elizabeth smiled at the older woman's sudden petulance. "But I would have chosen him regardless."

"Praise be that I am old for this nonsense they call love," Mrs. Pencarrow muttered. "Go, child. Leave me to my grumblings and go to your bedchamber to stare out of the window and dream of him. 'Tis a long time since I was one and twenty but I imagine this is still what young ladies choose to do in cases such as these."

With a low chuckle of her own, Elizabeth leaned over to kiss the wrinkled cheek.

"So it is, Aunt. And, to please you, for once I shall do just as you say."

Chapter 24

The small craft was skilfully manoeuvred towards the best landing spot in Landennis Cove and then the hired men, all but the one still at the rudder, unconcernedly jumped overboard into the shallow waters to pull the boat up high upon dry land.

Under any other circumstances Darcy and his two companions would have followed suit rather than wait to be conveyed ashore like as many damsels, but tonight was not a night for wading into salty waters. Darcy tried and failed to suppress a quiet chuckle. It was the first time in living memory that he was travelling to a ball by boat – but then again this spring seemed to have been one for doing a great many things for the first time ever.

Lantern in hand, one of the Falmouth men led the way towards the coastal path and, once they had secured the boat, the other two followed, in eager expectation of a tipple and a bite in the servants' quarters at Landennis.

The lantern was not needed. The waxing moon, well past its first quarter, was rising high over the dark waters, gilding the cliffs in a silvery light that allowed them to see well enough where they were going. Besides, by now they could have found their way blindfolded. The selfsame hired craft had brought them there to call above a dozen times before, ever since Darcy and his friend had relinquished Lord Trevellyan's hospitality for the lesser but untroubled comforts of a Falmouth inn.

Yet despite Elizabeth's light teasing, there had been no hope of rewarding secret assignations. Perversely, Mr. Bennet seemed intent to watch over their comings and goings with more determination than the keenest exciseman – and with greater success into the bargain. More often than not, he was already walking the cliff path on their arrival, like some lone sentinel set to guard his outpost, or was doggedly insistent upon accompanying his daughters on each and every one of their morning walks.

Privately Darcy suspected this had little to do with protecting them from smugglers or from a French invasion. Rather, it was as if he was determined to frustrate all hope of stolen privacy in the secluded cove. He was welcoming enough towards the callers – albeit in a dry and somewhat mordant way, that took some getting used to – but he was clinging to his daughters' hems like goosegrass, vexingly unwilling to relinquish either of them into their suitors' keeping a moment sooner than their prospective wedding-day!

Darcy's only consolation was that he was not the only one chafing under the imposition. Fitzwilliam was struggling mightily to bear it with the vaguest semblance of goodwill, particularly as he was already at a disadvantage and could not call as often as the other two, due to his many duties at the garrison in Falmouth. Even Bingley's proverbially easy temper was often stretched beyond endurance. But it was Elizabeth's clear exasperation at the heavy-handed chaperoning that Darcy found most soothing. And there was reason enough for exasperation as, of all the couples, it was by their side that Mr. Bennet always chose to walk. Not just by their side, but constantly between them, arm in arm with his daughter and endeavouring to engage them both in conversation.

Invariably they would soon be urged to make their way towards the house and, since there was little joy to be found in tarrying, Darcy – along with the other two irked suitors – would resign himself to trade walking shoulder to shoulder with the *father* for the doubtful delights of drinking tea with the *mother*. And even then Mr. Bennet would not retire to the library, but would persevere in the parlour with a tenacity worthy of better causes.

After a while, Darcy's frustration turned into mild amusement at the older man's transparent machinations. Galling as they were, he could not find it in him to dislike Elizabeth's beloved father, and if Mr. Bennet seemed disposed to cling to her until the inevitable separation, then this was a sentiment Darcy could easily understand.

There would be no hope for privacy tonight, *that* was quite certain – but it could not be helped. With renewed vigour, Darcy applied himself to negotiating the ascent. They soon reached the top, and neither he nor his companions stopped to admire the mysterious beauty spreading at their feet or the glinting path the moon traced upon the waters.

A very different lure called, to some of them at least, and they pressed on down the narrow stretch leading towards the carriage road and thence to the old manor-house that lay in a dip of the land before them.

Several torches were now fixed into the ground on both sides of the winding road to show the way and give bright welcome to the throng of carriages expected to convey Mrs. Pencarrow's guests to the first ball hosted at Landennis in two decades. Still, none were yet in sight. It must have been too early. With another chuckle at their boyish impatience, Darcy led the way down the shallow incline.

The house bore no resemblance to the night when himself and Bingley had hidden in the shadows, unknown guardians of the women they loved. The lower windows shone with bright lights in abundance and the old oak doors were thrown open wide.

Darcy's eyes drifted to the upper windows. Lights shone there as well, in most if not all – and breath caught in his chest at the unexpected sight.

No, it was not a figment of his imagination. In the third window to the right, he could espy a silhouette, nay, two, three, seemingly in conversation. Yet he had eyes for only one of them and a smile fluttered on his lips at the recollection of himself keeping a steady watch over the drive to Netherfield, half a year ago almost to the day, on the eve of another ball.

The thought that *she* was now doing the same – waiting for him, watching out for him – filled his heart with grateful wonder and hastened his steps towards the entrance. And then she saw him and she smiled, raised her hand in greeting, then vanished from the window. With no attempt to school his features into the proper show of civil reserve, Darcy stepped from the shadows into the bright light.

⁂

Landennis Manor had long since filled with guests. They had begun to file in shortly after his arrival, which could not fail to rile him for, as a result, *she* was forced to leave him and join her family in the receiving line.

They came in droves, filling the great hall and, as he impatiently waited for Elizabeth to be returned to him, Darcy wondered in passing if Lord Trevellyan would make an appearance.

Their parting a few weeks ago had been very civil but, on his lordship's side, understandably cold. Without any effort, Darcy found it in him to feel a great deal of sympathy for the other man. To have loved and lost – to have lost *her* – must be unbearable. Devastating.

Darcy drew a deep breath and drained his glass.

He had not lost, thank goodness! Shameful yet overwhelming, the relief was there – and much as he felt for Trevellyan in his grief, he blessed his stars that the other man's loss was his own gain.

Music filled the great hall around him – he had not noticed the minstrel gallery before. It was most noticeable now, crowded as it was with very skilled performers, and the vast room was becoming crowded too, with cheerful people in glittering apparel. Yet none could keep his attention for a moment, save for the figure trimly clad in cream-gold satin, still trapped in the devil's own invention that they called *'receiving line'*.

◦⚬⊙⊙⚬◦

The sight of her, her scent, her smile, her every move, were both a balm and a sweet torment, and it was only thanks to hours of relentless schooling that he did not misstep, for precious little of his thoughts were spared for the patterns of the dance.

The great hall – the set of a not so distant duel – was as different as could be from that horrific time of peril. Couples glided and bounded over the floorboards that had rung with his own and Wickham's footsteps, over the spot where the old suit of armour had collapsed and clattered, and flower garlands festooned the walls upon which long, fast moving shadows had danced their deadly dance.

The brief recollection forced itself upon Elizabeth as well, at the same time, making her shiver. Unconsciously, she tightened her hold on his gloved fingers as she twirled around her betrothed in a very different dance. She curtsied to his bow and her eyes misted at her unbelievable good fortune. He was alive and well – and he was hers. And very soon, yet still not soon enough, they would nevermore be parted. She wished it was tomorrow, their all-too-distant wedding-day and at the same time she incongruously wished that this magic night would never end.

"Would you stand up with me again?" she heard him whisper when the dance, their third set, had drawn to a close.

"This is hardly fair," Elizabeth smilingly chided. "You know that I would wish to, above all things."

"Then do!" he urged with fervour, his eyes unsettlingly burning into hers. "I have missed you dreadfully all morning."

"And I you, but you know I cannot. The other guests would be terribly offended."

"Let them be offended," he urged again – and nothing but levity and archness could provide recourse against the recklessness his words and tone engendered, against the wild drumming of her pulse beating fast and loud in her ears and drowning out every shred of common sense. Then levity and archness there must be, Elizabeth determined, and airily offered:

"Mr. Darcy! You used to be so civil and so very proper."

"I used to be all manner of awful things before I met you," he retorted warmly then lightened the tone, presumably for her benefit – or his. "Say no, if you must. At least I am relieved to know that you should then refuse to stand up with another."

"Not after three sets. Still, I imagine it would be meagre comfort."

He shrugged.

"A wise man would take comfort from such as he is given."

"I am pleased to see that you are being wise."

"'Tis but a crumbling *façade*, my love," he whispered, leaning closer. "Truth be told, right now I find myself most unwisely wishing that we could walk away from prying eyes."

"That is most unwise, I grant you," Elizabeth replied with a little breathless laugh, "and also bordering on the impossible, I fear."

Darcy's lips curled into something of a wistful smile.

"I know." He ran his thumb over the back of her gloved hand. "Go, then," he said at last. "Do your duty – but pray reserve your supper-dance for me."

A warm clasp of her fingers around his was her only answer, before she made her way towards her great-aunt and her mother. He might as well do his own duty and stand up with her sisters, Darcy decided, but upon inspection he found that they were all engaged, even Miss Mary, so he ambled towards the punchbowl instead.

He could not spot either his cousin or his friend, but a glance towards a nearby window alcove revealed Trevellyan, standing solemnly apart from the surrounding gaiety. Their eyes met and, after the briefest hesitation, Trevellyan acknowledged him with a bow.

Returning it, Darcy pondered whether civility required that he should walk to him, yet before he could bring himself to do so the other turned away, presumably to avoid that very outcome.

Relieved in no small measure Darcy went to select a cup and fill it, then withdrew out of the way to the spot that had been Trevellyan's. This is where Fitzwilliam found him a short while later, when his dance with his betrothed had come to an end.

"Abandoned, are you?" he good-naturedly remarked, having supplied himself with punch. "So, have you informed our esteemed relations of your upcoming nuptials?" Fitzwilliam added, only to be answered with a question:

"Have *you?*"

The Colonel shrugged.

"I have written Mater and his lordship."

"And?"

"I got the reply I was expecting."

"I see."

He did, with no effort of imagination. The Earl of Langthorne set great store by having suitable connections, much like his sister Lady Catherine de Bourgh. A union with an unknown quantity of a girl of meagre stock from Hertfordshire must have grated on his lordship's sensibilities.

Presumably Fitzwilliam had seen no purpose in informing his father that, to his great surprise, he had chanced to fall in love with an heiress. It was just as well, Darcy uncharitably thought. The intelligence would be most welcome in counteracting first impressions once Lord Langthorne made Miss Lydia's acquaintance.

Not for the first time, Darcy marvelled at his sensible cousin being ensnared by youthful but very senseless beauty. A pity, that!

Fitzwilliam would have done well to remember the old saying, *'Like mother, like daughter'*. But then the selfsame words of wisdom should have warned *him* against offering for Elizabeth, Darcy thought with something between a shudder and a chuckle.

The age-old warning held no sway of course. Besides, Elizabeth was as different from her mother as cheese from chalk. Praise be, she was her father's daughter far more than her mother's. The same, however, could not be said of her youngest sister. Miss Lydia was Mrs. Bennet through and through. Still, she was young. Fifteen. Sixteen maybe. With careful, loving guidance, there was *some* hope.

"I have written Georgiana," he suddenly offered, not just to change the unpalatable subject but also remembering that he had made no answer to his cousin's query.

"I should imagine she was as surprised as she was thrilled."

"Indeed. She is most eager to make Elizabeth's acquaintance and was distraught that I would not countenance her travelling at such great distance with only Mrs. Annesley for company and protection. At length, I pacified her with the assurance that she can join me at Netherfield as soon as Bingley opens up his house again."

"So you will not return to Pemberley until after the wedding?"

"I will not. I shall have to entrust Mrs. Reynolds with the preparations."

Fitzwilliam chuckled.

"'Tis a vast pity I am in no position to sit back and laugh at you for acting the part of the lovelorn fool."

"Indeed, you are not," was all that Darcy felt prudent to say on the matter. "So what of your commission?"

"I have resigned it. Young Stanhope is expected to come down and take my place. Once he arrives, I am free to wander off to Netherfield along with you two gentlemen of leisure. I trust your friend would tolerate the imposition."

There was no doubt of that. Cheerful, easy-going Bingley would welcome anyone to Netherfield, even Fitzwilliam's supercilious relations – although Darcy dearly hoped it would not come to that!

"Excuse me," Fitzwilliam offered lightly, presumably eager to rejoin his ladylove, as another set of dances had just ended and Miss Lydia was dutifully returned to her mother's side.

So was Elizabeth, and Darcy pondered whether he might stretch the boundaries of ballroom etiquette and ask her to stand up with him again. Or at least be near her and have the joy of her society, if there was little wisdom in defying norm. Though he failed to see the need for being so punctilious about it. After all, the betrothal – or rather betrothals – would be announced shortly before supper.

He drained his punch and turned to amble in Elizabeth's direction diverted by the passing thought that, oddly enough, Fitzwilliam and Bingley had not discovered yet that they could have great sport at his expense and tease him mercilessly for his newfound interest in country dancing.

He did not get far. To his vague discomfort, he noticed that Trevellyan was there before him. His lordship bowed formally as he made his request and was presumably accepted, though not without unease judging by Elizabeth's turn of countenance.

Darcy frowned. Much as he sympathised with Trevellyan for his loss, the man's presumption riled him in no small measure. What would possess him to impose upon her in this fashion? Surely he must see it brought her nothing but acute discomfort!

His jaw tightened – yet he endeavoured to school himself into some understanding for the other man's position. Put himself in his place. The unforgiving separation. The last evening. The last dance...

He barely suppressed a shudder and, with great determination, he turned on his heels and walked away, so as not to discomfit either his betrothed or his erstwhile rival with his presence or his searching glance. The parlour was quite full of merrymakers, and card-tables were set up in the adjoining drawing room. He did not linger there. Cards had never sparked his interest and were not likely to begin tonight. So he took another cup of punch from an obliging footman and returned to the parlour, steadfastly keeping his back to the great hall throughout – for he knew full well how badly he would have needed this final act of kindness, had the scales of Fortune been tipped the other way.

⁓⊙⊙⁓

The music reached her as though from a great distance and Elizabeth curtsied deeply as the dance began. She would not glance up to her partner – *she could not!* – yet as their hands met and held and they walked in slow measure around the axis of their entwined forearms, she looked up and almost faltered. It was inches away, his handsome face, tense and unsmiling; inches away, the dark eyes never quitting hers... A step, another step, a bow, a curtsy and they were separated, yet his gaze remained fixed on her with an anguished look that tore at her heart.

Their dance had perforce turned into a protracted parting. A long, harrowing adieu on the strains of far too poignant music. In any other circumstance, the piece might have been soothing. It was not. Its soft, alluring quality only deepened the sadness of the moment.

Despite herself, Elizabeth's eyes were drawn again into the pools of dark pain that were Lord Trevellyan's.

"I hope you can find it in you to forgive me," she whispered without thinking when the pattern of the dance brought them once more together.

At that, he shook his head.

"Say no more, I beg you," his words came in a ragged whisper. "Let it be thus – a dance and nothing more. As though we have not spoken of any of my wishes. As though I do not know that you will go to *him*."

It was the wrong thing to say – wrong even to listen! She did not wish it to be so. Much as his lordship's plight distressed her, she had pledged herself wholeheartedly to Mr. Darcy – to Fitzwilliam – and she *would* go to him, there was nothing that she wanted more!

Instinctively, her eyes roamed over the crowded hall in search of him. He was no longer in the window alcove where she had espied him talking to his cousin and she sought him now with something very much like panic, nearly losing her footing as she did so.

Surely he had not taken it ill that she had agreed to stand up with Lord Trevellyan! He would know it was a mere act of friendship and nothing, *nothing* more. Oh, she should have refused! And then sit out all the other dances, gladly. It mattered not one jot. She did not even wish to dance again tonight!

In every other instance she would have found jealous displays objectionable, offensive even. Not so now, when she knew full well that she had caused him enough pain already. He should not have another moment of distress or doubt because of her! If only she could catch his eye and gauge what he was thinking! Where *was* he?

Her companion's subdued tones drew her at last from her agitated musing.

"You are unwell, Miss Bennet. May I escort you to your father?"

"I… beg your pardon?"

"I believe I can see your father in the parlour talking to Mr. Darcy," Lord Trevellyan tactfully observed, his voice low and wistful. "This dance seems too taxing. Pray allow me to escort you to him."

So her anxious search did not go unnoticed. Indeed, how could it? Yet he had feigned no knowledge, and his delicacy of manner and generous suggestion well-nigh brought tears to her eyes.

Why was it that so many other women went to their graves as spinsters, or having spent their lives tied to unworthy men, while her lot was this: to be forced to choose between two of the most worthy.

Hurt one, so very deeply, so that she could have the other. But there was no choice. For her, there was no choice – there *had* to be Mr. Darcy and none other!

Her eyes darted in the direction Lord Trevellyan had indicated and she caught sight of her betrothed, over her father's shoulder. Surprisingly, he was laughing, presumably at something that her father must have said, and relief coursed through her to see him thus – at ease, oddly devoid of the reserve he uniformly displayed in her father's presence and moreover clearly unperturbed by her choice of dancing partner. And then his glance met hers and she found no shadow there, just a warm smile, which she joyfully returned.

Thus freed from fears which she could now dismiss as foolish, she was at last able to devote her full attention to her callously overlooked companion.

"I thank you," she said softly. "There is no cause for that. I am quite well."

"Are you certain?"

"I am. Pray excuse my earlier distraction."

"Nay, Miss Bennet. *I* should apologise for my untoward comment…"

"Do not concern yourself. Perhaps you were in the right. Perhaps we ought to have had this dance in silence. Some things are better left unsaid."

"Could you pretend then that I have not said them?"

"I could. Yet… now that we *have* spoken," she tentatively added as the dance brought them back together, "pray let me say that I wish you joy. I am distraught to have caused you pain and I pray that it will be of short duration."

Lord Trevellyan forbore to answer, presumably unwilling to distress her further with the stark admission that it was most unlikely. She pressed on, regardless:

"I pray that you will find your true match soon. Then you will know why I am not she."

He bowed and, incongruous as it might have been to the pattern of the dance, he lifted her gloved hand and pressed it to his lips.

"Be happy," he whispered and his pain-filled voice shook her to the core.

Mercifully, she was spared from having to make an answer.

The last strains of music rang, sweet and poignant and, with a final bow, Lord Trevellyan escorted her off the floor. He pressed her hand in his and left her standing by the dark-panelled wall watching his retreating back as he swiftly walked to the corridor that led towards the gardens. Without a backward glance, he vanished into the shadows of the night.

To Elizabeth's great comfort, she was never to know that he did not go far – just far enough to hide his overwhelming anguish from the eyes of others. He reached the end of the dark granite building and leaned his back and then his head against the cold damp wall. Moonlight fell on his face, revealing his ravaged features to a solitary figure that sat concealed on a wooden bench under a bough of jasmine, where she had retreated a short while ago to nurse her own bitter disappointment at her unkind fortunes.

Why was *she* not chosen? Granted, she was not as pretty as the others, but she was young and cheerful and amiable and *kind*. Why not her? *What* was she lacking?

Whatever it was, the others seemed to have it in abundance. Jane, of course – she was sweet and by far the best looking. But Lydia? She was no better than herself! And Lizzy! That was the most galling! Lizzy had won the hand of the handsome and wealthy Mr. Darcy but nay, that was not enough for *her*. She had gone and won this man's heart also – and had broken it too, if the sight before her was any indication.

The naked pain on Lord Trevellyan's features was so stark that suddenly Kitty was shaken out of her self-centred musings. He was not crying, surely! Nay, that was foolish – grown men did not cry.

He was not, but the frozen grief was worse even than tears and a moment later Kitty was almost glad she could not see it anymore, when Lord Trevellyan buried his face in his gloved hands.

She wished she could go to him and somehow soothe this awful pain. She did not. She knew full well that she would only mortify him further with her presence, in his very private anguish. So she leaned back, hiding deeper into the shadows of the fragrant alcove, until at last he vanished into the Cornish night.

∞◎◎∞

Back in the parlour, Mr. Darcy was having an incomparably better evening for reasons aplenty, one of them being that the quarter-hour in Mr. Bennet's company had turned out to be far more enjoyable than most of their previous encounters. It was the old gentleman who had sought him out and not the other way around. While Darcy was steadfastly feigning interest in the goings-on in the very crowded parlour purposely keeping his back to the great hall, he was suddenly distracted from his self-appointed task by a voice at his side:

"Let me offer you something stronger than punch, Mr. Darcy," his future father-in-law amicably said. "You seem in need of some pleasant diversion."

"I thank you, Sir. Your company will suffice."

"Handsomely said, young man," the other chuckled. "And handsomely done, if I may be allowed to say so."

Darcy all but arched a brow. Was Mr. Bennet attuned to the undercurrents between him, Elizabeth and Lord Trevellyan? The remark implied it and, upon reflection, that should not have come as a surprise, for the older gentleman had often showed himself a trifle too astute for comfort. Nevertheless, Darcy merely offered:

"I have not the pleasure of catching your meaning."

"Have you not? Well, we shall not quibble over it. Let me just say that I find myself in a most enviable position for a father of five daughters, Mr. Darcy."

"How so?"

"Unlike most, I am faced with the pleasant conundrum of settling upon a favourite son-in-law between three who are rather too worthy for an easy choice. Still, I think you might be beating the others to the post."

Darcy's lips twitched.

"That is highly gratifying, Mr. Bennet," he offered with a bow.

"Yes, well. I daresay there is great wisdom in sometimes turning a blind eye. Perhaps I should have seen it sooner. And while we are on the subject, I believe I owe you an apology," the other added and his tone of voice gave Darcy pause.

Over the last few weeks, a better acquaintance with Mr. Bennet had taught him to expect dry humour to colour virtually all of the gentleman's communications. There was no dry humour now, but a genuine ring that surprised him a vast deal more than the oblique reference to his act of kindness to Trevellyan.

"You do?" he asked, letting his surprise show. Whatever for?"

"Shall we say, for my heavy-handed approach to your courtship?" the older man chuckled. "I should imagine some might have found it rather vexing…"

Despite himself, Darcy echoed the other's chuckle. Over Mr. Bennet's shoulder, he caught Elizabeth's anxious glance and his smile grew warmer. She had no reason for concern – this interview with Mr. Bennet was going far better than the others. She would be pleased to hear it and presumably find the exchange diverting, once he got the chance to share it with her. He cast her a long reassuring look, then turned to his companion.

"I trust you do not expect me to admit as much, Sir. You will forgive me, but I shall do nothing of the sort. I should be loath to cede the advantage in this contest for your good opinion," he replied with a light-hearted hint of teasing that Mr. Bennet was pleasantly surprised to find in him.

So the rather solemn suitor had a sense of humour after all and, given some encouragement, he was not averse to showing it. The discovery cheered him. It was good to know he was a fair match for Lizzy's disposition. All in all, over the last few weeks, he had shown himself a good match for her in many ways, truth be told. Much more so than Mr. Bennet had originally thought, before he got to know the young man better. Perhaps he should have trusted Lizzy's judgement more – or sooner – he mused, then moved his glass to the other hand, so that he could pat Darcy on the shoulder:

"One satisfaction is left for me, if I live long enough, that is."

"And what might that be?"

"Watching *you* when your daughters are old enough for suitors."

Once more, Darcy echoed the mischievous laughter.

"Have you considered you might be thwarted in your amusements if we have sons only?" he cheerfully retorted. "But rest assured, you *shall* have your fun – and a great deal sooner than expected. You see, I have a sister to whom I have been more of a father than a brother. She is sixteen years of age and before too long there *will* be suitors to contend with. And when that time comes, I hope I can count on your assistance."

At that, Mr. Bennet burst out laughing – so heartily in fact that he all but spluttered in his port.

"Oh dear me! Gladly, my boy, gladly. The poor souls, then they are surely doomed." Still chortling, he dried his lips with a kerchief, then nudged the other into action. "Come now, let us find Mrs. Pencarrow – or rather let me find her while you fetch Lizzy and the others. Can you spot Mr. Bingley and your cousin? I should imagine they would be found cavorting somewhere in the great hall. Pray be so kind to seek them, Mr. Darcy. We have some happy tidings to announce."

⁓⊙⊙⊙⁓

The announcement of the three betrothals was duly made – and was of course greeted in the customary fashion – thus giving the three couples free licence to stand up together for the remainder of the dances.

At last, the supper dance had come and gone and, by now, so had most of supper – a pleasant albeit boisterous affair that was shown to have but one notable disadvantage: he could not feast his eyes on her without being conspicuous about it. Well, so be it, Darcy shrugged, and turned in his chair for a slightly better angle, to find her at his side, daintily spooning at her syllabub.

His fingers twitched and his chest tightened as the tip of her tongue flashed between her lips to catch a droplet of the creamy mixture. He swallowed hard and suppressed a sigh.

Did she not have the faintest notion of how maddeningly enticing she was as she did just that?

He reached for his glass and took a long sip of whatever liquid there was in it, yet his throat still felt unbearably dry. With any luck, before he became unhinged altogether, he might be allowed to tell her – *show her* – how much she meant to him and how her irresistible allure was driving him out of his senses!

He took another sip then set his glass down, his hand rather unsteady on the stem as thoughts that had no place in company and indeed at the dining table came to lure him into further depths of sweet insanity.

The lady at his left – a Mrs. Gower from somewhere north of Falmouth – said something which went woefully unheeded, until Elizabeth's light touch on his sleeve brought him back from his own brand of hell seasoned with heaven.

"Mr. Darcy? Mrs. Gower was just asking if you have ever travelled to Land's End," she quietly prompted. Then, once civil replies were duly made and Darcy apologised to the other lady for his inattention, Elizabeth added with an impish smile: "You were very far. May I ask where?"

"Several long weeks into the future," he daringly answered in a lowered voice.

"Yes, I have noticed your penchant for drifting a long way, either into the past or to the future. You should try the present sometimes. I often find it rather more appealing."

"Of course. Forgive me, I am a very poor companion. 'Tis a feeble excuse, I know, but you *were* in my thoughts."

"And were they pleasant?"

"Very."

And tormenting. But *that* he did not say.

"Then by all means return to where you were."

"I thank you, but I shall take your advice and keep to the delightful present. Or at least drift no further than tomorrow. I must say, I am looking forward to it with great anticipation."

"As am I. I hope the weather holds."

He had engaged a square-rigged ketch to take them sailing on the morrow. *The Rashley* was a good-sized craft, a great deal larger than the sloop bespoken to bring the three gentleman-callers daily to Landennis. It was after all due to accommodate more than three passengers at once, and besides Darcy would not have wished for Elizabeth's first experience of the kind to be overshadowed by the fears a small and seemingly unstable boat might cause her. For it *was* to be her first experience as, not surprisingly, the outing suggested by Lord Trevellyan all those weeks ago had perforce been abandoned.

Darcy could well remember his first day out sailing; the thrill of it, surpassing everything he had known before.

Unreasonably perhaps, it pleased him greatly to think that *he* would be the one to introduce Elizabeth to it, not Trevellyan – and his fingers drummed on the stem of his half-drained wineglass as he endeavoured *not* to dwell on all manner of experiences it would be his utmost joy to share with her.

Chapter 25

A cry of delight escaped her lips when the suddenly stronger breeze swelled the sails above, making them flap wildly as they trapped the welcome gust. The ropes grew taut, adding their hum to the muted tune of straining wood and the ship leaned windward, altering its course.

Instinctively, Darcy gripped the spokes to keep the wheel from spinning further than it should and the much-missed thrill coursed through him yet again, as the full power of the wind in perfect synergy with the man-made craft was channelled into his tightened muscles. The primeval joy reminded him once more of long-gone days out sailing with his father, but flashing memories of those distant times paled before the glory of the moment: the all-powerful sea, the breeze – and her proximity. She was before him, between him and the helm, hands clasped alongside his on the well-worn wood, her back warm against his chest, her scent intoxicating.

The old Cornishman, the skipper, had willingly relinquished the ship's wheel in his keeping and had made no comment other than a smirk half-lost in his greying beard when Darcy had chosen to share the privilege with his betrothed. He had left them to it and had withdrawn towards the bow alongside his crew, who were now going about their business tightening ropes and adjusting sails, with the odd covert glance up to the quarterdeck.

For once, this was insufficient deterrent and Darcy leaned closer, inhaling her sweet fragrance mingled with the salty air. She had long relinquished her bonnet and the strong breeze was blowing freely through her auburn tresses, ruffling them into an adorable tangle that swayed to and fro, in turns concealing and exposing the whiteness of her neck.

Temptation swelled like the high winds above them, wild and tantalising, until resistance became unthinkable. Impossible.

He lowered his head to press his lips against the fragrant skin and sharp desire coursed through him as he felt her quiver at the touch. With a breathless gasp, she tilted her head sideways, aiding and abetting him in taking the delicious liberty. His lips drifted to the corner of her jaw, then slid further to find a small velvety earlobe. A soft sigh left her lips, sending his senses spinning wildly – just as the ship's wheel might have done, had Darcy not tightened his grip on the spokes, as much to keep control of the craft as of himself.

"I love you," he murmured against the creamy skin, then leaned back in a futile quest for sanity that was destined to be thwarted even before she let her head rest on his chest.

"As I love you," he heard her whisper, and was thoroughly undone.

A blessing and a curse, this day together, alone but for a few weather-beaten Cornishmen!

Surprisingly – or perhaps not so much so, after their recent *rapprochement* – Mr. Bennet no longer felt compelled to shadow Darcy on the proposed outing. More surprisingly still, his views remained unaltered even when it had emerged that his second daughter and her betrothed were to sail alone.

Miss Bennet could not be persuaded, much to Bingley's secret disappointment, and Fitzwilliam was prevented from joining them due to some last-minute changes in his orders. He was to call at Landennis later in the day, though not early enough to catch the tide, and Darcy could only assume it must have been testament to Miss Lydia's affection for his cousin that, albeit grudgingly, she had relinquished the prospect of the eagerly-anticipated sailing trip. Insensitively perhaps, Miss Kitty had not been asked, and neither had Miss Mary – and so it came to pass that Elizabeth and Mr. Darcy found themselves alone.

Alone – and free. More so than ever. Not merely free from the constraints of convention or the reserve imposed by her family's presence but one with glorious nature, feeling the sun on their skin, the wind in their faces, tasting life as it must have been before so-called civilisation had put its stamp upon it, to adulterate it into something tame and bland.

A man, a woman, before the open world in all its glory, answering to no one – just the call of the sea.

Yet the selfsame freedom had its insidious dangers. For one, it made it devilishly hard to countenance returning to everyday constraints. Moreover, it fuelled all manner of wishes and unleashed thoughts that were best held in check.

There was another month at least until the wedding. The banns would be called once they returned to Longbourn. A special licence could be obtained of course, but then there were those lengthy preparations to contend with, as Mrs. Bennet's daily effusions claimed. Wedding clothes. Wedding breakfast. Invitations. Visits. Incursions to the warehouses. And the whole assortment of hindrances and delays – a curse on them all!

"Fitzwilliam?" her pensive voice drew him from his frustrated musings.

"Yes, my love?"

"I once heard it said that seafaring captains can read marriage vows. Is that true?"

Breath caught in his chest. What was she *saying?* His stark surprise melted into tenderness at the discovery that they were thinking the same thoughts, or at least thoughts that were to some extent related, he inwardly amended with a rueful smile. His chest swelled and fanciful imaginings took flight – then Darcy stopped the mad rush in its tracks, before he allowed himself to hope.

"I think so," he cautiously offered. "On merchant ships they can."

"And is *The Rashley* a merchant ship?"

"Hardly," he replied and forced out a chuckle.

"But Mr. Tregarrick *is* a seafaring captain."

"Of sorts."

"Then can he marry us?"

"Elizabeth!" he whispered, then pulled himself together.

With a glance and a nod, he summoned the helmsman, who was quick to come and take on his duties, thus freeing Darcy from the suddenly cumbersome task of paying attention to anything but *her.* They left the quarterdeck and withdrew to lean against the starboard rail. Their eyes met – his questioning, hers smiling. Before he could put his questions into words, Elizabeth spoke up:

"I would very much like to be married today, Fitzwilliam," she said softly.

"You *would?*"

Her hands were clasped in his, and none could have said how they came to be there.

"I would," she smiled again.

It was only with considerable effort that he resisted the wild urge to kiss her – especially when she playfully arched a brow:

"Unless you think me forward. If you would rather not – ..."

She trailed off and Darcy retorted promptly and with feeling:

"You know there is nothing I want more!"

The role of the devil's advocate was something he wholeheartedly resented, yet in good conscience he felt compelled to add:

"Still, I cannot vouch that having it performed by old Tregarrick would be in keeping with the law of the land..."

"We are not on land – but need I worry that you might be tempted to use this as an escape once we are ashore?"

"Minx," he smiled and kept to banter, yet the concern was real. "Your father might very well ask for my head on a platter. I am not saying that it would not be worth it, but I imagine it defeats the purpose."

"My father need not know," Elizabeth replied, soberly this time. "No one need know. It shall be our secret. For everybody else's benefit the wedding shall be held at Longbourn, yet you and I will know that we were united here and now, just off the very shores where we have reached our understanding."

The beauty of the thought and of her exquisitely romantic choice touched his soul – but, bless her sweet innocence, did she not know what she was asking? Married – but not quite. In word, but not in deed. How was he to leave her – *his wife* – at Landennis tonight as if nothing had happened and return to his empty chamber at the inn in Falmouth?

"You do not wish it," Elizabeth observed matter-of-factly and before any mistaken notions of rejection could take hold and pain her Darcy forced all selfish thoughts aside.

He would do anything for her, anything to make her happy – and by all that was holy, frustrated desire would *not* get in the way!

Darcy put an arm around her and called out:

"Mr. Tregarrick? A word, if it pleases you."

The old sailor looked up from the bow.

"Would you be so kind to marry us?" Darcy asked, his voice carrying over the loud flapping of the mainsail.

The man's bushy beard, thick enough to lose a ferret in, split widely into a toothless grin.

"Bless ye, m'ludd, Ah thort ye'd never ask." In a few long strides he was at their side and called out to his crew: "Ye pair o' loafers, get yerselves down 'ere. Come now, lively, lively! Belay 'em ropes an' come 'ere, sharply. An' take 'em caps off while ye're at it. Stand 'ere. Not there, lubber-'ead, 'ere, by the rail!" he admonished, then took his own cap off and mopped his balding head with a kerchief produced from his capacious pockets. "Tregony," he called up to the helmsman, who seemed mightily distracted by the goings-on. "Nose to the compass an' keep 'er steady as she goes, ye rascal! Ah've no min' ter be washed ashore in the gulf o' Biscay, if it be all the same to ye. Now then, 'ow does it go? M'ludd, Miss, 'old 'ands, will ye? Ha! Ye are. Good, 'tis as it ought ter be. Ahem! We're gathered 'ere onto this blessed ship an' under the Good Lord's clear skies ter join together this gent an' 'is willin' woman – ... Ah take it that ye're willin', Miss, a'n't ye?"

Tears mingling with laughter in her eyes, Elizabeth nodded.

"... ter join 'em together in the bonds o' matrimony. Ahem!" He mopped his head again with the bright-red kerchief. "Now, Sorr, yer name be – ...?"

"Fitzwilliam."

"That won't do. Yer Christian name, by Jove!"

"By Jove, that *is* my Christian name," Darcy retorted brightly and Elizabeth's lips twitched.

"Right ye are. Then, do ye, Fitzwilliam, take this woman 'ere ter be yer helpmeet an' yer wedded wife, ter love an' cherish 'er, an' keep thee only unto 'er, for as long as ye both shall live?"

It was hardly the Book of Common Prayer and the man's broad accent was so unfamiliar that of ten words Darcy could make out seven and understand less, yet despite the unorthodox officiant and the unusual location, suddenly the moment was as solemn as though they were standing before the altar of a vast cathedral. Or perhaps even more so, for there were no thick stone arches and man-made ornaments between them and the Lord's merciful eye.

"I do," Darcy firmly spoke the two words that encompassed a promise of a lifetime.

"An' do ye...?"

"Elizabeth."

"Do ye, Elizabeth, vouchsafe the same, an' take this man ter love 'im, an' keep 'im, an' obey 'im, an' stay true ter 'im till death do ye part?"

"I do," she answered, her voice clear, her eyes never leaving Darcy's.

"'Ave ye the ring?"

"No, I do not... I do not have it – I have not thought..."

"No matter," Elizabeth retorted, smiling through her tears.

"That fob'll do the trick," Tregarrick pointed at the one securing Darcy's pocket-watch.

"I believe it would."

The golden link was prized open in an instant and removed from its place, then hastily bent back into shape. It fit very snugly on Elizabeth's slender finger and she folded her hand to press it to her lips.

"As master o' this good ship, *The Rashley*, an' every blessed thing upon it, I send ye forth ter live as man an' wife together. An' now's the time ter kiss the bride, Sorr," Tregarrick muttered towards Darcy, who lost no time in doing just as he was told.

If nothing else – and perforce there *would* be nothing else, for a terribly long time – at least he had full licence to cup her beloved face in his hands and run his thumbs over her glowing cheeks as he leaned forward to freely claim her lips, without a care for their grinning audience.

Beside them, Tregarrick bellowed:

"Off wi' ye now, me lads. Go aft, an' leave 'em be. Off wi' ye, Ah tell ye!" Tregarrick barked again and walked away with his swaying gait, his booming voice still carrying over the raising wind. "Tregony, me man, Ah'll take the 'elm an' ye go below an' fetch me flask, there's a good lad. A slurp o' fine French stuff's what we be needin' now ter drink their 'ealth, son, an' Ah reckon we can all 'ave a tipple."

Under his, Elizabeth's lips curled into a smile at the old man's words and the cheer that followed, and Darcy leaned back to meet her laughing eyes.

"Mrs. Darcy," he said very slowly, tasting the words, savouring them.

Her eyes brightened.

"Mrs. Darcy," she repeated with something very much like blissful wonder and the joyous glow in her adored countenance made it impossible for him not to claim her lips again.

He turned by a fraction, in a vague endeavour to screen her from their four companions and his hands found their way into her hair, fingers tangled in soft tresses as the kiss deepened into wild, breathless abandon. A moment, just one moment more – and then another, and another – the taste of her sweet lips, the taste of *her* filling his senses and fuelling his desire into an all-consuming blaze. Her lovely form against him, warm and gloriously close, clasped to his chest, firm yet deliciously pliant, and more enticing than anything on earth.

"My love…" he whispered between kisses, savouring the flavour of her skin, the perfect essence that was all Elizabeth, mingled with sun-scented glow and the salty breeze.

His kisses drifted to her throat, only to feel the flutter of wildly rushing blood under her skin, under his hungry lips – a feverish rhythm that matched the forceful rush channelled through his veins.

"Elizabeth…" he whispered again, before his face was clasped between soft palms and his lips were silenced with yet another kiss.

And then she drew apart and turned towards the water, by far the wisest of the two. Yet she withdrew no further, but leaned back into his chest once more, raising a hand to reach over her shoulder and stroke his face and the tangled mess of curls above his neck.

His breath grew ragged at her touch and half-hearted withdrawal. His hands found and gripped the rail on either side of her, as burning temptation flared, unbearable, wreaking havoc through his senses. Explosively growing from mere desire into the sharpest need to hold her – and *not* have to let go. Feel her, soft and warm against him, and achingly perfect. Press his lips on her exposed throat again. And *not* stop this time. Indulge. Seek and give pleasure. Slowly guide her from love into passion. Claim her as his own.

'With my body I thee worship…'

"Sorr? Would ye come up fer a spell?"

He exhaled – a loud, forceful sound.

The gravelly voice that had just summoned him aft, to the helm, was something to be almost glad of, Darcy determined and, his breath still ragged, he made his excuses and left her by the parapet to bound up the steps at the old man's bidding.

When he was close enough, Tregarrick ran a gnarled hand over his beard then tentatively mumbled, his voice very low:

"M'ludd? If ye'd be willin', Ah'd be pleased to let ye 'ave me berth. Ah thort best to say naught afore, as it be ill-fittin' for a gent o' quality an' 'is missus, but – ..."

"Lord Almighty!" Darcy muttered.

"Beg pardon?"

"Nothing. Nothing. You are most kind and I appreciate it, but... that would not be necessary, thank you."

The old man shrugged, his beady eyes on the horizon, and then held out his hand, brandy flask in it.

"Then ye'd best 'ave some o' this instead."

With something of a chuckle, Darcy saw fit to turn down the second offer also. He rummaged through his pockets to find a purse, which he handed to the older man.

"This is to drink our health and to thank you for your troubles," he said and promptly left him to return to his bride.

Tregarrick did not open it, but briefly weighed the purse in his calloused palm and nodded his approval before letting it fall into his pocket. He took a swig from the rejected flask, then wiped his mouth with the back of his hand and deftly steered the craft into the wind as he quietly chortled:

"Bless yer 'eart, m'boy, but Ah reckon ye've got naught ter thank me fer. Looks ter me that *yer* troubles are only juss beginnin'."

⊷ ⊶

Perchance old man Tregarrick was not a proponent of the married state, hence his words. In any case they turned out to be prophetic – at least for the long weeks that followed, until that blissful day when the kindly vicar of Longbourn church finally declared Darcy lawfully married to the woman of his dreams. That day, Lady Anne's wedding ring came to rest on Elizabeth's fourth finger alongside the thin golden link which, to her family's surprise – though not so much Miss Bennet's – she had steadfastly worn ever since the day when she and Mr. Darcy had gone on their protracted sailing trip.

The service held in Longbourn church was of course for a triple wedding and, on the same day, Jane and Lydia were also united to the gentlemen of their choice.

293

Another pleasant surprise lay in store for Colonel Fitzwilliam, in the years to come. Not only had he unwittingly fallen in love with an heiress, but he eventually found himself enjoying the benefits of a country estate. The prospective mistress of Landennis was now the mistress of Pemberley and *there* was her life; there also were her joys and many duties. Thus, when Mrs. Pencarrow peacefully ended her days at Pemberley a few years later, Elizabeth was only too happy to suggest that Lydia and her husband should taste the delights of life at Landennis in her stead.

Lydia might have found limited pleasure in the said delights, for she never would have thought that life in a secluded part of the country and in an old-fashioned manor-house would suit her tastes and disposition. Fortunately for her, nearby Falmouth was a very lively place. More fortunately still, she eventually discovered that her husband was nothing like her father. Although similarly tempted into matrimony by the allure of youth and of a cheerful temper, unlike Mr. Bennet Colonel Fitzwilliam saw delight in guiding with affection, in sharing his understanding of the world and, more importantly, his thoughts. Moreover, despite the substantial difference in their ages, there was a boyish mischievousness about him that greatly appealed to his darling wife and a deep affection that could not fail to fuel hers until it far surpassed her youthful fascination for his regimentals.

To Kitty's material advantage, she often came to visit her dearest sister. Although she discovered, to her disappointment, that Lydia was strangely altered by her marriage – indeed, far too much for Kitty's taste – she also discovered bittersweet pleasure in the frequent society of Lord Trevellyan, the Fitzwilliams' nearest neighbour and their dear friend. Truth be told, Lord Trevellyan had long held her interest, ever since the night when she had been an involuntary witness to his dreadful anguish. This interest Kitty forced herself to keep in check, for she could think of no worse torture than labouring under the suspicion that Lord Trevellyan might bring himself to seek glimpses of Elizabeth in *her* and be resigned to share his life with a mere copy of the one he presumably still loved, but could not have.

In many ways, the Fates were as cruel to her as they had been to him for, despite her afore-mentioned fears, Kitty could not forget him, nor form an attachment to any of the other young gentlemen introduced to her acquaintance. By comparison, they seemed terribly dull and very bland indeed.

For the longest time, it did not dawn on her that she had neatly trapped herself into a vicious circle and the aura of a romantic hero that drew her irresistibly to Lord Trevellyan sprang from the very same anguish of unrequited love that made her recoil in fear of her own very likely heartbreak.

Fortunately though, in time, the Fates changed their minds and decided to deal kindly. Lord Trevellyan fell in love again, this time with a young woman who only wanted to be reassured that his affections were centred upon *her* in order to accept him. Thus, to everyone's satisfaction – and no less Mrs. Bennet's – a few years later Lord Trevellyan made Kitty an offer and they were married in the small church on the estate.

Mary never got her head out of her books. Yet, despite her father's opinion on the matter, she did marry. The partner chosen by fate was an Oxford scholar who, unlike most men of his day, could find great satisfaction in having been blessed with a learned wife.

No one ever doubted that Mr. and Mrs. Bingley would be happy. Well, perhaps his sisters *did* voice complaints and doubts, but the rest of their family and friends were not of a mind to listen – which was shown to be by far the wisest choice.

A vast deal was also said about Mr. and Mrs. Darcy and their unexpected marriage. That she had beguiled him. That she was beneath him. That he had no need and indeed no business to marry money instead of pedigree. Still, barking dogs have never stopped the passing coach and they could not even slow down this one, for Mr. and Mrs. Darcy could not care a jot about anyone's opinion but each other's.

Over the years, they found each other perfect, adorable, impossible, desirable, delectable, domineering, downright infuriating – or all of the above at once. But their love for each other never faltered, because it never does when two people are truly suited for each other – and *that* they were, without a single doubt.

The Darcy marriage was not in the least a modern one – not by the standards of *the ton* in any case – for they seemed inordinately keen to spend far too much time in each other's presence. Their fashionable acquaintances were astounded. They appeared to share everything: duties, pastimes, pleasures. Even more astounding still, they were clearly determined to go everywhere together.

The most puzzling of all, to those unfamiliar with the story of their courtship, was the allure of a very distant place, far into the deepest Cornwall, where they travelled often, though perhaps not quite as often as they wished.

It was a *very* long journey from Pemberley to Falmouth and it seemed longer still to those travelling with youngsters, even if they could afford a second carriage – for whoever said that the children of strong-willed people are often tame and meek was obviously not acquainted with the Darcys.

Yet discomforts paled before the joys that awaited at the journey's end. Friendly faces, very dear and long missed; cheerful people gathered round the dinner table; evenings spent before the fire sharing news and laugher; mornings' of watching hosts of little cousins – fourteen altogether – scampering through the gardens, running through the woods, careering down the beach or paddling with loud shrieks into the shallows.

And there was something else, of course. Like a book with pressed flowers safely kept between the pages, the place was fragrant with the treasured flavour of their earliest beginnings – and nowhere more than in a small, secluded cove unchanged by the years' passing where their happiness was born and where their brightest recollections lingered.

As for old Tregarrick, he eventually had cause to alter his views on the married state, at least where Mr. and Mrs. Darcy were concerned. He was captain of a very different ship now, a graceful three-masted schooner, which boasted of more than one cabin well-suited to accommodate a gentleman of quality and his adoring wife. And, to his way of thinking, the privilege of having full command of such a beauty for the best part of the year was well worth the inconvenience of having to play second-fiddle to its owner whenever Mr. Darcy chose to visit Cornwall – and *almost* worth subjecting himself, at his age and with his fiery disposition, to the self-appointed task of keeping a handful of young Darcys out of mischief, or at least out of water, while their parents stood on the quarterdeck, hair ruffled and as tanned as pirates, steering the ship together into the high winds.

The End

BY THE SAME AUTHOR

FROM THIS DAY FORWARD
A Pride & Prejudice Sequel

THE SUBSEQUENT PROPOSAL
A Tale of Pride, Prejudice & Persuasion

THE SECOND CHANCE
A Pride & Prejudice ~ Sense & Sensibility Variation

ABOUT THE AUTHOR

Joana Starnes lives in the south of England with her family.
A medical graduate, over the years she has developed
an unrelated but enduring fascination
with Georgian Britain in general
and the works of Jane Austen in particular.

You can find Joana Starnes
on Facebook at http://www.facebook.com/joana.a.starnes
on Twitter at http://www.twitter.com/Joana_Starnes
or on her website at http://www.joanastarnes.co.uk/